DR. KALBFLEISCH

&

THE CHICKEN RESTAURANT

Also by Cordelia Strube

Alex & Zee
Milton's Elements
Teaching Pigs to Sing

Dr. Kalbfleisch & the Chicken Restaurant

Cordelia Strube

A Phyllis Bruce Book
HarperCollins*PublishersLtd*

The author would like to acknowledge the support
of the Toronto Arts Council.

 For information address HarperCollins Publishers Ltd, Suite 2900, Hazelton Lanes, 55 Avenue Road, Toronto, Canada M5R 3L2.

http://www.harpercollins.com/canada

First edition

Canadian Cataloguing in Publication Data

Strube, Cordelia, 1960–
Dr. Kalbfleisch & the chicken restaurant

"A Phyllis Bruce book".
ISBN 0-00-648050-0

I. Title. II. Title: Dr. Kalbfleisch and the chicken restaurant.

PS8587.T72975D62 1997 C813'.54 C97-931233-7
PR9199.3.S77D62 1997

---

97 98 99 ❖ HC 10 9 8 7 6 5 4 3 2

Printed and bound in the United States

For Harold

If it be asked, what is the improper expectation which it is dangerous to indulge, experience will quickly answer, that it is such expectation as is dictated not by reason, but by desire; expectation raised, not by the common occurrences of life, but by the wants of the expectant; an expectation that requires the common course of things to be changed, and the general rules of action to be broken.

— Samuel Johnson
The Life of Samuel Johnson, James Boswell

DR. KALBFLEISCH

&

THE CHICKEN RESTAURANT

one

Raymond thinks about the deaf mute again. Her daughter thanked her for giving her life and not aborting her. She wrote on a pad that she respected any reasons her mother may have had for putting her up for adoption. When the deaf mute got cancer, the daughter wrote that she completely forgave her.

The social worker blows her nose. "What are you expecting, Raymond?" She tosses her crumpled Kleenex into a wastebasket already overflowing with her used tissues.

"I don't know what to expect," he answers.

It moved Raymond that, as the deaf mute took her last breaths, the daughter stayed at her bedside, holding her hand. Raymond hopes to experience a similar moment with his biological mother. Even if she isn't a deaf mute and doesn't have cancer, he believes that they will be able to communicate deep feeling wordlessly.

The social worker sniffs. "Everyone who has suffered birth-mother rejection has expectations."

Out the window Raymond sees the top of a tree being buffeted by the wind. A few of its branches rap threateningly against the glass.

"You never know," the social worker continues, "your birth mother may have become a nun. Or she could be severely disabled. You have to be prepared for this, Raymond."

It bothers him that she keeps repeating his name. When he was informed that "reunion preparation counselling" was mandatory, he'd expected to be greeted by someone kinder, gentler. This social worker has bristly hair and rodent eyes.

"Or she may want to mother you," she adds. "How will you feel if she suddenly wants to impose on your life?"

"I think I would like that. I mean, I want her to be a part of my life."

"But you don't *know* her, Raymond. You can't want her to be a part of your life until you *know* her. And that takes time."

Behind the social worker is a floral poster with the words "Forgive But Never Forget" printed on it.

"Adoptees fantasize about their birth mothers," she explains. "They imagine that there will be hugs and kisses all around, and that that will be the end of it. Well, far from it, reunion is just the beginning." The social worker keeps twisting her neck, as if trying to release tension. "We're here to mediate, and to maintain your anonymity, but once you sign the consent, there's no turning back."

Raymond nods. His mouth is still frozen from the dentist and he worries that he's drooling. He quickly wipes his chin.

"May I ask why you want to meet your birth mother, Raymond?"

"My mother's sick. I have no other family."

"Not married?"

"Not any more."

"Your father?"

"Gone."

She pulls another Kleenex from the box. "Do you understand that your birth mother may have married and had children by other men?"

"I hadn't really thought about that but yes, I guess it's possible."

"They may feel displaced by you. They may not welcome you with open arms."

Raymond hasn't had time to consider half-sisters and -brothers. When he applied to the adoption disclosure register he hadn't expected "a match" to be made so quickly, if at all. But his birth mother had also registered, which has hastened the process. That she wants to see him, has been waiting to see him, fills him with euphoria. For years he has told himself that she didn't matter, that she gave him up and therefore she should be forgotten. But in the Children's Aid Society reading material it explained how difficult it was for young women to keep their babies forty years ago, when there were no support systems in place for single mothers. Once they relinquished their infants they were told to "get over it" and "get on" with their lives. Raymond was particularly affected by one birth mother's account of her stay in the hospital. While in labour, she was isolated and left to her own devices. After her baby was born, they wouldn't let her hold him until she screamed that she would kill herself unless they brought him to her. She was advised by all concerned that her baby deserved a good home, and that she would forget him. But the birth mother said she never forgot him. He was constantly in her thoughts and dreams. She said his adorable little face as she handed him over to the social worker was "indelibly etched" on her soul. She carried her unexpressed grief for years and became afflicted by severe depression. She tried to replace her lost son by having more children only to discover that he was irreplaceable. Raymond has never considered himself irreplaceable. The fact that his birth mother could be out there mourning him — her surrendered baby — has caused Raymond to become genuinely concerned for her. She is no longer someone who didn't care about him. She is an innocent who was forced, by the conditions of the time, to give him up. His little face is indelibly etched on her soul.

"Raymond?"

"Yes?"

"Are you still with me?"

"Yes."

"If the truth be told, Raymond" — she twists her neck again — "reunions are not always easy. It's important that we alert you to the possibilities."

Branches rap harder against the window pane. Raymond waits for the glass to shatter, for a shard to skewer the social worker who stands between him and his severely depressed mother.

"Is that really all you can tell me about her?" he asks. He has already read what little non-identifying information is available: his birth mother's height, weight, place of birth, racial origins, religion. She was in good health, had a fair complexion, an oval face with even features, expressive eyes and long lashes. At the time she delivered she had not finished high school but intended to resume her studies and become a nurse. She loved animals. Her hobbies were dancing and reading historical romances.

The social worker blows her nose again. "Usually no information is added to the record after the adoption record has been signed. Unfortunately, in your case, not much information was collected to begin with." She looks at his file. "You know she was working as a waitress?"

"I thought she was going to be a nurse."

"Yes. But at the time she was waitressing to make ends meet."

He imagines the fair, oval-faced, long-lashed teenager slinging burgers while her belly grows. Impoverished, shunned by society, she returns to her rented room and stares at the cracked plaster walls, despairing as she feels the life growing inside her; a life she will be unable to share. "Would she have seen me?" Raymond asks.

"There were two of you."

Raymond nods quickly. He doesn't want to think about the fate of the other baby. "But would she have seen *me*? Before they took me away?"

"Obviously I can't say that, Raymond, as I didn't handle the case."

How his mother must have suffered, Raymond thinks. He sees her carrying plates in the burger restaurant, her shoulders slumped, tears rolling off her cheeks on to the fries. The sneering manager probably thinks he's doing her a favour by not firing her, since she's in disgrace. He probably treats her like shit and pays her less than minimum wage. What was minimum wage back then? Fifty cents an hour?

Raymond clears his throat. "The non-identifying information says her parents died in a car crash."

"That's right."

"That's all it says."

The social worker dabs her nose. "Obviously she didn't want to talk about it." She closes the file. "We can't force people to give information, Raymond. It is unfortunate that so little medical history was recorded."

"And you don't know anything about my father?"

"Only what was originally recorded which is that she didn't know who the father was."

"Do you think it's possible she was lying," Raymond asks, "to protect him?"

"Anything's possible."

Raymond suspects that his birth mother loved his birth father. She didn't tell him she was pregnant because he was from a good family and had a great future ahead of him. She understood that if she told him, he would sacrifice his education to marry her. He would be disowned by his family, forcing the young couple to live off his meagre earnings as an encyclopedia salesman. Determined not to ruin his life as well as hers, Gloria told him that she no longer loved him, that she never wanted to see him again. Raymond was a love child.

"Gloria," he mumbles. He enjoys saying her name. He has been saying it often.

"You'll have lots to talk about when you see her, Raymond. But it's important that we take things slow. Start with a non-identifying letter. Just think of it as writing to a pen pal, very informal. But don't seal the envelope because, before passing it on, we have to check to make sure that there is no identifying information in it. You might want to enclose a photo. We'll ask her to do the same." She collects her papers and smiles for the first time, revealing long teeth. "We'll be in touch."

❖

"How would you feel if *I* was going bald?" his ex-wife asks.

Raymond eats another nacho, wondering if she's serious. Even when they were married he wasn't sure when she was serious. "*Are* you going bald?" he asks.

"No, but if I was?"

"Women don't go bald."

"Some do." She dips a nacho into the sour cream. "Anyway, the point is you'd want me to do something about it, right? You wouldn't want to be seen with a *bald* woman."

Around him, in the bar, Raymond sees only unhealthy people with dried-up faces, hunched over tables. They too are eating nachos and drinking beer. Some of them smoke cigarettes. He wonders if he and Mara look unhealthy. "I can't help going bald."

"There's treatments you could try."

"They don't work."

"That's my point. You see, if *I* was going bald, I would try anything. That's the difference between men and women."

"What is?"

She waves her hand the way she does when she thinks he's being ignorant. "Forget it."

They had come to the bar because Raymond had discovered bones when he was planting a tree in her backyard. At first he thought they belonged to a dog but then he saw the skull.

"Mara," he shouted, knowing that she was doing her nails in the kitchen.

"What?" she shouted back.

"Can you come out here for a sec?"

"Why?"

"Just come out here. Please?"

Mara, spreading her fingers to protect her polish, walked carefully over the grass, avoiding the muddy spots, then stared into the hole. "What is that?"

"Bones."

She frowned. "Maybe a dog buried them."

"There's too many. And there's a skull."

She shook her head. "That's why this house was cheap. I knew it was too cheap." She'd been very excited about the house.

"It's got nothing to do with the house," Raymond told her, although he wasn't sure.

Suddenly the miniskirted waitress hovers over his shoulder so he orders two more beers. "I wouldn't worry about the bones," he says, watching the waitress's buttocks bounce as she walks away. "The tree's over them now. No one will find them."

"If people find bones in your yard, they assume you put them there."

"Not old bones. Those are old bones. They'd be able to tell that the bones got there before you did."

Mara slumps in her chair. "I have no energy to deal with this."

"Then don't deal with it." Raymond doesn't really understand his relationship with his ex-wife. Sometimes he thinks they spend time together because no one else will. When she threatened to move out west, he invented reasons why she shouldn't. When she didn't move out west, he wondered if maybe she should have; that maybe they had grown too dependent on each other; that maybe their relationship was sick.

Mara picks an olive slice off the melted cheese. "I knew I shouldn't have bought that house. I knew it was too cheap. I'm always fucking up. Just once I would like things to work out, you know, just once. That's all I ask." She grabs her beer glass, causing some to spill on the tablecloth. Raymond dabs at it with his napkin. She swallows more beer, then sets the glass down. "My brother says I'm making a mess of my life. He says I have to plan my life like a business. He says I have to make a business plan for my life."

Her brother wears berets and has a goatee. Retired now, he spends his time in cafés offering financial advice to anyone who will listen.

"He says I should determine my strengths and weaknesses and plan accordingly. He says I must do what I do well or I will never be happy. Because you're only happy when you're doing what you do well." She picks off a jalapeño pepper. "Does that make any sense to you?"

"Sure," Raymond says, knowing that he isn't required to say more.

"The problem is I don't know what I'm good at. Do you?"

He scratches behind his ear. "Know what you're good at or what I'm good at?"

"What I'm good at."

This is what he doesn't like about their relationship. She wants him to tell her she's good at something. In return she'll tell him that he's good at something. But they won't really believe each other. They'll just say nice things to make each other feel better. Sometimes he feels as though they're a pair of monkeys picking off each other's fleas.

"That's probably a monkey in the backyard," he remarks.

"Did you see a tail?"

"I don't think monkeys have a lot of bones in their tails. The bones might have disintegrated."

Mara leans heavily on the table and pulls another nacho from the melted cheese. Strands of cheese stretch between her nacho and the plate. Raymond waits for them to break and fall on to the tablecloth. Mara has always had difficulty handling food. When she eats spaghetti she stains anything or anyone within a three-foot radius. Even with the table between them he occasionally gets a spot of her tomato sauce on his shirt.

Still chewing her nacho, she wipes her fingers on a napkin. "My brother says life is very complex."

Raymond clears his throat and narrows his eyes. He often does this when he is preparing to annoy her. "He put oven cleaner on his pimple, didn't he?"

"On his leg. That was years ago. It wasn't a pimple, it was a growth."

"Does that seem intelligent to you?" Raymond asks. "Using Easy-Off to remove a growth on your leg? He had to have a skin graft, didn't he?"

"Don't try to make it sound like he's stupid, Raymond. He's a very wealthy man. He built up his business from nothing." She pushes the plate of nachos away from her. "At least he doesn't work in a *chicken* restaurant."

She knows that this hurts him; that just hearing the word "chicken" distresses him. He tries to avoid it in general conversation. At the restaurant he calls them "birds." "Are those birds ready yet?" he asks the cooks. Or "Hurry up those birds," or "We need more birds here." Some of the customers have begun to look like chickens to him. Particularly when they're pecking at items from the salad bar.

"If that house is haunted," Mara warns, "I will die."

Mara often says that she will die if certain things happen. It used to worry him. "I didn't think you believed in ghosts."

"It doesn't matter what I believe if the house is haunted, does it? I mean, ghosts don't care if you believe in them or not. They're used to people not believing in them, that's why they throw furniture and everything."

"Well, if it was a monkey, it probably wouldn't do that. It probably wouldn't even come into the house. It would probably prefer to hang out in a tree. I wouldn't worry about it."

❖

In his high-rise apartment, he looks down at the city and thinks about his loneliness; about how being with his ex-wife isn't helping him. Even when they were married it wasn't helping him. He can't remember not being lonely. As a child he invented an imaginary friend because the real ones kept disappointing him. When he whispered to his "friend" in class, his teacher made him stand in the corner. This didn't bother Raymond, because his "friend" stood in the corner with him.

Maybe he should invent an imaginary wife.

Burt nudges his feet. Raymond squats beside him, pats his head and pulls on his ears. Burt was the only dog at the pound who didn't bark when Raymond approached. He just stared very sadly, as though certain that no one would ever choose him. Even when Raymond put him in the car he looked sad. In fact, he always looks sad. The vet says he's part basset hound.

Raymond balances a biscuit on Burt's snout and watches him flip it into his mouth. "Good pooch."

Mara says that Raymond lives in a high-rise because no one can reach him up there; touch him up there. She calls it his ivory tower.

Raymond wonders if he would be as lonely if his twin were with him. Often he fantasizes about him, imagines them sitting around talking. Or not talking because they wouldn't need to because they'd have this bond. They'd know what the other was thinking even before they said it. Raymond has read that some identical twins have telepathic powers and can communicate over great distances. Some twins can induce the other to phone just by thinking about them. Some experience each other's pain. One can be perfectly healthy but if the other is having a gall bladder problem, its twin will feel it too. Raymond loves the idea of sharing pain, of knowing that you are not alone with your pain. Identical twins often die around the same time. Raymond didn't die with his twin. In fact, he's afraid that he murdered his twin. He has researched the subject and learned that twins who share the same placenta compete for nourishment and space. They wrestle with each other, which explains why many of them become professional wrestlers. Even if they don't fight, depending on where the umbilical cords are inserted into the placenta, one twin can receive more nourishment than the other. If one cord is centrally placed and the other only drains from one side, the first baby is overfed while the other is starved. The poorer blood supply can retard his brain maturation, and leave him less able to fight infections. Even if the blood supply is equal in the womb, decreased oxygen during birth can damage the last twin to be delivered as the placenta begins to shut down after the birth of the first. In cases where the twins don't share the same placenta, one placenta can be much larger than the other, providing one baby with better nourishment.

Raymond doesn't know which of these scenarios applies to his and his brother's prenatal existence. He does know from the non-identifying information that he was born first and had the higher birthweight. But it doesn't state whether or not they shared the same placenta, although Raymond is convinced that this was the case. He fears that he wrestled his twin, strangled him, then drank all his blood. Over the years he has asked his adoptive mother for more details, but she's always claimed ignorance. "The social worker gave you to me and that was that," she told him. "You had big blue eyes and I fell in love with you on sight." Raymond has always enjoyed the thought of being loved on sight. But he has never understood why his brother had to die. "It's not uncommon," his adoptive mother explained. "Survival of the fittest. You were the stronger." At first this information sent Raymond into spirals of grief. He imagined cinching his brother's umbilical cord so that he'd have all the blood to himself. He imagined shoving his fist into his brother's throat, his foot into his groin. As a kind of therapy he began apologizing to his dead twin in the mirror. He formed a bond with his reflection. His twin became someone he could count on. More than his adoptive mother, even though she'd always assured him of her love, insisting that he was as good as her own. But he wasn't her own. He was someone else's. Someone he'd thought didn't want him.

He still talks to his twin in the mirror. He thinks this may be one of the reasons Mara left him. He wishes he could forget the night he almost strangled her. It hadn't been his intention, they'd been wrestling as they often did when they argued. It was play fighting — he never hurt her really, he doesn't think. But that night he just couldn't get his point across, she just wouldn't listen, wouldn't understand, no matter how many times he explained himself. He knew that he was losing control and this upset him. He'd never thought of himself as a violent man. It made him think again about being trapped in the womb with his brother, losing patience with him for not understanding, then strangling him.

He has also read that chromosomal aberrations or gene mutations can take place in one embryo but not the other after the egg divides. The twins continue to be identical except for the mutant gene or the altered chromosome. One fetus may reject the other because of these genetic differences. If the rejected twin doesn't die, it fights the other for survival.

His research has led Raymond to believe that his time in the womb was relentlessly violent. In his dreams it is a bloodbath. He wakes gasping for air, his arms and legs straining against tangled sheets.

He feeds Burt another biscuit and starts to think about what to write in his non-identifying letter. The social worker said to treat it as though he were writing to a pen pal. He's never had a pen pal. He thinks he should be polite in the letter, and not too prying. Raymond's adoptive mother raised him to believe in the importance of common courtesy and respecting the privacy of others. He doesn't know what he'll do about a photo. He has wedding pictures but he doesn't want Gloria to see those because she'll assume that he's still married. He could get a shot professionally done. But that might look contrived.

He finds a pen and some paper, sits at the kitchen counter and begins to write. *Dear Gloria, I hope you are happy to hear from me. I'll certainly be happy to hear from you. It's been a long time.* He crosses out *It's been a long time* and continues, *I'm very well.*

What if Gloria, after reading his letter and seeing his photo, decides she doesn't want to meet him? He doesn't think he could withstand being rejected by her twice. He probably wouldn't even be doing this if his adoptive mother hadn't developed Alzheimer's disease. Or if his adoptive father hadn't moved to Michigan to sell motor homes. Or if Mara hadn't left him.

I hope you're well too.

He can't think of anything to say about himself; what is there to say? Burt lies beside him, rests his chin on his feet.

I'd like to assure you that I'm not angry with you for putting me up for adoption. I understand that it was difficult for you, that things were different back then.

He pats Burt's head, then looks back at the paper.

I've had a good life. No hard feelings. He crosses out *No hard feelings* and writes, *I hope you've had a good life too.*

He's left-handed and has always been embarrassed by his handwriting. He crumples the piece of paper and starts again. *Dear Gloria.*

If she does agree to a reunion, he hopes, he prays, that she will love him on sight. He hopes, he prays, that he will feel less alone.

two

"What is it?" Raymond looks up from his desk as Jeff pokes his head around the office door.

"The savoury freezer's busted again."

"How long?"

"I don't know, some stuff has thawed."

"How many birds?"

"Maybe fifteen, twenty. I'd better cook 'em." Jeff pulls a Kleenex out of his pocket, spits on his glasses, then attempts to wipe grease off the lenses. "Hope it's a slow Saturday, otherwise we're going to run out of fresh chicken. Mrs. Kalbfleisch took a whole bunch home last night."

"What?"

"She came by for chicken. Took maybe ten, twenty. Barney saw her. She had a mah-jong party."

"How many cooked birds have we got left over from last night?"

"Maybe five, ten."

"Okay, well get them ready for hot-chicken sandwiches. We're going to have to offer a special if we run out."

"Right, Captain." Jeff salutes and starts back upstairs. "Oh and one of the dishwashers called in sick."

"Which one?"

"The Filipino guy."

"Okay, well we're all going to have to put a hand in then."

Jeff wrinkles his nose. "Can't you call what's-his-face?"

"Who's what's-his-face?"

"The Paki."

"Sharif. Try to learn their names, alright? You better get moving."

Raymond spends an hour on the phone trying to locate a dishwasher and the contractor for the freezer. While leaving messages he pictures rotting chicken and irate customers and heaps of dirty plates. When Dr. Kalbfleisch comes in, Raymond doesn't acknowledge him right away. But he knows he's there because he can hear him sucking on his dentures.

Dr. Kalbfleisch stares at Raymond. "How's business?"

Raymond closes his desk drawer. "Oh hello, sir. We're just getting ready for lunch."

"How were the numbers yesterday?"

"Twenty-eight hundred."

"On a Friday? Friday should be busy."

"It was busy. Twenty-eight's good for a Friday."

"When the weather's nice like this, it should be four. Chicken Villa was busy, not one empty seat."

Raymond clears his throat and narrows his eyes. "Well, sir, as I've explained, if we computerized the system, we would have a higher turnover. The waitresses could punch in their orders at their stations, and by the time they got to the kitchen, the orders would be up."

Dr. Kalbfleisch holds his hands over his ears. "Don't start with the computers, Raymond. I don't want to hear about the computers."

"Well, Chicken Villa has computers. You're always comparing our numbers to Chicken Villa's. Chicken Villa seats three hundred people, Chicken Villa is part of a chain. They own the chicken farms, the packers . . ."

"I don't want you lecturing me, Raymond. I know the chicken business. Your numbers are down."

To avoid strangling Dr. Kalbfleisch, Raymond opens his drawer again and shuffles through papers. "Sir, I have to ask you to please suggest to Mrs. Kalbfleisch that she give us advance notice when she wants chicken. We're short today because she took twenty chickens with her last night. It's the weekend. I can't get more chicken."

Dr. Kalbfleisch shrugs. "So tell her no."

"I wasn't here. Barney was working. And, anyway, we're not really in a position to tell her she can't take chickens, sir."

"Why not? You're the manager, tell her no. Tell her to pay for them. I didn't open this business for her entertainment. Tell her to pay for the chicken. Full price."

"I don't feel comfortable about that, sir. I would prefer that you speak with her."

"You think she'd listen to me? She won't listen. Don't give her chicken, end of story. I'm going upstairs. When you have a minute, come and talk to me. Tell Jeff I want a quarter-chicken dinner with no bun, just fries. And tell him I want it *crispy*."

Raymond knows that if he had any self-respect, he would not work for Dr. Kalbfleisch. When they were still married Mara often told him to look for work elsewhere. "Who would hire me?" he'd ask. "You won't know until you try," she'd reply. Occasionally she'd snip employment ads from the papers and leave them for him by the phone. He never called. He knew they wouldn't hire him. They'd hire someone younger with a university degree; someone computer literate. Raymond advises Dr. Kalbfleisch to computerize the system because he knows he won't, because he's too cheap. But secretly Raymond is afraid of computers and knows that most decent jobs require computer skills. Mara works with computers and has offered to teach Raymond. But he doesn't want her teaching him anything.

When the phone rings he hopes that it's the freezer contractor or a dishwasher. Or the social worker with news of his birth mother.

"Hi," Mara says.

"Hi."

"It's me."

"I know."

"Something's been after those bones."

"What do you mean?"

"Something's been digging under the apple tree."

"Probably a cat burying its crap."

"Can you come over later and look? I'm scared."

"I'm supposed to visit my mother."

"Come after that. I'll make spaghetti. Please, Raymond?"

"Alright."

❖

Dr. Kalbfleisch has chicken grease on his chin. "Why doesn't that waitress smile? I've been sitting here half an hour and I haven't seen one smile."

"She's too busy to smile."

"She should smile. She's lucky to have a job. Tell her to smile."

Raymond sips his coffee, trying to avoid watching Dr. Kalbfleisch ripping apart a chicken wing. "Her mother just died of cancer," he tells him.

Skin hangs off the bone. "Whose mother?"

"Beth. The waitress. Her mother just died."

"So? Do I bring my tears to work? Is that professional?"

"She isn't crying. But her mother's death could be why she isn't smiling."

Dr. Kalbfleisch grips the wing between his dentures. "She never smiles, that one. Unless she gets a big tip. Then she smiles." He gnaws on the chicken. "I ask for crispy and what do I get? Soggy chicken."

❖

Raymond streams with sweat from the dishwasher steam. He drops a plate, swears, then tries to prevent more plates from sliding off the pile. "Jesus fucking Christ," he mutters.

Beth, her arms loaded with dirty plates, hesitates in front of him. "What do you want me to do with these?"

"Just hang on to them a minute, will you?"

"You don't have to shout."

"Sorry, was I shouting?" Then he notices that she's crying. "Are you okay?"

She shakes her head. "It's nothing."

"It can't be nothing if you're crying."

Beth sniffs. "It's just usually I call my mom about now, you know, to tell her I'll be there for dinner tomorrow." Raymond carefully takes the plates from her. "It's just I keep expecting her to be there, you know, it's like I can't believe she's not going to call me."

Raymond rinses the plates. He has always liked Beth. She has nice breasts and is usually in a good mood. "Is there anything I can do?"

Beth shrugs. "Like I say, tomorrow's Sunday, right. I always go over there on Sunday. It's like it's the only day I eat healthy food."

Bruce, the other waiter, pushes plates at Raymond. "If we don't get clean cutlery out here, I'm going to ca-ry."

Jeff pokes his head into the dish room. "Yeah, boss, we need more finger bowls, and we're running low on birds. You better start pushing those hot-chicken sammies."

Beth begins to sob. Jeff, surprised, stares at her. "Beam me up, Scotty," he mumbles.

Raymond hands him a stack of finger bowls. "Here."

"She's my *mom,*" Beth emphasizes. "I'm not old enough to have no mother. It's like everyone's got one, right, and they don't even like them. Their mothers could die and they wouldn't give two shits. I *loved* my mother."

Raymond stacks more plates in the rack, then closes the door and starts the washer. He tries to wipe sweat from his forehead with his sweaty forearm. "Beth, listen, what if you have dinner with me tomorrow night? We can go somewhere healthy. Wherever you want."

"With you?"

"Well yeah. If you want." He wipes his hands on his apron. "I just don't want you to be lonely."

She squints. "You mean like on a date?"

"No, just friends." He's thinking about her breasts. "So you won't have to think about your mother."

She pulls a napkin from her apron and wipes her tears. "I don't know if that's such a great idea."

"See how you feel. I'm here till seven. Meet me here. If you want."

She looks at her bill pad tucked into her apron. "I've got to get this toad some pie."

"Only if you feel like it," Raymond insists. "See how it goes."

He hasn't had sex since the divorce. He looks at porno magazines and masturbates, telling himself that this will suffice, that he doesn't need live women. In his experience, live women are too complicated, too demanding, too unpredictable. He tells himself that he is finished with all that.

❖

The smell of the old people's home always nauseates him — the stench of decay. Like a battlefield, the ward is littered with broken bodies. Some of them twitch, some of them moan. A few babble to anyone who'll listen. Raymond becomes fearful in this place, aware that the "retirement home" has become the inevitable precursor to a natural death — his death.

It's his adoptive mother's birthday. A pudding, moulded to resemble a cake, has been decorated with a single candle.

"We made it out of pudding because she can't chew," a rotund attendant explains. "Blow it out, Belinda." She holds it in front of Raymond's mother's gaunt face.

"She can't blow," Raymond points out, extinguishing the flame between his thumb and index finger.

"I can feed her if you want," the attendant offers. Raymond sees "volunteer" printed on her smock. "Happy birthday, Belinda," she says cheerily. "Make a wish."

Raymond takes the "cake" from the volunteer. "Thank you, maybe later." He sets the pudding on the bedside table, then holds out the roses he brought to his mother. She grips his wrist and pulls him towards her, struggling to say something. Pleased that she recognizes him today, he leans close to her, trying not to be repulsed by her smell. After listening intently for some minutes he discerns that she's talking about his twin. She seems to be trying to say that he is not dead. But Raymond finds it hard to believe her, not only because she has Alzheimer's, but because she is drugged. The head nurse warned him that they had been giving her "something" to stop her from shoving her fingers up her rectum and digging out excrement. "She makes herself bleed," the nurse explained, rubbing her chin as though there was dirt on it. Raymond already knew that his mother was shitting wherever the urge came upon her and wiping her hands on whatever was available. "She's very consistent about wiping her hands," the nurse told him. This didn't surprise Raymond because Belinda has always been a lady. She used to iron napkins. She wouldn't leave shit on her hands. The nurse also insisted that they had to sedate her because she was biting attendants. Raymond suggested that if the attendants didn't charge at her with toothbrushes, combs and Q-Tips, she might not need to bite them and they might not need to drug her. The nurse only stared at him as though he were a demented patient himself.

But drugs aside, Raymond can't think why Belinda would come out of her fog to tell him his twin is alive if it weren't true. Maybe she's telling him now because she wants him to know. Because she's dying. Because she doesn't want him to be alone.

He would like to get more information from her, but already her mind has vacated her body. Her eyes scan the ward as though she's looking for something but can't figure out what. The staff haven't even bothered to dress her. She lies stranded in her hospital gown, her withered arms and legs exposed. Raymond tucks the sheet around her. "Mum . . . ?" he asks. But she only stares at him as though he has done something incomprehensible. Her bewildered condition no longer upsets Raymond. He has grown accustomed to the disease that is dissolving her brain.

The woman in the next bed begins tweeting. Raymond knows from experience that she may continue making bird sounds for hours and that this disturbs his mother. When the bird-lady twitters, his mother winces. Not wanting to watch her discomfort, and seeing the attendants bringing in the dinner trays, he decides to leave while she has food to distract her. When he bends down to kiss her cheek, she pushes him away. He tries not to take it personally.

❖

He checks in at the restaurant, even though it's Barney's shift, because he's worried about the chicken shortage. He finds Barney in the washroom, squeezing his pimples. "Can't you do that at home?" Raymond asks.

"It's pus, man, I gotta get it out. You don't want customers seeing pus leaking from my face."

Above the sink a sign reads "For Health Reasons Please Wash Your Hands." Raymond suspects that his staff are inconsistent about washing their hands but he has stopped worrying about it. He washes his, hoping that Barney will follow his example.

Barney points to a pimple. "This is *stress*, man. Last night my girlfriend made her eyes bleed inhaling some nose spray. I had to take her to hospital. Her eyes were bleeding, man."

"I'm sorry to hear that," Raymond says. "But you're needed upstairs. I think maybe you should squeeze your zits on your own time. How's the bird situation?"

"We ran out. I sent Bubba to buy some from IGA."

"How much?"

"You don't want to know. The receipt's on your desk. It was either that or turn customers away. And you know how excited old Kalbfleisch gets when you turn customers away."

"What did Gus say about the freezer?"

"He said it's old. He says we should get a new one."

"It's working though?"

"Yeah, but he offered no guarantees."

"What about the hot-chicken sandwiches?"

"Sold out."

Raymond looks at his watch. "Well at least the rush is over. We'll just have to hope it's a slow day tomorrow."

"In your dreams, man. Sunday's church day."

Bruce, the waiter, shouts down the stairs. "If somebody doesn't make me three Bloody Marys I'm going to ca-ry!"

"Coming right up," Barney shouts back.

Alone in the washroom, Raymond turns to the mirror and is about to commiserate with his reflection when he remembers that his brother might be alive. Suddenly the mirror reflects only Raymond, short of chicken, working for a man he despises in a business that will kill him. Because one night, out of desperation, he will move a chair into the savoury freezer and sit very still with a bottle of scotch until he can no longer move. They will find him in the morning covered in frost, surrounded by frozen chickens.

❖

Mara's spaghetti sauce spots his shirt. "So this monkey," she explains, "crawls out of the earth and knocks on my bedroom window. Actually, it claws the window. And I can't move. I'm absolutely paralysed. I keep thinking I should call 911 but I can't reach the phone. I'm just waiting for the monkey to open the window. And it has these teeth. I can't remember what monkey teeth look like but these are like fangs. And his tongue. God it was gross."

"It was just a dream."

"You don't know that. I don't know that. That's what we *assume.*"

"What else could it be?"

"I have no idea. It was completely realistic, Raymond."

He sprinkles more Parmesan over the sauce. "Did the monkey climb in the window?"

"I can't remember."

"So you woke up. So it was a dream."

"Who's to say it wasn't something paranormal trying to communicate with me?"

"Saying what?"

Mara twists her fork into her spaghetti. "That's what I don't know."

Raymond clears his throat and narrows his eyes, preparing to annoy her. "Squirrel monkeys demonstrate their male dominance by thrusting their erect penises in each other's faces."

Mara stops twisting her fork and stares at him. "What's your point?"

"No point."

"Squirrel monkeys are small, which is why they are called *squirrel* monkeys. This monkey was huge."

"In the dream. Not in real life."

"I knew you wouldn't take this seriously. I don't know why I brought it up." She drops her fork and begins to clear the table even though Raymond hasn't finished.

"My mother," he says, "told me that my identical twin is still alive."

"When?"

"Today."

"And you believe her?"

"Why would she lie?"

"She doesn't know what she's saying. Last week she was singing you the alphabet song. The week before she was going to her high school prom."

"I think she was lucid when she was talking about my twin. I think she was telling me for a reason."

"Which is?"

"She doesn't want me to be alone."

"Oh Raymond, that is so sentimental. This twin thing, it just goes on and on, doesn't it? You won't let it go. It's like a crutch or something."

Once, when they were still married, they saw a TV documentary that showed an ultrasound of twins sucking each other's thumbs in utero. Moved by the shadowy image, Raymond reiterated his longing for his twin, but Mara told him he was romanticizing the "twin thing."

"I think it's sad," she continues, "I think you should get past it." She looks out the kitchen window. "Your dog is shitting in my yard again. I wish you wouldn't let him do that."

"I'll scoop it up later."

"You always say that and you always forget and I step on it."

"It's organic matter."

"Try scraping it off your running shoes."

Raymond wipes his mouth with his napkin. "Anyway, I think I'm going to try to find him."

"Who?"

"My twin. He isn't registered but I'm going to search for him."

Mara groans. "Just because your weird mother said he was alive? Ask her next week, she'll probably say he's dead."

"What do you mean 'weird'?"

"You know what I mean."

"No, I don't."

Mara puts the Parmesan in the fridge. "I don't want to get into this."

"You started it."

"I didn't start anything."

"You said she was weird."

"Raymond, she'll say anything to please you. She's in love with you."

"According to you."

"Fine, okay, let's not get into this, alright? We don't have to fight about this. We're not married any more." She runs water in the sink. Raymond has noticed that since the divorce she often insists that they don't have to fight any more.

He scratches behind his ear. "Why don't you think I should try to find him?"

"I didn't say that. Do what you want. It's your life."

She never used to say this when they were married. He hates it when she says it because it makes him feel as though he doesn't exist. At least when they were married and fought, he felt that he existed.

She squirts dish-washing liquid into the sink. "What am I going to do about that monkey?"

"Do what you want. It's your life."

three

"Like I say," Beth explains, "he told me he was a hermaphrodite."

"What's that?" Raymond tries to stuff alfalfa sprouts back into his pita sandwich.

"It means he was supposed to have a penis and a vagina. Not fully formed, right? Like not normal."

"Did he have . . . both organs?"

"No way. Like I say, he lied to me. He *used* me. There was me feeling all sorry for him and all the time he was a woman." She rips apart her multi-grain roll.

"Why would he say he was both?"

"He said he was more man than woman. That's why he had his breasts cut off. Anyways, that's what he said. And he said he took testosterone to make his penis bigger than his vagina. He said he couldn't even get a Q-Tip up his vagina, which is why he decided he was more man than woman."

Raymond clears his throat. "I guess what I find confusing is that you two lived together, didn't you? So I mean, wouldn't you know what sex he was?"

"He wouldn't let me look. I said *please* let me look, but he wouldn't let me. He told me he was embarrassed because his penis was so small." She shakes her head. "He had no penis."

Raymond is trying to understand how they could have sex without a penis. He doesn't want to ask because he feels that this would be prying.

"With a dildo," Beth explains. "That's what you're thinking, right? He said it was a prosthetic, but it was just a dildo."

Raymond scratches behind his ear. "Why would he — I mean, she — lie to you like that?"

"Because he's a dyke."

Raymond nods slowly, hoping to imply that he understands because he doesn't want to hear any further explanations. He wants to remember Beth as he imagined her before she mentioned her abusive boyfriends, and her girlfriend posing as a boyfriend. He has been noticing that often he imagines that people are what they're not. He'll meet them once and think they're interesting. Then he'll meet them again and find out they're boring. While he's listening to them talk about their exes or their cats, he'll be wondering if they're realizing that *he's* boring. If they're thinking, This guy is so boring I have to talk about my ex and my cat.

"Well," he offers, "people do the strangest things."

"You were married, right?"

"Yeah."

"What happened there?"

"Hard to say."

She smears hummus on her roll. "It's all bullshit anyway, don't you think? All that wedding crap. Who needs it. I quit going to them. I say, if you still love each other in twenty years, I'll come celebrate."

While she chews on her roll, Raymond glances around the restaurant, noticing that even here the customers look unhealthy. He would have thought people would look healthier in a health-food restaurant.

"Do I look like a dyke to you?" Beth asks.

"Not at all."

She jabs at her lettuce with her fork. "Like I say, that's what worries me, that people will think I'm a dyke."

"I don't think they do."

She shakes her head again. "I might just as well've been raped. Even though she's got no penis, she *raped* me."

"Well," Raymond says, "I'm sure there will be other men. I mean, real ones."

Whenever a girl rejected Raymond, his mother always said there would be "other girls." She seemed to believe that there was an endless supply.

Raymond always felt in short supply and couldn't understand why his mother would encourage him to think that girls were expendable. Mara confused him even more by insisting that his mother didn't want him to have a lasting relationship with another woman. "She wants you to herself," she'd say. This would upset Raymond, and they would wrestle until she screamed at him to stop because he was hurting her.

❖

He takes Beth to a movie that is billed as a thriller but it seems to Raymond that most of the action on-screen occurs between naked men and women. Ordinarily this wouldn't bother him, in fact, it might arouse him. But sitting beside Beth, thinking about dildos and severed breasts, he feels embarrassed. Periodically their hands touch as they reach into the popcorn carton and Raymond worries that she will think that he's coming on to her. A waitress at work thought Raymond was coming on to her. She sent her boyfriend after him, who threatened to kick in Raymond's headlights. Fortunately that waitress got pregnant and went to live in the suburbs. As a rule Raymond doesn't date the waitresses. He realizes now that asking Beth to dinner was a mistake. Already he's planning a clean exit. He'll behave brotherly towards her, drive her home and tell her that she can call him any time she misses her mother; any time she needs a shoulder to cry on. He'll pat her shoulder and say something like, "You'll get through it," or "You're young, you have your whole life ahead of you." He'll watch her unlock her door and will wait until she is safely inside. Then he'll drive away.

❖

He can't believe he couldn't sustain an erection. After the scotch, Beth's breasts appeared fuller to him, her face prettier, her personality softer. Now, sitting on the toilet with his head in his hands and a limp penis between his legs, Raymond is stupefied. What to do now, he wonders, now that she can sue him for sexual harassment; now that she can say he made her pregnant and force him to pay child support. Now that she can blackmail him, extort money from him, discuss his impotence with Barney and the boys.

He stands, startling himself in the mirror. His reflection glares back at him. He throws water on his face and rinses his mouth to wash away the taste of Beth. Looking at his twin he sees no compassion, only disdain.

The lights are still off in the bedroom but her smell is everywhere. An hour ago the scent had been alluring. Now it is a stench that he imagines only steam cleaning will remove. He can't bring himself to get back into bed with her so he tiptoes into the living room and pours more scotch. He puts on his trenchcoat, then picks up the converter and channel surfs. The Juice Man elaborates on the effectiveness of spinach and pear juice on irritable bowel syndrome. John Wayne rides a horse and shoots Indians. A man and a woman rub crotches on a Harley-Davidson. A fitness instructor demonstrates how Raymond too can have buns of steel. A newsman tells him that more people have massacred more people. Raymond turns off the TV and listens to the night: the expressway humming, the fridge gurgling, Burt snoring.

He decides he must tell Beth now, get it over with, get her out of his apartment. He can blame his ex, say that he is still in love with his ex. Beth will understand.

He turns on the bedside lamp and sees that there is no body under the pile of blankets. He checks the bathroom, then searches for traces of her clothes. "Beth?" he calls, but she's gone. He can't even smell her. He begins to worry about what she'll say at work. What should he say at work when he sees her? Should he say anything? He's the boss, he could just ignore her. He could pretend the whole thing never happened. If she tells anybody, he could say she's nuts. This wouldn't be very nice though. His mother wouldn't like it.

He takes one of the sleeping pills that Mara left behind because he wants to be drugged, free of thought, free of conscience. He studies the label on the bottle. The prescription is three years old. Mara stopped sleeping after the sixth miscarriage. She paced, she sat, she paced, drank scotch, paced, sat. It drove Raymond to distraction because there was nothing he could do to stop it, nothing he could do to relieve her pain. The first five times he was able to say that miscarriages were normal, that they could try again. But by the sixth time even her doctor looked worried. He suggested that her uterus may have become too scarred from the repeated D & Cs to carry a pregnancy to term. He suggested that she might want to consider "other options."

The look on her face after the last D & C will never leave him. It was as though they had cut out her heart. There were no words that he could say, no touch that he could give, that had any meaning in the face of her suffering. He almost wished that she were dead, that her expression was the result of some horrible accident. An expression that could be repaired by a mortician.

She never spoke about it, never speaks about it. The first five times she railed about the injustice of it. "All I ever wanted was babies!" she screamed. But after the sixth time she became silent and snapped at him when she felt that he was pitying her. "This has nothing to do with you," she'd insist, "this is *my* problem. You can do what you want, I won't stop you." He tried to explain that he wasn't interested in having babies with anyone else; that, in fact, babies weren't a priority with him. But she accused him of lying to make her feel better. "Nothing will make me feel better," she informed him. "I have a defective womb. That's the way it is. I have to live with it." Just as he had allowed her to lead them into parenthood, he allowed her to lead them out of it. And when she told him that she was getting her tubes tied, he didn't argue.

As his eyelids grow heavy he wonders if a better marriage could have withstood the miscarriages; if a better man could have prevented his wife from nearly killing herself with scotch and sleeping pills. That morning when she lay curled up on the bathroom floor like a fetus, he thought she was dead. The ambulance took forever. Raymond knelt beside her, gripping her hand, pleading with her not to die. In the hospital, after they'd pumped her stomach, he didn't know what to say or how to touch her. The doctor told him that he might as well take her home because if she was determined to kill herself, staying in the hospital wouldn't stop her.

While Raymond was tucking her into bed he asked if she had intended to kill herself. She said nothing, only stared at him with lifeless eyes. He tried to hold her hand but it felt cold.

"Go to work," she murmured, "I'll be alright." He didn't argue because he didn't want to stay, didn't know how to deal with it, her, life.

In a moment he knows that he will be asleep. He rolls on to his side and feels himself sinking into sand.

❖

He never knows what to do on his days off. He looks forward to them, then finds out that he has nothing to do except laundry and housecleaning.

He phones the social worker again but she's in a meeting. He phones his adoptive father, hoping but fearing that he will be home. Raymond lets it ring ten times before hanging up.

He looks in the paper for something to do. The air and aviation show is on at the airport. Raymond has always liked planes, always thought it would be exciting to be a pilot, so he drives out to the airport. The first thing he notices is that there are very few planes on exhibit. There are many kiosks selling ice cream, souvenirs and memberships to flight clubs, but hardly any planes. He stares at the helicopters and the few small planes. Around him many other people do the same thing. He wonders why they aren't at work and what they're doing here; if they're rich and fly planes or if they're just people with nothing to do like himself. A tall woman strides by in a flight suit. Raymond wonders if she has clothes on underneath and if she flies planes. A child bumps into him, drops his ice-cream cone and begins to wail. Raymond quickly ducks behind the B25 bomber and looks into the cockpit. It would be great, he thinks, to fly a bomber; to know that at any second you could kill or be killed. There would be no time for guilt, no time for blame. He studies the bubble that houses the gunner and marvels at how exposed he was. Who were the gunners? Were they like front-line men, dispensable? Did they climb into their bubbles expecting to die? How did the pilot feel when the Jerries knocked off his gunner? Did it make him more determined or more afraid? Any time Raymond is reminded of his own vulnerability he becomes more afraid. He worries that eventually he will be so afraid he won't be able to leave his high-rise. A man down the hall suffers from an obsessive-compulsive disorder and can't leave his apartment without going in and out of the door several times. Then he has to take a step backwards after every three steps forwards. When Raymond passes him in the hall, he doesn't hold the elevator for him because he knows that the man has an even more complicated ritual involving the elevator doors. He has considered his own rituals involving oral hygiene and toilet sanitation. He worries that he too could become handicapped by his own compulsions.

He stares at boxes of miniature model planes, wondering why he has come to an air show when he used to hate going to car shows with his father. His father could discuss cars for hours with anyone who seemed interested. Sometimes, when he remembered Raymond was with him, he would buy him a hot dog. But usually Raymond lost sight of his father. He'd get into a panic, thinking that his father had left without him; that he would never find him; that he would be stranded among the Barracudas and Mustangs. But then he'd hear his father shouting his name and he would run towards his voice. It didn't bother Raymond when his father cuffed him on the back of his head for wandering off. He liked it because it meant that he existed.

Raymond climbs into a skydiving harness that lifts him a few feet above the ground. He hovers suspended from a machine that is supposed to simulate skydiving. Staring down at the Astroturf he feels silly and knows that people are watching him. He jerks his arms and legs, causing him to tip. He feels like a fly caught in a web. "Head up," the man operating the machine tells him. But Raymond finds it difficult to keep his head up, and the harness is hurting his crotch. He knew that getting into this contraption was a bad idea. All his life he has had bad ideas that he knew beforehand were bad, but he did them anyway; like sleeping with Beth.

"That's enough, thank you," he says, but the operator isn't paying attention. Raymond knows that he will have to hang here, strung up like a marionette, until the operator decides to let him free. Raymond could shout or scream but he doesn't want to cause a scene. Resisting other people's control, in his experience, only causes them to dislike him. Or worse still, ignore him. Sometimes when his father ignored him, Belinda would as well. Later she would explain that she'd ignored him not because she wanted to, but because she didn't want to anger Gord. "You know what he's like," she'd say. Raymond did know what he was like; he was mean and stupid. But he never said this. He only quietly hated Belinda for not defending him from Gord. Raymond swore that he would never ignore anyone, that no one deserved to be ignored. But then he ignored Mara. For days he wouldn't converse with her, would just grumble greetings. She'd break down in frustration, but he'd continue to ignore her. Because in his mind she had become his mother, his father, the entire ignoring world.

After the sixth miscarriage she ignored him back. After she had her tubes tied, nothing he did seemed to matter.

❖

He finishes his pizza, then phones again. When his father answers, Raymond becomes speechless.

"Who's this?" Gord asks. "Hello?"

"It's Raymond."

"Raymond. How are you? How's your mother?"

"She's alright. I think. I mean the place seems pretty clean, she seems to be cared for."

"Glad to hear it."

Raymond knows that Gord isn't interested in Belinda, that he's only asking to be polite. He wonders what he's doing, if he's watching TV, if he's drinking rye.

"How can I help you, Ray?"

"Well, it's about my twin."

"Your what?"

"My twin." He knows that already Gord is bored. Raymond thinks he can hear a football game in the background. "Mum says that he's still alive."

"She said that?"

"Yes. And I was wondering if maybe you knew anything about it — him, I mean — being alive." Words become stumbling blocks when he talks to his father.

"Alive hunh?"

"That's what she said."

"Well isn't that something."

"Is it true?"

"Raymond, if I told you once, I told you a hundred times, I never knew what your mother was up to."

"I just thought you might know about this, because, I mean, you were there." He hears Gord swallow something liquid.

"You want to know my gut feeling about this?" Raymond feels his father losing patience, wanting to close the deal. "I think that you should let sleeping dogs lie. You're a grown man. You've got other concerns."

"Like what?" Raymond demands, startled by his own impudence.

"Kid, if you don't know that, I can't help you." Raymond always hated it when his father called him "kid." It was as though he couldn't remember his name. And when he said "kid" he made it sound as though he owned Raymond, as though Raymond were his slave and had no choice but to obey. Which Raymond believed was true. Because being adopted had meant that they weren't obliged to love him, since there were no blood ties.

They could decide that they hated him and send him back and order another kid, one who would obey.

He felt this when Gord accused him of stealing his cigarettes. Raymond was only ten and didn't even smoke. "You don't deserve to be in this family," Gord shouted. "From now on you can live here, but we don't have to talk to you, or eat with you. I'll put a roof over your head but that's it. I've had it with you." Then he sent Raymond to his room. Huddled under his blankets with his pillow over his head, he could hear his mother sobbing. But he didn't care because she hadn't stuck up for him. She had betrayed him. He knew he could never completely trust her again. Or anybody.

In the morning Gord found his cigarettes but he didn't apologize to Raymond, he just left for work. Belinda apologized and begged him for forgiveness. She dropped to her knees before him. But it was too late.

"So you don't remember anything?" Raymond asks. "About the twin?"

"I remember what your mother said, same as you."

Raymond senses that his father knows more, that he's lying. Even with miles between them, his parents stand united against him. "You don't understand," he persists. "She wants me to know, she told me he was alive. She doesn't want me to be alone."

"Then she's the person to talk to, isn't she?"

"She's demented."

"Raymond, I left her and that life a long time ago. I don't mind you calling me, but I'm not going to start digging around in the past. It's over and done with. Best forgotten. Trust me on this."

Raymond would like to shout that he wouldn't trust him further than he could piss. He would like to call him bastard and asshole and selfish prick. But it's as though his chest is bound in rope. Every breath hurts.

"Gotta go, kid," Gord says. "Take care of yourself and that wife of yours." Raymond hears the click, then the dial tone.

His father doesn't even remember that he is no longer married. He doesn't even care.

Raymond puts the phone down, then crawls into bed. He huddles under the blankets and puts his pillow over his head.

four

Dear Son,

I hope things worked out good for you. Those social workers told me you was going to a good home. They said your new mother couldn't have babies of her own and was very happy to have you. I hope they brought you joy as I'm sure you brought them. All the same I'm so happy you decided to register because I knew one day you would. Your horoscope is very good this month. It says you have often worried about the future but not done anything about it. It says this month you'll have an opportunity to make big changes if you are willing to take risks. You may have to work hard but the rewards will be great. The people that you meet could make an impact on your life that will help you in the future, if you get involved. That could be me. It says pay attention to what your inner feelings tell you. Live a little.

Here is a picture of me from when I won a trip to Disney World. I hope to see you soon.

Love,

your real Mum

The woman in the photo is standing beside a man in a Pluto costume. Pluto has his arm around her shoulders. It's difficult to see the woman's face because she's wearing dark glasses and a floppy hat. In her left hand she holds green cotton candy.

Raymond looks hard at the photograph. She seems to have pleasant features. She's slightly overweight but not unattractively so. He can't see her hair under the hat but she looks fair. It does alarm him slightly that she's wearing platform shoes. Perhaps it's because she's quite short and feels the need for extra height. He wonders how old the photograph is, tries to remember when platform shoes were fashionable. He had a short boss once who wore them and stomped around snapping his fingers at the staff. That was ten or fifteen years ago.

Bruce, the waiter, barges into the office. "Raymond, can I use the phone?"

"What's wrong with the one upstairs?"

"This is a private matter."

"Well, I'm right in the middle of something."

"Oh, well *excuse me.* I only happen to be experiencing a crisis."

"Craig?"

Bruce nods. "I know you don't take our relationship seriously because we happen to be gay."

Raymond folds Gloria's letter. "That's not true."

"It's just like any other marriage. We have problems."

"You seem to be having a lot of them lately."

"You should talk, Raymond. How long were you married? Five minutes?"

Raymond slides the letter into his back pocket. "Try to keep it short."

"Just get Beth to call me if it gets busy."

Raymond rereads the letter in the corridor, trying to connect it with the slender waitress with the oval-shaped face and long eyelashes who wanted to be a nurse. Obviously she's changed, he tells himself, this is to be expected. She's aged thirty-seven years. It just surprises him that she seems to have some difficulty with grammar. Perhaps she has cataracts and finds it nearly impossible to put pen to paper. The horoscope business concerns him. He has always been uncomfortable around people who believe in horoscopes.

Beth shouts downstairs. "I need two brown cows and a half-litre of white."

"I'll be right up," Raymond calls back. He thinks about his own letter. It wasn't particularly well written either. He doubts that Gloria was impressed. In fact, it surprises him that she has gone ahead and signed the consent. The social worker told him that "the ball is in his court," that Gloria is willing to meet him wherever, whenever, he wants.

It also bothers him that she went to Disney World. Why would a grown woman go to Disney World? She says she won the trip. Raymond has never won anything. Maybe he would go to Disney World if he won a free trip. But would he pose with Pluto?

Jeff stops him at the top of the stairs. "Boss, we're out of apple pie again."

"That's impossible. I ordered a case of them."

"See for yourself." He pulls open the sweet freezer and points to the two remaining apple pies. "Highly illogical, Captain."

"Do you think someone is stealing them?" Raymond asks.

"No comment."

"Jeff, you're supposed to be managing the kitchen. You're supposed to pay attention to who's walking in and out of the freezers."

"To the best of my knowledge, no one is stealing pies."

"Well then where are the rest of them?"

"Beats me." Jeff spits on his glasses, then uses a Kleenex to wipe the grease off the lenses.

"Is it too much to ask that you pay attention from now on?"

He puts his glasses back on. "It's hard to dismember chicken and watch the freezers at the same time."

Beth glares at Raymond while she picks up her orders. "I asked for two brown cows and a half-litre of white half an hour ago."

"It was more like ten minutes," Raymond says. "I'm getting it."

"You explain to the customers why they're getting their drinks *after* their chicken."

Raymond follows her into the dining room and steps behind the bar to mix the drinks. It startles him to see Dr. Kalbfleisch at a table eating hot-fudge cake. Usually the staff warn him when he arrives. "Raymond," he calls, beckoning him with his hand. Beth takes the drink order without thanking Raymond.

"What can I do for you, sir?" he asks, approaching the table.

"Sit down, Raymond." He does, noticing some ketchup on the chair. He doesn't wipe it off because this would give Dr. Kalbfleisch an opportunity to complain that the staff never clean the chairs.

Dr. Kalbfleisch spoons five sugars into his coffee. "There is no energy in this restaurant."

"Energy?" Last night Raymond dreamed that Dr. Kalbfleisch was ordering him to get into his Mercedes. Raymond knew that if he got into the car, he would never come out alive. But he didn't want to annoy Dr. Kalbfleisch and lose his job. So he pretended to be getting into the car but then acted as though he'd just remembered something he needed to do in the restaurant. Once inside the restaurant he peered through the blinds to see if Dr. Kalbfleisch would leave, but he didn't. He was waiting for him.

Hot-fudge sauce coats the corners of Dr. Kalbfleisch's mouth. "God forbid we should sell any chicken. God forbid we should turn a profit."

"Tuesdays are slow days. We could try offering ten-cent wings. That would bring people in."

"And they'd sit around all day eating three dollars worth of food. Is that the way to run a business?"

"It's just an idea, to bring people in."

"You think Chicken Villa offers ten-cent wings?"

"Chicken Villa offers midweek specials."

Dr. Kalbfleisch holds his hands over his ears. "Don't start with the specials, Raymond."

"You always say that Chicken Villa is crowded midweek. It's crowded because they offer midweek specials."

It worries Raymond that he has begun to dream about Dr. Kalbfleisch on a regular basis. When he mentioned this to Mara, she said that it meant that Dr. Kalbfleisch had entered his subconscious mind. "He's controlling you," she said sadly, as though there were no hope for him.

"There's going to be changes around here," Dr. Kalbfleisch warns him.

Beth approaches to clear Dr. Kalbfleisch's plate. "More coffee, sir?"

"A smile would be better," he says. "How much for a smile?"

Beth ignores him and stares at Raymond. Until now he has managed to appear preoccupied around her; too busy to talk. "Do you want something?" she inquires.

"No thanks."

She swiftly clears a neighbouring table, then takes the plates to the dish room.

"Why can't you find friendly waitresses?" Dr. Kalbfleisch asks. "Bubbly girls. There's lots of bubbly girls who want jobs."

Raymond scratches behind his ear. "Beth is our best waitress."

"Is it any wonder nobody comes into this restaurant? With waitresses like that I wouldn't come into this restaurant. I couldn't eat looking at that face."

"Her mother just died," Raymond reminds him.

Dr. Kalbfleisch holds his hands over his ears. "Don't start with the dead mother, Raymond."

❖

Beth corners him while he's changing a ribbon on the take-out cash register. "I'm willing to forget the whole thing," she declares, "but there's no way I'm going to be treated like a second-class citizen."

Raymond glances around to see if anybody's listening.

"Nobody's listening," she tells him.

He clears his throat. "I'm sorry you feel that way."

"Like I say, I'm willing to forget the whole thing, but don't go acting like it was my problem."

"I don't think it was anybody's problem. These things happen."

She jabs her finger into his chest. "It was *your* problem, pal. Don't go blaming me for your problem. Men always do this. When they can't get it up, all of a sudden it's everybody's problem. When the woman isn't into it, she's frigid. Well fuck you. Fuck all of you." She strides to the order shelf and shouts into the kitchen, "Where's that order? This toad's been waiting twenty minutes."

Women impress Raymond. Because they can endure pain and continue on with their lives. Nothing stops them: raping, pillaging, childbearing. In spite of their suffering they forge ahead. Raymond has happily followed in their tracks. Now, without his mother or Mara for guidance, he feels directionless. On his own he inevitably chooses the path of least resistance. And inevitably it leads him nowhere.

He wonders if he should attach himself to Beth. If she's headed anywhere that he would like to go.

He thinks about Gloria again and imagines that she must be a powerful woman. Because of hardship she surrendered sons. But now she is willing to take them back, to welcome them into the fold. Raymond can already imagine the pies that she will bake and the roasts that she will roast. Beth said she always went to her mother's for Sunday dinner. Raymond would like to take Beth to his birth mother's for Sunday dinner. This might improve her mood. Although it would mean that he would have to explain that he was adopted. Usually he doesn't tell anyone. In his experience, telling people only causes problems. Suddenly they act as though he has been lying to them, pretending to be someone else. Without biological parents he becomes unidentifiable. He could be anybody: a serial killer. Raymond finds this hard to understand since he rarely meets other people's parents. And he doesn't believe that if he did meet them, he would feel any differently towards anybody. But saying the words "I'm adopted" has always dampened conversations. Because it means that he shouldn't have been born, that he was a mistake.

If his twin is alive, he too will be feeling these things, and they'll be able to talk about them. And as a result of sharing their feelings and experiences, they will feel less isolated. They will have each other.

Of course, his twin may not know that he is a twin, which would explain why he hasn't searched for Raymond. Their reunion with each other and their birth mother will not only be joyful, but will end their lives as outcasts.

Beth returns and deftly balances an order on her arms. She is the only waitress who can carry six plates at once. "Phone for you," she snaps. Raymond worries that she will never be in a good mood again.

"She's got nice gazoombas anyway," Dr. Kalbfleisch observes over Raymond's shoulder.

"I thought you'd left."

"You want me to leave?" Dr. Kalbfleisch takes out a handkerchief, wraps it around his index finger and pokes it into one of his nostrils.

"I didn't say that."

"Don't worry, I'm leaving. Jeff's giving me a chicken."

Jeff comes out from behind the broiler and hands Dr. Kalbfleisch a wrapped chicken. "Crispy, sir, just the way you like it."

"I've heard that before." He stuffs the handkerchief into his pocket. "Raymond, think about the numbers. The numbers are down. Go eat at Chicken Villa, see if you can learn something."

Mara has told Raymond many times that eating shit is all right if you're making lots of money doing it. But for what Raymond is making, she says, she wouldn't eat tapioca. It used to bother him that she made more money than he did. They'd be considering buying a new TV, or a microwave. He'd suggest that it was too expensive and she'd say, "Don't worry about it," and whip out her gold American Express card.

He notices the "hold" light blinking on the phone and remembers that it's for him. "Hello?"

"It's me." She sounds small, as though she's shrunk.

"What's up?"

"The police are digging up the bones. My brother called them. He said I couldn't live with unidentified remains in my yard. He said it would compromise my soul. They're making a mess of the yard. Can you come over later?"

"Where's your brother?"

"He's at the track. He bet on Superstition, he had to go."

Raymond glances at his watch. "I'm pretty tired."

"Please? I'm scared."

"Alright. It won't be for a while though. I have to wait for Barney to show up. And I have to walk Burt."

"That's okay."

He finds Barney talking to Jeff in the washroom. Jeff's shift is over, but Barney should be on the floor. Raymond tries to look authoritative. "Barney . . ."

Barney holds up his hand. "Just a sec. He's talking about William Shatner."

"Who?"

"Captain Kirk."

"So he's inspecting this location," Jeff continues, "where they're going to shoot this movie. And his handlers send memos to the entire staff, saying that they're not, under any circumstances, to address him as Captain Kirk."

"Why not?"

"Identity crisis, I don't know." He tosses his apron into the laundry bin. "So he's doing this inspection and a girl who didn't read the memo runs up to him, pointing and shouting, 'Captain Kirk! Captain Kirk!' He totally freaks out and starts running from her, but she chases after him shouting, 'Captain Kirk! Captain Kirk!' So finally he turns and points at her and says, 'Don't *ever* call me that again.'"

"What's his problem?"

"Barney," Raymond repeats.

"Yes sir, how can I help you?"

"By getting on the floor for starters. You're twenty minutes late."

"My girlfriend had an abortion yesterday, man. Without even telling me.

She just went and did it. It took way longer than it was supposed to because she's so tiny. She was one sick pup."

Raymond isn't sure that he believes this story, although it's more convincing than Barney's usual the-dog-ate-my-homework excuses. "That was yesterday. You're late today."

"Have some pity, man. It's not something you get over in a day. She didn't want me to leave her."

Raymond knows that he should find another assistant manager, but he hates firing people. "Just get upstairs."

He delays going to Mara's by eating at Chicken Villa. The waitress is bubbly and keeps asking if she can get him anything else. Her breasts perch very high on her chest and he wonders what happens when she takes off her bra. He orders a chocolate sundae for dessert just so that she'll keep asking him things. When she brings it, he asks if she likes working at Chicken Villa.

"Oh yes. They're pretty decent here. I'd probably make more in a bar, but then I'd have guys slobbering all over me."

Raymond tries to disguise his own slobbering by spooning ice cream into his mouth. "So you've got the hours you want?" he asks, hoping that she'll say she wants more hours and he can offer her a job.

"Oh yes. Well, I'm not full-time. My fiancé likes me to cook for him, so I only do lunches. Today's different because one of the girls called in sick."

"Hunh."

"Can I get you anything else?"

"Some more coffee would be nice. Thank you." At Chicken Villa they offer free refills. When Raymond suggested to Dr. Kalbfleisch that Chez Simon offer free refills, Dr. Kalbfleisch said, "Is that the way to run a business?"

Raymond rereads Gloria's letter. "Pay attention to what your inner feelings tell you. Live a little." He's touched that she signed it "your real Mum." First thing tomorrow he'll get the consent in order. And apply to the Children's Aid Society for a search to locate his twin. The social worker warned him that the waiting list for searches was very long. Maybe Raymond and Gloria can find him on their own.

When the waitress bends over to refill his cup he notices that she smells of strawberries. "You smell good," he comments.

She jerks herself straight and stares at him, suddenly hostile. "Excuse me?"

"Sorry." He wipes ice cream from his mouth with a napkin. "I just couldn't help noticing that you smell nice."

"Will that be all?" Already she's whipping his bill out from her apron.

"Yes, thanks."

She slaps the bill on the table and does not look in his direction again during the ten minutes it takes to finish his coffee. Why do women wear perfume if they don't want men to notice it?

He leaves her a three-dollar tip.

❖

Mara sits at the kitchen table, trembling.

"What's going on?" Raymond asks.

"It's horrible."

"What is?"

She drops her head into her hands and leans her elbows on the table. Raymond opens the back door for Burt.

"Don't let him out there," Mara gasps.

"Why not? Didn't they take the bones?"

"There might be more."

"What do you mean?"

"They think there might be more. They're going to keep digging." She covers her face with her hands. Raymond admires her perfectly polished fingernails. He's never understood why she paints her fingernails, but he admires her handiwork anyway.

"Digging for what?" he asks.

"More bones."

"What sort of bones?"

She lurches out of her chair and runs to the washroom. When he hears her throwing up, he understands that something horrible has happened. He reaches down and pulls on Burt's ears and scratches his belly. He hears her flush the toilet and run the taps. While he waits for her to come out, he opens the back door and looks at the yard. What was grass is now mud. The apple tree he planted for her has been dug up and left with its roots exposed. He considers going out and wrapping a garbage bag around them but then notices the yellow police tape. He closes the door and sits at the kitchen table. Mara has been drinking scotch so he sips from her glass. When she doesn't come out of the washroom, he knocks gently on the door. "Mara?"

"Give me a second." Her voice sounds hoarse, almost like the voice of the possessed girl in *The Exorcist.* He sits back at the kitchen table and drinks more of her scotch.

When she comes out she walks stiffly with her bottom lip tucked under her upper. She doesn't look at him but stares at the floor. She sits very straight at the kitchen table. "It was a baby."

"In the yard?"

She nods, still not looking at him. "They think there might be more. They think some woman lived here who kept getting pregnant and didn't want the babies. They don't know if she starved them, or strangled them, or if they just got sick and died." Raymond pours more scotch into the glass. She starts to shake her head and doesn't stop. "It's like they were my babies. I can't stop feeling like they were *my* babies." Her straight back buckles and she begins to sob. Watching her bent over, her delicate ribs heaving, he tries to think of how to help.

"They weren't your babies," he mumbles.

"I said they *feel* like my babies. Of course they're not my babies. How could they be my babies?" Always, when she cries, she fights her tears with anger. Often he has been caught in the crossfire.

She stands abruptly, goes to the sink and throws cold water on her face. She rips paper towel from the dispenser and pats her face dry. "I've got to sell the house."

"You love this house."

"I hate this house."

"You won't get back what you put into it in this market."

Suddenly she's shouting at him. "What does it matter? As if it fucking matters! There's dead babies in the backyard!"

"Only one. They've only found one baby."

"If they find six, I will die."

He offers her the scotch but she ignores him. He drinks some.

"All my fucking life," she says, "all I wanted was a husband, a house and babies. All my fucking life. I've got the house and I've got the babies. The only problem is, they're dead."

"Mara . . ."

She starts to sob again and pull on her hair. She grips it close to the skull.

"Sweetheart . . ."

"What a fucking joke," she says in the *Exorcist* voice. "A fucking joke. My entire life."

He reaches across the table and grips her forearms, hoping to prise her hands loose from her hair, but she won't let go. "Mara, baby, please, please, honey, you're scaring me."

"Don't call me baby. I hate it when you call me baby." Her grip loosens and she drops her hands into her lap. She stares back at the floor. "I can't be alone tonight."

"I know."

"I can't be alone."

"I know, sweetheart." He moves his chair so that he is sitting directly in front of her. She won't look at him. He can see that she's trembling again. He holds her hands and waits for her to look at him.

five

Driving to meet Gloria at the Howard Johnson's, Raymond feels sick. All afternoon he has had diarrhea because of his nervous state. When Dr. Kalbfleisch told him that the Chez Simon sign needed to be cleaned, Raymond planned to ask one of the dishwashers to do it. But then it occurred to him that being up on the ladder, in the air — away from Dr. Kalbfleisch — might make him feel better. This was true except that Raymond had to climb down the ladder several times to use the washroom. Eventually, Dr. Kalbfleisch followed him outside and scurried around the base of the ladder, shouting instructions to him. From up above, Raymond found it easy to ignore him and instead thought about Mara, and how she was doing at work; if she was telling anyone about the baby bones. This morning, her brother had phoned and was not happy when Raymond answered. Raymond decided not to explain that he and Mara had not had sex. Instead he asked if Superstition had won at the races.

"No," Arthur said.

Raymond cleared his throat. "Did you lose a lot of money?"

"May I speak to Mara, please."

When Mara got on the phone she immediately became pathetic and girlish. Raymond has always despised her relationship with her brother, has never understood why he has such power over her. She was still on the phone when he left. She didn't even say goodbye.

At the Children's Aid Society things moved very quickly because the social worker had a flood in her basement and had to return home. She called Gloria who said she wanted to see Raymond right away because she'd been "waiting thirty-seven years and didn't want to wait another minute." The social worker offered to be present at the reunion but Raymond didn't want her around. At least he thought he didn't. Now he isn't so sure. What will he say to Gloria? What if he can't think of anything to say? It's not as if they know each other and have things in common. And he's mildly disappointed that she chose to meet him at a Howard Johnson's. He would have preferred that their reunion take place in more pleasant surroundings; a restaurant with flowers on the table and linen napkins. Perhaps Gloria chose Howard Johnson's because she suspected that he would insist on paying the bill, therefore she didn't want it to be high. She was tactfully saving him money. The social worker said that Gloria would be wearing a magenta turban. Raymond didn't admit that he wasn't certain what magenta looked like, or that he thought it was weird that his mother would be wearing a turban. This afternoon he looked up magenta and learned that it was a reddish purple.

While he's stopped at a light, he sniffs his shirt to determine if he smells of chicken. Of course he does. He should have brought a clean shirt and changed at work. He glances at his watch, considering if he has time to buy a new one. Around him he sees only fast-food restaurants and gas stations. Then he remembers that he told the social worker he would be wearing a brown corduroy shirt. What are the chances of finding a brown corduroy shirt in a hurry? Besides, he realizes, if he buys a shirt, it will look brand new. It will look as though he bought the shirt specifically to meet his birth mother. He would rather not leave this impression. He would prefer to appear casual, as though it won't devastate him if she doesn't like him.

Pulling into the Howard Johnson's parking lot he feels even more sick. He parks, then rests his forehead against the steering wheel, waiting for the dizziness to pass. He feels sweat on his forehead and temples and worries that he will look sweaty to her. He wipes it off with a Kleenex and puts some extra tissues in his pants pocket. In the rearview mirror, he scrutinizes the pimple forming beside his nose and his shaving cut. He doesn't look healthy in his opinion. There are dark circles under his eyes and a pallor to his skin: raw chicken skin, his face is the colour of raw chicken skin.

He walks up and down the dining room of the Howard Johnson's but sees no woman with a turban. Three Sikhs are sitting by the window and he looks twice at them. When he sees the squat, turbanned woman coming out of the ladies' room, his first instinct is to run. She's wearing a peacock blue and orange sleeveless blouse with brown stretch pants. She trudges towards a table with her chin jutting forward. As she walks, her slip-on sandals flap against her heels and she repeatedly tugs the blouse down over her hips. She looks poor, like the woman who comes into Chez Simon, orders the cheapest food on the menu, then occupies the table for hours. She looks like the kind of woman he feels sorry for. When she sees him she waves her arms as though she's just won a prize. "I can't believe it."

Raymond tries to smile as he approaches her. "Hello, Gloria."

"Don't you look nice. All dressed up. All Dwayne ever wears is jeans."

"Who's Dwayne?"

She puts her hand over her mouth. "I'm not supposed to say anything."

"About what?"

"Oh Raymond, I'm so proud of you. What you've done for yourself."

As he sits across from her, he notices that some of her red lipstick has bled into the wrinkles above her upper lip. "I haven't done much," he admits.

"Sure you have. I was worried, see. Because you didn't send a photo. I thought maybe something had happened to you. Like you was missing an arm or something."

"No. Nothing like that. I just didn't have a recent photo."

"Well, you look just like him," Gloria says. "Only nicer, cleaner looking. He don't shave no more."

"Who?"

"Oh for heaven's sake, there's me spilling the beans again."

"Is Dwayne my father?"

"Heavens, no. He's your brother. They told me not to tell you right away but I figure we might as well get it out in the open."

"Dwayne's my twin?"

"That's right."

"He's alive then?"

Gloria frowns. "Who told you he was dead?"

"My mother."

"Now why would she say that?"

"I don't know. I guess she was afraid of losing me."

"Poor thing. Well you tell her we're not taking anybody from nobody. We're all family here."

"Actually, recently she told me he was alive." There's something very strange about Gloria, besides the turban. Raymond isn't sure what it is.

"The thing is," she says, "he don't know about you. He's got two sisters, see."

"Two sisters?"

"They're not real sisters. They've got a different dad, see. Dwayne *hates* them. Don't know how he'd feel about a brother. Specially one that looks like him." She turns her head slightly and looks at him primarily out of her right eye. "He's a little shorter than you, maybe."

Raymond is having difficulty absorbing all this information. "I guess what I don't understand is . . . weren't we both put up for adoption?"

"It started out that way. Then he got sick, see. He came out all skinny and white. They wasn't sure if he was going to make it, or if he'd be retarded or whatnot, so the people who were supposed to take him got scared."

"Why was he skinny and white?"

"I don't know. He just came out that way. So I told them to go to hell, I was keepin' him. I didn't want him shopped around, see. I didn't want people feeling sorry for him and taking him on like a charity case. I knew he'd be alright if I looked after him."

Raymond feels a pang, a yearning to have been the feeble one that the mother refused to give away.

"Don't feel bad about it, Raymond. You was lucky they took you. Dwayne and me haven't exactly had it easy."

But how could you give me up? he wants to ask. As much as he understands that things were different back then, he still can't understand how she could give up one son and keep the other. If she could care for one, why not two?

"Are you going to have a cocktail?" she asks.

"Ah, sure. A scotch with ice."

Gloria waves at the waitress. "Two scotch on the rocks."

Raymond realizes that he must say something, otherwise it will become obvious that he is hurt and he's not sure that this is appropriate. Gloria did the best she could under the circumstances. "What are my half-sisters' names?"

"Tammy and Tory. They lived mostly with their dad. Dwayne never liked them." She grabs a menu. "I'm hungry, are you hungry?" She puts on glasses and looks at the menu. "I feel like some chicken. What're you going to have?"

He wishes she wouldn't eat chicken. "I think I'll just have a salad."

She looks over her glasses at him. "You one of those people don't eat meat?"

"I eat meat. I just don't feel like any right now."

"Dwayne eats meat. I buy pork chops supposed to last the whole week, the next day they're history. He just fries them up and eats them. No vegetables. I tell him, 'You've got to eat vegetables.' But he don't listen to me."

"He still lives with you then?"

She pokes her index finger under her turban and scratches. "Well that's one of the problems, see. He got laid off, and his UI ran out, so he's back home. I don't mind, it's just feeding two costs money, know what I mean?"

"Of course." It surprises Raymond that his twin, at thirty-seven, is living with Gloria. "Is he looking for a job?"

"Don't get me started," Gloria says. "I tell him he's got to go out there and hustle, but he don't listen to me. What's *your* job, Raymond?"

"I work in a restaurant."

"You the manager?"

"Yes." He can see this pleases her. Her eyes crinkle and the creases leave her forehead. Only now has he figured out what is strange about her. She has no eyelashes or eyebrows. What happened to her long lashes?

The tired waitress brings their drinks. Gloria holds up her glass. "Cheers, Raymond."

"Cheers." They clink glasses.

"I was hoping you'd done better for yourself." Gloria takes off her glasses and puts them in her handbag. "Like, that's why I gave you up, see, so's you'd have a better future, know what I mean?" He notices that she has pencilled-in eyebrows. "What restaurant you work in?"

"Chez Simon."

Again she looks pleased. "A French restaurant."

"No, actually, it's a chicken restaurant."

"A *chicken* restaurant?"

"Yeah, well the owner's first name is Simon. That's why he called it Chez Simon." He watches her consider this information.

"Is he French?"

"No."

She nods slowly, trying to comprehend why someone who wasn't French would name their restaurant Chez Simon. "I'm going to have the chicken."

The waitress takes their order. At the table behind Gloria, a child screams and tries to climb out of his booster chair. His father pushes him back down.

Gloria opens her napkin and spreads it on her lap. "So that's good. That you're manager."

"It's okay."

"See, I figured you was the one that got all the brains since Dwayne don't got any. He's a good kid, know what I mean? But he don't know how to look after himself. I was hoping he'd find a girl and get married and she could look after him. But girls don't do that no more."

"What was he doing before he got laid off?"

"Security guard."

"There must be jobs for security guards."

"That's what *I* say. I say, 'You're not even looking.' He's got his welfare cheque and me to look after him, so why bother, know what I mean?"

"It's a tough job market out there," Raymond concedes, not wanting to think of his brother as a layabout. He's beginning to recognize himself in Gloria. The wrinkles deepening around his eyes match hers. The pronounced chin is familiar, so is the bump on the bridge of her nose. On her, the features belong as they never have on Raymond. He has always felt uncomfortable about his looks. He runs his finger over the bump on his nose.

She looks at him out of her right eye again. "Do you get sinus headaches?"

"No."

"Dwayne does. Certain times of year he gets headaches so bad nobody can talk to him. He just stays in his room with the lights out. All he'll eat is pudding cups. Chewing hurts his head, he says. You don't get none of those?"

"No."

She nods, squinting. "Makes me wonder if maybe he's making it up, know what I mean? Makes me wonder if he gets sinus headaches so's he don't have to do nothing. Help around the house or nothing. He wouldn't even go to Tammy's wedding."

Raymond has also noticed that she has no hair around her ears or at the back of her neck. He suspects that she's wearing a turban because she's bald. He clears his throat and narrows his eyes. "So are you going to tell him about me?"

She nods. "I was just waiting to make sure you was alright, see. I'm hoping you can make him see some sense. You being just like him, I'm hoping he'll listen to you. I was hoping you'd show up years ago and straighten him out. I was waiting for you to show up. I knew you would. And I knew you'd be successful. Because you was more aggressive than him as a baby, see. I knew you'd do alright without me."

Raymond tries to take consolation from the fact that she gave him up because he was strong. Handing him over to social services was a demonstration of her belief in him. She loved him so much she could part with him.

The waitress serves their order and Gloria begins to eat. Consuming her food absorbs her. She seems to forget about Raymond. He would like to ask her why she's bald, but decides that this might be too intimate at this point. It occurs to him that she may have cancer, and endured a course of chemotherapy. If so, he wonders if that's why she wanted to see him immediately; because she's afraid that she's going to die soon. Watching her eat, it's hard to believe that she's afraid she's going to die soon.

Once she has finished the chicken and has only a few fries left on her plate, she again turns her head slightly and looks at him primarily with her right eye. "There's something you should know about your brother." She stops chewing and swallows. "He tried jumping off a bridge."

"How do you mean 'tried'?"

"This fellow was walking his dog and he saw Dwayne and he shouted, 'Don't jump!' Dwayne was throwing ten-dollar bills into the water. Before the man got to him, he threw his wallet into the water. He'd just cashed a welfare cheque, so I don't know what he was thinking."

"So he didn't jump?"

"Nah. The fellow took him to the hospital. They wouldn't admit him because they didn't think he was really suicidal. So the fellow drove him home." She picks up the last of her french fries and soaks them in the gravy. "Which was nice of him, I thought."

"What did Dwayne say?"

"About what?"

"Jumping off the bridge."

"Nothing. He said he had a sinus headache and went to bed. He don't talk much, you know, he's not a talker."

Raymond can relate to this. He's not a talker either. The suicide attempt suggests that Dwayne is crying out for help. Raymond watched a TV documentary about a depressed stand-up comedian who killed himself. His wife said sadly, "He was too sensitive for this world." Maybe Dwayne is too sensitive.

"Does he know his father," Raymond asks, "I mean, our father?"

She wipes her mouth and fingers on her napkin, then bunches it into a ball. "There's something you should know about your father. I mean, you've got your own father, right, that adopted you and looked after you. That's what I wanted, see. The problem with your real dad is that I don't know exactly who he is. I mean, he could be a couple of people."

"Which people?" Is she still trying to protect his father?

"Well, there was Joe down at the station. He's dead now. We were going steady. Then there was Phil who worked for the Petersons."

"Where's Phil?" Is she still afraid that the scandal would destroy him? Surely, after all these years, he would accept his sons, maybe even rejoice in them.

"Phil turned homosexual. I haven't seen him for years." She pokes her index finger under her turban again and scratches. "Then there was the *other* incident."

The boy in the booster chair throws a french fry on to the floor. The father slaps his hand and the child begins to cry.

Gloria leans over the table and stares at Raymond. "I was raped, see. I never told this to Dwayne because I didn't know how he'd take it. I told him his dad could be Joe or Phil and he was happy with that. He don't ask questions about it."

Raymond stares at her, realizing that he should be more affected by this information. But at the moment, it doesn't seem real. His fantasies about being the love child of the oval-faced, long-lashed waitress and the young-man-with-a-future seem more real. The woman in front of him has nothing to do with the waitress or the young man. "Did you know the man that raped you?"

"Nah. It happened so quick, see. I came home and he was in the closet. He forced me from behind. I know he had a ski mask on because I could feel it against my neck."

The boy in the booster chair throws another french fry on to the floor. The father grabs his shoulders and shakes him. The child screams.

Gloria waves her hand. "Don't go worrying about it. That was years ago. I'm over it now, see, but I don't want you thinking I know where your father is. You got a father, the one that adopted you. Don't go wasting your time worrying about the other one."

The father cuffs the head of the boy in the booster chair. The boy howls. Raymond looks into the black hole of the child's mouth and feels that it is his soul. The child's screams belong to his soul.

"You feel like dessert?" Gloria asks. "They got good pecan pie here."

"You have some."

"You on a diet?"

"No, I just don't feel like pie."

"That's different from your brother, that's for sure. He loves pie. Anything sweet. I bring home cookies and the next day they're history." She signals the waitress and orders a piece of pecan pie with ice cream and a coffee. Raymond can't believe that he is going to have to watch her eat the pie. He tries to think of reasons to leave; if only he had a beeper. When she sips her coffee, she sucks in air at the same time making a slurping sound. He tries to ignore it. The child in the booster chair has crumpled into a heap.

Gloria looks at him with her right eye. "You get arthritis?"

"I get a few aches and pains. I don't know if they're arthritis."

"Dwayne's got bad joints. Every one of them. It's because you're long and skinny, see. Joe was short and so was Phil. And Joe was fat. Neither of you is fat. So makes me think maybe it was the *other* incident."

Raymond nods. His head feels dislocated, as though it were floating above his neck. He watches the child, searching for signs of life.

❖

He drops Gloria off a block from her house. He tells her he'll call her in a few days. Gloria's dismay fills him with guilt. She adjusts her turban. "You won't call."

"I will."

"Nice meeting you." She slams the car door, hooks her handbag over her wrist and trudges homeward. Without looking back.

Raymond watches until she turns the corner. He doesn't know what to do, where to go. He drives. Everywhere he looks he sees people who belong; people talking to each other, hugging each other, holding hands. They smile, they laugh. They belong. He is the product of violence. He should not have been born.

The cop flags him down, then walks towards him in slow motion. He stands by Raymond's window. Raymond looks up into the reflector sunglasses. The cop begins to write out the ticket. "I clocked you at sixty-five."

"Really?"

"What speed did you think you were going?"

"I don't know. I didn't think that I was speeding."

"That's twenty-five over the limit. That's three demerit points." He snaps the ticket from his pad and shoves it at Raymond.

"Thanks," Raymond mutters, but the cop is already walking back, in slow motion, to the patrol car.

❖

It's getting late, but he picks up Burt and goes to Chez Simon because he doesn't want to stay home. Home belongs to his old life — the one in which he was a lovechild. He doesn't want to be reminded of his old life. At the restaurant he has no life, and therefore nothing to lose.

"Hey, boss," Barney says, chewing on a chicken wing.

"Barney, don't eat in the dining room."

Barney gestures grandly towards the tables. "Do you see any *diners* here, sir?"

Raymond looks around and sees that there are no customers. "I ate at Chicken Villa last night."

"No kidding." Barney glances at his reflection in the window and slicks back his hair.

"They're busy as hell."

"Must be the pretty waitresses."

"It's their specials, they've got a different special for every night of the week."

"Kalbfleisch drove by to look at his name in lights. He went around twice tonight. One day we should block out one of the letters. See if he notices."

Raymond scratches Burt's belly. "He'll notice."

"He wants us all to wear chicken hats."

"He what?"

"Some promotional guy came by and told him he could get him a deal on chicken hats. Just the thing on top, right, of a chicken, the red bit."

"The crest."

"Right. Kalbfleisch wants us to wear them."

"Only roosters have crests."

"Whatever. He wants us to wear them."

"Jesus." The only good thing about this life is that it's so horrible he forgets about his other one. "Do you have any idea who's stealing apple pies?"

"Somebody's stealing apple pies?"

"They're missing. We aren't selling that much pie."

"Maybe one of the dishwashers?"

"They don't go into the freezers."

"You think it's one of us?"

"I don't know what to think. All I know is that we keep running out of apple pie. There's cherry but no apple."

Barney glances at his reflection again and adjusts his hair. "Don't look at me. I hate pie."

"I'm not looking at you, I'm asking you to pay attention and see who's taking them."

"Maybe Mrs. Kalbfleisch. She was in last night."

"She went into the freezer?"

Barney nods. "I thought she was just checking things out."

"Did you see her leave?"

"No, I was up front doing bar."

"Jesus."

"What am I supposed to do? Tell her she can't take stuff? It's her restaurant, man."

"He wants her to pay full price."

"Yeah, sure."

"That's what he said."

"She took two heads of lettuce the other day. We're her grocery store, man."

After the cop had stopped him, Raymond didn't drive off right away because he saw a cat mauling a bird. He got out of the car and tried to chase the cat away. It backed off slightly, but Raymond knew that it was just waiting for him to leave. He chased it again and stamped his feet. The bird struggled in the dust on the side of the road. Its wings were dirty and one of them was broken. The bird couldn't fly. The cat slithered past Raymond and began batting the bird around with its paw. When Raymond shouted at it and pretended to kick it, the cat backed off again. Raymond didn't know what to do about the bird. It hobbled towards a bush. Raymond kept praying that it would fly, that it would free itself from this hell on earth. But it only stumbled. And the cat was waiting.

He feels as though he is that bird.

six

Raymond finds Mara standing in her backyard, tugging at the yellow police tape. He clears his throat. "I don't think you're supposed to do that."

"Don't you think I know that? Don't you think I *fucking* know that?"

"So, leave it alone."

"Don't tell me what to do. This is my fucking yard and I can do what I want with it."

"They might consider it tampering with evidence."

"Like I fucking care."

He has never heard her swear so much. And her hair is dirty. Usually she washes it every day. He puts his hands in his pockets. "Did you go to work today?"

"Oh yeah. Like I have any choice. It's either work or hang around with the bones." Burt noses around the grave. "For god's sake, Raymond. Control your fucking dog. All we need is dog shit in the grave."

"It's not a grave any more. They took the bones. It's just a hole."

She shakes her head. "There's more."

"How do you know?"

"I know."

Raymond looks around and notices her neighbour pushing back his curtains and staring at them. Raymond stares back. The curtains close.

"It's late," Mara says. "What are you doing here?"

"I thought you might've called me."

"I didn't."

"I just wanted to check and see how you were."

She stares at the hole. "I'm major wonderful."

❖

At the kitchen table she says nothing. She stares out the window at the yard.

Raymond clears his throat and narrows his eyes. "Did you eat today?"

"How could I eat?"

"You've got to eat."

She waves her hand the way she does when she thinks he's being ignorant. "Yes, yes, yes." She pours more scotch. Burt scratches his belly with his back paw. Outside, the neighbour mows his lawn. "Why's he doing that now?" Mara demands. "He's always fucking mowing his lawn." She slams the window shut. "He's crazy, you know. I've seen him naked in the backyard."

"When?"

"At night. He prowls around naked, and beats off."

"You never told me that."

"I didn't think you'd be interested." She tears open a bag of pretzels and offers them to Raymond. He shakes his head. She takes a handful and eats the pretzels slowly, one after another. Raymond looks out the window to see if the neighbour *is* naked or beating off. He isn't. Burt heaves a huge sigh.

"I had this idea . . ." Mara begins.

"What?" Raymond leans closer to her so that he can hear over the mower.

"I had this idea that I was comfortable with who I am. I mean, what I've become. Which isn't what I planned to be." She brushes salt from the pretzels off her hands. "I had this idea that my life was okay. I had my house. I had my job. I was *independent.* I thought . . . I thought that I could forget the past. The awful parts. I thought that I could bury them. I'd know that they were there, but they wouldn't bother me. Because they'd be buried." She wraps her hands around her scotch glass and stares down at it. Raymond notices that her nail polish is chipped and ingrained with dirt. She's been digging in the dirt.

"That's all true," he says.

She stares at him. He's afraid that she's going to start shouting at him again. But instead she touches the side of his face. "You're so sweet. The good guy. The guy who's always there. What do you get out of this?"

"I want to know that you're alright."

"Why?"

"I just do. I care about you."

"That's very sweet." She drinks more scotch. "But you see, I'm not alright. I'll never be alright. I realized today that I will never be alright. And I'm going to stop trying to be alright. I'm going to be *fucking* depressed. I'm tired of trying not to be depressed." She holds her hands over her eyes. "Like why fight it, you know? Like what's the point? I use up all this energy trying to convince myself that it's alright that my babies died. That there are *other* things in life. Well, what are they, that's what I'd like to know. What the fuck are they?"

The neighbour's mower shuts off and suddenly it's quiet. Deathly quiet. Watching the tears leaking between her fingers, Raymond wonders why it is that he can so badly want to help her — more than he wants to help himself — and yet he can't. He tries to think of "other things in life" for her to live for. For him to live for. He used to live for his imagined twin. Now his twin is alive and wants to be dead. And doesn't sound like somebody Raymond wants to know. "I met my biological mother tonight."

"You're kidding?"

"Her name is Gloria."

"Is she everything you expected her to be?"

He can tell that she isn't really interested, that she's just asking to be polite. "She's bald."

"Why?"

Raymond shrugs. "She has no eyelashes or eyebrows. Apparently she did at one time."

"Maybe she has cancer."

"That occurred to me."

"What did she say about your twin?"

"He's alive."

"Wonderful, that's what you wanted."

"He nearly jumped off a bridge."

"What stopped him?"

"A man and his dog."

She nods as though this makes perfect sense, then stands, wavering slightly. "Well, I've got to go to bed."

"Do you want me to stay?"

"I don't want you to stay because you think you should. Stay if you want."

"Maybe I'll sleep down here."

"If you want."

❖

Looking at her things that used to be their things, he thinks he hears noises. He has always lived in concrete structures. Mara's house is wood and seems to be constantly shifting. He can't sleep. Even Burt is having a bad night. His feet jerk and he emits small yelps. Raymond keeps hearing noises in the backyard. He tries to ignore them. Suddenly Burt's entire body shudders, then lies still. Without switching on the light, Raymond creeps into the kitchen and looks out at the backyard. The neighbour is naked and swinging from a tree. The rope creaks against the bark as he swings. Raymond can hear him whistling.

He lies back on the couch and tries to determine what is important in life. What is essential to the planet: animals, plants, trees? Certainly not humans. Animals, plants and trees can survive without humans. In fact, they would be better off without them. Humans, on the other hand, need animals, plants and trees to survive. And yet humans constantly destroy them. Why did God create humans? He was doing fine until he invented humans. Maybe he realized his mistake too late. Maybe he has turned his back on planet earth and is focusing on Mars. No one likes to dwell on their mistakes. And there can be no doubt that humans were a mistake; a waste of space. Maybe, after creating man, God had a nervous breakdown. Which explains why earth has gone to hell.

The swinging neighbour sings, "You are my sunshine, my only sunshine. You make me hap-py when skies are grey."

A waste of space. The neighbour is a waste of space.

"You'll never know, dear, how much I love you. Please don't take my sunshine a-way."

Why did the babies have to die? He never cried in front of her. He was trying to be strong. But he imagined them, small bloody creatures with tiny fingers and toes. His grief lives in his stomach like an ulcer.

Why didn't his twin jump off the bridge? What stopped him? Fear? Hope? Is his twin too sensitive for this world? From Gloria's description, Dwayne doesn't sound very agreeable. In fact, he sounds as though he may contain impulses that Raymond has tried to suppress for years. Impulses like trying to strangle his wife.

"You are my sunshine, my only sunshine . . ."

In her medicine cabinet he finds some sleeping pills. While filling the glass he avoids looking at his reflection. He turns his back on the mirror to swallow the pill.

❖

Barney leans on Raymond's desk, waiting for his paycheque. "So what were you doing snooping around last night?"

Raymond hands him the cheque. "What do you mean?"

"Around midnight, you were snooping around out front. We thought you were checking up on us."

"I didn't come back. I was at Mara's."

"Oh. So we're supposed to pretend like we didn't see you?"

"I didn't come back."

Barney folds the cheque and slides it into his back pocket. "Whatever you say, sir."

"Who was out front?"

"Somebody who looked just like you." He slicks back his hair. "I might be a little late tonight. My girlfriend bought this couch. It's COD, so I gotta be there."

Raymond doesn't bother to suggest that Barney's job should be more important than a couch; that without a job, there would be no couch. He says nothing because he's too tired. And because he's trying to understand why his twin would show up late last night to snoop around the restaurant. And why Gloria would tell Dwayne about him now, after all these years. What does Gloria want from him? What does Dwayne want from him?

"Raymond," Dr. Kalbfleisch calls from the stairs. "Come up here. Where's the Chicken Deal-icious sign? It should be out front."

❖

After putting the Chicken Deal-icious sign outside, Raymond joins Dr. Kalbfleisch who is eating a sundae. Chocolate sauce coats the corners of his mouth.

Raymond scratches behind his ear. "I just don't think it's a great idea."

Dr. Kalbfleisch scrapes the sides of the sundae glass with his spoon. "You have a better one?"

"I ate at Chicken Villa last night. They offer specials all week long. And free refills."

"Don't start with the refills, Raymond. I've already ordered the hats."

"If you don't mind my saying, sir, chickens don't have crests. Only roosters have crests."

"You think anybody cares? They want entertainment, they want waitresses who smile. Where's what's-her-name, with the hooters?"

"Beth. It's her day off."

"Tell her to smile more." He drops his spoon into the sundae glass and wipes his mouth with a napkin. Raymond tries to picture his twin snooping around out front. What was he wearing? What did he think of Chez Simon? Was he envious because Raymond was manager of a restaurant? Or did he pity him? Or despise him? He clears his throat and narrows his eyes. "Sir, there's something I've been meaning to talk to you about."

"So, talk."

"Well, as you know, Mrs. Kalbfleisch has been taking chickens."

"I told you to charge her."

"I really don't feel that we can do that."

"You're the manager. Charge her. Let her have them at cost."

"Well, you see, sir, she's also been taking apple pies. And lettuce. In fact, we can't keep track of what she's taking. She just comes in and goes into the freezers."

"So? Tell her to stop."

"I really think it would be better coming from you, sir."

Dr. Kalbfleisch holds his hands over his ears. "I don't want to hear this,

Raymond. You're the manager. Take care of it." He flaps his hands around. "The windows are dirty. Get somebody to clean the windows."

Jeff signals from behind the bar that the phone is for Raymond. Grateful for an excuse to leave Dr. Kalbfleisch, he takes the call in the kitchen. Jeff has the radio turned up so he presses a finger over his ear to hear. "Raymond speaking." He hears breathing. "Hello . . . ?" he says. More breathing. "Who is this?" More breathing, then the person hangs up. Raymond looks at Jeff. "Who was that?"

Jeff bobs his head to the beat of the music. "Who was what?"

"On the phone. Did they give a name?"

"Negative, Captain."

"Was it a man or a woman?"

"Male. Caucasian."

Raymond knows it was his twin.

Seymour, an obese regular customer, stands at the take-out counter. "Raymond, my good fellow, how are you?"

"Alright, yourself?"

"I've been better. Somebody threw burning newspapers into my convertible."

Jeff whistles from behind the broiler. "The beemer?"

"Yes, sir."

"Who would do that?"

Seymour shrugs. "Somebody who wants it, can't get it, doesn't want anyone else to have it. Give me a half-chicken dinner, will you?"

Jeff throws a chicken on to the cutting board. "Is it totalled?"

"Absolutely."

"Those bastards."

"Whoever they are."

"You seem pretty calm about it," Raymond observes.

"Yes, well, you'll notice that, as you age, these things don't upset you in quite the same way. Other things upset you, like angiograms revealing clogged arteries. Things like that."

"It's a shame though," Raymond comments. "A nice car like that."

"Yes. It is a shame. It's even more of a shame that they felt they had to burn it. They didn't steal it so that they could enjoy it. They destroyed it. Somehow, if they'd stolen it, I would have felt better."

Jeff hacks the chicken in half. "Senseless violence."

Down the street, in a bar, a guy was knifed in the throat. Nobody knows why.

"I should probably have salad with that chicken," Seymour says.

Raymond wonders if his twin is capable of senseless violence.

"On second thought," Seymour adds, "give me fries."

It's the rape part that Raymond can't accept. How could that happen? How could products of rape survive when Mara couldn't carry products of love?

"The curious thing about it," Seymour continues, "is that I had a minor accident yesterday. I was lugging six bags of groceries when I stumbled and fell. On to my knees, on the pavement. I couldn't get up. Two firemen had to help me. I felt fortunate to be rescued by two firemen. I felt kindly towards the human race. Which is unusual for me. Then they burn my car." Raymond punches his order into the cash register. Seymour hands him a fifty.

"That's really too bad." Raymond closes the register and gives Seymour his change.

"Yes. I have to go back to despising mankind. It's unfortunate."

Raymond wonders if he himself despises mankind. Or if he just despises himself so much it spills over on to mankind. He takes the half-chicken dinner from Jeff, bags it, then hands it to Seymour. "Enjoy your dinner."

"Thank you. It won't do much for my arteries, but at this point, do I care? *Buenas noches,* my friends."

What kind of man commits rape? Forces his penis into a terrified, helpless woman? That man's genes are inside Raymond. Raymond is that man. So is Dwayne. He wipes the take-out counter with a damp cloth. Bruce drops off plates in the dish room, then sees Raymond. "I've got two tables full of Salvation Army losers," he tells him.

"What's the problem?"

"They never tip. They drink glasses and glasses of water and they *never* tip. Cheap bastards."

Raymond scratches behind his ear. "Listen, Bruce. I've been meaning to talk to you."

"What is it?"

"Would you mind not asking the dishwashers out?"

"Why, were they complaining?"

"Well, the thing is, they're not gay. So they don't like it when you ask them out."

"They don't have to say yes."

"I know, but as a rule we shouldn't date people we're working with."

"Oh really? Tell that to Beth." Bruce snatches an order off the shelf and saunters back into the dining room. Raymond makes eye contact with Jeff who looks away.

"So," Raymond says. "Everybody knows?"

"About what, boss?" Jeff skewers a raw chicken on to a spit.

"Me and Beth?"

"Affirmative, Captain."

Raymond looks at the floor, at the grease encrusted on the grout between the tiles. He wants to hide. "I'll be downstairs."

"Okay, boss."

❖

After work he decides to check in on Mara. She's in the living room, watching TV. On the screen a plastic surgeon is cutting a woman's face off. He stretches her skin away from her skull and slides a cannula under it. "He's vacuuming out her jowls," Mara explains.

Raymond sits beside her. "Why are you watching this?"

"I should probably do it."

"What?"

"Get a facelift."

"You don't need a facelift."

"Not now. Later. What are you doing here?"

The plastic surgeon pulls some skin tight over the woman's cheekbone and begins to stitch it behind her ear.

"I came to see how you were."

"I'm swell."

It relieves him to see that she has washed her hair and done her nails. A different colour, almost purple. Magenta.

"They found three more babies," she says.

"Where?"

"In the yard, where do you think? The apple tree's dead."

"We can get another one." The plastic surgeon stretches more skin.

"He's going to suck out fat from her belly," Mara explains, "and stick it in her upper lip."

"Why?"

"To make it fuller."

Raymond nods and looks around. The place is tidy. Her briefcase is open, which means she brought work home. This is a good sign.

"Raymond, we're not married any more, remember? You don't have to keep checking up on me."

"I worry about you."

"Worry about yourself."

Raymond hears the toilet flush and sees her brother come out of the washroom. Raymond can tell that he is not pleased to see him.

"Good evening, Raymond."

"Good evening, Arthur."

Arthur looks at Mara. "Were you expecting him?"

"No." The plastic surgeon is cutting off the other side of the woman's face.

Arthur pulls on his goatee. "For a divorced couple, you seem to be spending a considerable amount of time together."

"What business is that of yours?" Raymond demands, startled by his own anger.

"She *is* my little sister, after all."

"Then why do you go off to the races when she's having a nervous breakdown?"

Arthur looks at Mara. "Were you having a nervous breakdown?"

"Of course not. He always exaggerates."

"You were fucking shaking," Raymond says, surprised by his own swearing.

Arthur raises his eyebrows. "Shaking, really?"

"Raymond, go home. *Please*, just go home."

"Why do you listen to this asshole?" Raymond shouts. "What has he ever done for you?"

"Am I going to have to call the police," Arthur asks, "or are you going to leave peacefully?"

"Go ahead, call the police, you fucking loser, you can't even defend yourself." Raymond wants to grab Arthur's neck and throttle him. He wants to throw his dead body into the baby grave and burn it. Mara's face appears in front of him, very close and very red. She's screaming. "You're not wanted here! Leave! Now!"

It's as though the air has been let out of him. Barely able to stand, he stares at the plastic surgeon shoving the cannula into another woman's thigh and sucking out fat. There's a lot of blood and bruising. Raymond feels sick. Mara gently takes his hand and leads him out the front door. "I'll call you," she whispers, then closes the door behind him.

He sits in the car and looks up at the darkening sky. A plane streaks a white line across it and Raymond wants to be on it. He drives across town to Gloria's house where he parks a short distance away, behind a truck. There are garden gnomes in her front yard, and a miniature windmill that spins in the wind. A plastic bird bath has blown over and lies on its side. The lights are on but the blinds are drawn. He can't see in. He drives home through the dark city. He looks at the light on the answering machine. It isn't flickering. Mara hasn't called.

seven

Raymond swims the backstroke one way, then crawls on the return lap. The pool is small and he can't stand it when other people are in it. But tonight, like most nights, nobody's around. The water cools his mind. He imagines the grey mass of his brain suspended in a pool of blue.

When he visited Belinda today, she didn't know who he was. He tried not to let this upset him. But he had this sense that he only existed in her mind; that she was the only person who cared enough to remember him. And now that her mind is fading fast, so is he. He is being erased. He will disappear and no one will bother to remember him. Usually when people die, they are mourned. Relatives bring flowers to their graves, and think fondly of them at Christmas. No one will mourn Raymond. It will be as though he had never been born.

He dives down below the surface, feeling his lungs expand, and touches bottom. He used to do this as a child. Touching the floor of the swimming pool behind his building made him feel strong and in control. It proved that he was unafraid of the depths of the water, even at the deep end. As he bobbed to the surface he would look around to see if anyone was watching. Usually nobody was. There was a girl named Sherry who watched him for a while. But she had pimples on her thighs and a mother who was always asking her to fetch things: cokes, suntan lotion, gum. Sometimes Sherry would ask Raymond to fetch things. He would but he hated doing it. It made him feel like a servant.

There were good times though. He didn't really notice that his father wasn't around. Sometimes his mother would come down and applaud when he did handstands, or difficult dives off the board. Occasionally his father would drink rye by the pool. He'd lie on a lounge chair, sunbathing. Raymond, wet and shaking, with his towel wrapped around his shoulders, would watch Gord's hairy belly rise and fall with his breathing. Once in a while he would muster enough courage to disturb him by asking for money for a popsicle. Gord always complied. In fact, he bought Raymond just about anything he wanted. All Raymond had to do was ask. A baseball bat, a tennis racket, a basketball, all could be his. But he didn't ask, because he knew his father wouldn't play with him.

Sometimes people Raymond didn't know would sit beside Gord, who would start up a conversation with them. Sitting on the edge of the pool with his legs in the water, Raymond would listen. At first it upset him to hear his father lie. He'd sit very still while Gord told his ever-changing stories about where he was born, where he went to school, what kinds of jobs he'd had. But then Raymond got used to it, the lies. It was just another thing his father did.

He has tried to forget walking in on his parents having sex. They were in the bathroom. His mother's bathing suit was pulled down and his father was sucking on her nipples. He had lifted her on to the sink and had his fingers in her vagina. Raymond was only seven and didn't understand what was happening so he started to yell. "It's alright, Raymond," his mother assured him, tugging up her shoulder straps. His father swore, pulled his hand out of her and turned his back on Raymond. After closing the bathroom door, Raymond could hear them fighting. He ran out of the apartment, took the elevator down and sat on the steps of the building. While watching what he considered to be happy people walk by, he tried to comprehend what he had just seen; if his father had been hurting his mother. She hadn't looked as though she was in pain. And her voice was very calm when she told Raymond it was all right.

He has always wanted to believe that his mother hated having sex with his father. But he isn't sure that this is true.

In the change room he masturbates into a towel. Swimming always makes him horny; the cool water rushing against him. Immediately he feels guilty for masturbating and wonders why he can ejaculate into towels but not into Beth. Or any woman. It's not as though there aren't any women out there. If he made an effort, he should be able to find one. He has a job, he has a car, he's not that ugly.

Does he really want one though?

Walking back to his apartment he passes the obsessive-compulsive man in the corridor, taking three steps forwards, one step backwards.

He boils some water and throws ravioli into the pot. He gives Burt a couple of biscuits, then turns on the television. According to the TV guide, there is a movie on about two rival reporters — one male, the other female — who hate each other. While competing for the same news story, they fall in love. Raymond eats his ravioli watching this, wondering how much clothing the actress is going to take off. Early in the movie, the two reporters get caught in the rain and her erect nipples show through her blouse. Then she goes skinny-dipping and the male reporter hides her clothes. When the network breaks to commercial, Raymond wonders if they're going to cut out the parts where they have sex.

He phones Beth because he can't stand worrying about what she has told people at work. She doesn't sound friendly when she answers.

"What do you want?"

"I just wanted to clear up a few things."

"What things?"

"Between us."

"There's nothing between us."

"Well . . . what did you tell people?"

"About what?"

"Us."

"Nothing. I told Bruce because he happens to be my best friend."

The two reporters are on a speedboat and her dress blows up in the wind.

"Well the thing is," Raymond continues, "Bruce must have told somebody. Because everybody knows."

"Knows what?"

"About us." The male reporter lets the female reporter steer the speedboat. He puts his arms around her to offer assistance. Her hair blows in his face and she laughs.

"What's to know?" Beth demands.

"You tell me."

She sighs. "Like I say, Bruce knows. I don't know what he told anybody else. Anyways, what difference does it make?"

"I prefer that people at work don't know the details of my personal life."

"Well then maybe you should think twice before you try stuffing one of the waitresses."

"I'm sorry."

She says nothing. He can hear her cracking something in her teeth, maybe pistachios.

"I guess the question is," he says, "where do we go from here?"

"I'm not going anywhere. You can fire me but there's no way I'm quitting."

"I wasn't suggesting that."

"What were you suggesting?"

"I don't have any suggestions."

She cracks another nut. "Like I say, so long as you don't treat me like a second-class citizen, I'll do my job, same as always."

"Good. Well, I'll try not to treat you like a second-class citizen."

"You do that."

"Goodnight then."

"Goodnight." She hangs up. Raymond rubs Burt's belly with his foot. Now the reporters are running. She trips and hurts her ankle, so he carries her. Her dress falls away from her legs, revealing bikini panties. Raymond feels himself becoming aroused again so he turns off the TV and takes Burt for a walk.

It's raining and everywhere people are scurrying for shelter. Raymond enjoys the pressure of the downpour on his head. It drives out his thoughts. But Burt cowers in a bus shelter. "Alright," Raymond concedes, "just do your business and we'll go home."

A man in ragged clothing ducks into the shelter and squats on the floor. Burt watches him but the man pays no attention. He pulls a half-eaten hamburger out of a styrofoam container and gobbles it. Raymond wonders if he got it out of the garbage. Burt starts to drool. "Come on, Burt," he urges. "Time to go home."

❖

He steps into the photo booth, pulls the curtain, sits on the stool and tries to smile. But the flash makes him blink. He makes an effort to sit up straight and tries to relax his face, to appear casual. Flash. He quickly attempts to tidy his hair. Flash. Once more he tries to smile but feels only one side of his mouth turning up. Flash. Teenaged girls are waiting outside to use the booth. They smoke cigarettes and giggle. Raymond gets out and waits for the shots to be developed. He's not sure why he's doing this, since he's already met Gloria. He just thought it might be interesting to see a picture of himself. The teenaged girls pile into the booth, shrieking. His photos slide into the ready slot. Raymond carefully pulls them out and studies them. He looks guilty, as though he's afraid of being found out. He looks like a criminal.

❖

He pulls down one of the blinds to stop the sun from shining in his eyes. Dr. Kalbfleisch wraps his handkerchief around his index finger and pokes it up one nostril. "Get your repairman to fix it."

"He fixed it last week. He offered no guarantees. It's an old freezer."

"Get a new repairman."

"Gus is a good repairman. That's not the problem. We really should look into getting a new savoury freezer."

"Get a second opinion. Always get a second opinion."

"The service calls alone cost a hundred dollars."

"Get a second opinion. End of story."

Beth shoves two boxes of coffee creamers at Raymond. "These are all sour."

"What's the date on them?"

"They're supposed to be good until the sixteenth."

"Call the supplier," Dr. Kalbfleisch commands. "Don't pay him a cent, get a refund."

"If you'll excuse me, sir." Raymond takes the boxes from Beth and goes back with her to the kitchen. "Can you not bring up problems in front of him?"

"What am I supposed to do? Serve sour cream?"

"No, but I mean, just wait till he's gone."

"You're pathetic. You grovel in front of him."

She never spoke to Raymond this way before he failed to penetrate her.

"Just calm down," he mumbles. Sharif, the dishwasher, is watching from the dish room.

"It's going to be like this, isn't it?" Beth demands. "Suddenly you're acting like you have special rights over me. Well let me tell you something, pal. You got no rights over me." She glares at Sharif. "What are *you* staring at."

Raymond has absolutely no idea how to remedy his relationship with Beth. She's not even his wife and yet it feels as though there are years of misunderstandings between them. "He wants you to smile more," he tells her, hoping to take the heat off himself.

"He *what*?"

"Kalbfleisch says he wants you to smile more."

"Bullshit he said that. I always smile. You're just looking for reasons to fire me."

"I'm not. Honestly, he said that."

"Then why doesn't he tell me himself?"

Raymond doesn't want to say that it's because Kalbfleisch is scared of her. "I don't know."

"You're pathetic." She grabs some finger bowls and strides into the dining room. Raymond looks around and sees that Sharif is still staring at him. "Don't you have work to do?"

"Yes, sir."

Downstairs Raymond sits in his office without windows and calls the supplier of creamers. A Mr. Hayhoe explains that the creamers could not have been sour because they had not reached their expiry date. Mr. Hayhoe insists that someone, perhaps a waitress, left the creamers out of the fridge. It would be easy to do, on a busy day. Perhaps she took the boxes of creamers out of the fridge and forgot about them. These things happen all the time.

Raymond is too tired to argue with Mr. Hayhoe. He orders more creamers. Then he phones upstairs. "Is Kalbfleisch gone?"

"Affirmative, Captain."

Raymond hangs up and stares at the concrete wall. Maybe if he just stayed here, he'd be safe. He could lock himself in and slowly dehydrate. In a few centuries they'd find him petrified.

A tiny, pale yellow bug lands on his hand. How did it get in here? It has four legs and tiny feelers that continually wave in all directions. The bug is always on guard. What kind of a life can that be, Raymond wonders, then realizes that it is not unlike his own. He takes the bug down the hall and lets it out the back door.

He knows that he must call Gloria; that he cannot, now that he has opened the door, close it. He has had a glimpse of what's behind it. If he tries to ignore it, it will haunt him. He dials the number given to him by the social worker.

"Hello?"

"Hi, Gloria? It's Raymond."

"Who?"

"Raymond. Your son?"

"Oh yeah. What do *you* want?"

"I thought maybe we could have dinner together. All three of us. Some time this week."

"You buyin'?"

"Of course." He hears her cover the mouthpiece with her palm while she talks to someone. He hears a male voice that resembles his own.

She takes her hand off the mouthpiece. "What restaurant?"

"Anywhere you like."

"We like steak."

"Okay, a steakhouse. Can you think of one?"

She puts her palm over the mouthpiece again. The muffled voice says something. She argues with it, then she takes her hand off the mouthpiece. "How about the Ranch House? They got good steaks there."

"Which Ranch House? There's a couple of them."

"The one near us. In Everglade Mall."

"Okay. What night?"

She puts her hand over the mouthpiece again. More arguing. She removes her hand. "Tomorrow's good."

"Fine. Say . . . seven-thirty?"

"We'll see you then." She hangs up.

❖

Barney's late as usual. Raymond doesn't even wait to hear his excuse. He goes home to see if Mara's called. She hasn't. He read in a magazine that you never stop loving your ex-wife. He's afraid that this is true. It also said that in every divorce there is hatred. Raymond knows this to be true. Even now there are times when he hates her. Especially when she doesn't need him.

He walks Burt, feeds him, then goes to a bar because he doesn't want to stay home. The bar offers free peanuts in shells so Raymond takes a handful and sits in a corner beside a plastic plant. He drinks his draft and cracks open peanuts. Two tables away, three middle-aged men and one young woman smoke cigarettes and drink beer. All three men talk at length to the young woman who nods. She's wearing a sleeveless denim shirt and large earrings. She's chubby, but because she's young, it looks sexy. The older men surround her like wolves. Raymond wonders which one will get to sleep with her. None of them can have done so yet because they're trying too hard to impress her. When she gets up to use the washroom, they all watch her. Then they light more cigarettes.

At another table, a man in his thirties sits with two women in their thirties. One of the women has a twitching eye. The other won't put down her beer bottle. She holds it against her body, drinks, then holds it against her body. The man has acne and is wearing a suit. Listening to the two women, his head rotates from side to side.

The waitress asks Raymond if he wants another beer. He says yes, noticing that the veins stand out on her legs, even though she's young. He knows that waitresses often get varicose veins because they spend hours on their feet. At Chez Simon they wear pants.

He can feel the beer relaxing him, making things look better. At another table, a man in a cowboy shirt talks on a cellular phone while another man waits. The waiting man also has a twitching eye. Raymond wonders if the woman with the twitching eye has noticed the man with the twitching eye and vice versa. The waitress brings his beer and tells a joke that Raymond doesn't understand. He laughs anyway, even though he doesn't get the joke. He'd like to tell her that she doesn't have to be funny, he'll tip her anyway, but he worries that this will offend her.

He's trying to remember if Beth had varicose veins. Mara had a couple but she had a doctor inject a solution into them to make them disappear. Why is Beth so angry with him? How can he make her less angry? She did have nice breasts. He shakes his head and drinks more beer.

He remembers Belinda's breasts, from when he walked in on his parents in the bathroom. They were large and pendulous and they frightened Raymond. When his father stopped sucking on them, they flopped against her body. He hates his father. As much as he tries to pretend he doesn't, he hates him. That time his father couldn't blow up a long, sausage-shaped balloon. Raymond waited patiently at his knee, expecting him to finish blowing it up so that there was no dangly bit at the end. "Here, son," his father said, panting, tying a knot in the balloon.

"Blow it up bigger," Raymond said.

"What's wrong with it?"

"It should be bigger." He felt the sagging nipple. "Blow this up."

"It's too late. I already tied the knot."

That was the first time his father really disappointed him. The first time Raymond realized that his father could fail.

Doesn't everybody, though? He can't hate his father just because he's a failure. Most people are failures. In their own eyes, anyway. Because they didn't turn out to be who they wanted to be. Like Mara. She considers herself a failure. And yet Raymond considers her to be the finest person he has ever met. He has told her this. Many times. It makes no difference. She still thinks she's failed. At what exactly? Procreating? So what? So fucking what? Look at all the idiots who procreate. Are they successful? Are their lives filled with meaning because they screwed and got a baby out of it? Babies they slap, and curse, and lock in their rooms? Babies that grow up with scars so deep nobody can see them?

Why can't he say any of this to her? Why is his mouth wired shut around her? And would it make any difference now?

"You ready for another?" the waitress asks.

"No thanks. Just the bill."

He leaves her a three-dollar tip.

❖

He drives to Mara's to see if her brother's car is out front. If it is, Raymond intends to gash it with keys. He turns his lights out so that she won't see him. No sign of her brother's Jetta. She's home though. She hasn't pulled shut the curtains on the living-room window and he can see that her TV is on. Is that what she's going to do with the rest of her life? Watch plastic surgeons suck fat from women's bodies? And movies about screwing reporters?

He would like to charge in and scream at her that she's worth so much more than that. But she won't listen. And they'll start to fight. And he'll almost strangle her.

He starts the engine and drives home. In the elevator a man stinking of whisky stumbles. He slouches against the wall, muttering to himself, or to someone who isn't there. Raymond looks up at the floor numbers.

Burt wags his tail so much that his rump jerks from side to side. Raymond knows that he shouldn't leave him like this. He feeds him three biscuits, then throws his ball around. But Burt grips it in his teeth and won't let go. He understands that as long as he holds on to the ball he will have Raymond's undivided attention.

Outside, while Burt does his business, Raymond notices an apartment across the street. A man bends down to look in a fridge while a woman sets things on a table. The man leans on the open fridge door. The woman joins him. They both stare into the fridge. Then she bends down and rummages inside it. On their balcony a dog barks. Burt's ears prick up. "Easy boy." Raymond puts Burt's turds in a plastic bag, then looks back at the window. The woman straightens and the man bends down, reaching into the fridge. What can they be looking for, Raymond wonders. Don't they know what's in it? What are they hoping to find?

"Come on, boy. Let's go home."

Tomorrow, he thinks, he is going to be nicer to Gloria. And to Dwayne. Tomorrow, he thinks, he is going to begin to forgive.

eight

On the way to meet Gloria and Dwayne, Raymond feels a tension headache coming on and decides to stop at a drugstore for some Tylenol. While he's waiting to pay, an old man shouts at the cashier that he needs a laxative for his wife. "The cheapest laxative," he emphasizes. While the cashier leads the man to the laxatives, Raymond looks for some breath mints. "Is that the cheapest?" he hears the old man shout.

On the whole, Raymond is feeling more positive about the prospect of meeting his twin. He has decided that Dwayne is probably very shy, which is why he didn't come into Chez Simon. After all, he didn't know he was a twin. It must have come as a shock to him. More shocking than Raymond finding out that his twin was alive. A period of adjustment is to be expected. Raymond plans to be very gentle with him, to set him at ease.

The cashier and the old man return with several boxes of laxatives. The old man takes Raymond's place in line. Raymond sucks on a breath mint and glances at the newsstand. There's a headline about a woman pregnant with eight babies because she took fertility drugs. He leans in closer to read the small print. Trying to carry all the babies to term could result in her death, as well as theirs. Yet if she tries to abort some of them, she may lose them all. The woman has been offered a movie deal if she tries to have all eight. Raymond can't imagine how eight babies can fit into a uterus. It would be all-out war. He must mention this story to Dwayne, to break the ice. It might enable them to talk freely about the experience of being twins.

❖

Gloria's turban is scarlet this evening, as are her lips. "Dwayne got a nosebleed," she says. "He's going to be late."

"Is he alright?"

"He always gets nosebleeds. I tell him he takes too many pills for those headaches of his. But he don't listen to me."

"How long do they usually last?"

"Oh not long. He's just got to lie down, take it easy."

"Well . . . should we wait for him?"

"Heavens, no. I'm starved." She grabs a menu. "They got good steaks here. They don't fry 'em up like leather." She peers over the menu at him. "You feel like a cocktail?"

"Ahh . . . okay."

She looks around for a waitress. When she can't flag one down she chases after them. They're dressed as cowgirls and much taller than Gloria. Raymond can tell from their grim expressions that they are not pleased to be pestered by the turbanned customer. Her mission accomplished, Gloria returns to the table. "I ordered you scotch on the rocks and a steak, rare."

"Thank you," Raymond says, although he's not hungry. The thought of his twin languishing with a nosebleed upsets Raymond. He feels that he should do something for him. "Are you sure Dwayne's going to be alright?"

"Heavens, yes. He stuffs Kleenex up his nostrils and is better in no time. Anyways, he really wants to meet you."

"I really want to meet him." Raymond keeps glancing towards the entrance, hoping that a man identical to himself will appear. "He phoned me at work."

"Who did?"

"Dwayne. He didn't speak to me."

"Then how do you know it was him?"

"I heard his breathing."

"You can't know for sure that was him, Raymond. Could've been anybody."

One of the cowgirls sullenly sets down their drinks.

"Do you think it's possible he's nervous about meeting me?" Raymond asks. "I mean, I've known I was a twin for years. He just found out."

"Could be. I told him he should dress up, look nice. I told him you always wear a shirt and tie. He said wearing a tie is like being hanged. All he ever wears is sweatshirts. It's because he's a bachelor, see. Half the time they don't even change their underpants. You're married, right?"

"Divorced."

"Oh. That's too bad. I thought you had a wife and whatnot."

"It said in the information that I was divorced." The cowgirl serves their steaks.

"I didn't read none of that, Raymond. I figured you'd tell me what you wanted me to know when you was ready." She drips ketchup on to her fries.

"Is Dwayne married?"

"Nah." She stabs a fry with her fork. "He used to have a girlfriend. Sheena. Nice girl. Thing about Dwayne is . . ." She eats the fry. "If things don't work out just the way he wants, he quits, see. He don't understand that if things don't work out exactly right, you got to make do with what you've got. There's no sense crying over spilt milk. The way I see it, you could spend your whole life waiting for things to work out exactly right, and they just don't." She stares at Raymond primarily out of her right eye. "You over the divorce?"

"Not really . . . completely."

She chews on some steak. "She have the kids?"

"No kids."

"So, you're a free man. You can start over. That's what it's all about, see. New beginnings. If I went around crying over all the things that've happened to me, nobody'd want to talk to me."

A man comes through the doors, wearing a sweatshirt and jeans. Raymond stops breathing as he looks more closely at him. They share the same hair colour and height but the face is different.

"Did you go to college, Raymond?"

"No."

Her face flattens. "You're kidding me."

"No. I'm not."

"The whole point of you going with a good family was so's you'd get educated." Her right eye fixes on him. "Didn't they have the money?"

"Umm, I'm not sure. It just didn't work out."

She squints. "That don't seem fair to me, being adopted and not getting educated. Those people was checked out by the social worker. They was supposed to look after you."

"They did. I just didn't go to college."

It shocks him to see that Gloria has tears in her eyes. Because she has no eyelashes, the tears spill immediately on to her cheeks. "All those years of me thinking you was getting nice things and an education."

"I got nice things." Raymond offers her his napkin. "Really. It was very nice. I just didn't go to college. My mother wanted me to go. I went for a couple of semesters, but it just didn't work out."

She takes the napkin. "That breaks my heart."

"I'm sorry."

She blots her tears. "Anyways, you've got a good job now, that's the important thing."

Raymond looks down at his steak. He rarely eats red meat. It looks like flesh to him, like somebody's thigh. "Did Dwayne go to university?"

Gloria scratches under her turban. "He got a security guard diploma."

"That's useful."

"That's what I say, but do you see him looking for work? All he does is eat me out of house and home."

Something shatters. One of the busboys has dropped a tray. The cowgirls gather around to scold him.

"Gloria, what happened after you had us? What did you do?"

Gloria eats another french fry. "I don't like talking about the past, Raymond. That's all over and done with."

"I understand that but, you see, I'd like to know more."

"About what?"

He watches her knife her steak. Blood seeps out of it. "Well . . . the birth, for example."

"What about it?"

"Did Dwayne and I share the same placenta?"

"The same what?"

"Did we come out of the same sac? Or were there two sacs?"

"What's that got to do with anything?"

"I'd like to know."

"Heavens, Raymond, I can't remember stuff like that."

A birthday is being celebrated two tables over. The sullen cowgirl presents a cake in the shape of a cowboy hat. The other cowgirl hands out little party cowboy hats.

Raymond clears his throat. "You can't remember if you had to push out two afterbirths?"

Gloria butters her roll. "How would I know that? It's not like you know what's going on down there."

"But you were there. The doctor must have told you if you had to push out two placentas."

"That doctor was red in the face. I think he was a drinker. He wasn't paying much attention. All I know is you came out, then Dwayne started coming feet first, so the doctor pushed him back in and tried to turn him around. But he couldn't, so he cut me so bad I haven't been the same down there since. I don't even think he was looking when he stitched me up."

"How horrible."

Gloria bites her roll. "Would've been a whole lot easier if they just fished you out of my belly, know what I mean? But things was different back then. They didn't cut you open at the first sign of trouble. They cut Tammy open and nicked her bowel. She almost died. Poor little Mickey wouldn't even nurse because he knew her milk was poisoned. They had to open her up again right away."

Raymond senses that Gloria is trying to direct the conversation away from his and Dwayne's birth. "So, do you think Dwayne might have been deprived of oxygen?"

"Nobody told me nothing about that. They thought I was no good, see. The drunk wouldn't give me drugs till he cut me. They didn't even give me ice packs afterwards, or painkillers or whatnot. I was bleeding like a pig. I thought I had one foot in the grave, know what I mean?"

"I'm so sorry."

"It wasn't your fault, Raymond."

That he was born in such a barbarous manner horrifies him. Pools of blood form around his steak.

"It was crowded in there too," she adds. "And only one bathroom. All us poor girls trying to make it to one toilet."

The cowgirls half-heartedly sing "Happy Birthday." The people in the party hats join in.

"What happened to us?" Raymond asks. "Did you see us?"

"They made me nurse you to start off with. I told them I didn't want to because I had to give you up, but they said it was important for your health, so I didn't argue. I wanted you to be healthy, see. I nursed you more than Dwayne. They was doing all kinds of things to Dwayne. Sticking tubes in him and whatnot. He turned all yellow. I didn't think he was going to make it either. But God never closes one door but he opens another, know what I mean?"

Raymond hasn't heard her mention God before. He wonders how someone who has endured such torment can believe in God. "But we were the products of rape? How could you care about the products of rape?"

"We don't know that for sure, Raymond. Could've been Joe or Phil."

"You said Joe and Phil were too short."

"Short people get tall kiddies sometimes. Anyways, you was still babies, *my* babies."

"Well then how could you give me up?"

"Now Raymond, you said in your letter you wasn't going to get mad at me for putting you up for adoption."

"I'm not mad at you."

"You are too."

At the birthday table the sullen cowgirl opens a bottle of champagne. The pop is feeble.

"My wife and I tried to have children," Raymond explains. "I just . . . it's difficult for me to understand how someone could give up babies."

"It's not like it was easy for me. I cried for two days."

He would prefer that she say she never stopped crying; that his adorable little face is indelibly etched on her soul. But she's looking at the dessert menu. "I feel like pie. They got good coconut cream here."

"Maybe I should call Dwayne. Make sure he's alright."

"You got to call him on his cell. He don't answer my phone."

"Why not?"

"He wants separate lines. He thinks I listen in. Like I don't have anything better to do."

She gives him Dwayne's cellular number. At the back of the restaurant, under some steer horns, he finds a phone. Dwayne picks up almost immediately. His voice unsettles Raymond because it is his own. He sounds tired and not pleased to be disturbed. "I was just worried about your nose," Raymond explains.

"My what?"

"Your nosebleed."

"What are you talking about?"

"Gloria said you had a nosebleed. We're here at the Ranch House waiting for you."

"Oh."

"Do you think you can make it?"

"I'm not feeling too good. I've got a headache."

"Gloria says you get a lot of those."

"Tell that stupid twat to shut the fuck up."

It shocks Raymond to hear Dwayne refer to his mother in this manner. "I think she's just worried about you."

"She's a fucking busybody."

"Anyway, I'd love to meet you, when you're feeling better. Can I give you my number?"

"Gloria's got it." He hangs up. Taken aback, Raymond listens to the dial tone. One of the men in party hats is staring at him, apparently waiting for the phone. "Sorry," Raymond says.

"Are you Russian?" the party man asks, obviously inebriated.

"No."

"You have a Russian face."

Raymond, hoping to avoid further contact with the drunk, starts his return to the dining room. But the man calls after him. "So what are you, a fucking Martian?"

Back at the table he sees that Gloria is almost through another scotch. "He doesn't have a nosebleed," Raymond says.

"He doesn't?"

"No. Did you make that up because you knew he wasn't coming?"

"He said he was coming, Raymond. When his nose got better."

"Right. Well he doesn't remember any of that." In a way, it touches him that Gloria has lied to shield him from disappointment. He wonders how she would feel if she knew that Dwayne referred to her as a stupid twat and a fucking busybody.

"Thing about Dwayne is," Gloria cautions, "sometimes he says things he don't mean."

"What do you mean?"

"Sometimes he don't mean what he says." She wipes her mouth with her napkin, pulls out her compact and lipstick and reddens her lips. "When he's not nice, it don't mean nothing."

"Not nice?"

"Sometimes I wonder if maybe he's one of those antisocial types."

"What antisocial types?"

"Those people with no feelings who go around hurting people for no reason."

"You mean a sociopath?"

"Is that what they call them?"

"Sociopaths kill people."

"Do they? Oh I don't mean them then. It's just sometimes his bite's bigger than his bark, know what I mean?"

"Not really."

Outside the window, in the parking lot, a man is standing with his arms outstretched, balancing a ball on his temple. Slowly he tips his head causing the ball to roll over his crown on to the other temple. He pauses, steadying the ball. Then he tips his head again, rolling the ball back to the other temple. "What's he think he's doing?" Gloria asks.

Raymond clears his throat. "I guess he's some kind of juggler."

"What kind of dummy juggles with his head?"

"I don't know. Maybe he's trying something new."

Gloria gets up to pursue one of the cowgirls for pie. The juggler throws three balls in the air and catches one in his mouth.

It shouldn't be like this, Raymond thinks. This is all wrong. He's not sure he wants to know any more about his biological history. The more he knows, the more he feels filthy and unloveable. The steak nauseates him, he pushes it to one side. He's afraid he's going to be sick and hurries to the washroom. He runs the taps and throws cold water on his face. The drunk in the party hat is jerking off at a urinal. Raymond pretends not to notice him.

When he returns to the table Gloria's eating her coconut-cream pie. "I didn't know what you wanted."

"Nothing. I don't want anything." Raymond opens his wallet and takes out his credit card.

Gloria slurps her coffee. "You should try the pecan. Dwayne always orders pecan with ice cream."

The juggler has dropped the balls and is on his belly searching for them under a car.

Gloria points her fork at Raymond. "Maybe you boys could go to a ball game together."

"I don't enjoy sports."

"Dwayne loves sports. All day long he watches it. He likes that wrestling. I don't understand it."

Raymond waves his credit card at the cowgirl who snatches it. He watches her, hoping she'll go immediately to the cash desk. But a customer stops her to ask for something. The cowgirl hovers by the table, taking a long time to answer. Finally she goes to the cash desk. But on the way back she stops to refill a table's water glasses.

"You got a picture?" Gloria asks. "Maybe if I show him a picture, he'll get more excited about meeting you."

"I thought you said he really wanted to meet me."

The juggler can't find one of his balls. He keeps crouching to look under cars.

"He does, Raymond. It's just he's shy. What with you being successful and whatnot."

"I'm not successful. Please don't tell him that." Raymond feels around in his pockets for the photo-booth shots. "Here." He hands them to her.

"Now don't you look nice, all dressed up."

The cowgirl returns with the bill tray and his card. He fills out the slip, tips her four dollars, then puts the card back in his wallet.

"Thanks for the din-dins," Gloria says, fitting the photos into her purse. "I've got to use the ladies'."

"Do you need a ride home?"

"Nah. I've got shopping to do in the mall. Dwayne needs undies. He's got holes in every one of them."

That she buys him underwear while he calls her "twat" baffles Raymond. "Okay, well . . ."

They both stand. Raymond envies Dwayne for having a mother who cares enough to buy him underwear. He always had to remind Belinda when he needed new underwear, and she would always sigh as though keeping him in underwear was a major chore.

"Don't work too hard now, Raymond. It said in your horoscope you work too hard." She pokes her finger under her turban and scratches. "Come for din-dins on the weekend. I'll get Dwayne to give you a ding."

In the parking lot he spots the juggler's ball behind a trash can. "It's here," he calls. He picks it up and tosses it to the juggler who catches it in his mouth and then bows to Raymond.

❖

The light is flickering on the answering machine. Raymond hopes it's Mara, but it's Barney telling him to call the restaurant. Raymond dials. Barney answers. "Chez Simon."

"It's Raymond."

"Oh, hi. Big news. Kalbfleisch's wife just kicked off."

"What do you mean?"

"She came by, stole pies and chickens and died. They couldn't even get her to the hospital."

"Who?"

"Her mah-jong buddies."

"Jesus."

"So Kalbfleisch wanted to let you know he wouldn't be in tomorrow."

"Why didn't he call me himself?"

"You know how he doesn't like mixing professional and personal lives."

"How did he sound?"

"Like Kalbfleisch."

"Was he crying or anything?"

"Shit no."

Raymond can tell that Barney is chewing gum. He has asked him not to chew gum on the job.

"Oh the other thing is," Barney adds, "the chicken hats have arrived. Kalbfleisch was wearing one earlier. Before she kicked off. Anyway, at least now we won't keep running out of apple pie and chickens."

"Jesus."

"I gotta go do cash."

"Right. Thanks for calling."

Raymond doesn't get off the couch. He feels unbearably heavy suddenly. The fact that someone can die, just like that, astounds him. That she could steal pies and chickens and then die. Pie and chicken is still inside her corpse. He feels nauseated again. Maybe he should see a doctor about feeling sick all the time. Burt nuzzles his feet. "Okay, boy, give me a minute."

What can Kalbfleisch be doing right now? What can he be thinking? How can he sleep with one half of his life dead? The void must be intolerable, it must be draining the life out of him. Even if he hated his wife, he could count on her. She was there, always there. Now there's nobody.

Raymond feeds Burt, then takes him for a walk. He stares at the pavement, having difficulty feeling his feet connect with the concrete. A man wearing a baseball cap sits cross-legged in the grass. His shirt is unbuttoned to his navel. He nods at Raymond. "Good evening to you, sir." Raymond looks at him, thinking that he should recognize him, that maybe he's a customer. "How are you?" the man asks.

"Fine," Raymond replies, still unable to identify the man.

The man smiles. "Happy holidays to you and your family."

Raymond realizes that he doesn't know the man, that the man is insane. He tugs Burt's leash, urging him along.

The man tips his baseball cap. "Thank you, sir."

What happens after a body dies? How long does it take to decompose? When the savoury freezer breaks down overnight, in the morning there is chicken blood over everything, and it stinks. They have to disinfect the freezer to prevent cross-contamination. Does Mrs. Kalbfleisch stink yet? Does the chicken inside her stink?

He can't believe she's not going to come in to the restaurant any more. Usually she shows up alone to steal food. But sometimes she comes with Dr. Kalbfleisch who repeats everything she says. She'll tell Raymond to clean the chair seats. "Clean the chair seats," Dr. Kalbfleisch will repeat. She'll tell Raymond to clean the light fixtures. "Clean the light fixtures," Dr. Kalbfleisch will repeat.

It can't be that she's just vanished. It can't be that it can end just like that. There has to be something else. Something after life, before death.

❖

Raymond balances a biscuit on Burt's nose and watches him flip it into his mouth. He turns on the TV and channel-surfs. He stops when he sees a bare-chested man in jodhpurs pick up a woman and hold her in his arms. They're in a stable, surrounded by horses. When Raymond's phone rings he picks it up immediately, hoping it's Mara. "Cute photo," Dwayne says. The man in jodhpurs glistens with sweat as he carries the woman towards a pile of hay. "So, what do you think of our mother?"

Raymond clears his throat. "She seems quite nice."

"She's a whore."

"That's a terrible thing to say."

"It's true."

"Are you saying she's a prostitute?"

The jodhpured man lies down with the woman in the hay and begins to unbutton her blouse. The woman's husband shows up and wields a pitchfork at the man in jodhpurs.

"Put it this way," Dwayne says, "I had a whole bunch of different daddies. She never had a job but somehow bought a house. You figure it out."

The husband chases the jodhpured man around the barn. The woman, buttoning her blouse, runs after them screaming.

"That doesn't mean she was a prostitute," Raymond points out. He remembers Gloria saying that Dwayne says things he doesn't mean, or doesn't mean what he says. "Lots of people have several spouses over a lifetime," he adds.

Dwayne burps. "You're married, right?"

"No. I mean, I was. We're divorced."

"What's her name?"

"Mara."

"Mara who?"

"Moretto." He wonders where Dwayne is. It sounds like a bar. He can hear rock music and people talking. "Were you and Sheena planning to get married?"

"How do you know about me and Sheena?"

"Gloria told me."

"That fucking twat."

The husband has pinned the jodhpured man to the wall with the pitchfork. A prong rests against either side of the man's neck. The woman, hysterical, has her hands over her mouth.

"Sheena's a slut," Dwayne says.

A cook at Chez Simon always referred to his ex-girlfriends as sluts. While they were dating he called them his "baby" or his "honey" but as soon as they rejected him, they became sluts. Raymond understood that the cook was trying to hide his pain by acting macho. Maybe Dwayne is trying to hide his pain by acting macho.

"I'm sorry to hear that," Raymond says. He wishes it were easier for them to talk. He remembers the social worker's warning that his siblings might feel displaced by him. "Dwayne, I don't mean to interfere in your life."

"Then don't." The jodhpured man feigns unconsciousness, then, when the husband isn't looking, kicks him in the groin.

Dwayne burps again. "That chick with the great tits in your restaurant, she your girlfriend?"

"No."

"Too bad. I bet she gives good head."

Raymond is offended by this kind of language. He reminds himself that Gloria warned him that when Dwayne isn't nice, it doesn't mean anything. He suspects that Dwayne is using coarse language out of a fear of intimacy. Or maybe he's slightly brain-damaged due to oxygen deprivation since Raymond hogged all the blood. He must be patient and make allowances.

"Gotta go," Dwayne says and hangs up. Raymond feels bereft. He calls Mara. She isn't home. He sinks into the couch and remembers that Mrs. Kalbfleisch is dead. He tries to feel happy that he's alive. The jodhpured man yanks the pitchfork from the wall, grabs the woman's hand and pulls her out the stable doors. They run across a field. He lifts her over a fence, then hurdles it himself. She says that she loves him and that they must always be together. He agrees and says that he will never let that son of a bitch touch her again. Raymond misses Mara. He changes the channel. A hockey game is on. He decides to try to watch it, to see if he can learn to enjoy sports so that he can at least share that with his twin. One hockey player is smashing his stick over the head of another hockey player. Raymond picks up the phone and redials Mara's number. It rings for a long time. When she answers she sounds drugged. He panics and quickly hangs up. If she's done it this time, he won't interfere. Then he realizes that she answered the phone. People committing suicide don't answer the phone.

nine

Dr. Kalbfleisch sits motionless by the window. Raymond was downstairs and didn't know that he was in the restaurant. Usually Dr. Kalbfleisch asks him to come upstairs as soon as he arrives. Raymond hadn't expected him to come in today and doesn't know what to say to him. It doesn't seem to matter since Dr. Kalbfleisch hasn't noticed him. Raymond goes back to the kitchen. "Kalbfleisch is here."

Jeff raises his eyebrows. "No shit? I thought we'd get at least one day off." He turns down his Beatles music. "When's the funeral?"

"I don't know. Soon I guess."

"Do you want me to make him a dinner?"

"No. Let's just wait."

A half an hour later Dr. Kalbfleisch still hasn't moved. Beth, looking worried, whispers to Raymond, "Maybe he's dying. People do that, you know. After losing a loved one, they will themselves to die. Like, he could be dead in his chair."

"Do you think he loved her?" Raymond asks.

"Who loves anybody? They were married, right? That must count for something. I mean, they were married for like . . . for ever."

"That's true," Raymond agrees. "Maybe you should go see if he wants a sundae or something. Or a cup of coffee. Bring him a cup of coffee."

"You bring it."

"You're the waitress."

"He doesn't happen to be a customer. Waitresses serve customers."

Raymond doesn't want to fight with Beth so he pours the coffee himself and takes it to Dr. Kalbfleisch. "Hello, sir. I thought you might like a coffee."

"Thank you, Raymond." Slowly he pours his usual five teaspoons of sugar into the cup and slowly he stirs it.

"I'm very sorry to hear about your wife, sir."

"Thank you, Raymond."

"It's a tragedy."

"Yes." He nods several times. "At least she went fast. We should be thankful."

"Yes . . . was it a . . . I guess it was a heart attack?"

Dr. Kalbfleisch nods again. "A million times I told her to lay off the fats, but she loved food. She grew up hungry. You never forget that."

"No."

Sharif the dishwasher mops the floor around them. Dr. Kalbfleisch doesn't seem to notice. "She never had it easy," he continues. "I did what I could. But you never forget what happened in your childhood."

"No."

It hadn't occurred to Raymond that Mrs. Kalbfleisch stole pies and chickens for any reason but greed. It hadn't occurred to him that she stole because of an ingrained fear of starvation. It bothers him that he assumed that she was greedy; that he couldn't see beyond the obvious. Had he known she grew up hungry, he could have overlooked her pie fetish. He feels that people's histories explain who they are and that, without knowing their histories, he can do nothing but misjudge them.

"You're a good man, Raymond. I know I can be a little tough at times."

Raymond knows little about what happened to Dr. Kalbfleisch in the concentration camp because he never talks about it. Mrs. Kalbfleisch mentioned it once while she was taking chickens. She said that Dr. Kalbfleisch's mother and sister were gassed, and he and his father were forced to do menial labour. Dr. Kalbfleisch had to watch helplessly as they took his mother away. Since then, when Dr. Kalbfleisch has really irritated Raymond, he has tried to imagine the boy, torn from his mother, lifting rocks with bloodied hands. He believes that if he can see the boy, he won't be bothered by the man. He still is though. He clears his throat. "The chicken hats have arrived."

Dr. Kalbfleisch nods.

"We can try them out tonight if you like."

"Whatever you say, Raymond. You're the manager." Dr. Kalbfleisch stands with more difficulty than usual, pulls out his handkerchief, wraps it around his index finger and pokes it inside one nostril. "I'll see you tomorrow." He puts the handkerchief back in his pocket and starts for the front door.

"Would you like to take a chicken home, sir?"

"No. No chicken."

Watching him walk through the glass doors, Raymond can't believe that he has allowed himself to hate this frail man. He remembers Mara telling him, "It's easier to hate than to love. Love you're never sure about. You never doubt hatred."

Jeff charges towards him, pushing his hair up into a hairnet. "The health inspector's here again. The bastard came in the back door. I wasn't even wearing gloves."

"Jesus."

"He's checking the temperatures. He already saw Beth sticking a glass into the ice maker."

"Why won't she use the tongs?"

"She says it takes too long." Jeff pulls on plastic gloves. "And Bubba's lost his contact lens again. He's on his knees back there."

Through the window Raymond sees Gloria speedily crossing the street, heading towards Chez Simon. His first instinct is to run, but then he remembers the health inspector.

"And he's already bitching about that light fixture," Jeff adds. "We were supposed to cover it." Gloria halts abruptly, backs up a few paces, then bends down to pick something up off the pavement.

"Tell him there's been a death in the family," Raymond says.

"You tell him. You've got to stall him. I've got to check temperatures on the salad bar. All I need is another lecture on botulism."

Gloria pushes through the glass doors, spots Raymond and waves. He waves back. "I'll just sit here," she calls to him.

"Okay. I'll be with you in a minute."

In the kitchen the inspector is staring hard at some shelves that Raymond put up at Mrs. Kalbfleisch's request. Dr. Kalbfleisch had been with her and they'd argued about the shelves. Raymond knew that the porous material wouldn't pass a health inspection but he didn't want to take sides in the argument. Finally Dr. Kalbfleisch raised his voice so much the entire staff could hear. Unperturbed, Mrs. Kalbfleisch told him that he had shit for brains and ordered Raymond to put up the shelves.

The inspector taps one of them with his pen. "Would you call this an impermeable surface?"

"No. Those are just temporary."

"They'll be out of here next time I drop by."

"That's right."

The inspector jots something on his clipboard. "Your cook's a bit slow on the gloves."

"I'll talk to him."

"Not to mention the hairnet."

"I know." Raymond scratches behind his ear.

"Ray, I want to cut you some slack here but your steam table wasn't even at a hundred and forty."

"Yeah, well, we're just getting ready for lunch."

The inspector, looking skeptical, fondles his tie as he continues walking around the kitchen. Raymond follows behind. "You got rid of that three-hundred-pound compulsive eater?"

"Yes," Raymond says.

"Never seen anything like it."

"He was a good cook."

"Good cooks don't eat all the food. It was disgusting."

Raymond doesn't argue. He's worrying about what Gloria's doing in the dining room.

"Fumigator been by?"

"Yeah. I called him the week after you saw the cockroach."

"Good." He looks back at his clipboard and sighs heavily. "You've got to do something about this grease-laden vapour. I can't keep pretending I don't notice it." He jots something else down.

Beth dumps dirty plates in the dish room, then looks at Raymond. "There's some woman out here says she's your mother."

"Just serve her."

"She says she'll only eat what you recommend. I think she's expecting free food."

"Give her a quarter-chicken dinner."

The inspector stops and grimaces at the floor. "I cannot believe the grime between these tiles."

"We do the best we can," Raymond says. "They're old tiles."

"You might want to suggest some renovations to your owner. Has he heard about stainless steel?"

"His wife just died."

"I'm sorry to hear that. I'll be even more sorry if I have to close down his restaurant." As he walks into the dining room, Beth sticks her tongue out at him. While he inspects the salad bar, Raymond sits with Gloria.

"I had a hair appointment downtown," she tells him, "so I thought I'd drop by." Raymond wonders how she can have a hair appointment when she's bald. She stares at him out of her right eye. "And I was worried about you."

"Why?"

"Did Dwayne call you?"

"Yes."

"What'd he say?"

"Nothing much." He wonders how she would react if he told her that Dwayne said she was a whore.

She picks at something between her teeth. "The trouble with Dwayne is he got in with the wrong people."

"What people?"

"Bad people. Sometimes I worry maybe he does drugs. I've never seen any. But sometimes I wonder. He's so moody, see. Could be he's taking drugs."

"Drugs are expensive," Raymond points out.

"Well what's he do with his money? The cheques come in one day, next day they're history. Last I heard, he was throwing money off a bridge."

"Has he talked about suicide since then?"

"Nah. I don't think he'd do it. He's just a talker, know what I mean?" She opens her purse, rummages inside it and pulls out a lipstick. Suddenly the inspector stands over them. Raymond notices a grease stain on his pants near his crotch and wonders if he should mention it. While Gloria freshens her lipstick, the inspector passes Raymond the clipboard to sign. The inspector tears off the top sheet and gives it him, then fondles his tie again.

"My advice to you is to get a grip, Ray. Things are getting out of control here. I don't want to give you a hard time but I've got a job to do."

"I understand."

"Mind if I grab a coffee?"

"Go ahead. Ask Beth."

Gloria puts her lipstick back into her purse. "One time he wouldn't go to work and I said why and he said he was having a nervous breakdown. All he did all day was play with those fuzzy dice. They were hanging in his car before he sold it. All day long he'd play with them, throw them in the air and whatnot. He said he was glad to have time to do what he wanted for a change. All he did was play with those damn dice." She adjusts her turban. "He's one of those people always dreaming about what they don't have. Then they get it and it's no different than what they've already got."

Beth approaches with Gloria's chicken dinner. "Don't tell me to serve people that aren't customers, Raymond. I only serve customers."

"He's the health inspector."

"Like I don't know that. I don't give two shits who he is. He's not a paying customer. He's taking up a whole table for a cup of coffee."

"He'll leave in a minute."

"I'm Raymond's mother," Gloria interjects.

"So you said. Enjoy your meal." She glares at Raymond. "Like I say, don't treat me like a second-class citizen or I'm out of here." Behind her, a toothless man is trying to get her attention.

"A customer wants you at table six," Raymond advises her.

"He's a toad."

"At least he's a paying customer."

"That's so funny I forgot to laugh."

Gloria watches Beth stomp over to table six to negotiate with the toothless man. "Nice girl. She your girlfriend?"

"No."

"Give me your hand."

"What?"

She takes his hand and presses a penny into his palm. "I just found it. It's lucky."

"How do you know it's lucky?"

"Found pennies are always lucky." She picks up her knife and fork and begins working on the chicken. "Usually I prefer white meat."

"You should have specified."

"Don't worry about it. It's just there's more fat in the dark meat, see. I got to be careful."

"Is there a history of heart problems in the family?"

"Nah." She picks up the leg and chews on it. Raymond notices the health inspector talking with Beth. He wonders if he's trying to pick her up. Gloria puts the chicken leg down and eats a french fry. "Anyways, don't go believing everything your brother says. Half the time he don't know what he's saying. It's growing up without a dad that did it. You're lucky you had a dad."

Raymond clears his throat and narrows his eyes. "He told me he had a whole bunch of different daddies."

"Now why would he go and say a thing like that?"

"I don't know."

Gloria pokes her finger under her turban and scratches. "I had a couple of boyfriends and he got jealous, simple as that."

"Just a couple of boyfriends?"

"I was lonesome, Raymond. I'm not one of those women don't like having men around."

"How many were there though?"

She dips her dinner roll into the barbecue sauce. "Just a couple. He makes like there was more to get attention. He's always acting like I was mean to him. It's all lies. He was spoilt, see, he was my pride and joy."

"It doesn't seem that way."

She points her roll at him. "That's because he's *different* now. He's changed. That's why I'm hoping you can help him."

"How?"

"Maybe you could get him a job here? If he had a job here, he might get some self-respect, know what I mean? And you could keep an eye on him. You're stronger than him, see, you could help him. He needs help."

Raymond notices Beth writing something on a napkin. She smiles and hands it to the health inspector. He looks at the napkin, smiles and puts it in his breast pocket.

"Why can't *you* help him?" Raymond asks.

"He don't listen to me."

Raymond suspects that Beth has given the health inspector her phone number. He feels betrayed.

"Anyways, you're coming over Saturday," Gloria says. "Tammy and Tory want to meet you. Tory's cooking a chicken and Tammy said she'd make potato salad. We'll get some weenies for the kiddies. Maybe, if Dwayne's feeling better, he'll bake some brownies. Right now his neck's bad."

The health inspector ambles out the front doors, slapping his clipboard against his thigh and jangling his car keys. Raymond notes Beth watching him. "I've got to get back to work," he says.

"Thanks for the chicken. You got pie here?"

"Yes. Ask the waitress. I've got to go." As he walks past the health inspector's table he sees that he has left a dollar tip for Beth. A dollar tip for a free cup of coffee. She's in the kitchen sticking a glass into the ice machine. "You're supposed to use the tongs," Raymond tells her.

She sets the glass on her tray and shoves another one into the ice bin. "Give me a break."

"The health inspector said you have to use the tongs. It's not hygienic to use your hand."

"Fuck the health inspector."

"Are you going to?"

"What?"

"Fuck him?"

Suddenly the kitchen seems very quiet. Jeff stares at him, Bubba the line cook stares at him, Bruce the waiter, even Sharif the dishwasher. "Forget it," Raymond mutters. "I'll be downstairs."

In his concrete cell he cries. He has no idea why. For some reason he can't stop thinking about his puppy, Buster. When the older boys called Raymond a crybaby and wouldn't let him play, he went home and kicked Buster. That's what he does. When he feels humiliated he lashes out at the wrong people. Not the people who humiliated him but innocent bystanders. Buster never trusted him after that, and one day he ran under a car. Raymond's mother found him and wouldn't let Raymond see the body. He wants to hold Buster, to protect him from himself. As he wants to protect himself from himself. He feels Gloria's lucky penny in his hand and looks down at it. It's dirty and tarnished. He drops it into the wastebasket.

❖

The For Sale sign on Mara's front lawn jolts him. He feels himself perspiring again. If she did commit suicide, he will never forgive himself. The singing neighbour who runs around naked is watering his lawn. He's wearing trousers but no shirt. His belly hangs over his belt like a melon. Raymond tries to ignore his stare as he gets out of the car to ring Mara's bell. It relieves him that he can hear her TV. He rings again but she doesn't answer. He walks around to the backyard and finds her sitting on a lawn chair by the grave. It surprises him how happy he is to see her, even though she's drinking scotch again. She notices him before he has a chance to say anything.

"What are you doing here?" she asks.

"I just thought I'd come by to shoot the breeze."

"Shoot the breeze?" She drinks more.

"I'm trying to be casual."

She nods and stares at the grave.

"Your TV's on."

"Is it?"

"Were you watching it?"

She raps her nails against her glass. Raymond clears his throat. "Are you seriously selling the house?"

"If someone seriously wants to buy it." A few houses over someone is having a party. Raymond hears laughter and rap music. Mara leans forward in her chair and pulls up a weed. "My brother says that we should make a clean break."

"Who should?"

"Who do you think?"

Raymond pictures chicken bones splintering. "Is a clean break possible?"

"Anything's possible if you make it possible."

This sounds like something her brother would say.

"It's like a scab, Raymond. Our relationship. We keep picking at it."

"We're friends."

"No we're not. We're damaged people. Seriously damaged people hanging around each other because we're afraid to be alone."

He likes being an ex. It's safe being an ex. It's an excuse to avoid commitment; because you've been there. You've been burned. You have a reason to be cautious. He doesn't want to lose his ex. There's no other woman he can talk to without complications. "Is that so bad?" he asks.

"We're not helping each other."

"Says who, your brother?"

"Leave him out of it."

"How can I leave him out of it? It's as if he's controlling your mind. Maybe I should just talk to him and leave you out of it."

She holds up her hands. "I have no interest in having this argument."

Glass smashes at the party and a man howls with laughter.

Raymond clears his throat and narrows his eyes. "I just don't see why two lonely people can't be friends."

"Two lonely people who haven't been married and watched their babies die can be friends. We're too fucked up, can't you see that? We're both *totally* fucked up."

Raymond unfolds the other lawn chair and sits on it. The weave on the seat is shredding and he can feel his butt slipping through it. But he stays on it because it's the only chair available and he hopes to appear casual. "Mrs. Kalbfleisch died yesterday." A woman at the party squeals.

"Was anyone surprised? She was old, wasn't she?"

"Older than he is."

"Was he distraught?"

"I don't know. I think so. I mean who's he going to talk to now?"

"Do you think they talked?"

"I don't know."

Mara pulls up another weed. "People stick together for the sickest reasons. They feed off each other's misery. Their spouse is the only one who'll put up with their shit, so they keep doling it out. It's like nobody else can stand them so they stick together, torturing each other."

The woman shrieks and a man shouts, "Fucking totalled!"

"I don't think that's necessarily true," Raymond says.

"No? What do you think is necessarily true, Raymond? You tell me. I'd like to know."

He tries to think. The party is distracting him. Mara doesn't seem to notice it. "Well it's subjective, isn't it? Everybody's truth is different."

"So what's your truth?"

Raymond grips the arms of the lawn chair. "I don't know."

"Isn't that something? Here we are, we've been adults for twenty years and we don't even know what the fucking truth is."

"Is that so important?"

"I think it would be nice not to bother with the distorted shit, don't you?"

"What is the distorted shit though?"

"I don't have a fucking clue. It's all starting to look the same. I can't even remember what I used to think was the truth. Whatever it was is so distorted now it looks like all the other shit." She drinks more, then looks at him. "I can't get excited about anything any more, do you know how awful that is? Nothing excites me."

Raymond scratches behind his ear. "I don't think anything excites me either. I mean, I can't think of anything." The singing neighbour drags his hose to the backyard and starts watering.

Mara brushes a bug off her leg. "I saw you creeping around earlier."

"What?" Raymond asks.

"You were here earlier. It's beginning to look like you're stalking me."

The neighbour begins to whistle.

"I wasn't here earlier. I was at work."

"Right."

"I was. I just got here."

"Well somebody who looks an awful lot like you was prowling around my house this afternoon."

He'd like to tell her that it must have been his twin, but this might frighten her. The woman at the party screeches again and men laugh. Raymond isn't sure if she's having fun or not. "Do you think she's alright?"

"Who?"

"The woman at the party."

"Don't change the subject."

"I'm not. I'm worried about her."

"Well maybe you should go over and save her, Raymond. Because you know what? I'm tired of being saved. I want you to leave me alone. I don't want you calling me or creeping around my house. I'm sorry. But that's the way it is." As she stands her ankle rolls over on the grass. Raymond can tell that she's drunk. "It's not that I don't care about you," she insists. "I just need to be left in peace. Can you do that for me? If you care about me, you'll do that for me." She tries to steady herself on the back of the lawn chair but it tips and she falls to her knees. "Shit."

Raymond wants to reach out and help her but stops himself. The only way she will understand that she needs him is if he is no longer there. "Alright," he says, "I'm going." He leaves her in the dirt beside the grave.

As he walks across her front lawn for what may be the last time, it feels as though the blood has dried up in his veins. While driving away he tries not to worry about Dwayne stalking her. Dwayne is harmless. He's a loser. He's got a bad neck and sinus headaches. Dwayne won't do anything.

ten

Raymond's in an old folk's home with Mrs. Kalbfleisch. She's ordering him to do things but she has no voice. Her lips move but no sound comes out. He clutches the skirt of a nurse and tries to explain that he doesn't belong in a home; that he shouldn't be here; that there's nothing wrong with him. The nurse smiles politely and tells him not to worry. "But you don't understand," Raymond insists, "I shouldn't be here." The nurse tries to prise his fingers loose from her skirt, but he won't let go.

The doctor places the ends of his stethoscope into his ears. "Are you alright, Raymond?"

"What?"

"You left me for a moment there."

"Oh, sorry. I was remembering a dream."

"I see." He holds the stethoscope against Raymond's back ribs. "Take a deep breath, please." Raymond does. "Again, please." Raymond does. "Sounds fine." He wraps a blood-pressure gauge around Raymond's arm, then pumps it up. "Blood pressure's fine," he says. He takes off his stethoscope and picks up an otoscope. "Open wide, please." He looks down Raymond's throat. Then, with the otoscope, he looks in Raymond's ears.

Raymond clears his throat. "I just found out that I have an identical twin."

"Really. How interesting."

"It's kind of stressful, really."

"How so?"

"Well . . ." Sitting on the examining table, wearing just his underpants, Raymond feels like a child. He doesn't know why he's confiding in this doctor. He doesn't even know him. He only sees him once a year for his physical. "I guess he's not the type of person I usually hang around with."

"Twins are often quite different."

"He gets sinus headaches. And has a bad neck. I don't have any of that."

"There's no reason that you should."

The doctor is wearing a very thick gold wedding band. And there are pictures of his children on the wall. They smile broadly, revealing perfect teeth.

The doctor jots something on Raymond's chart. "Any problems you want to discuss?"

"Problems?"

"With your health."

"It's just the nausea. When it comes over me I feel like I'm going to faint."

The doctor nods and looks down at the chart. "Well, I can't find anything wrong with you at the moment. We'll get some blood work done. See if anything shows up."

"Right."

"You might try taking some Gravol. That usually does the trick."

"Okay."

"Anything else?"

"No."

❖

Back at the restaurant everyone is wearing the chicken hats. Bruce, whose hat is on crooked, bustles past him carrying dinners. "What's going on?" Raymond asks.

"Kalbfleisch told us to wear them. The bitch has only been dead two days and already he's back to being an ultra-asshole."

In the kitchen Dr. Kalbfleisch is talking to Gus the serviceman. Raymond called Gus to fix the seals on the fridges. It was one of the instructions left behind by the health inspector.

"Raymond," Dr. Kalbfleisch says, "I was watching from outside for ten minutes and not one person was doing anything, filling ketchups, nothing. They were just standing around."

"It's a slow day."

"Slow days should be workdays. I don't pay these people to stand around. Why don't they clean the windows? How many times do I have to tell these people to clean the windows?"

"We did clean them."

Dr. Kalbfleisch points to the take-out window. "You call that clean?"

The window is greasy. "Maybe they forgot to do take-out."

"What's wrong with these people?" He takes out his handkerchief, wraps it around his index finger and pokes it into one nostril. "They've got shit for brains."

Raymond wonders if now that Mrs. Kalbfleisch is dead and unable to accuse Dr. Kalbfleisch of having shit for brains, he will use the term on a regular basis.

"I'll talk to them," Raymond says.

"Have you ever seen a dirty window at Chicken Villa? Never. Every day they clean the windows."

"They have a larger staff."

Dr. Kalbfleisch holds his hands over his ears. "Don't start with the staff business, Raymond. Ten minutes I saw them standing around."

"As I said, I'll talk to them."

Dr. Kalbfleisch sucks on his dentures. "And tell them to smile more. Not once did they smile. You'd think they were in prison."

Raymond considers how close to the truth this is, but says nothing. Gus, working on the fridge, looks bored. Dr. Kalbfleisch points at him. "And why can't he fix the savoury freezer so it won't break down every five minutes? You should offer guarantees. What kind of serviceman offers no guarantees?"

Gus shrugs. "It's an old freezer, sir. If you buy a new freezer, I'll give you a guarantee."

"Why would I need a guarantee if I had a new freezer? A new freezer would put you out of business."

Gus shrugs again, picks up his tools and moves to the next fridge.

"Sir," Raymond interjects. "Why don't we talk in the dining room?"

After the Mrs. Kalbfleisch dream, he dreamed he was in a chicken restaurant even seedier than Chez Simon. The smell of grease was overwhelming and all the customers looked cruel. He wanted to leave but couldn't find his ID. He always keeps his driver's licence, social and health insurance cards separate from his wallet so that if his wallet is stolen, he will not be without ID. But somehow, in the seedy chicken restaurant, he'd lost his ID, not his wallet. Panicked, he tried to get a waitress to help him but she only stared at him with loathing. He was forced to search under the tables himself while the cruel customers sneered at him, calling him jackass and saying he had shit for brains. He ponders this dream while Dr. Kalbfleisch tells him once again that his staff is lazy, and that this is no way to run a business.

❖

When Dr. Kalbfleisch leaves, Raymond tells everyone to take off the chicken hats. He sits very still at the table, wondering why he feels so incomplete, and if this matters. He notices Seymour, the customer with the burned-out BMW, watching him. "Has somebody taken your order?" Raymond inquires.

"He really shouldn't speak to you that way, Raymond."

"Who?"

"The owner."

"His wife just died."

"I'm sorry to hear that. Even so, he shouldn't speak to you like that."

"It doesn't bother me."

"That's what I said for years. Then I became a food addict."

"He wants me to cut back on inventory. Maybe he's right."

"What he wants is for you to sell your soul. It's not worth it. Take it from me."

When people talk about souls, Raymond feels uncomfortable. Because he's not sure that he has one. Which is one of the reasons he liked being married to Mara. She had a soul. The troubles of the world pained her. She sent money to world organizations intent on feeding the hungry. The only thing that pained him was the thought of losing her. And now he has.

Beth brings Seymour his half-chicken dinner. "Jeff gave you extra fries because he loves ya." She uses the friendly tone she saves for her best-tipping customers. She has never used this tone with Raymond.

"Thank you, beautiful one." Seymour watches her walk back to the kitchen, then begins dripping ketchup over his fries. Raymond looks down at his inventory sheet, trying to find something to cut. Seymour tears the drumstick away from the breast. "Don't you ever long to be in love,

Raymond? Head over heels in love? The kind of love that makes your knees wobble?" He makes sweeping gestures with the chicken leg. "The kind of love that takes over your thoughts, your life. Leaving you with nothing but this feeling, this . . . debilitating but glorious feeling."

It surprises Raymond to hear Seymour talk this way, since he is obese. Raymond imagined that the fat insulated Seymour from feelings; except for food. He realizes that this is an unfair assumption and he wonders if Seymour was in love once.

"You're single, aren't you, Raymond?"

"Yes."

"How is it?"

"It's alright."

"I hate it. But then, when I'm with a woman, I see everything that's wrong with her. Poorly applied makeup, flabby arms, flawed skin. It's terrible."

Raymond wonders how Seymour can be so picky about women when he himself is so gross.

Seymour shakes his head. "Most of all it's the aftermath I can't get enthused about."

Raymond's pen is running out of ink. He shakes it. "Aftermath?"

"Of love."

"Oh."

"The wreckage."

"Yeah," Raymond agrees.

Seymour picks up his knife and fork and starts cutting into the breast. "Too many romantic movies, I think. I've got to stop watching movies."

Raymond isn't sure that he was ever in love with Mara. He knows only that he used to worry about her being killed in a car accident. He would give himself diarrhea worrying about her. He wonders if he will worry about her less now that she no longer wants to see him.

❖

After driving home to walk Burt, he goes to Chicken Villa because he wants to be served by the bubbly waitress. If she recognizes him, he intends to apologize for commenting on her perfume. And he plans to congratulate her on her engagement. But when she prepares to take his order, smiling warmly, he realizes that she doesn't recognize him; that he must look like any other male customer suffering from pattern baldness. "I'll have the chef's salad," he tells her. "Can you ask him not to put chicken in it?"

"Sure, but it'll cost the same."

"That's fine. Just no chicken."

"Would you like something to drink with that?"

"Ahh . . ." He wants her to stay there asking him things. He wants her to like him. "What would you recommend?"

"Well, the shakes are good. Unless you want something from the bar." He knows that she will like it if he orders from the bar because it will mean a higher tab, meaning a bigger tip. "Maybe I'll have a scotch," he says, hoping this will please her. But her face reveals nothing and he worries that maybe she has had a bad experience with scotch. Maybe her father was an alcoholic, or her fiancé.

"Certainly," she says. "Will that be all?"

"Yes. Thank you."

"My pleasure."

Why can't Beth speak to customers like this? He studies the paper place mat. It is a map of the city. Treasure chests mark places of interest. Raymond hasn't been to any of them. There is a memorial not far from here. Maybe he'll go look at it later.

When the waitress brings him his scotch, he smiles. "Thank you."

"Is ice alright? I forgot to ask how you wanted it."

"This is perfect."

She smiles. He knows that she still hasn't recognized him. Today she smells of apricots.

Because he was at the doctor's office and missed lunch, the scotch moves quickly through him. He is glad for this, glad to feel relaxed. No one else in Chicken Villa seems relaxed. Mothers and fathers cut chicken for their kids. Sometimes they slap their kids' hands. Sometimes they exchange angry looks. A man behind Raymond must have some kind of health problem because he wheezes. His wife is discussing the need for tax reform in this country. The man doesn't respond, only wheezes.

When the waitress brings Raymond his salad, he smiles again. "Thank you."

"You're welcome."

"Do you mind if I ask your name?"

"Claire."

"What a beautiful name."

"Can I get you anything else?"

"Not for the moment. Thank you."

She doesn't say "my pleasure" this time and he senses that he has offended her. He swirls the ice around in his glass and drinks some more. A father is taking his little boy to the men's room. The little boy insists that he doesn't need to go. Raymond tries to remember if his father ever escorted him to the men's room. He can only remember needing to pee while waiting for his father to pick him up after the movies. Initially, his father was supposed to take him but then he'd change his mind. "What time does it get out?" his father would ask. "I'll come pick you up and we'll go for ice cream or something." Raymond would give him the exact time the movie finished. But his father would always be late anyway. Raymond would worry that he'd forgotten to pick him up. He'd wait, sitting on the steps of the movie theatre. Everyone else would have left the cinema. There would be cats picking at garbage and drunks sleeping in corners but no sign of Raymond's father. He'd wait on the steps to the movie theatre. Before closing up, the projectionist and ticket girl would ask if he was all right. "My dad's picking me up," Raymond would explain, wondering if he should ask them if he could use the washroom before they closed the theatre. He never did though, he was too embarrassed. After they turned off the lights on the marquee and locked the doors, Raymond would watch them walk down the street. The sounds of their footsteps receding desolated him. Occasionally, if his father completely forgot about him, the police would take Raymond home. If his father did remember, there was never any ice cream. Only the smell of rye on his breath. Raymond did not get angry with his father. He understood that he was forgettable. You're only forgotten if you're forgettable.

The salad has no taste. The lettuce is wilted, the radishes and carrots are dry and the edges of the egg yolk have gone grey. He moves the lettuce around on the plate so that Claire will think he has eaten some of it. He tries to decide what to order for dessert. He doesn't want any but understands that if he increases his tab by ordering an expensive dessert, she will not resent him for occupying a table all by himself. He studies the menu. The strawberry shortcake seems to be the most expensive. He'll order that. He puts the menu back behind the ketchup bottle, considering that strawberry shortcake might be quite pleasant. But then he sees Beth coming through the front doors with the health inspector. Raymond grabs the menu again and tries to hide behind it. Beth is wearing tight jeans and gold appliquéd cowboy boots with a matching purse. Her tight pullover is low-cut and emphasizes her breasts. She didn't dress like this for Raymond. They glance around the restaurant, deciding where to sit. They choose a window seat by the door. Raymond will have to walk past them.

"Can I get you anything else?" Claire asks.

"Ah, no. Nothing else. Just the bill, please."

Before she has time to hand him the bill he gives her fifteen dollars. "Keep the change."

"Thank you, sir."

"You're welcome." It saddens him to be leaving Claire but he feels that he has no choice. If Beth sees him eating alone, she will feel superior towards him. At least, if he hurries out now, it might appear that his dinner companion has already left and is waiting for him outside. He wipes his mouth with a napkin to make certain that there is no salad dressing on his chin. He heads towards the door, hoping to look preoccupied because he plans to appear as though he has just noticed them. The health inspector sees him first. "Hello, Ray, how's it going?"

"Fine."

"You just can't get enough of that chicken, can you?"

"Actually, I had a salad."

"On a diet, are you?"

"No."

Beth just stares at Raymond.

"You should get some exercise, Ray," the health inspector advises. "It's not good to be cooped up with the chickens all day." He smirks at his own joke and looks to see if Beth is amused. She isn't.

"I'll see you later," Raymond says.

The health inspector winks at him. "Ciao, baby."

❖

The memorial is in a park about the size of Mara's backyard. The general, who died for his country, has a paper bag over his head. Raymond would like to remove it but is afraid he'll fall off the general's pedestal. A dog urinates at the base of the statue while its owner speaks on a cellular phone. On the street, two cars screech to a stop. One of the drivers gets out and shouts at the other driver. "Get out of your car, asshole." The driver still in the car only shrugs. "Come on," the first man repeats. "Let me see you get out of your car." The driver rolls up his window and pulls around the shouting man who kicks the car. "Cocksucker," he shouts.

Raymond looks back at the general. According to the plaque, he died in action. Raymond would really like to see his face. He starts to climb the pedestal. Because of the scotch, he takes extra care to make certain that he has a firm hold before hoisting himself up beside the general. He grips the general's ankle, then his calf, then his thigh. When his foot slips he wraps his arms around the general's waist, pressing his face into his bullet belt. He slides a hand up over his medals, then grips the general's shoulder. He pulls himself up, removes the paper bag and stares into the blank eyes of the general. He looks as though he has forgotten what he is supposed to be doing. He has a moustache, and a scar over his left eye. Raymond begins to climb down. The shouting driver shouts at him. "What the fuck do you think you're doing?"

Startled, Raymond loses his toehold. His leg dangles. He clutches the general's gun. "I took a bag off his head," he explains.

"What?"

"Somebody put a bag over his head. I took it off."

"Probably some fucking nigger."

"I don't know who it was."

"The place is crawling with niggers."

Raymond gets one foot on the ground, then the other. He wipes his hands on his slacks, trying to figure out how to escape from the shouting man. "Well, I guess I'll be going," he says, but the shouting man has already lost interest and is striding back to his car. He gets in and slams the door. Raymond notices that his bumper sticker reads, "To all you virgins . . . thanks for nothing." As he accelerates, his tires screech.

❖

When he gets out of the elevator Raymond sees the obsessive-compulsive man stepping in and out of his apartment door. While Raymond unlocks his own door he can hear the man counting.

The light flickers on his answering machine. It is a message from Mara. She sounds angry. "Raymond, if you don't stop creeping around my house, I'm calling the police. I'm not kidding." Then she hangs up. He doesn't know what she's talking about. He hasn't been around her house. He's been avoiding it. He rewinds the tape, then plays the message again. "Raymond, if you don't stop creeping around my house, I'm calling the police. I'm not kidding."

It must be Dwayne.

eleven

Dwayne phones him from a sports bar. Raymond hears him order more beer and call the waitress "Angel Puss." He tells her that he's on the phone with his identical twin. He says he and his twin could double her pleasure. Then he shouts, "Gas it up, asshole!"

"Who are you talking to?" Raymond asks.

"You watching the fight?"

"What fight?"

"Jesus, you're not watching it? Turn on twelve, man."

Raymond has been watching a movie about a male prosecutor and a female defence lawyer who are working on the same case. They're arch enemies but attracted to each other. They just had a scene in an elevator in which the woman lawyer told the man lawyer to drop dead, and he responded, "See you in court."

"I can't believe you're not watching the fight," Dwayne says. "It's fucking amazing."

"I am now." On-screen two huge black men are swiping at each other. One of them is bleeding from his right eye.

"What a nimrod this guy is," Dwayne says. "Thanks, baby." Raymond assumes he's talking to the waitress who has brought him his beer.

"Who's a nimrod?"

"Garcia. He's fucking slow on his feet."

Raymond decides it wouldn't be prudent to broach the subject of

Mara immediately. "Dwayne, I've been meaning to ask you about a few things."

Dwayne makes hissing sounds as the boxers pound each other. Periodically he says, "Ouch."

"For starters," Raymond begins, "why is Gloria bald?"

"All her hair fell out."

"Why though?"

"She got some disease that made it fall out. She has no hair anywhere. Not even on her fucking twat."

Raymond wonders how he knows this. "When did this happen?"

"I don't know. A couple of years ago. It came out in clumps. It was all over the place. It clogged the sinks, the vacuum cleaner. She acted like it wasn't happening. She thinks nobody notices it. She talks about her hair like she's still got it."

"What colour was it?"

"I don't know. Red, black. For a while there it was yellow."

On-screen the bloodthirsty crowd is revealed. They jeer and roar.

"And what's wrong with her eye?" Raymond asks.

"What do you mean?"

"She always stares at me with her right eye."

"Oh that. One of her sugar daddies hit her. Well, they all hit her. But this guy struck a bull's eye."

"You mean she was abused?"

"If being swatted means abuse, yeah."

It appears to Raymond that the slightly larger boxer is repeatedly punching the other in the bleeding eye. "Is she blind in that eye?"

"She'd never admit to it. She never admits to anything. Her life's been hunky-dory as far as she's concerned." Raymond hears him swallow more beer. "Ask her about her arm."

"What's wrong with her arm?"

"One of the daddies twisted it. She had it in a sling for months. Now it won't straighten. She always carries her handbag over her wrist so no one will notice it. Ouch!" The boxer with the bleeding eye stumbles and falls against the ropes. The slightly larger boxer continues to pummel him. The crowd cheers.

Raymond clears his throat. "She told me she only had two boyfriends."

"Get moving, asshole! Jesus, this doofus is an amateur. It's got to be a setup. He's supposed to lose."

"He looks injured."

"He's a putz." The man with the bleeding eye staggers, then crashes to the floor. The referee stands over him and begins counting. "Get up, you stupid fuck!" Dwayne shouts.

"If he's supposed to lose," Raymond inquires, "why should he get up?"

"Show business." The bleeding man writhes on the floor like a beetle that's been crushed. The referee holds up the larger fighter's hand. The crowd roars.

"The other thing is," Raymond begins, "have you been watching my ex-wife?"

"Why would I do that?"

"I don't know. She says somebody who looks like me has been creeping around her house. You're the only person who looks like me."

"Unless Gloria had triplets."

"It's not funny, Dwayne. It's upsetting my wife."

"Is she frigid or what?"

"That's none of your business."

"I bet she's frigid. I bet you had to beg for it. I bet ramming your cock into her was like humping a bucket of ice."

Raymond really doesn't know how to deal with this kind of language. "I wish you wouldn't talk about her that way. I wish you'd leave her alone."

"Don't whine, brother. Nothing gets a rise out of me like whining."

"If you keep bothering her," Raymond warns, "she's going to call the police."

"Now that's a scary thought."

On-screen the larger boxer is shown in close-up. Dripping with blood and sweat, toothless, with a nose flattened from previous fights, he grins idiotically.

"That fuck's got a lot of dough coming to him."

"Seriously, Dwayne, please leave her alone."

"I don't know, she looks awful lonesome to me, brother. Maybe she needs a guy like me. Maybe I could do things for her you couldn't. Maybe I could make her smile."

Raymond feels nauseated again. And helpless, as if his arms and legs were in irons.

"What do you think?" Dwayne continues. "Do you think she'd spread her legs for me? If she thought I was you? Is she hot for you? Or maybe I should tell her I'm not you. Maybe you're the reason she's frigid."

"Shut up," Raymond says. "Or I'll . . ." Medics are loading the crushed boxer on to a stretcher, his face is contorted with pain.

"What?" Dwayne asks. "You'll what?"

"If you go near her, I'll kill you."

Dwayne burps. "Well I just hope you're a man of your word, because I'm kind of tired of this planet. I wouldn't mind getting off it."

"So why don't you kill yourself?"

"Then I'd have to make a decision. And I don't like making decisions. You've met our mother. She makes decisions for me. Which is why I'm such a charming person. So, if I fuck your wife and you kill me, I won't have to make a decision. You'll make it for me."

The larger boxer is hopping around the ring with his arms outstretched in victory. The crowd roars.

❖

Gloria's kitchen isn't very big but everyone is in it. Tammy and Tory sit at the table while the children play under it. It disturbs Raymond that Tammy is crying. "Don't worry about her," Gloria tells him. "Once she gets a few drinks in her, she always starts crying. Don't pay any attention. Her baby fell in the pool, see. So every time she comes over she thinks about it."

"You have a pool?" Raymond asks. He's still recovering from his phone call with Dwayne. He plans to confront him today regarding Mara. He's hoping that Dwayne's sexual references to her were intended to be humorous. Dwayne is obviously the kind of person who tells dirty jokes. Raymond has never laughed at dirty jokes.

"Out back," Gloria says, "above ground. Nothing fancy. But her kid fell into it. Tammy was on the phone and didn't notice."

"Was the baby alright?" Raymond asks.

"I wasn't on the phone," Tammy protests.

"I told you never to leave those kids alone by the pool."

"I was watching them."

"You was on the phone."

"How do you know, you weren't even there."

"You were on the phone with that man you been seeing."

"Would you please stop?" Tory asks. "How many times do you have to go over it?"

Gloria shakes her head. "She's always saying Dickie lives in the past. But it's her that's living in the past."

Tory, whose smile slits her face in half, clasps her hands together and holds them at chest level. "Please, please, please, can we not fight? This is a family reunion, remember?"

Earlier it seemed to Raymond that Tory was flirting with him. This made him uncomfortable, since she is his half-sister. She asked him about Chez Simon and kept repeating "How interesting" when he replied. She also informed him that she is an oral hygienist and that she was going to get married once, to a dentist, "but then he died."

Gloria forks fried chicken on to a serving dish. "You got to live your own life. All you young people go around expecting other people to wipe your behinds. You got to go your own way in life, simple as that." Tammy starts sobbing again.

"Where's Dwayne?" Raymond asks.

"In the pool."

"It's a bit cold to be swimming, isn't it?"

"He loves it. Now it's getting warmer, he'll spend all day floating around. Don't wear no sunscreen, nothing. I tell him he'll get cancer. But he don't listen to me. Raymond, go tell him dinner's ready."

Since the phone call, he has been less enthusiastic about meeting Dwayne because he's afraid that he will turn out to be as callous as he sounds; afraid that there will be no future to their relationship, that no bonding will take place, that he will once again be left alone with his reflection. But Belinda always told him not to judge people by appearances. It's entirely possible that Dwayne too is afraid, that he is intimidated by the prospect of a brother and is simply trying to act tough. As Raymond pushes open the back door it occurs to him that he might suggest they seek counselling together.

But Dwayne isn't in the pool. Only an inflatable raft shaped like a dolphin bobs in the wind. A pair of dripping swimming trunks decorated with peace signs hangs over the ladder. Raymond looks around the yard and down the driveway. "Dwayne?" he calls. "Dwayne?"

❖

"He's not in the pool."

"Are you kidding me? Where'd he go?"

"I have no idea. His trunks are there."

"That boy." Gloria shakes her head.

"Didn't he know I was coming?"

"I told him and he said he could hardly wait."

"Maybe he's coming back," Tory suggests.

"Thing about Dwayne is," Gloria explains, "he's shy. He just don't want nobody to know about it."

"Well," Raymond says, "I just think it's strange that he keeps avoiding me."

"He's not avoiding you, Raymond. Maybe he went to the corner for some Coke." She takes a framed photograph from a shelf and hands it to Raymond. At first he recognizes himself as a child but then realizes that it's a picture of Dwayne. He's standing in front of a lopsided sandcastle, holding a plastic shovel and pail. He looks unsure about the person behind the camera, as if he's not convinced that the person should be taking his picture. He offers a tentative smile but there is no joy in his expression, only uncertainty. Where is that little boy now? Raymond wonders. What happened to that little boy?

"Cute as a button, isn't he?" Gloria says.

"Who took the picture?" Raymond asks.

"What's that?"

"The photo. Who took it?"

She adjusts her turban. "Oh I don't know. Some friend of ours. We always had people around."

Raymond imagines that if he could find that little boy, if he could bring him out of hiding, the callous Dwayne would soften.

Gloria shows him another photograph of the man who looks like himself. That it isn't himself but someone who looks exactly like him unsettles Raymond, even though he knew that this would be the case.

"You look just like him except for the 'stache," Gloria points out. "Except now he's shaved it."

"He did?"

"And went and got his hair cut like yours. He wants to look like you,

Raymond. That's what I mean, he likes you. You wait, next he'll start wearing a shirt and tie."

Raymond can't decide if he should consider this emulation a compliment or a threat. He looks back at the photograph. Dwayne's holding up a turkey leg and grinning maniacally. Because it's a Polaroid, his eyes look pink. "What colour are his eyes?"

"Same as yours." Gloria puts a chicken leg on a plate and hands it to Raymond. "That was last Christmas. He promised Tammy and Tory he'd dress up like Santa, then he copped out. The kiddies was so disappointed."

"Why did he cop out?"

"Thing about Dwayne is, you can't count on him. One day he'll be sweet as sugar, the next day you're history."

Raymond looks down at the chicken leg. The skin is soggy. Dr. Kalbfleisch wouldn't like it.

"He killed his own bunny," Gloria adds, as if to emphasize her point.

"Can you believe that?" Tory asks, still smiling. Her teeth are very white.

"Fluffy," Gloria explains. "He *loved* that bunny. He was always cleaning his cage and hugging him and whatnot. Then one day I come home and Fluffy's dead." She nudges Raymond. "Help yourself to potato salad."

"How do you know Dwayne did it?" Raymond asks.

"Who else? Nobody else was around."

Raymond clears his throat and narrows his eyes. "One of your boyfriends maybe?"

"None of my boyfriends did nothing for no reason. When Dwayne was bad he got punished, simple as that."

Raymond wonders what the punishment was; if he was locked in closets, deprived of meals, beaten. "You said you only had two boyfriends."

"I did? Well neither of them did nothing for no reason."

Raymond looks at his half-sisters to see if their faces will reveal anything. But they're preoccupied with eating chicken. One of Tammy's children is crying but no one pays any attention. Raymond looks down at his chicken. Grease is congealing on the plate. "Why would he kill his own bunny?"

Gloria dollops potato salad on to Raymond's plate. "For attention."

Raymond wonders if it's true that Dwayne killed the bunny. And, if so, he killed it for the same reason that Raymond kicked Buster — because people were horrible to him.

"After that he was always wanting a dog," Gloria adds. "I said, 'What do you want a dog for, so you can kill it?'"

"Dwayne isn't like other people," Tory explains.

"Why not, though?" Raymond asks.

No one seems to have an answer. Tammy is still sobbing intermittently while her children squabble under the table. Tory daintily eats a pickle. Gloria tears skin off of a breast. "Some days he's nice as pie," she tells him. "Other days you just want to lock him up and throw away the key."

"Was he locked up?"

"You mean, was he in prison?"

"No, I mean did you send him to his room."

"We were all sent to our rooms," Tory explains. "This was different."

"How was it different?" Raymond feels as if he's speaking a different language and unable to make himself understood.

Gloria shakes her head. "Dwayne watches too many of those morning shows, see. Those shows about child abuse and whatnot. He makes up stories about what happened to him from those shows. One time he told me he had multiple-personality disorder. He was three people, he said."

Raymond scratches behind his ear. "Why would he make up something like that?"

"To get attention."

Tory nibbles on a chicken wing. "The way he explained it to me was that he could only cope with what happened to him as a child by becoming different people. He told me he completely forgets things that happen to one of his personalities when he becomes another personality. He says he blacks out, can you believe that?"

"He's just making excuses," Gloria insists. "Ever since he killed Fluffy, all I hear from him is lies."

❖

After dinner Gloria shows Raymond Dwayne's room. Baseball cards cover one wall. Gloria points to a stack of porno magazines on his dresser. "He don't even hide them like normal people." On another wall he has pinned up *Playboy* centrefolds. The room is tidy, the bed made. He has folded the sheets back over the blankets in the same way that Raymond does. On his bedside table is a book on stress management. Beside this, a John Grisham novel. Underneath this, *Introduction to Yoga.*

"He likes reading anyway," Gloria says. "See, what I don't get is, if I was so mean to him, how come he's still living here?"

"That's a good question." Raymond looks at the shoes neatly arranged at the bottom of the closet. Raymond arranges his shoes in exactly the same manner. "He's pretty tidy."

"Yeah. I never had to tell him to clean his room. Sometimes he goes at it with Ajax. I've never seen anybody clean a bedroom with Ajax. And the bathroom. Heavens, he can spend two hours in there scrubbing and spraying. I told him he should get a job as a cleaner. But he said he don't want to touch other people's dirt. He won't clean the rest of the house. Just the bathroom and his room."

Raymond considers his own fastidiousness where bathroom hygiene is concerned. It used to irritate Mara, since they only had the one bathroom. She would need to use it but he wouldn't let her until he'd sanitized all of its surfaces.

Out the window he sees the dolphin drifting in slow circles. "I wish I'd known him a long time ago," Raymond says. "Before the bunny."

Gloria's examining one of the porno magazines with her right eye. "What's that?"

"A long time ago Dwayne and I might have been friends."

"It's never too late to start fresh. Life's only over when you're dead." She closes the magazine and puts it back on the pile. "Looks to me like you're pretty lonesome yourself, Raymond. What with being divorced and whatnot. Seems to me you could use a brother."

Raymond thinks of Mrs. Kalbfleisch dying just like that. Dwayne could die. Suddenly he doesn't want to lose his brother. Even though he can't find him. "I guess he's not coming back."

"Could be he's off some place meditating," Gloria says. "Did you check the garage?"

"No."

"Could be he's in the garage. When he's done diving and doing handstands and whatnot, sometimes he meditates in the garage. He says he's got to get spiritual after being physical."

It comforts Raymond that both he and his twin enjoy swimming and doing handstands and diving; that both he and his twin make their beds in the same way, arrange their shoes in the same way, clean their bathrooms in the same way. At least they have this in common.

The garage is overcrowded with old sports equipment. Raymond picks up a battered and dusty hockey helmet and tries it on. It fits perfectly. He tries on a pair of hockey gloves. They also fit perfectly. Three bicycles in various states of disrepair lean against one wall. A torn basketball net hangs above them. *Playboy* centrefolds are taped above a workbench covered in disassembled electric trains. There is an order to the disarray on the table. It is clear that the person in charge has left it with the intention of returning and completing his task. Raymond sits on the stool facing the bench, aware that Dwayne must sit here. He reaches for a tiny screwdriver before realizing he's still wearing the helmet and gloves. He removes both and puts them back where he found them. One corner of the garage is furnished with an old mattress and cushions. Above the mattress is a picture of a long-haired East Indian man sitting cross-legged. Raymond suspects he is a yoga guru. Taped beside the guru is a small, very worn photograph of a bunny. Raymond bends over to take a closer look at it. The bunny's nose is crinkled, its ears perky. In its paws it grips a carrot.

"Not here either," Gloria observes. "Heavens, what a mess. I tell him it's a fire hazard but he don't listen to me."

Raymond clears his throat and glances at his watch. "Well, I guess I'd better head home. I've got to walk my dog. Thanks for the dinner. Give my regards to Dwayne."

"He'll be sorry he missed you, Raymond."

"I'm sure."

"Too bad he didn't make brownies."

"Maybe some other time."

❖

Raymond gives Tory a lift home. She lives downtown in a condominium. Raymond realizes that she must be well paid as an oral hygienist. "So," he asks, "did you and Tammy spend much time with Gloria when you were growing up?"

"Not really. My dad didn't want us to see her at all at first. He calls her white trash. But my stepmother thought it would be a good idea. So in our teens we started spending time there over the summer."

"Did you get along with Dwayne?"

"Oh sure. He can be nice."

Raymond clears his throat. "He hasn't been very nice to me."

"He's probably intimidated by you. I mean, it's not like he's done anything with his life."

"He hasn't been very nice to Gloria either."

"What do you mean? He's crazy about her."

"It doesn't seem that way."

"That's because," Tory explains, "he's one of those guys who thinks being vulnerable is being weak. It's really sad. But seriously, he can be a charmer. He dated a girlfriend of mine a couple of years ago and she was nuts about him."

"Really?"

"She said he was amazing in bed, can you believe that? With all the porno you'd think he'd be into S & M or something. She said she would have married him if he'd gotten a proper job and settled down. But Dwayne's always been a drifter."

Stopped at a light, Raymond rests his forearm on the car door. A gaunt man walks by and spits on the sidewalk. "Why does he live with Gloria?"

Tory shrugs. "Economics, insecurity. I think she's always been overprotective of him, I guess because he didn't have a father. But ever since he chased her around the kitchen with a fork it's been a little different. I think before that she thought she could control him. The fork changed that."

"What did he do with it?"

"Held it at her throat. Anyway, that's what *she* says. It's hard to know what's true and what isn't with Dwayne and Gloria."

The traffic slows again and Raymond notices a woman in a very tight miniskirt and stiletto heels leaning against a building. She stands with her pelvis thrust forward and her shoulders slouched. She looks sick and tired. Raymond suspects that she is a prostitute. "Were there a lot of men around?"

"When?" Tory asks.

"When you visited. Did Gloria have boyfriends?"

"Sometimes."

"Didn't you think that was strange, that she had so many boyfriends?"

"She didn't have a husband. Why shouldn't she have boyfriends?"

A car in front pulls over. The prostitute approaches it and says something to the driver, then gets into the car. How can the driver want her, Raymond wonders — want to do things to her — when she is so sick and tired? Raymond would prefer to take her to the hospital. He looks to see if Tory has noticed the exchange, but she's chewing her fingernails. The traffic begins moving again. "Dwayne says she slept with men for money. He says that's how she paid for the house."

"Yeah, well Dwayne says all kinds of things."

Raymond nods although he isn't sure what this is supposed to mean. "And why is Tammy always crying?"

"Oh, well she's never gotten over her baby drowning. And her husband never forgave her. He hardly speaks to her. She's taking Prozac but it doesn't help." She points to a high-rise. "That's my building." Raymond is surprised to see that she has a doorman. "Good evening, Ms. Spalding," the man in uniform says.

"Hi, Chuck." She gets out of the car and smiles. "Well, nice meeting you, Raymond." She hands him her card. "If you want company, call me."

"Thanks," he says, although he isn't sure he wants to see her or any of them again.

❖

Outside his building two cats are fighting. They screech horribly as they claw at each other's faces. Raymond stamps his feet, hoping to startle them and break up the fight. But they ignore him. Raymond tells himself not to care since he doesn't like cats. They kill birds, let them kill each other instead. One of the dogs in the building has to be destroyed because he bit a tenant. Raymond knows the bitten tenant, what an asshole he is, and doesn't think it's fair that the dog has to die. He remembers the dog as a puppy, joyful and curious, until his owner started beating him. Suddenly the dog was wearing a muzzle and walking with his head down. Suddenly he was sneaky and snarling all the time. Just like his owner. Raymond often wondered what would become of the dog if he were freed from his tormentor. Would he become joyful again? Or is he beyond repair? Is Dwayne beyond repair?

On his couch he holds Burt on his lap. Burt hasn't sat on his lap since he was a puppy and must find it uncomfortable because he keeps wriggling around. But Raymond won't let go. He hugs Burt as he wishes he'd hugged Buster. He hugs him so hard that Burt starts to wheeze. Raymond loosens his hold. "Sorry, buddy." Burt turns to look at him with sad eyes. He's drooling, probably because Raymond was squeezing the life out of him. Raymond puts him on the floor. Burt sits and watches him apprehensively. His tail wags slightly. "It's okay, pooch. I'm okay." He gets up and grabs Burt's leash. "Come on, boy, let's go for a walk." Burt trots excitedly to the door.

In the elevator, looking up at the floor numbers, Raymond ponders this business of loving; maybe the key is not to reveal the need for love. Because once they know you need it, they can tear you apart. Loving is too scary, Raymond thinks. And being loved is even scarier. Being loved can be like standing by a river that's overflowing. You could be pulled into the rapids. You could be smashed against rocks. You could die.

twelve

Raymond sits at the picnic table behind Chez Simon waiting for Barney. He doesn't want to have this discussion inside the restaurant because he doesn't want any of the other staff members to hear it. He breaks up a dinner roll and sprinkles the crumbs at one end of the table for the sparrows. Accustomed to Raymond, they quickly swoop down and peck at them. He sits very still so as not to disturb them. It astonishes him that they are constantly in motion; always cocking their heads from side to side or up and down; always on the alert. If he makes the slightest motion, they fly off. He wonders how they tell one from the other, as they look identical. He wonders how people will tell Dwayne and himself apart, now that Dwayne has cut his hair and shaved his moustache. He imagines that it wouldn't be difficult — once a person began talking with them — to tell the difference. He can't believe that anyone who knows him well could mistake him for Dwayne.

A familiar garbage picker is digging methodically through Chez Simon's garbage. He looks dirty but sober. A few weeks ago Raymond tried to say hello to him, but the man only scowled. He wanted to be left alone. He doesn't even glance in Raymond's direction.

Last night he removed his mirrors from the walls and covered the one on the medicine cabinet. He no longer wants to see his reflection because he sees Dwayne, not his imagined twin. And Dwayne, unlike his imagined twin, offers no comfort. For shaving purposes Raymond uses the small mirror. It reveals only one aspect of his face at a time. He sees himself in pieces. Individual pieces that make up an individual whole. A whole different from his twin. He studies his palms. Everybody's palms are different, aren't they? Everybody's fingerprints?

He hasn't heard from his biological family for days. He's hoping that they are as disappointed in him as he is in them.

After removing the mirrors, he saw Dwayne on his TV. The TV was off but Raymond saw his twin's head lying sideways on the screen. His mouth was gaping and his eyes were closed. He looked dead. Frightened, Raymond looked away, then back at the TV to see if he was imagining it, but Dwayne was still there. Raymond took one of Mara's sleeping pills. This morning the TV screen was blank.

"Sorry, sir," Barney says, getting out of his Firebird. "The frigging alarm clock is busted."

Raymond hates it when Barney calls him "sir" because he knows it is said without respect. "I don't want to hear excuses."

Barney straddles the bench of the picnic table. "Sorry, sir. How can I help you?"

"You were giving free drinks to your friends again last night."

"Who told you that?"

"Bruce saw you do it. Saw that they didn't pay."

Barney scoffs. "And you believe that little faggot?"

"Don't call him that, and yes, I do believe him. Because you've done it before. I've tried to ignore it. But that's it. No more."

"I'll replace the bottle. It was like . . . two drinks."

"You know it was more than that."

"I'll replace the bottle."

"Do that. Today."

Barney slicks back his hair. "The thing is, we're kind of low on cash right now, what with the abortion and the couch and all that."

"Replace the bottle today. Or don't bother coming to work."

"You have to give me two weeks notice."

"If you don't replace the bottle today, consider yourself notified." It surprises Raymond to hear himself speak with such conviction. He doesn't want Barney to quit. He's used to Barney. Even though he is an asshole, at least he doesn't steal cash. The last assistant manager stole from the till.

"I'm sorry, man," Barney says. "I didn't think it was such a big deal. Like I said, I was going to replace it."

The garbage picker drops a brown paper package back into the garbage bin and shakes his head in disgust. Raymond suspects that it contained chicken organs. He gets up. "That's it. I've got to get back to work."

"Like I said," Barney insists, "I'll replace it."

"Tonight."

❖

Dr. Kalbfleisch is waiting for him in the dining room. He spoons five sugars into his coffee. "Raymond, last night I was watching for ten minutes and not one person was wearing the chicken hats. I spend money on promotion, and nobody's wearing the hats."

"They were wearing them earlier," Raymond says.

"They should be wearing them all the time. It looked like a funeral parlour in here. Not one person was smiling."

"I think the death of your wife has had an effect, sir."

"What kind of an effect? She's *my* wife. It's my business to be affected. This is a business. It should be professional."

Raymond clears his throat and narrows his eyes. "The elastics hurt their chins."

"What?"

"The elastics that hold the crests on hurt their chins. They're too tight."

"So get more elastic. How difficult is it to get more elastic?"

Raymond looks down at his notes. He doesn't want to argue. Sharif's wife had a baby three months early last night. He made the mistake of telling the taxi dispatcher that his wife was in labour. No cabs were eager to respond to the call. While Sharif called 911 the baby was born on the bathroom floor. Its lungs weren't fully developed. Sharif tied the umbilical cord with a shoelace and watched helplessly while his baby struggled to breathe. Finally an ambulance arrived and took them to the hospital. The baby's in an incubator in critical condition. Sharif came to work distraught but determined to do his job. He cupped his hands to demonstrate to Raymond how he held the infant, how tiny it was. "He looked at me," he said. "My son." Raymond insisted that he go back to the hospital to be with his wife and child. He explained that he would pay Sharif for the day regardless. Sharif had difficulty comprehending this; that an employer would pay him for not working. "It's okay," Raymond insisted. To prove to Sharif that he would get paid, Raymond punched in his time card and signed him out at six. "See," he said, "according to the card you've worked the whole day." Sharif repeated "Thank you, sir" many times. Raymond envied him for having a baby that is still alive; that may survive because Sharif held him and tied the umbilical cord. Raymond never had a chance to save his babies. His babies never looked at him. He didn't even see them. He's never asked Mara if she saw them. He was too afraid.

Dr. Kalbfleisch sucks on his dentures. "Did you cut back on inventory?"

"I'm doing what I can."

"Don't order at the end of the month. Order at the beginning so we don't get the bill right away."

"I'm already doing that, sir."

"Good. Now see what you can cut."

Raymond tries to picture the boy in the concentration camp so that he won't be annoyed by Dr. Kalbfleisch. He clears his throat. "I've got to help with the dish-washing. One of our dishwashers called in sick."

"What's wrong with the dishwashers? They're always sick."

Raymond gets up, leaving Dr. Kalbfleisch talking to the air. He has never done this before. It feels strange, as if he had just walked through cobwebs. Bruce is in the dish room and not happy about it. "Can't you call the Filipino guy?"

"I did already," Raymond says.

"If we don't get a dishwasher by tonight I will ca-ry."

"We'll get through it if everybody puts a hand in." Raymond takes the hose from Bruce and begins rinsing and fitting plates into the racks.

"Why aren't there any decent dishwashers any more?" Bruce asks.

"Sharif's good. He just couldn't make it in today."

Bruce stacks finger bowls on a tray. Bubba, the line cook, comes into the dish room and takes the few clean plates from the shelf. "Oh," Bruce says, "so did you hear about Beth's date with a certain powerful individual?"

Bubba stops still. "Beth had a date?"

Bruce puts one hand on his hip while the other holds the tray. "With none other than our very own health inspector."

"No shit," Jeff comments, over Bubba's shoulder.

"My sources tell me they had a really good time," Bruce adds. "A repeat performance is in order."

Jeff takes off his glasses, spits on them and tries to wipe grease off the lenses. "Does this mean he's not going to lecture me on botulism?"

Bruce stacks more finger bowls. "Don't count on it. More than likely he'll be even more particular about Chez Simon, otherwise it might appear that he's extending special favours because of her."

Bubba shoves his hand into his pants pocket and adjusts the crotch of his underwear. "That guy smells weird."

"It's his cologne," Bruce explains. "It's not exactly top of the line."

"So, are they, like, serious?" Bubba asks, looking worried.

"Let's hope so. The poor dear could use a break. She's had one long streak of losers. This guy actually *owns* a house."

"Wow," Bubba mutters.

"His car's leased by the government," Raymond points out.

Bruce looks at him. "Be careful where you cast aspersions."

"I wasn't casting anything. It's a fact."

"What's aspersions?" Bubba asks.

Raymond wonders if Beth told the health inspector about her relationship with the hermaphrodite. Or about his failure to ejaculate.

❖

Barney arrives only five minutes late for his shift with a bottle of scotch. He works hard at dish-washing. Raymond is relieved. He stays for the dinner rush anyway because they are short-staffed and it's a show night. He appreciates the rush, not only because the numbers will be up, but because it takes his mind off his life. The demands of his customers come first. He can satisfy their needs, unlike his own. Tonight his restaurant runs like a well-oiled machine. The staff move in sync. He wishes Kalbfleisch could see it.

Afterwards he picks up Burt, then goes to see Claire at Chicken Villa, because he doesn't want to be at home in case his twin appears on the TV screen. She recognizes him this time and offers a smile he suspects she saves for her best-tipping customers. "Hi, Claire," he says.

"What can I get you?"

He orders a chef salad, without the chicken, and a scotch. He watches her walk back to the bar. He loves the way she moves. Her buttocks swish from side to side, actually swish. She'll marry her fiancé and they'll have beautiful babies together. They'll buy a nice house and live happily ever after. Raymond doesn't really believe the happily ever after part. But certainly the house and babies part. When she brings his scotch, he smiles. He'd like to tell her that she's beautiful but he knows she wouldn't like it. He scratches behind his ear. "What are they saying about the weather tomorrow?"

"I think it's supposed to rain. Why?"

"Just curious."

"Can I get you anything else?"

"That's fine. Thank you."

Why hasn't he ever been able to attract girls like Claire? Normal, pretty girls who don't know about computers and hermaphrodites? He's getting older. Soon he won't be able to attract any girls at all. He drinks more scotch.

Tonight, after the rush, Barney slapped him on the shoulder. Raymond knew that it was intended as a comradely gesture, but he hated it. His father always slapped him on the shoulder. Raymond was never sure what it meant. Sometimes Gord would do it when he was angry with him, other times he would do it when he wasn't. Raymond couldn't tell the difference. Either way it hurt. It wasn't a touch. Raymond has always longed to be touched. Mara understood this. She'd hug and hold him without expecting that they jump into bed together. Sometimes, when they were watching TV, he'd rest his head on her lap and she would massage his head. He misses being touched. He feels as though he will never be touched again. He feels untouchable. He can't even feel himself any more. When he holds his hand against his face he feels Dwayne. When he rests his hands on his knees he feels Dwayne. He can no longer feel or see himself. He feels and sees only Dwayne.

Claire brings his salad. Again it looks inedible. He tries to appear enthusiastic.

"Can I get you anything else?"

"No, that's fine. Thank you."

"My pleasure."

If she would just hold him, hold his head in her hands and say that everything will be all right, he might be able to believe her. But she's gone to serve another customer. Raymond drinks more. Burt's outside tied to a mailbox. This isn't fair. Raymond shouldn't be doing this to Burt, his only friend.

What he hated most was that he felt diminished in his mother's eyes when his father was around. When his father was around, Raymond ceased to exist. Sometimes he did things purposefully to annoy her so that she would notice him. He broke her china teapot, shoved it off the counter and pretended it was an accident. She made him pick up the pieces. They cut his hands. She didn't care, she wanted to fuck his father. He hates his father, wants to kill him. He drinks more scotch. Claire smiles. "Is everything alright?"

"What?"

"You're not eating your salad."

"Oh. Right. I'm getting to it."

"No rush."

"Could you get me another drink?" He's almost afraid to ask because she might disapprove. But at this point he doesn't care. He knows that she's beyond his reach.

What was so strange about growing up in high-rises was that when he left them, stood on the ground and looked up at them, he felt insignificant. There was nothing he could climb — no monkey bars, no trees — that would make him rise above the buildings. He didn't matter to the buildings, he was just another speck to them. He could never be king of the castle. So he didn't like going out. He preferred staying in where he didn't feel insignificant. But his father, when he was home, wanted him to go out. "Go out and play," he'd tell him.

A teenaged boy and an older man argue at the table in front of Raymond. The older man looks pregnant. "I'd kick him in the solar plexus," the teenager insists, thumping his chest.

"That's the sternum," the pregnant man responds.

"I'd kick him in the nuts then."

"You don't want to kick him in the nuts."

"Okay, so I'll kick him in the solar plexus."

"That's the sternum."

"Same thing. I'd kick him there."

Claire sets down Raymond's scotch. "How's the salad?"

"Fine."

"Can I get you anything else?"

"I wouldn't mind some strawberry shortcake."

"Certainly. Are you finished with your salad?"

"Yes, thank you."

"Would you like a coffee with your cake?"

"Please."

Raymond wonders about Claire's fiancé: if he's handsome, if he has a good job, if he hits her. One of Raymond's regular customers asked him if he thought she should tell her girlfriend that the man she's dating used to beat his wife. "Should I tell her?" she kept asking. Raymond didn't know what to say, because he didn't know if it was true that the man had beaten his wife. He thought about Mara saying that she can no longer tell the difference between the truth and the distorted shit; how the distorted shit looks like all the other shit. Even if he asks Claire about her fiancé, he won't know if she's telling him the truth. She'll probably insist that they're very happy, very excited, very in love. But should he believe her?

The pregnant man and the teenager are arguing about losing muscle mass, and protein powders to build muscle mass. Claire brings the strawberry shortcake. "Here you go."

"Thank you."

"Just let me know when you want a refill."

"I will. Thanks."

Now that he has consumed two scotches, it occurs to him that he could impress Claire as being the strong-and-silent type. The kind of man who suffers pain but can take it; a broken marriage, a sociopathic twin brother, an alcoholic adoptive father, a demented adoptive mother and a bald biological one. A product of rape. Would she serve him so pleasantly if she knew that he was a product of rape?

He looks down at his strawberry shortcake. It looks quite nice, fluffy. He thinks of Fluffy the bunny. How could you kill a bunny? *Did* he kill the bunny? And if he did kill Fluffy, why has he taped his photograph beside the yoga guru?

The cream is synthetic and the strawberries taste of fridge. But he eats the cake anyway to please Claire. The pregnant man is demonstrating weightlifting exercises to the teenager. His belly bumps the table as he lifts his arms over his head and then brings them down again. "I wouldn't do it like that," the teenager insists. "I'd bring it in front. Like over my chest."

"That's to build your pecs," the pregnant man argues. "This is to build your lats and your traps and your delts."

"So, I want to build my pecs."

If they are father and son, Raymond wonders if they ever agree about anything. Or if disagreement is the basis of their relationship. Raymond never disagreed with his father because he wanted to be liked. It didn't work though. Maybe Raymond should stop trying to be liked. Maybe he should be mean to Claire, tell her that she's nothing, just a dumb slut waitress. Tell her that when her tits fall her husband's going to start looking elsewhere. He'll leave her at home with the screaming kids. She'll get fat and watch TV and wonder what happened to her youth. Raymond could say all these things, and they could be true. But would she like him any better for showing aggression? Would his abuse interest her? Because at the moment she is definitely not interested.

She leans over him to refill his cup. He inhales her strawberry smell. "When's the wedding?" he asks.

"Pardon?"

"You told me you had a fiancé."

"I did? Oh . . . umm. Next May."

"If everything goes as expected."

"What do you mean?"

Raymond clears his throat and narrows his eyes. "If nothing goes wrong."

"What could go wrong?"

He thinks about the news item regarding the man who knifed his girlfriend to death, then hanged himself from a tree. "Probably nothing," he says. He can see that she is back to disliking him.

"Will that be all?"

"Yes. Thanks."

He leaves her a four-dollar tip.

❖

In the all-night supermarket he buys Shreddies, dog food and milk. At the check-out counter an old lady with her roots showing asks him if he knows why the brand-name grated Parmesan is more expensive than the generic brand. When he suggests that perhaps she should compare the ingredients, she asks him to do it. She tells him to hold her place in line while she gets the generic brand so that he can compare the ingredients. Raymond can't understand why this woman has selected him from the lineup. What is it about him that invites any stranger to talk to him? She comes back with the generic brand. He compares the ingredients, then holds up the generic brand. "This one has more chemicals in it."

"You're jokin'? That's the only difference? It's a buck cheaper."

"That's the only difference."

"Do you think I should buy it?"

"It's up to you."

"What do *you* think?"

The other people in the lineup are ignoring her and Raymond.

"It depends on how you feel about chemicals."

She turns her head slightly. Raymond suspects that she is deaf in one ear. "How I feel about chemicals?"

"Right," Raymond says loudly. "If you mind eating them."

It's her turn in line. He tries to urge her along but she thrusts a jar of blueberry jam at him. "What about this? Is this good? Ninety-nine cents. Do you think I should buy it?"

"It's your turn to cash out," he advises her.

"Usually I buy raspberry but I thought I'd try blueberry."

"Good idea." Raymond takes her items out of her hands and gives them to the cashier. He would like to scream, he would like to yell. He would like to break store windows.

❖

At home the light is flickering on the answering machine. He hopes it's Mara. It is. "Thank you for the flowers, Raymond. It was really sweet of you. I don't think you've ever sent me flowers. Anyway, I'm calling you at home because I know you'll be at work and I can't talk to you right now. I can't explain why. I just wanted you to know that I received them and that . . . that I appreciate it. But please don't call me. Bye." At the end of the message it sounds as though she's fighting tears. This could be a good sign, Raymond thinks. Except that he didn't send her any flowers. He has never sent her flowers. Somebody else sent them and had the florist sign Raymond's name.

He goes straight to bed without looking at the TV because he knows that his twin will be on it.

thirteen

The head nurse phones Raymond to tell him that Belinda died in her sleep. He puts her on hold because he's on the other line with Mr. Hayhoe. He assures Mr. Hayhoe that the creamers arrived and were not sour. "Well," Mr. Hayhoe says, "if you have any problems, let us know. A happy customer is a repeat customer."

Raymond stares at the concrete wall. His mother is dead.

"Have a wonderful day," Mr. Hayhoe says.

"Thank you. Goodbye." Raymond releases the hold button. "Hello?"

"Yes, Mr. Gage?" the head nurse asks. "As I explained, she passed away in her sleep."

Passed away where? Where did she go?

"We don't believe that she suffered," the head nurse adds.

"How can you be sure?"

"We can't be sure, sir."

"What makes you even think she didn't suffer?"

"As I've explained, it was in her sleep."

"You don't know that she was asleep. She could have been awake. Just because it happened at night doesn't mean she was asleep. She could have been crying out in pain and nobody noticed." His throat is tightening, in seconds he will have no voice.

"We have a night staff, Mr. Gage. If she had been crying out, someone would have heard."

"How do you know that for sure? You can't know that for sure. She might have been trying to call out but was in too much pain."

The head nurse sighs. "I really can't give you any more information, Mr. Gage. Would you care to see her?"

"No. I mean yes."

"As soon as possible would be best."

"Yes."

"Which funeral home do you intend to use?"

"I don't know."

"We can't keep her here, Mr. Gage. You'll have to contact a funeral home."

"Yes." He hangs up and plays with the elastic he bought for the chicken hats. He stretches, then releases it. It slaps his hand. He stretches, then releases it. It slaps his hand. The turtles, he tells himself, remember the turtles. She let them die. Because Gord hated them, said they were reptiles, said they belonged in a swamp. She let them go; into the wilderness, she said. Raymond knew this meant outside where they would dehydrate and die, be mauled by cats. He ran to the elevator, then outside to find them. He searched until dark. Nobody came to look for him. Mrs. Gillespie, the super's wife, asked him if everything was all right. He didn't tell her that his mother had killed his turtles. He didn't tell her because he didn't want her to know how horrible his life was. He didn't want her to know that he was adopted, and that his parents didn't care if he came home; that his parents were probably in their bedroom with the door closed and the stereo playing.

"Did you eat your supper yet?" Mrs. Gillespie asked.

"Uh-huh," Raymond lied.

"You look pale, boy. You make sure you eat your veggies."

Raymond nodded, his eyes still scanning the ground for turtles.

"You go home now," Mrs. Gillespie said.

"I will." He watched her waddle to the bus stop. When her back was turned, he rushed behind the building to continue his search.

It wasn't until days later that he found one of the shells. There was no turtle left, only bits of skin clinging to the shell. Ants were crawling all over it.

The snapping elastic is beginning to burn his hand. Small welts are forming. He focuses on the pain, is glad for it because it's real; something he can feel, without doubt. Clean, indisputable physical pain. No emotion. He's tired of emotion. It grinds him to pulp.

He kept the turtle aquarium. She'd put it in the garbage, but he found it. He put it under his bed. Later she came into his room, kissed his forehead and said she was sorry. It meant nothing to him. She smelled of Gord. He turned away from her. She pleaded with him, insisted that it was for the best, turtle germs were dangerous, they would be happier outside in the wilderness. His pillow became wet from his tears but he made no sound, was determined to make no sound. After she was gone, he turned the pillow over.

Now she's dead.

"Raymond's no trouble," she always said to people. This was true because he understood that it was good to be "no trouble," to keep quiet, to obey. Once, when they were in the bathroom, Mara screamed at him to stop being so fucking polite.

No trouble.

So he fucked her on the bathroom sink. "You're hurting me," she said. He stopped immediately, became himself again, not his father. He carried her to the bed and kissed her hands, atoning for the beast inside him.

Remember that she wasn't your real mother, remember the bad things about her, remember that she was demented and that she is better off dead. Except that he can't fantasize about his biological mother any more. Before, when he was angry at his adoptive mother, he could fantasize about his biological one: how she would love him, cherish him, once she found him.

Jeff pokes his head in the door. "You coming up, Captain?"

"In a minute."

"What's with your hands?"

"I burned them, hot water."

Jeff takes off his glasses and tries to clean them. "We couldn't believe you were eating chicken last night."

"What are you talking about?"

"You eating chicken. We couldn't believe it."

"I wasn't eating chicken."

"It looked like you were eating chicken."

"When was this?"

"Last night. You left, then came back for a half-chicken dinner with extra fries. We couldn't believe it."

"That wasn't me."

Jeff puts his glasses back on. "It wasn't?"

"It was my twin."

"No shit. You have a twin?"

"An identical twin brother."

"No shit. I knew you wouldn't eat chicken. Bubba watched you the whole time. Watched you chew on the bones. You know the wing part? You even ate that. The crispy part. We couldn't believe it."

"That was my brother."

"Holy shit. How come you never mentioned him before?"

"He wasn't around."

"He ate cherry pie à la mode."

Raymond clears his throat. "I think you better get back upstairs."

"Okay, boss. Can I tell the gang about the twin?"

Raymond nods because he can't think of an alternative.

❖

The staff look at him strangely, differently. He makes them wear the chicken hats.

"So, boss," Jeff says. "It occurred to us that maybe you'd better have a code name. Unless you don't mind your twin getting free food."

Bubba shoves his hand into his pants pocket and adjusts the crotch of his underwear. "Yeah, like what if he comes in and takes money? We won't know if it's you. He could take money and go off to Mexico or some place."

Bruce empties a packet of coffee into a filter. "*I* knew it wasn't you. You never drink milk shakes."

Raymond looks at him. "He had a milk shake?"

"Chocolate. And he eats like a pig. I was nearly sick watching him. I thought, if that's Raymond, there's something going on, he's repressing something and now he's binging. I thought maybe it had to do with the Beth thing."

Bubba puts a stick of gum in his mouth. "What Beth thing?"

"Forget it," Raymond says. He hands out lengths of elastic so that they can adjust their hats.

"Can't we just wear them when he's here?" Bruce asks.

"He spies," Jeff cautions. "He was spying again last night. I saw him driving around."

Raymond feels as if he is no longer anchored by the force of gravity; he spins directionless above their heads. He tries to reach out to something, grab hold of something.

Bubba pulls off his hairnet and scratches his head. "So what about the code name?"

"How about gator burgers?" Jeff suggests.

"Gator burgers?"

"Alligator meat's only one per cent fat compared to chicken which is six per cent. I thought we could suggest to Kalbfleisch that we offer gator burgers as a low-fat alternative."

Bruce starts the coffee machine. "That's disgusting."

Raymond's afraid that nothing can hold him, that he will spin indefinitely, that he will never rest.

"So like . . ." Bubba puts his hairnet back on. "What are we supposed to do when we see Raymond, ask him about low-fat alternatives?"

Jeff shrugs. "Just wait for him to say gator burger. Right, boss?"

Raymond nods. "Gator burger."

❖

They haven't bothered to put his mother's teeth back in. They haven't had them in since she forgot how to chew. Raymond has grown accustomed to her lips caving in and hugging her gums. But it's worse now that her skin is grey and depleted of fluid. She never wanted to be seen without her teeth. Before she became ill, Raymond had never seen her without them. She made a point of cleaning and inserting the denture in her locked bathroom. She had her bottom teeth. Just the upper were false.

He stares at her, waiting for her eyes to open. An object of desire, who would believe it? He has won in the end. All the harm she has done him she has paid for. He can hate her now. She looks like a carcass to him. Revolting. Carrion waiting for vultures. The head nurse approaches and folds her hands over her stomach. He notices a gold cross at her throat. He wants to ask her if she believes in God. If she can find some justification for all this. Her mouth opens. "My sincere condolences, Mr. Gage. Did you decide on a funeral home?"

"Where are her teeth?"

"Her teeth? With her personal effects, I would presume."

"Please find them."

"I'll have someone collect her belongings for you."

"No. Her teeth. I'd like them now. They should be in her mouth."

"Mr. Gage, I know that this is a difficult time for you."

"Find her fucking teeth. I'm not giving you the name of a funeral home until you put her teeth back in her mouth."

The nurse twists the wedding band on her finger, then abruptly turns and leaves the room. Her heels snap against the linoleum. He expects to see sparks.

❖

He stops his car in front of Mara's house. The lights are out, indicating that she's not home. He doesn't care, he'll wait. He parks behind a van. On the radio they're playing the Beach Boys. My mother's dead and they're still playing the Beach Boys. We could all be dead and they'd still be playing the Beach Boys. He turns off the radio. The singing neighbour comes out to water his lawn. What about *his* mother? Raymond wonders. Where is she? Does he love her? Is it possible to really love your mother? Or do you secretly hate her, resent her, because she made you? You spend years thinking that you are growing away from her; becoming who you are, separate from who she is. But all the while she's pulling at you in ways that no one else can. Because she gave you life.

But that's not the case with Belinda. She didn't give him life. She's a stranger to him. He doesn't need to love her, or hate her. He should let her go in peace. Forget about her.

A car parks behind Raymond and laughing people get out. A man grabs a woman's behind. She slaps his hand, still laughing. Another man and woman get out. They don't laugh but stand with their arms crossed watching the laughing couple stumble across the street. Laughter can be very ugly, Raymond thinks. It can signal carelessness and scorn. Gord laughed at him. And at Belinda when they fought. Then he'd leave and she'd weep as she'd turn her attention to Raymond. She'd give him back rubs and read him stories. Mara said Belinda was in love with him. He couldn't see this, could see only that he was never able to fill the space left behind by Gord. Mara also insisted that Raymond was in love with Belinda. He couldn't see this either. He cared for her as any loving son should. But he found fault with her. She kept disappointing him. How could he be in love with her? And what about Dwayne and Gloria? Do they love each other? They talk as though they want to be free of each other and yet they live together.

He looks back at Mara's and tries to understand why people are dying all of a sudden. People he knows. What if Mara dies? What if Dwayne stalks her, breaks into her house, ties her up, rapes and dismembers her? He imagines Jeff hacking apart a chicken. He hears the crunch of gristle resisting blade. He would have to kill Dwayne. He would have no choice. He doesn't want this to happen. Wants to stop this from happening. Dots of light collide in front of his eyes. He's afraid he's getting a migraine.

He sees her coming home alone, carrying her briefcase. She walks as though a heavy load were on her shoulders. She unlocks the door and goes inside. The lights come on. She's home now, he tells himself, he can relax now.

This affection he feels for her, he's not sure if it's what she would call distorted shit. He's not sure that he isn't making it up. Not sure if he isn't hanging on to her because there's nothing else.

A stereo goes on inside the house belonging to the laughing couple. Electric guitars and drums assault Raymond. His headache is getting worse. When Mara's lights go out he waits to see if the man who mirrors himself will appear from behind the trees. It starts to rain again, blurring his vision. The dots of light reappear. He knows that he must go home and take some codeine. He knows that he must leave her. She whom he swore to love and protect until death did them part.

❖

In the pool he floats on his back. The codeine is beginning to take effect. The dots no longer collide but merge into symmetry, then dissolve. He breathes deeply, calmed by the water lapping against him. It occurs to him that maybe he has lost the capacity for happiness. It must be a skill that improves with practice. He tries to remember being happy. Maybe when he was promoted from bag boy to candy boy. He was only fourteen. Usually the candy boy was older, more responsible, less likely to steal. But Mr. Clarizio trusted Raymond and paid him fifteen cents more an hour. His first day filling the candy bins was happy. Although he was tempted, he did not eat one candy; not even a jujube, not even a gummy bear. Wesley, the new bag boy, watched him with envy. Raymond very much wanted a jawbreaker so he bought one. When he paid Mrs. Clarizio, she smiled and said, "*Grazie.*" Happiness, was that what he was feeling? Why can't he feel that any more?

He ran home, his cheeks bulging with jawbreaker, to tell his parents. His father was watching sports. "Good, kid," he said, without taking his eyes off the TV. His mother was in the kitchen fretting over a new recipe. She needed paprika. She asked Raymond to go to the store for some. He wasn't even sure she'd understood about his promotion. She said, "That's wonderful, Plum," but she didn't take her eyes off the recipe book. She twisted a lock of her hair in her fingers. Raymond knew that she was worried that she wouldn't cook a good dinner for his father. When Gord was home, she cooked special meals. Raymond went to the store for paprika.

That's more than twenty years ago. He must have felt happy since then. He must have.

He flips over, dives down and touches bottom. He stays down feeling his heart swelling in his ears. He worries that he has missed opportunities to be happy. Because he hasn't been paying attention, has let things slip by. Too much time spent worrying about chicken hats and savoury freezers. At least, when his mother was with his father, she was happy. At least she's dying after having lived.

When his lungs can endure no more he surges to the surface. His splash echoes against the tiled walls. He grips the pool's edge and hoists himself out of the water. He sits on a deck chair and watches the water become still again. As though he'd never been in it.

❖

In the kitchen, the staff watch him warily. Jeff salutes. "Morning, Captain."

"Gator burgers," Raymond mumbles.

"He's not the body snatcher," Jeff announces.

Bruce and Beth resume their argument over who should get the window section.

"Like I say," Beth says, "most times I don't mind but today I need the money."

"We *all* need the money," Bruce points out.

"Who had it yesterday?" Raymond asks.

"I did," Bruce admits, "because Beth switched shifts with Bonnie so that she could go for a drive in the country with a certain individual."

Bubba stops chopping onions. "What individual?"

"The point is," Bruce insists, "you missed your turn."

"That's not fair. I worked anyway, and Bonnie had the window."

"Toss a coin," Raymond suggests.

"Just because I'm going out with the health inspector," Beth says, "you guys are all ganging up on me."

Bubba wipes onion tears from his eyes. "You're going out with the health inspector?"

In the dining room Raymond is greeted by Seymour, the food addict. He has finished his chicken and is consuming a piece of hot-fudge cake. "Raymond, my good fellow," he says.

"How are you, Seymour?"

He wipes his mouth with a napkin. "Well, to tell you the truth, I'm a little disillusioned. I've been reading about Vivien Leigh and it turns out she was a very unhappy lady."

"Is that right?"

"She did drugs, alcohol, the whole bit."

"That's too bad."

"Yes. She who seemed to have it all. Amazing how that works." He picks up the book and studies Vivien's picture on the cover. "And, bless her heart, she had to act opposite Clark Gable's stinking dentures."

"He had dentures?"

"Apparently. And never cleaned them. All those two-shots of them in *Gone with the Wind* were torture for poor Viv."

"Hunh." Raymond finds it curious that Seymour reads biographies of movie stars. Every week he's reading a new one.

"Bogie's teeth also stank," Seymour adds. "But you'd expect that of Bogie."

Raymond steps behind the bar to check stock and the ice supply.

Seymour sighs heavily. "Nothing is what it seems. Remember that, Raymond."

Raymond goes to the kitchen to get more ice. When he returns, Seymour is still talking. "Bruce told me that you have found your long-lost twin."

"That's right."

"That must be peculiar."

"It is."

"Are you the nice twin or the nasty twin?"

Raymond empties ice into the bin. "Pardon?"

"There's always a good twin and a bad twin. Did you see the movie about the twin gynecologists? You should rent it. Maybe you'll get some insights."

"What happens in it?"

"They do horrible things to women."

Bruce appears with the coffeepot. He always gives free refills to his best-tipping customers. "More coffee?"

Seymour holds out his cup. "Thank you, señor."

"So," Bruce says, pouring, "I had this chocolate carrot cake with cream-cheese icing at Decadent Desserts that was to die for."

"How many calories?" Seymour asks.

"Forget calories. Eighty-five grams of *fat* per slice."

"That sounds about right," Seymour says. "I must go there." Raymond suspects he is planning to eat himself to death.

In his office he starts to do payroll but has difficulty concentrating. He's remembering Seymour's words, "Nothing is what it seems." This is a common enough phrase. People use it all the time. It must be based on truth. He thinks about Dwayne, how he seems. Which might not be what he is. Raymond remembers the little boy in the photograph. The little boy who may or may not have killed Fluffy. Maybe Dwayne too has lost his capacity for happiness. Maybe the two of them can find it again together. Two brothers awakening joy in each other.

Mr. Pyper from the funeral home calls. Raymond explains again that he wants no service, no fuss, a simple cremation. Mr. Pyper doesn't seem to believe him. "Well let us know if you change your mind," he says. "There's still time."

"I won't change my mind."

"Would you like to be present?"

"No. I want you to burn the body and put the ashes in a jar."

"As you wish, sir."

"I wish." Raymond knows that Mr. Pyper is annoyed because he isn't going to make more money — more fuss, more money. "No fuss," Raymond repeats, then hangs up. He looks at his hands that belong to his brother. He thinks of those nuclear holocaust movies in which the survivors gradually realize that they are the only people left on the planet. They turn to each other because there is no one else. They love, they hate, they fight, they embrace. But they survive. In the movies.

fourteen

Dr. Kalbfleisch comes in with a woman Raymond has never seen before. She has straw-coloured hair piled high on her head. Dr. Kalbfleisch pulls a chair out for her, then waves at Raymond to get his attention. "Raymond," he says, "this is Mrs. Bumby."

Mrs. Bumby smiles at him. She has a gold tooth. "Simon's told me all about you."

"Raymond, Mrs. Bumby will have a chicken breast à la carte with the salad bar."

"Sure."

"And I'll have the leg, but make it crispy. And extra fries, no bun."

"Yes, sir."

"And two very dry martinis." He looks at his watch. "Make it quick because we're going to a show."

"Certainly."

Raymond gives Beth the order, then goes to the bar to mix the martinis. Bruce is sitting on the stool doing the crossword. "Who *is* that woman?"

"Mrs. Bumby."

"Is she his tart or what?"

Raymond scoops ice into the shaker. "I don't know."

"His wife isn't even cold yet."

They hear Dr. Kalbfleisch laugh. They have never heard him laugh before. He sounds like a vampire. Raymond pours gin, then vermouth into the shaker. Beth comes back from the kitchen and leans on the bar. "Like I really want to serve Kalbfleisch."

Raymond shakes the shaker. "He's in your section."

"You wanted the window, remember?" Bruce smirks and looks back at his crossword.

Raymond sets out two chilled martini glasses. Beth drums her fingers against the bar. "She's pretty old," she observes.

"Not for him," Bruce points out. Dr. Kalbfleisch laughs again. Beth scribbles something on one of her bills. "She's got to be after his money."

Raymond spears olives and sets them in the glasses. "Maybe she likes him."

"Yeah, right." Beth arranges the drinks on a tray and takes them to the table. Raymond pours himself a glass of water and sips it while watching Dr. Kalbfleisch and Mrs. Bumby. She sits with her legs crossed, leaning over the table as she talks. She talks a lot, swinging her leg. She has a large bosom. Because she's short-waisted, her breasts rest on the table. Raymond wonders what will happen when there's a plate in front of her. Beth comes back to the bar and wrinkles her nose. "She stinks of something."

Bruce looks up. "Liz Taylor's Passion perhaps?"

Raymond clears his throat. "Did you tell her to help herself to salad?"

"He can tell her."

Mrs. Bumby pokes Dr. Kalbfleisch. He laughs again.

"Scary," Bruce comments.

"You'd better tell her to help herself to salad," Raymond advises Beth. "Otherwise the chicken's going to be ready before she is."

She glares at him. "Don't tell me how to do my job." She strides back to the table. Mrs. Bumby smiles at her before getting up to walk to the salad bar. Her skirt is very tight, forcing her to take tiny steps. Dr. Kalbfleisch trails her, pointing out various salads.

"Did Jeff check the salad bar recently?" Raymond asks.

"Jeff," Bruce explains, "is absorbed in baseball. He's got his miniature TV going."

Dr. Kalbfleisch hurries towards them. "Raymond, the lettuce is wilted."

"I'll get some fresh."

"And the tomatoes."

"Alright."

"And two more martinis."

"Sure." In the kitchen Raymond switches off Jeff's TV. "Not when we're busy," he explains.

"It's the top of the ninth."

"Too bad."

Bubba has lost a contact lens again and is crawling around on the floor.

"If Kalbfleisch comes back here," Raymond warns, "he's not going to be too happy."

Beth shoves glasses into the ice bin. "He's not coming back here. He's got a woman with him."

Bubba looks up from the floor. "He's got a woman with him?"

"No shit," Jeff says. The two of them come out from behind the broiler and peek into the dining room.

"Wow," Bubba remarks.

"She's got a lot of hair," Jeff observes.

Beth snorts. "It's a wig."

"Really?" Raymond asks.

"The top part. The bottom is hers."

"Wow," Bubba repeats.

Raymond clears his throat. "Can we get back to work, please?"

"Sure thing, Captain."

Raymond doesn't understand why he is unable to instil a work ethic into his staff. They seem completely unconcerned about whether or not they do their jobs well. He wonders how the managers at Chicken Villa motivate their staff.

Bruce storms in with an order. "I can't believe I've got those fucking Salvation Army losers again." He slaps the order on to the wheel.

"Can you keep your voice down?" Raymond asks.

"They're going to make me refill their water glasses fifty times, then stiff me."

"That's their prerogative," Raymond points out.

Bruce continues to curse under his breath. Bubba holds up his contact lens. "Found it!"

In the dish room Sharif is praying again. His lips are moving and his eyes are closed while he's rinsing dishes. Although this concerns Raymond, he doesn't want to disturb Sharif because his baby may be dying. He goes back behind the bar where Beth is chewing on a toothpick. She stares at Dr. Kalbfleisch and Mrs. Bumby. "He's not going to leave me a tip."

"He might," Raymond offers, "to impress her."

"I'll bet you five bucks he doesn't."

Raymond begins slicing a lemon. He can't understand how Dr. Kalbfleisch can be dating Mrs. Bumby so soon after the death of his wife. Does this mean that he didn't love Mrs. Kalbfleisch? Does this mean that he was just waiting for her to die so that he could go to shows with Mrs. Bumby? Or was Mrs. Bumby there all along, in the shadows? Maybe Mrs. Kalbfleisch knew about her, which is why she repeatedly told Dr. Kalbfleisch that he had shit for brains. Maybe Mrs. Kalbfleisch stole chicken and pies because she was angry with her husband, not because she grew up hungry.

Beth delivers the chicken to their table, then comes back to the bar. "They're talking about musicals."

"Really?" Raymond watches to see what transpires between Mrs. Bumby's bosoms and the plate. She sits taller and leans back slightly, tucking in her chin while she cuts the chicken.

Beth flips through her bills. "She says she *loves* musicals."

"Do you think they know each other well?" Raymond asks.

"In what way?" She stares at him and he feels himself blushing. She tosses her toothpick into the garbage. "Do I think she's his chicky-babe? Is that what you mean?"

"It's not important. Forget it."

"God, Raymond, you really are thick." She goes back to the kitchen. He isn't sure what she means regarding Dr. Kalbfleisch and Mrs. Bumby: if, in fact, they have slept together. If they do sleep together, what happens to the top part of her hair? He scratches behind his ear. Nothing is what it seems.

❖

Raymond has never been to a strip club, would never, under normal circumstances, go to a strip club. But Gloria told him that Dwayne would be here. And Raymond understands that he will have to surprise his twin, otherwise he will elude him again. A neon sign above the entrance reads, "Lap Couch Dancing New Girls Weekly." Raymond looks over his shoulder to see if anyone is watching because he doesn't want to be seen entering such a place.

A short man with strong body odour pushes past him to open the door. Raymond quickly follows him and, for a moment, sees nothing until his eyes adjust to the low lighting in the club. Naked women seem to be everywhere. He would have thought they would be wearing at least G-strings. He feels himself flush as he begins to search for his brother. The clouds of cigarette smoke gag him, the stench of stale beer nauseates him.

He spots the man who looks like himself sitting at a table with a naked woman on his lap. Seeing the face that is his staggers Raymond. He stops still, but the short man with the body odour, now behind him, nudges him forward. "Move it," he says.

When Dwayne expresses no surprise at seeing him, Raymond surmises that Gloria phoned to warn him he was coming. This angers him. She can't be trusted, just as Belinda couldn't be trusted, just as Dwayne can't be trusted. "You sent flowers to my wife," Raymond says loudly to be heard over the rock music.

"Yeah. So?"

"I told you to leave her alone."

The short man with the body odour shouts at him, "Sit down, ya' knob!"

Raymond sits. "Why did you send her flowers?"

"Don't make a federal case out of it," Dwayne responds. The lap dancer, rubbing her buttocks into his groin, looks bored. Dwayne gyrates his pelvis in tandem with the dancer. Raymond doesn't understand why he feels so powerless; as though his twin is a cyclone and he has no choice but to be sucked in by him.

Dwayne narrows his eyes in the same manner that Raymond does. "I thought you said she was your ex-wife?"

"She is."

"It's open season on exes, pal."

"As a favour to me then," Raymond says, disgusted by his feeble tone. "Can you please leave her alone?"

"What's wrong with sending her flowers? Your name was on them. I would've thought you'd be grateful. She liked them, didn't she?"

"I don't know." Raymond remembers that she thanked him for the flowers, said it was really sweet of him, that she really appreciated them. He wishes *he'd* thought to send her flowers.

"See, the problem with you, Ray, is that you've got no romance in you.

The chicken business has robbed you of romance." The dancer gets off Dwayne and holds out her hand for payment. He gives her some bills. She turns to Raymond, apparently unfazed by the fact that he looks exactly like her previous customer. Her skin is too white and her hair too black. She looks like a corpse. "What about you?" she asks.

He shakes his head, thinking that maybe Dwayne's right, that maybe the chicken business has robbed him of romance.

"Try it," Dwayne urges, "you'll like it. Pure physical contact. No attachments, no diseases."

The dancer continues to stare at Raymond. "No thanks," he says. She turns and walks away. Her buttocks sag. Raymond wonders how she can stand to do what she does.

"Alright," Dwayne agrees, "I won't send her any more flowers. Just don't go ballistic on me." He eats some potato chips from a bag. "You know what I think? I think you take things too seriously, Raymond. I mean, I was joking around. A lot of the time I joke around. I don't mean anything by it."

"Then why do you do it?"

"For fun. You've heard of it. Fun? Good times?"

"Is it fun to frighten people?"

"Who've I frightened?"

"My ex-wife."

"Oh come on now. She thought I was you. She wasn't frightened. She liked it that you cared enough to hang around her yard. Nothing excites a woman more than knowing a man is broken up over her."

The cigarette smoke forming a fog around them is stinging Raymond's eyes. "Can we go somewhere and talk?" he asks.

"Where do you want to go?" Dwayne finishes the chips and brushes the crumbs off his hands. "Are you hungry?"

"No."

"Let's go to Burger King."

❖

Dwayne eats one Double Whopper and then another while people stare and point at them. Only now does Raymond realize that Dwayne is wearing a shirt and tie just like his, and similar trousers. With his moustache gone and his hair cut like Raymond's he now looks exactly like Raymond.

"Dwayne," Raymond ventures finally, "Gloria said you had a bunny."

"She said what?"

"She said that when you were a child you had a bunny."

Dwayne stops chewing. "A bunny?"

"Called Fluffy."

He starts chewing again. "She's off her nut."

"She said you killed it."

"She said *what*?"

"She said you came home one day and killed the bunny."

Dwayne shakes his head. "Fucking unreal." He takes another bite of his burger.

"It's not true?" Raymond wants it to be untrue. He remembers the photo of the bunny clutching the carrot — its little nose, its fluffy ears. How could he kill it?

"Do I look like a bunny killer to you?"

If it's not true, Raymond can start fresh with his brother. They can talk things over, work things out. "I don't know what a bunny killer looks like," he admits.

Dwayne shakes his head repeatedly, indicating that he can't believe that Raymond could mistake him for a bunny killer. Raymond expects him to protest his innocence, but Dwayne only stares at a woman in worn clothing sitting at the table beside them. She takes coins out individually from a rumpled plastic bag and stacks them into little piles.

"Why would Gloria lie about something like that?" Raymond asks.

"Because Gloria is an insane person. She is deluded."

The woman starts counting the change, moving it into new piles. Raymond figures she can't have more than two dollars. "Well," he continues, "I still can't understand why she would make up something like that."

"So that you would think that I'm mentally ill and that it's not her fault. Because she gave me a bunny."

Raymond would like to remind him about the photo of the bunny in the garage. But it would reveal that he had been snooping around and he doesn't think Dwayne would like this. He scratches behind his ear. "She also told me that you said you suffer from multiple-personality disorder."

Dwayne narrows his eyes. "She said *what*?"

"And Tory agreed. She said you told her that you have three different personalities. That you said that was the only way you could cope with what happened in your childhood."

Dwayne finishes his fries, unfolds a napkin and wipes his hands. "Let me try to explain something to you. Those women hate my guts. I don't know why. But ever since I was a little kid those sisters of mine have had it in for me."

"They weren't even around that much. Only in the summer."

"Who told you that?"

"Tory."

Dwayne bunches up the napkin and tosses it across the table. "Well, believe what you want, brother. But those sisters hated my guts. They did things to me that would make you shudder."

"Like what?"

"Suffice it to say that they experimented on me with a variety of implements. I was a boy, they were girls. Go figure."

If this is true, it is too horrible to contemplate. Feeling faint, Raymond leans both elbows on the table. The woman starts counting her change again.

"You eating your fries?" Dwayne asks.

"No. Go ahead."

Dwayne pushes several fries at a time into his mouth. "You were lucky, Raymond. To be the adopted one. You have no idea what you missed."

"What about our father?"

"What about him?"

"Don't you ever wonder who he was, what he was like?"

"No."

A man on crutches joins the lineup of people waiting to order. His legs flap below the knee, seeming to make no contact with the floor. Raymond can't figure out how he balances on the crutches without pivoting on a foot. He clears his throat. "I wonder about him often."

"I'm sure he was a delightful human being. Who else would fuck Gloria?" He sucks the straw on his milk shake.

"She told me he raped her."

"And you believed her?"

"Why wouldn't I?"

Dwayne shrugs and stares at the man on crutches.

"Who do you think our father was?" Raymond asks.

"I don't think about it."

"Why not?"

"Because he's gone. Whoever he was. He's probably dead."

"She said he wore a ski mask. She felt it on her neck."

Dwayne shrugs again and starts tapping his foot against the floor. He taps hard, sending vibrations into Raymond's feet. He scratches behind his ear in the same way Raymond does.

"She said," Raymond persists, "he was hiding in a closet when she came home."

Dwayne doesn't respond, only taps his foot. Raymond suspects that he is repressing emotion, that really he is as disturbed as Raymond is about being the product of rape. "I think it would be good for us to get to know each other," Raymond says. "Do you think that's possible?"

"Anything's possible."

"But I think we have to make an effort," Raymond explains, "to be friends. I think we have to be honest with each other."

"I am being honest with you, brother. It's the three witches you have to watch out for."

Raymond notices a cat outside on the sidewalk. Its chest is heaving and its mouth is open. It looks possessed. Raymond wonders if it's dying. Suddenly it vomits white liquid.

"You want a coffee?" Dwayne asks.

"Sure." Watching Dwayne stride over to the counter, Raymond admires his confidence; confidence that he himself lacks. He watches him take his cell phone from his pocket and, while standing in line, dial a number. Raymond wonders who he's phoning. During the conversation he gesticulates vehemently, then smiles almost tenderly. The cat looks down at its pool of white vomit. Apparently unperturbed, it walks away.

Dwayne returns with the coffees and grins at Raymond. "Cream, no sugar."

"That's right." Raymond wonders how he knew this, if this is the twin connection at work. They sit sipping in silence. Rain begins to fall, making it feel almost cosy in the Burger King.

Dwayne narrows his eyes. "Are you particularly attached to the chicken business?"

"Not particularly."

"That's what I thought. You can do better than that, Ray. You should be working for yourself."

"How?"

"Start your own business."

"I don't have the money."

"The money's not important, it's the idea. You can always get money for the right idea."

He wonders if Dwayne really believes this. Raymond has always had trouble getting money. He wonders how Dwayne can say money's not important when Raymond had to buy his Whoppers. "Why don't *you* start your own business?"

"Ditto." Dwayne pulls a worn copy of *Popular Science* from his coat pocket and places it open on the table. He points at a photograph of a geodesic dome. "Ever seen one of those?"

"It's a geodesic dome."

"That's right."

"What about it?"

"What do you think of it?"

"What you do mean?" Raymond notices the change-counting woman searching for something under the tables.

"Is it a good idea?" Dwayne persists.

"I don't know."

"What's your gut feeling about it?"

"I don't have one."

Dwayne taps the photograph with his finger. "There's money in the dome."

Raymond realizes that the change-counting woman is looking for change. "I don't know much about them. My impression is that they didn't work."

Dwayne grins. "That's right. They leaked, collapsed, people punched holes through them."

Raymond clears his throat. "So how does this translate into money?"

"With the technology available today, you could manufacture a super dome that could stand up to hurricanes, tornadoes, you name it."

Raymond looks at the front cover of the magazine. "This is from nineteen seventy-three."

"So?"

"If it's such a great idea, don't you think someone else would've gotten rich from it by now?" The change-counting woman picks up something that she must have mistaken for change, then quickly drops it.

"Maybe. Maybe not."

"Anyway," Raymond adds, "no one wants them now. People don't want to buy a used idea."

"North Americans, yeah. But what about *other* countries?"

"Which countries?" Raymond notices the man with legs that flap below the knee pivot off his crutches on to a chair.

"Where," Dwayne asks, "do you think they need cheap, efficient housing?"

"I don't know. Third World countries?"

"Bingo."

Dwayne's enthusiasm disarms Raymond. He himself can't remember being enthusiastic about anything. The man with floppy legs must be very hungry. He doesn't seem to swallow between mouthfuls but steadily injests burgers and fries.

"I'm talking about marketing directly to the Third World," Dwayne emphasizes. "You want to know the amazing thing?"

"What?"

"With these babies, you don't need air-conditioning. You ventilate the bottom and the top and — presto — you've got airflow. Perfect for the Third World."

"So how does this translate into money?"

The change-counting woman has left the Burger King and is checking a phone booth for change.

"I know a guy," Dwayne explains, "who's selling used gas stoves to the Third World. Stoves nobody here would buy, they're buying like hotcakes over there. This guy *loves* the dome idea."

Raymond scratches behind his ear. "Is he going to put up the money?"

"Nah. He's the distributor. He's how we get the domes to the market."

"We?"

"I need someone who knows about management, Ray, who knows how to keep things organized. I need someone I can trust. Also, you're family."

The change-counting woman starts checking the parking meters.

"So," Raymond offers, "I guess you want me to invest."

"Nope. I want your expertise. You know how to talk to people. You know about business."

"Then where does the money come from?"

"Julio, from the sports bar. He's looking to turn a fast buck. Something offshore. No taxes."

Raymond wants to believe in this idea, wants to believe in his brother. "What makes you think the people in the Third World want to live in domes?"

"American. They love American. If we make the domes high-tech, they'll buy. You want to know the other amazing thing?"

"What?" No one has ever made a business proposition to Raymond before. As much as he suspects that the domes might not be a great idea, it's nice to be included in a plan — especially a plan that doesn't require his money. Certainly there is no future in the chicken business.

Dwayne leans forward to make his point. "Solar heating. The domes will work in cold climates. The potential for solar heating is incredible. Think about the igloo. The Eskimos were on to something." He sits back again. "Anyway, it's just an idea."

"It sounds interesting." Raymond has never taken a chance, never dreamed a big dream. Maybe Dwayne's right, maybe now's the time. After all, isn't this what brothers are supposed to do: make plans, share their hopes and dreams? He imagines handing in his notice to Dr. Kalbfleisch, the surprise on his face. No more could he take Raymond for granted. No more would Raymond sweat to make somebody else rich.

Dwayne's cell rings. He answers it and says "no problem" several times while becoming increasingly agitated. Abruptly, he puts the phone back in his pocket. "Anyway, think about it, Ray. I'm outta here."

❖

Raymond is so tired of feeling ashamed: of failing to give his wife babies, of failing to keep his wife, of failing to protect his wife, of being adopted, of working in a chicken restaurant, of failing to be a good son. This shame doesn't motivate him to succeed where he has failed. It only coats him with filth. Filth as immovable as the grime between the tiles of Chez Simon.

"Use your fucking head," his father used to tell him when he fumbled at simple tasks. Tasks that he would have completed with ease if Gord hadn't been watching. But under his father's stare he grew clumsy. And ashamed.

He's so tired of it. He's so tired of not understanding anything. He always seems to be the last to know about anything. Ever since he can remember he's been on the outside looking in, trying to understand. Maybe Dwayne can help him out of this, if he's telling the truth — about what his sisters did to him, about what Gloria did to him, about the dome idea. Raymond must find out if he's telling the truth.

He looks down at Tory's card and dials.

❖

The bartender has a curly blond toupee. As he pours their drinks, Raymond notices that he's wearing a wedding ring. What does his wife think of the toupee? Raymond wonders. Does she think he looks better with it? When does he take it off? Does he do what Mrs. Bumby does, whatever it is she does? Leave it on the bedside table, inert, like a dead animal?

"Life is hard," Tory admits. Her mascara is crumbling, leaving shadows under her eyes. She plays with a book of matches, opening and closing it. "I think I'm going to have to put my poodle down. He keeps peeing in the condo. I actually hit him the other day, can you believe that? It was devastating. I've never hit him."

"If he's old, he can't help himself."

"I know. That's why I have to put him down. It's not fair to him."

"Why don't you just not hit him? It's only pee. We don't kill people when they become incontinent."

"Maybe we should."

Tory hasn't smiled for about five minutes. Her face looks entirely different when she isn't smiling. She has jowls. It occurs to Raymond that she smiles to prop up her face.

"Anyway," she adds, "believe what you want."

Raymond clears his throat. "I'd just like to know the truth."

"I already told you that he lies."

"Yeah, but that was before he told me that you lie. You and Gloria and Tammy."

Jeff told him that alligators only eat at night, that you can swim in alligator-infested waters during the day because they're not hungry. Raymond thought of all the movies he'd seen in which alligators chewed up humans in broad daylight. It was all lies.

Tory puts the matchbook down and leans on the bar. "Well I guess you're going to have to make a decision then, about who to believe."

"I just don't understand why anybody has to lie."

"Everybody lies. Half the time they don't even know it. I ask people if they eat a lot of sugar. They say no. I can tell from their teeth they eat sugar."

"That's different, though."

"From what?"

"From lying about what happened to you."

"How is it different?"

Raymond isn't sure. He remembers Gloria saying that Dwayne lies to get attention. Raymond doesn't think it can be as simple as that. He stares into his scotch. The man sitting beside him is discussing art with the bartender. He talks about surrealism, letting the unconscious take over, freeing yourself of preconceptions. "Being controlled by reason is self-imprisonment," he says. The bartender eats an ice cube.

"It's the same as pretending that you're someone else," Tory insists. "Someone who doesn't eat sugar, someone who was abused as a child. Same difference."

When Raymond was small he always pretended to be someone else. He told people that he lived in a house, not a high-rise. He said he had parents who didn't drink. He said his father took him fishing. How is this different from his biological family's lies? How can he condemn them for lying without condemning himself? He lied to protect himself. Are they protecting themselves? From what?

Tory shakes her head. "I can be staring right at their plaque and people will tell me they floss regularly. Can you believe that?"

"What do you say to them?"

"Nothing."

"You could say it doesn't look like they floss regularly."

"What difference would it make? They'd still come to me with garbage mouths. You wouldn't believe the mouths I have to clean. The smokers are the worst."

Raymond nods. The man beside him is now talking about impressionism. "What the painter sees is not necessarily what is actually there."

Tory picks up the matchbook again. "Some people don't even bother to brush regularly. They show up once a month and expect me to clean them up. Can you believe that? It's disgusting."

The bartender asks Raymond if he wants another. Tory lifts her face into a smile. "Just the bill, thanks."

Raymond reaches for his wallet. "I'll get this." She doesn't argue.

❖

It relieves him that Dwayne isn't on the TV screen. He turns it on and sees Clark Gable talking to Doris Day. She looks upset. "I would have told you the truth," Clark explains, "but I didn't want to hurt you." Doris refuses to look at him. Raymond wonders if she's thinking about Clark's stinking dentures. Why didn't anyone tell him about their odour? They could have put it nicely, something like, "You're a great actor but please soak your dentures daily." Clark holds out his hands. "Please, try to understand." It would have been so easy to tell him. Why didn't anybody tell him?

Burt nudges his foot, signalling that he wants a biscuit. How simple, Raymond thinks as he goes into the kitchen. Why can't humans be more like dogs? He considers the women he sees walking their dogs. They exude love for them, call them "sweetums" and "poochkin." They love them because they know what they want, can give them what they want. Dogs can be satisfied. Unlike men.

Suddenly Doris and Clark are kissing. They must have worked something out while Raymond was in the kitchen. As usual he missed the crucial moment. He thinks of Mara, tries to understand Mara — why she doesn't want him around any more. He balances a biscuit on Burt's nose who flips it into his mouth. "Good pooch," Raymond says.

When he entered the building, after dropping off Tory, the obsessive-compulsive man was going in and out of the front doors, counting. Raymond thought of himself, how many times he has gone in and out of doors; how many more times he will go in and out of doors. He pictured doors, both familiar and strange: swinging inwards and outwards, slamming, locking, jamming, sliding, creaking. He felt overwhelmed by doors. In the elevator, after the doors closed, he told himself to stop thinking these thoughts because they might drive him mad, as mad as the obsessive-compulsive man.

He looks at the door of his apartment, imagines putting his hand on the knob, turning it. He knows that he will do this, will have to do this, again and again. Unless he were to die immediately. He looks at his hands that could be his brother's, who may or may not be a liar; hands that were fondling burgers and potato chips and lap dancers. He gets up to wash them, runs hot water over them, scrubbing hard to remove the grease. He scrubs until his hands burn. He's afraid he won't be able to get it off. What if he can't get it off?

fifteen

Mr. Pyper becomes very upset when Raymond insists that he has changed his mind, that he wants to be present at his mother's cremation; that he wants to see her put into the oven and burned. "The oven is closed," Mr. Pyper points out.

"So open it. Whoever operates it can open it. I want to see her consumed by flames." He is speaking like a deranged person because he suspects that this will intimidate Mr. Pyper. Being polite will not.

"Mr. Gage," he persists, "I promise you, you will be much more comfortable waiting in the chapel."

"No payment until I see her burn."

Mr. Pyper sighs. "I'll see what I can do." He hangs up.

Raymond wants to see his mother's cremation because he wants to experience something real, something finite. He wants to be certain that she is dead and gone. He wants to know the truth, feel the truth. He's tired of lies.

Beth stands in the doorway with her hands on her hips. "That woman who says she's your mother is here. She wants chicken, should I give it to her?"

Raymond stares at her. She looks familiar but unfamiliar to him, as though he knew her a long time ago.

"She's got a woman with her," she adds. "She says she's your sister. Do I feed her too?"

Raymond nods because words won't form on his lips. Beth turns abruptly and goes back upstairs. He's finding that he's experiencing delayed reactions. This morning he nearly ran over a puppy who sat in the middle of the road looking at him. It took a moment for Raymond to register that the puppy wasn't going to get out of the way. He jammed on his brakes, relieved to see no one behind him. The puppy skipped around the car and studied Raymond, cocking its head and wagging its tail. It didn't seem to have noticed that it had almost been killed.

Jeff appears in the doorway. "Captain, we seem to have a problem with the washroom."

"What problem?" Raymond feels his words echo off the walls. He looks to see if Jeff has noticed this.

"Dr. Kalbfleisch is in the can and won't come out, and I need to go."

"Use one of the dining-room washrooms."

"Looking like this?" He gestures to the grease and chicken blood on his uniform.

"How do you know he won't come out?" Raymond asks. "Did you knock?"

"Affirmative."

Raymond looks at the cement wall, then back at Jeff. "Well how long has he been in there?"

"At least twenty minutes, which is weird. I mean, he's old. He could be dead."

Raymond walks down the corridor to the washroom and knocks gently on the door. "Dr. Kalbfleisch? Sir?" He hears a tap running, then it stops. "Sir? It's me, Raymond."

"I know who it is."

"Are you alright in there?"

"Of course I'm alright."

"Do you think you might be coming out shortly? Because Jeff needs to use the facilities."

"He what?"

"He needs to use the toilet."

Silence. Jeff, attempting to restrain his bladder, crosses his legs.

"I'll be out in a minute," Dr. Kalbfleisch says. "Don't bother me."

Jeff rolls his eyes and grimaces. Beth shouts down from the kitchen. "We've got orders up here!"

"Just go through the dining room," Raymond tells him. "It's not that busy. No one will notice." Jeff scrambles back upstairs. Raymond goes back to his office and tries to remember what he was doing before he got interrupted. After a moment he hears the washroom door open and Dr. Kalbfleisch approaching. He stands in the doorway, sucking on his dentures. "Raymond, Mrs. Bumby was not happy with the washrooms."

"Not happy, sir?"

"She said nobody is cleaning under the rim."

Raymond notices a damp patch on the crotch of Dr. Kalbfleisch's trousers. He wonders how it got there; if it's water, or semen or urine. Raymond thinks about Tory's incontinent poodle; how she's going to put it down. How she thought incontinent people should be put down. "They're cleaned daily," Raymond assures him.

"Not under the rim." He starts to leave, then stops. "And another thing, Mrs. Bumby said her chicken was pink."

"Really? That surprises me because the temperatures are very strictly regulated."

"She said close to the bone it was pink." He takes out his handkerchief, wraps it around his index finger and pokes it into one nostril. "We could get sued, Raymond."

"By Mrs. Bumby?"

"By someone who gets sick from the chicken. It can't be pink. Make sure it isn't pink. End of story."

"We've never had complaints before, sir."

"There's a first time for everything. Make sure it doesn't happen again." He puts his handkerchief back in his pocket and starts down the corridor. Raymond has been noticing that Dr. Kalbfleisch seems increasingly rumpled since his wife's death. His shirts are not pressed and there is dandruff on his jacket. Soon, Raymond imagines, his dentures will start to stink.

❖

Tammy, in leopard-spotted leggings, is tearful. Her children pummel each other under the table. Gloria freshens her lipstick. "We was hoping you'd be working today, Raymond. We wasn't sure."

"I always work," he says.

"We just wanted to clear up a few things." Gloria puts the lipstick back in her handbag. "Tory told us about last night."

"What about it?"

"You siding with Dwayne."

"I wasn't siding with anybody."

"She's all upset because she has to put down Curly, and you go telling her she lies. Is that nice?"

"I didn't tell her she lied. I asked her to tell me the truth." Gloria's lips are orange today, matching her turban.

"We *told* you the truth," she insists. "Seems to me you're spending too much time with that brother of yours."

"He's been bothering my ex-wife. I was trying to stop him."

"There's no stopping Dwayne once he gets an idea in his head. You'd best not see him, best forget about him."

"I can't. He's bothering my wife."

"I thought you said you was divorced?"

"My ex-wife. He's stalking her and sending her flowers."

Gloria pokes her finger under her turban and scratches. "That's no business of mine. Just don't go taking it out on Tory. She gave Curly a lickin'. She's never hit that dog in her life. That's how upset you got her."

"She hit the dog before I talked to her."

"That's not what *she* said."

"Well then she was lying."

"There you go saying people are lying again."

Tammy seems to want no part of this conversation. She wipes her eyes and studies the menu. One of her children bites her ankle. She doesn't appear to notice.

"I'm just trying to find out what's really going on," Raymond explains.

Gloria fixes her right eye on him. "Where?"

"In your family. What really happened."

"Where?"

"In your life. In Dwayne's life."

"I told you already." She adjusts her turban. "Don't fight with me, Raymond. That's just like your brother."

Beth brings their dinners. Immediately mother and daughter descend on the chicken. Raymond takes this opportunity to seek refuge in the kitchen. Seymour is standing at the take-out counter discussing forms of Chinese torture. "The emperor," he explains, "would order the traitor to be wrapped in a carpet. The torturers would swing the carpet, beat it, until the man was asphyxiated."

"No shit," Jeff comments.

"Beats getting your balls cut off," Bubba remarks.

"It was a slow death," Seymour emphasizes. "Only the elite were entitled to be executed rolled up in carpet. It resulted in very little bruising."

Jeff hacks a chicken in half. "You want fries with that?"

"Please."

Bruce slices a piece of pie and puts it in the microwave. He looks at Raymond and shakes his head. "I can't believe your sister is wearing leopard-skin tights. Leopard skin should be outlawed."

After the lunch rush is over Raymond inspects the toilets and cleans under the rims, even though it's Sharif's job to maintain the washrooms. Raymond has already observed that Sharif's idea of clean toilets differs from his own. But he hasn't pressed the issue because he recognizes that cleaning public washrooms is a horrible job. He has decided to clean the bowls himself rather than ask Sharif to do it because his baby may be dying. Also, cleaning the toilets keeps him out of Gloria's line of fire. She has glowered at him all through dinner, even during the hot-fudge cake. He gave the children extra cherries on their sundaes, but still she glowered. Tammy seems to enjoy white wine. She has had several glasses. He'll have to pay their bill because it will be large. And he'll have to tip Beth.

When he returns to the dining room he finds Mrs. Bumby searching for Dr. Kalbfleisch. "Have you seen Simon?" she inquires.

"No, ma'am." Her perfume is very potent.

She looks around. "I was supposed to meet him here."

"Did you ask in the kitchen?" She seems to have very little neck. Just the bosoms, then the hair.

"They say they haven't seen him," she says. "Isn't that odd?"

"Well, he comes and goes."

"He's absent-minded?"

"You could say that."

"I'm a little worried about him. Do you mind if I use the phone?"

"Go ahead." He hands her the bar phone. She takes a Kleenex from her purse, picks up the receiver and wipes the mouthpiece with it. While she dials, Raymond looks across the restaurant at his biological family. The children, their faces smeared with chocolate sauce and whipped cream, butt each other with their heads. Tammy stares out the window, sipping her wine. Gloria has opened her compact and is powdering her nose.

Mrs. Bumby puts the phone down. "There's no answer."

"I can tell him you were looking for him," Raymond offers.

"Oh don't bother. I'm sure I'll catch up with him later." She smiles a smile he knows she doesn't mean, then walks, taking tiny steps, out of the restaurant.

Back in his office he discovers Dr. Kalbfleisch hunched over his desk. "Hello, sir. Mrs. Bumby was looking for you."

Dr. Kalbfleisch flinches. "Did you tell her I was here?"

"I didn't know you were here."

"Good. Don't tell her I'm here."

Raymond notices that the wet patch on Dr. Kalbfleisch's trousers has dried. Maybe he hid down here because he didn't want Mrs. Bumby to see the wet patch. Or maybe he hid down here because he didn't want to see Mrs. Bumby. "I'll get out of your way now, Raymond."

"That's okay, you don't have to leave." He can't believe he's feeling protective towards Dr. Kalbfleisch. "Anyway," he adds, "she said she'd catch up with you later."

"That's fine. Just don't tell her I was here."

"Okay." More lies.

"I'll be on my way. See you tomorrow, Raymond."

"Okay, sir."

❖

The men in charge of cremating the bodies wear baseball caps. One is stooped, the other pigeon-shaped. They look at Raymond with suspicion. The stooped one opens the cardboard box containing his mother. She looks grey and withered in a floral dress she bought years ago when the disease began destroying her brain. She repeatedly asked the salesgirl the price of the dress, and studied her reflection in the full-length mirror for at least half an hour. Raymond wondered what she saw — the beauty she had been or the crone she had become? He wanted to shield her from her reflection, and kept trying to distract her by suggesting she try on something else. But the floral dress entranced her. She would not take it off and nearly left the store without paying for it. He took her for a sandwich and watched while she dribbled egg salad on to the new dress. She didn't notice and he didn't tell her. He couldn't admit to himself that he was losing her. The grease stain from the mayonnaise is still there.

He closes the box. "That's fine." The men look at him, then each other, and nod. One end of the box is marked "head." They slide the other end down the cart fitted with rollers until it's in front of the oven. The pigeon-shaped man presses buttons and the oven door opens. The firebrick is stained with ashes. They roll his mother into the oven. More buttons are pressed and the oven door closes. On either side of Raymond are two more boxes marked "head." The men check the documents of identification and receipt, sign them, then wheel these bodies into the two other ovens. Raymond watches even though he knows they don't want him in here. The stooped man smells of cigarettes. The pigeon-shaped man chews gum. They work in silence, exchanging looks. Abruptly the pigeon man turns to Raymond. "Okay, I'm gonna start her up. I have to keep the doors closed right off, otherwise the fire won't take. Mr. Pyper said you should go wait in the chapel for twenty minutes or so, till it gets going."

"Okay." This relieves him. He didn't want to see her bubbling and blistering. He didn't want to see her hair ignite. He wants her charred, unrecognizable; a burnt log.

In the chapel he hears a hum. He can't figure out where it's coming from. It seems to grow louder. He feels it closing in on him, consuming him. He needs air, walks out to the lobby, through the front doors on to the steps. May breeze buffs him. Tulips, many of their flowers chewed off by squirrels, line either side of the walk leading to the crematorium. Spring again. He doesn't know if he can take it.

Mr. Pyper startles him. "Mr. Gage?"

"Yes."

"They're ready for you now, if you wish to view the body. Certainly we'll understand if you've had a change of heart."

"I haven't." He goes back to the ovens. The two men continue to stare at him.

"The head takes longest to burn," the pigeon man advises. "And the heart." This seems appropriate; that the heart and mind resist extermination.

"I'm just opening it for two seconds," the pigeon man warns, "so's we don't lose too much heat."

"I understand," Raymond says. The man pushes buttons and the oven containing his mother opens. Heat blasts him, and the smell of roasting meat. He hears the spitting sound of burning fat. Without her skin and hair she still looks like his mother. She seems animated, as though the flames have given her new life. Her head is tossed back, her mouth gapes. She's either in ecstasy or agony. She could be laughing or screaming. She could be fornicating. She could be fucking his father. She could be crying out in orgasm. The door closes. "You okay?" the pigeon man asks.

"Okay."

"Mr. Pyper's waiting for you in the lobby."

Raymond nods and walks slowly through the humming chapel to the lobby where Mr. Pyper has his invoice ready. "Everything alright, Mr. Gage?"

"Fine." Raymond takes out his wallet and hands him a credit card.

"Thank you, sir." He scurries into his office.

She's definitely dead. No question. He sits on a straight-backed chair waiting for the heat and burnt-meat smell to leave him. Mr. Pyper scurries back with his credit card and receipt to sign. "The ashes will be ready tomorrow afternoon. We have to let the ovens cool, you understand. Before we can collect the ashes." Raymond signs and Mr. Pyper hands him his copy. "I hope you're satisfied with our service."

Raymond realizes that Mr. Pyper is waiting for him to leave. "Fine," Raymond says. "Everything's fine."

As he walks away he looks up at the smoke spiralling from the chimneys. She's definitely no longer of his world. Maybe of another; out the chimney into another cosmos.

❖

He doesn't know what he expects from Claire, what she can possibly give him. He watches her taking orders, delivering chicken. She smiles when she sees him. He knows that she's remembering his tip.

"Chef salad, no chicken?" she asks.

"Please. And a scotch."

"Hard day?"

It pleases him that she is being intimate, but then he notices her checking the order she took before his. She's asking about his day to be polite, she isn't really interested. In reality she's calculating how long the various items ordered will take to prepare and in what order she should bring them to the table. "I watched my mother burn," he tells her.

"Pardon?"

"My mother was cremated today."

"Oh I'm sorry. That's terrible." She holds her hands over her mouth. He notices bruises on her wrists. It looks as though someone was holding on to her, shaking her, not letting go. At a loss for words, she shifts her weight from one leg to the other.

"I'll have my scotch whenever you can manage it," he says, knowing that this will give her an excuse to leave him, in spite of his mother's cremation.

"Right away."

He doesn't know why he told her about his mother, what he expected her to say. He slouches down in his seat, resting the back of his head against the banquette. Behind him two women discuss another woman who is not present. "She goes through one guy after another. Like, after Bill there was Gary, right?"

"Gary was nice."

"She got bored with him, that's what she told me. You know what else she told me? She put deodorant up her vagina to make it tighter."

"Does that work?"

"I don't know. I mean you'd have to be psycho to do it."

"I guess."

"I mean it could be dangerous."

Claire brings him his scotch. He smiles. "Thank you."

"My pleasure."

At the table in front of Raymond sits an older woman with a pained expression. She eats slowly, methodically, her expression unchanging. She has a carafe of wine to herself which is half empty. Raymond would have thought the wine would have reduced her pain by now. She notices him staring at her and stares back. "Do you believe that Jesus Christ is our saviour?" she asks.

"No," Raymond replies.

She continues to stare at him, then abruptly looks back at her chicken, her expression still unchanged. She drinks more wine. Raymond drinks more scotch, wondering why, if everyone is in pain — and as far as he can tell everyone is — they can't be nicer to each other. In the paper there was a story about two six-year-old boys kicking a five-year-old girl to death. How could this happen?

"Here's your salad," Claire says.

"Thank you." It looks awful. "What happened to your wrists?"

She looks down. "Oh. I fell."

"Where?"

"At home. There's lots of stairs." She speeds away. He knows that she's lying, that her fiancé is responsible for the bruising. He got shit on at work so he came home and shit on his future wife, the only person who would take it. This afternoon, when Raymond was walking Burt, there was a man reprimanding his whippet. The whippet had been chasing squirrels. The man caught up to the dog and turned it over on to its back so that it was helpless, its skinny legs pointing skyward. The man shoved his hand into its chest, then wagged the finger of his free hand in the whippet's face. "*I* am the master, not you," he told it. "*I* will decide when you can go for squirrels." Raymond wondered why the man had to take his frustrations out on his little dog. Because he didn't have a wife?

Is that what it's all about then? Being master? Master of what? A woman weaker than you are, a dog smaller, a child? Is that what it's all about? Proving your superior strength, then inflicting suffering? To what purpose? All over the world men are trying to prove their superior strength. Some of them control armies. Men who were once little boys, who may have had bunnies and who may have killed them, are tearing the world apart.

"Nobody's putting their fist up my ass," one of the women behind him declares.

"Me neither," the other agrees.

Claire glances his way in passing. "Everything alright?"

"Fine. Thank you."

What about death in a carpet? It wouldn't be so bad. You couldn't see, the blows would be muted. Death in a carpet might be better than life in a chicken restaurant. It would be over quickly, you wouldn't have to face your executioners. Raymond feels that he must repeatedly face his executioners, and that it won't be over quickly. Maybe Dwayne feels the same way, which is why he's tired of this planet and wouldn't mind getting off it. Raymond ponders their time together in the Burger King. Maybe he should stop listening to what Gloria and Tory say about Dwayne and just spend time with Dwayne. It wouldn't hurt to at least find out more about geodesic domes.

Outside, Burt is tied to the mailbox.

Claire breezes by. "Are you finished with your salad?"

She just looks stupid to him now: a pretty woman lying to herself; a pretty woman who will lock herself inside a life with a man who will torment her.

How is that different from me? Raymond thinks. He can't free himself from his torturers. He puts his knife and fork on the plate. "That's fine. Thanks."

"Can I get you anything else?"

"No. I've got to go. My dog's outside." He gives her fifteen dollars. "That's fine."

"Thank you."

❖

At home there is a message from Mara. "I don't know what you're trying to pull, Raymond, but I don't think it's funny. If you send me anything else, I'm calling the police." He stares at the machine a moment before replaying the message. "I don't know what you're trying to pull, Raymond, but I don't think it's funny. If you send me anything else, I'm calling the police."

He didn't send her anything else. He has never sent her anything. He plays the message again because he doesn't want to believe it, doesn't want to believe his brother is doing this to him. He feels his heart sinking. He has read about hearts sinking but has never felt it. The brother he wants to love is becoming one of his torturers. Raymond sits very still in front of the coat closet, watching the living room. He doesn't want to go into the living room because he knows that Dwayne will be on the TV screen, laughing at him. He goes into the kitchen to find something to soothe him: food, drink, pills? There's nothing. There's nothing he can do. Except kill him. And he doesn't know how to do that, is afraid to do that — of the remorse, of what would happen when he was caught. He fears the consequences of his actions. His brother does not.

sixteen

Dr. Kalbfleisch has begun to smell. Beth notices it first and asks Raymond to do something about it. "It's bad for the restaurant," she insists.

"How is it bad for the restaurant?"

"To have a stinking owner? Use your head, Raymond." This is what his father used to say.

Raymond clears his throat. "The customers don't necessarily know that he's the owner."

"The way he parades around they do."

The health inspector gave Beth a gold chain and pendant which she has shown to everyone. It's a heart and a horseshoe combined. Bruce advised Raymond that it's tacky.

"At least he's forgotten about the chicken hats," Raymond points out.

For the past three days Mrs. Bumby has been driving Dr. Kalbfleisch to the hospital for "tests." She hasn't explained what the tests are for and Raymond feels it would be rude to ask. It's very strange to see her behind the wheel of Dr. Kalbfleisch's Mercedes. He wouldn't even let Mrs. Kalbfleisch drive it.

"Just say something about the importance of personal hygiene to him," Beth persists.

"You say something."

"You're the manager."

Sharif's baby is still alive. But Sharif told Raymond that every time his phone rings he's afraid that it's the hospital telling him his son is dead. He still prays while washing dishes but has opened his eyes, which relieves Raymond. As much as he pities Sharif, he also envies him for experiencing deep feeling. Raymond feels that he himself has only experienced shallow feelings — even over the death of his babies. He was concerned less about the babies than about Mara. He despaired over her despair, not his own. Even with his mother dead, he does not despair. Even with his brother turned torturer, Raymond can get up in the morning and order chickens. Mara once accused him of being selfless. "You're so busy trying to keep everybody happy," she said, "you can't even help yourself." When she said "self" he wondered if he had one. He'd been looking in the mirror for so many years, imagining his twin, that he wasn't sure if he had a self, or if the self he had belonged to his twin. He realizes now that he must have a self because he certainly isn't Dwayne. His brother can steal his appearance, but he can't steal his self.

He's not sure that this is true.

Now that his mother is definitely dead and he doesn't have her concerns to worry about, and now that Mara doesn't want him around, he feels more anger than despair — about the injustice of it all. He finds himself hating people for no particular reason, people he hardly knows; customers. A man with trembling hands complained about the small portion of french fries included with the chicken dinner. Normally Raymond would apologize to the customer and get him more fries. But he hated this man and would do nothing for him, in spite of his trembling hands. What surprised him was that the man looked fearful, and actually shut up and ate his dinner. Raymond hadn't expected this. He'd expected a fight, wanted a fight. But the man backed off. All his life Raymond has been the one to back off, because he has been afraid.

He called Dwayne and invited him out for a coffee to discuss the geodesic dome idea, but really he intends to offer Dwayne money to stay away from Mara.

At take-out, Seymour is discussing Queen Elizabeth and Sir Walter Raleigh. "He called her Cynthia," he informs them.

"No shit?" Jeff comments.

"And when she found out he was fornicating with one of her ladies-in-waiting, she tossed him into the tower for three months."

"Wow," Bubba remarks.

"Wouldn't that be nice," Seymour continues, "to toss annoying people into the tower."

Bubba drops more fries into the fryer. "I like the royal family."

Dr. Kalbfleisch comes in the back door, followed by Mrs. Bumby. He holds up one hand weakly. "Raymond . . . ?"

"Yes, sir?"

"Can you get Mrs. Bumby a dinner?"

"Of course."

"Simon," Mrs. Bumby says, "aren't you eating?"

"I'm not hungry."

"You have to eat, Simon."

"Maybe later. I have work to do in the office."

Raymond doesn't know what "work" Dr. Kalbfleisch can be referring to. He never does work in the office.

Mrs. Bumby grips Dr. Kalbfleisch's elbow. "Do you want me to help you?"

"No. You go eat. Raymond, she wants white meat. Make sure it isn't pink."

❖

After mixing Mrs. Bumby a dry martini, Raymond goes downstairs to check on Dr. Kalbfleisch. He isn't doing any work. He's leaning back in the chair with his feet up on the desk. "Are you alright, sir?" Raymond asks.

"I just need to sit for a minute."

"Wouldn't you be more comfortable in the dining room?"

Dr. Kalbfleisch waves his hand dismissively and closes his eyes. Raymond clears his throat. "Was everything alright at the hospital?"

"They took so much blood from me, I need a transfusion."

"Were they testing you for anything in particular?"

"It's a hospital. They want to find something wrong with me."

Raymond leans against the wall. "I don't mean to pry, Sir, but I'm having difficulty understanding why, all of a sudden, you're going for tests."

"Mrs. Bumby thinks we'd be better safe than sorry."

Raymond says nothing, only stares at a *Star Trek* poster Jeff has taped to the wall.

"Mrs. Bumby is a very energetic woman," Dr. Kalbfleisch emphasizes.

"Yes."

"When you get to be my age, Raymond, it's nice to have company."

Raymond would like to point out that Dr. Kalbfleisch has only grown weaker in the face of Mrs. Bumby's energy. He would like to ask, "What is Mrs. Bumby to you and what are you to Mrs. Bumby?" But he feels that this line of questioning would be too intimate.

"Mrs. Bumby has many children," Dr. Kalbfleisch admits. "My son isn't going to like it."

All that Raymond knows about Dr. Kalbfleisch's son is that he's a fashion model in Paris and never comes home to visit. He scratches behind his ear. "Are you thinking of marrying her, sir?"

"Raymond, when you get to be my age, you don't like to be alone."

Raymond would like to point out that Dr. Kalbfleisch has been seeking refuge from Mrs. Bumby on a regular basis. He would like to suggest that he hire a professional companion rather than marry a woman who frightens him.

"She's my *joie de vivre*," Dr. Kalbfleisch insists. "She knows how to have a good time." He looks extremely depressed when he says this. Raymond can't figure out why he's convincing himself that he needs Mrs. Bumby to be his wife.

"You don't have to marry her right away, sir. You could just date for a while."

Dr. Kalbfleisch shakes his head. "I don't have much time, Raymond. You saw what happened to Ava. One minute you're eating chicken, the next minute you're dead."

Raymond would like to say that the possibility of sudden death shouldn't be a reason to marry someone. But he suspects that none of his reasoning would have any effect on Dr. Kalbfleisch because he has decided that there is a hole in his life that must be filled. He has created a need where there wasn't one. Which makes Raymond consider his own needs, the ones he has created; like having a twin and a biological mother. He was doing all right before he established these needs, before he dug himself these holes. "Well," he says, "I think I'll go back upstairs. Can I get you anything?"

"Just tell her I'm busy."

"Okay." He suspects that once you have dug the holes you can never forget them; you'll be staring into them your whole life, wishing you could fill them.

His stomach is upset because he's meeting Dwayne after work, so he opens the kitchen's first-aid kit and takes out some Gravol.

"You bleed from all your orifices," Bubba explains.

"No way," Jeff argues.

"It's true. It was on TV. It's a monkey virus."

Bruce, smoking a cigarette, leans out the back door. "Bubba, maybe you haven't noticed this, but there are no monkeys here."

"It's the virus. It's carried on air particles, right, like all the way from Africa. Some nuns died from it. All you have to do is, like, be in the same room with an infected person. It could wipe out the entire human race."

Beth storms in carrying a plate. "That bitch says the chicken is pink."

"Impossible," Jeff says, coming out from behind the broiler. Raymond fills a glass with water and swallows two pills. Beth sets Mrs. Bumby's plate down on the take-out counter and they all study it. Bubba pokes it with his fingers. "That's not pink. That's chicken-coloured."

"That's what I told her." Beth fondles her pendant.

Jeff scratches under his hairnet. "Does she want another dinner?"

"No. She's doing the martyr thing. Like we forced her to eat here so she's suffering through it. You'd better go talk to her, Raymond."

"Why do I have to talk to her?"

"Because you're the manager."

Mrs. Bumby is swinging her leg and resting her bosoms on the table. In front of her bosoms is a fashion magazine. She flips through it while Raymond is talking. Her perfume smells like bug spray.

"Health standards, Raymond. We don't want Simon getting into any trouble."

Raymond clears his throat. "The health inspector comes by once a month and says everything's fine." Another lie.

"Then he obviously doesn't take his job very seriously."

"Mrs. Bumby, the temperatures are strictly regulated. We wouldn't pass an inspection otherwise." He remembers the health inspector complaining about the temperatures on the salad bar.

"Well . . ." she continues, still flipping through the magazine, "I don't want to tell you how to do your job."

He wonders why she's telling him then.

"But it's obvious to me that things have been a little slack around here. The chicken business is very competitive, Raymond. We can't afford to lose business."

How did they become "we" all of a sudden? Raymond wonders what kind of future Dr. Kalbfleisch envisions with this woman. Does he anticipate that they will have good times, since she "knows how to have a good time"? Or is his idea of a good time having a wife who frightens him and tells him that he has shit for brains? Maybe that's all he knows. Maybe he's afraid of what he doesn't know; more afraid than he is of Mrs. Bumby.

She closes the magazine. "I think we all have to do what we can for Simon."

"Of course."

"Is he downstairs?"

"He's busy."

"I'll talk to him." She takes tiny steps, in her high heels, across the dining room and into the kitchen. Raymond finds himself hoping that she'll slip on the greasy tiles and break her neck.

He totals the day's receipts at the bar register. He's hoping to finish the cash report early because he wants to pick up his mother's ashes. Bruce and Beth are behind the bar eating maraschino cherries and discussing what killed their mothers.

"Can you not eat all the cherries?" Raymond asks, but they ignore him. Bruce tosses a stem into the garbage. "It's the same thing they use to kill rats," he explains. "They fed her rat poison to thin her blood."

Beth reaches for another cherry. "And that killed her?"

He shrugs. "They say the disease killed her."

Beth shakes her head. "With all the drugs they give them, it's hard to know what's doing the killing."

Raymond pulls out the cash drawer. "Can't you guys find something to do? Check the ketchups or something?"

Bruce wipes his hands on his apron. "In my opinion, certain people are better off dead."

Raymond waits at the top of the stairs because Mrs. Bumby is leading Dr. Kalbfleisch up them. Raymond has never noticed Dr. Kalbfleisch having difficulty climbing the stairs before and he wonders if there really is something wrong with him. If there is, and he dies, Mrs. Bumby will be his boss. Raymond couldn't stand this. He'd have to find another job. Suddenly he wants Dr. Kalbfleisch to live forever; a man whom only a week ago he hated.

At the top of the stairs Dr. Kalbfleisch turns to him. "We'll see you later, Raymond." He hasn't even asked about the numbers.

"Okay, sir."

Mrs. Bumby offers one of her insincere smiles. "Don't forget to check the washrooms."

"I won't."

He's forty-eight dollars short on the cash report but he doesn't care. He goes home, walks Burt, then drives to the funeral home. Mr. Pyper seems very happy to see him and tries to sell him an urn.

"I haven't decided if I want an urn," Raymond says.

"We have some very attractive models." He shimmies towards a display case filled with ceramic urns, metal urns, marble urns.

"Not today," Raymond insists. "Maybe later."

He takes the tin of ashes to the general's memorial. He sits on a bench with the tin on his lap and looks up at the general. Fortunately there is no paper bag over his head, although someone has spray-painted "douche bag" on his podium. Why would someone do that? Raymond wonders. He knows that removing the spray paint would be very difficult. Maybe it doesn't matter to the general, maybe he is above all that. Which is what Raymond dreams of being: above all the avarice, ignorance and cruelty of mankind. He suspects that you can only rise above it when you're dead. He pictures his mother spiralling out the chimney, rising above it. He looks down at the tin and shakes it gently. "Where would you like to go?" he asks her, although he's not sure that he can part with her yet. He thinks he might just hang on to her. Since she's all he's got.

❖

"They told me I was growing breasts," Dwayne tells him. A football game is being televised on the large screen and all the men in the bar are watching it. They shout and groan and hiss at the players.

"What's that got to do with anything?" Raymond asks.

"I want you to have some idea of where I'm coming from. I mean, imagine being this little kid, and your sisters are telling you you're growing breasts. I mean, you'd have to believe them because they're girls, right? So you're constantly looking at your chest to see if they're growing. You're convinced that they're growing so you spend your days trying to hide this development. Gym class is a nightmare because you're sure all the other boys are looking at your tits."

Football players run after another football player and fall on top of him. Men in the bar cheer. Raymond wonders what happens to the man under the pile of men. Can he breathe? Are his ribs crushed?

Dwayne starts to eat another chicken finger. "Then they start telling you that your dick is going to drop off. So you spend a lot of time looking at that too. So do your mommy's boyfriends. They like looking at it."

"Alright," Raymond interjects, "you don't have to tell me any more." He didn't want to come to the sports bar but Dwayne insisted he meet Julio, the bartender with the cash. But Julio isn't around.

"Why not?" Dwayne asks. "Does it upset you? You who lived with nice middle-class parents in a nice middle-class neighbourhood?"

"It wasn't that nice. We lived in a high-rise."

"Oh, my heart bleeds."

The football player who was under the other players can't get up. Attendants rush out with a stretcher and load him on to it.

Dwayne dips his chicken finger into the plum sauce. "Then they tell me that I'm going to get a cunt and blood's going to pour out of it."

Raymond watches the attendants carry the unconscious player off the field. Batter drops off Dwayne's chicken finger on to his lap. He brushes it off with his hand. "So I'm waiting for that to happen too. Meanwhile the daddies are exploring my member with their fingers."

"Alright," Raymond insists, "I get the picture."

"Ask my sisters what they did to me with coat hangers."

"They'll deny everything. That's all your family ever does. Accuse each other of lying."

"Well there's a reason for that. Would you want to admit that you poked hangers up your brother's anus?"

"Can we not talk about this any more?" Raymond reaches for his beer.

"What would you like to talk about? The weather? The chicken business?"

"I want you to leave my wife alone."

"I haven't touched your wife."

"You sent her something. What did you send her?"

Dwayne swallows more beer, sets his glass down and narrows his eyes. "Lingerie. Actually, *you* sent her lingerie."

"What?"

"It was nice stuff. Victoria's Secret. I hope I got the size right."

"You sent my wife lingerie?"

"Your ex. She thinks you sent it." He picks up another chicken finger and dips it into the sauce. "I bet she got all warm and runny when she saw it. I bet she thought, Gee, he really loves me."

"She didn't think that. She was pissed off."

"So she says."

"She's not that kind of woman."

"Oh? What kind of woman is she?" Dwayne stares at him. "And if you know her so well, why did she dump you?"

"That's none of your business."

Dwayne leans back in his chair and stretches his legs into the aisle. "All women want to be desired. It doesn't mean they'll fuck you. They just want you to want them."

Above the bar there are trophies. Raymond wonders who won them, and why they left them in a bar. He clears his throat. "What if I pay you to leave her alone?"

Dwayne folds his hands behind his head. "How much?"

"I don't know. Five hundred dollars?"

"Wow, that should keep me going for about a week."

"Alright, I can pay you more but it would have to be in instalments. And if you broke your word, I wouldn't pay you."

"Wow, you drive a hard bargain."

The Gravol is making Raymond sleepy. He hardly knows what he's saying. He's angry but he has no energy for it. He knows that he should threaten his brother, hold a gun to his head, something. But he's too tired. He just wants it to end. He leans his elbows on the table. "If you were abused by anybody, I'm very sorry. But lots of people were abused and they get help. They get over it. Why don't you go see somebody about it?"

Dwayne just stares at him. His eyes look dull, as though he's not even listening to him. There is no trace of the man who was enthusiastic about geodesic domes. More football players chase another football player down the field and fall on top of him. The men in the bar boo.

"Please," Raymond says, "I'll do whatever you want, just leave her alone."

"Don't beg. I hate begging." Dwayne finishes his beer and wipes his hands with a napkin. "Look, I promise I won't send her anything else."

"Or call her, or watch her house?"

"Right."

"Thank you."

Dwayne looks at the TV. "I was only joking around."

"Alright, just don't do it again."

This time the fallen football player is able to get up. His teammates pat him on the back as he limps to centrefield.

Dwayne burps. "You buying the beers?"

❖

His apartment door is unlocked. Raymond can't believe that he forgot to lock it. He assumes that he has been robbed and hurries into the living room to see if they've stolen the TV or the stereo. Nothing has been touched. He looks in the bedroom and sees that, again, everything is as it was. Only then does he realize that he hasn't seen Burt. He calls for him, waiting to hear the soft jingle of his dog tags. Nothing. He looks under the bed, the couch. He searches all the closets, the bathroom, the kitchen. Burt is missing. They took Burt. Raymond runs down the hall to the elevator, nearly knocking over the obsessive-compulsive man. "Have you seen my dog?" he asks him. The man starts and stares at Raymond, but he doesn't stop counting.

Raymond presses the superintendent's buzzer. He can hear the television and the super shouting at his wife to answer the door. She opens it a crack and peers out at him. "Hi," Raymond says, "I'm Raymond Gage from twenty-one ten."

"Yes?"

"My dog's missing. I came home and my door was unlocked and my dog was missing."

"What is it?" the super shouts from the living room.

"Mr. Gage from twenty-one ten says his dog's missing."

"Of course it's missing, he took it out earlier."

"Yes," Raymond agrees, "but I brought him back. Then I went out again." He hears the fat super huffing and puffing as he approaches the door. He opens it wider, forcing his wife to step back. "Did you find your keys?" he asks.

"My keys?"

"Did you find them? You couldn't lock your door without your keys. If you forgot to lock your door, that's not my problem."

"I never lost my keys."

The super looks at his wife, then back at Raymond. "You came by earlier to get keys because you was locked out."

"Today?"

The super nods.

"That wasn't me."

The super scratches his belly. "It wasn't?"

"It was my identical twin."

"Is that right? Well I guess he took your dog then. Maybe you'd better call him."

Raymond wants to shout but he doesn't. "Please don't let anyone who looks like me into my apartment unless they have ID with my name on it."

The super's wife pulls her cardigan tightly around her neck. "How many of you are there?"

"Just two. Sorry to trouble you." He starts down the corridor. He wants to kill his brother, wants to wrap his fingers around his neck and squeeze the life out of him.

Dwayne doesn't answer his cell and there is no response at Gloria's. Raymond sits on his couch, shaking. He doesn't understand, can't understand, why this is happening. Why does this have to happen?

If his brother killed Fluffy, what will he do to Burt?

He phones the police but they don't care. He drives to Gloria's and searches the bushes. He rings the bell but no one answers. He tries to see in the windows but it's too dark. He gets back in the car and waits.

seventeen

The Gravol put him to sleep. He wakes with his head against the steering wheel. There is still no light at Gloria's so he gets out of the car and pounds on the door. He doesn't know why he didn't do this before: he was trying to be polite, didn't want to disturb anybody. He pounds harder and sees lights go on in the front window. Gloria, in a pink fuzzy bathrobe and matching turban, peers at him across the safety chain. "I told you if you come home all times of night, I'm not letting you in. I'm not running a hotel."

"I'm not Dwayne. I'm Raymond."

She pauses. "You are not."

"I am."

"Raymond wouldn't pound on my door at two o'clock in the morning."

"I'm looking for my dog. Dwayne took it."

"Raymond don't have a dog."

"I do. A mongrel. Actually he's part bassett hound."

Gloria stares at him with her right eye, then unhooks the door. "Come in, Raymond."

"His name is Burt. Have you seen him?"

"No." She sits on the couch.

"When did you last see Dwayne?"

"This morning. He ate twelve Eggos, then took off."

"Where did he go?"

"He don't tell me nothing. Sit down, Raymond. You want some cocoa?"

"I want my dog."

"Maybe he took him for a walk."

"For five hours?"

"Seems to me you could use some cocoa." She shuffles into the kitchen. He hears her set the pan on the stove and pour milk into it. Beside the couch, hanging from the ceiling, are two bird cages, each containing a budgie. "Why don't you keep them together?" Raymond asks.

"What's that?" Gloria squints at him from the kitchen.

"Why don't you keep the budgies in the same cage?"

"Oh, well they were for years, see, but then Tee-Kee started trying to have his way with Chow-Chow. Poor little Chow-Chow, it got so bad he hurt her, know what I mean? So I had to separate them."

Raymond can't imagine how a budgie has "his way" with another budgie. He doesn't even want to think about it. Gloria brings in the cocoa and hands him a cup. "So Tory's changed her mind about Curly, says she couldn't do it, says she loves that dog more than anything. Says she's going to start putting newspapers down. Maybe get the carpets cleaned more regularly."

Raymond clears his throat and narrows his eyes. "Dwayne told me there was no Fluffy."

"No Fluffy?"

"He said you never gave him a bunny."

"He's lying." She blows on her cocoa. "He wants to make out like he had this difficult childhood and nobody gave him nothing. It's all lies."

"He says his sisters sexually abused him, and so did your boyfriends."

She sips her cocoa, making a slurping sound. "Did he mention his multiple-personality disorder?"

"He said he never claimed to have that."

"Well he's lying." The sound of their voices must have excited the budgies because they start to squawk. Gloria squawks back at them. Raymond puts his cocoa on the coffee table because he doesn't want it. Gloria pokes a finger into one of the cages. "What is it, Chow-Chow? It's only Raymond. He's come by to visit. He won't do nothing. You go back to sleep now." She fixes her right eye on Raymond. "Chow-Chow don't like Dwayne, see. She thinks you're Dwayne."

"Why doesn't she like Dwayne?"

"He pours bleach in her cage."

"Why?"

"To sanitize it."

"That's crazy."

"He *is* crazy."

Raymond hasn't seen Gloria without makeup before. Without her pencilled eyebrows she looks constantly surprised. Without her lipstick her mouth becomes a small slit. "So you have absolutely no idea where he is or when he'll be back?" Gloria shakes her head. Raymond tries not to imagine what Dwayne might be doing, or might have done, to Burt. In the paper there was a story about a man pouring boiling water over a puppy, burning and blinding it. It had to be destroyed. Raymond tries to think about something else. He stares at the two oil paintings of horses' heads above the couch.

"Aren't those nice?" Gloria asks. "Tammy did those. She's so talented. She's been selling her horse paintings at the Ranch House. Now she's started painting on saw blades, kittens and whatnot. People love them."

"Why is she always crying?"

"Well . . ." Gloria sighs and adjusts her turban. "Dickie's a darkie, see. He's very nice but you shouldn't mix colours. It's too hard on the kiddies."

"Her kids are white."

"That's from her first marriage. Then she met Dickie and had another one, see, the one that died in the pool. Dickie's never forgiven her. She thinks he thinks she let it drown because it was a darkie too. But I seen her with that baby. She *loved* that baby."

The horses in the paintings seem to be staring at Raymond. He scratches behind his ear. "You said that the reason the baby drowned was that Tammy was on the phone to some man she'd been seeing."

"I said that?"

"Yes."

Gloria sniffs. "Well . . . it was hard for her, see, what with Dickie always working."

"So why doesn't she divorce Dick?"

"She *loves* Dickie."

"But she's always crying."

Gloria shrugs, then sips more cocoa. "One thing you got to understand about Tammy is she's had a hard life. First she married Dougie thinking he had a good job and would be a good husband. Then he gets laid off and goes to work in a titty bar. So he's feeling up the girls and whatnot, and not coming home nights, and she's left with the kiddies. Think how you'd feel if you was a woman and your husband was hanging around a titty bar." The budgies start squawking again and Gloria squawks back. The horses glare at Raymond. He looks at his watch, wondering how much longer he'll have to wait for Dwayne. "Then she met Dickie," she continues, "and he was so nice to her, used to call her 'princess.' Everything was going great between them. Trouble is, the baby drowned. He's a good provider though. Those kids never go hungry. Even though they're not his."

"So why does Dick stay married to Tammy?"

"What do you mean?"

"If he can't forgive her, why does he stay married to her?"

"He *loves* Tammy."

Raymond can't understand this family. Why they complicate things, why they dig themselves these holes. "So why don't they have another baby?"

"Well, that's a problem, see. He wants sex all the time and she's tired, looking after two kids. So they fight and he goes out and she thinks he's sleeping around."

"Then why doesn't she leave him?"

"She *loves* Dickie. People don't leave just because there's trouble, Raymond. What kind of world would it be if people took off every time there was trouble?"

Probably a better one, Raymond thinks. None of what she's saying makes any sense to him. It's all lies. These people make up stories to fool themselves that they're having lives. They make up stories to justify doing nothing. They sit around telling each other stories because no one else will listen. Raymond doesn't want to listen. He wants to find Burt. "How late does he usually stay out?"

"Who?"

"Dwayne."

"There's no telling. Some nights he don't come home at all. Did you try him on his cell?"

"Many times."

Gloria nods. "He switches it off, see, so he don't hear nothing. I say what if there's an emergency, but he don't listen to me."

Raymond doesn't know what to do. If he stays here and Dwayne doesn't come home, he'll have to listen to Gloria. He should get some sleep. If he doesn't get some sleep, he'll be a wreck at work tomorrow. But he can't sleep here. He hates it here. Gloria never opens the windows. The air never moves. It is the same air that was breathed this morning and the morning before that. The same air that his biological family has been breathing for years. He thinks of the monkey virus travelling on air particles, wiping out the entire human race. He'd like the monkey virus to travel into this house.

"I've got to go," he says. "When Dwayne gets home, tell him I want my dog."

"I'll tell him to give you a ding. You want to have din-dins with us Sunday?"

"I'll let you know."

"Tammy's cooking a roast and Tory said she'd make scalloped potatoes. Maybe, if his neck's better, Dwayne'll mix up some brownies."

"I'll call you."

"Don't be a stranger, Raymond. You're family now."

He closes her front door behind him for what he hopes is the last time.

❖

After sleeping fitfully for five hours, dreaming intermittently about the horses' heads, he hears Burt howling outside the apartment door. When Raymond opens it, Burt hardly moves, only his tail wags slightly. There is a pool of dark brown vomit at his feet. "What's wrong, boy?" Raymond carries him into the living room and puts him on the floor. "You okay?" Burt rests his head on his paws. His ears lie flat and his tail stops moving. Raymond, trying not to panic, goes into the kitchen for paper towels and starts to clean up the vomit. It's not regular vomit, the kind Burt coughs up after eating grass. It's too dark. Raymond suspects it's poison; that his brother has poisoned his dog. He puts the soiled paper towels into the garbage, then looks in the phone book for an all-night emergency veterinary clinic. When he finds one he wraps Burt up in blankets and takes him downstairs to the car. The clinic is across town. When he turns corners

Raymond has to steady Burt with his hand to prevent him from rolling off the seat.

The vet looks somnambulant and examines Burt with little interest. "Have you been feeding him human food?"

"No. Well, actually, I don't know what he's been eating. My brother had him."

"Did you ask your brother what he fed him?"

"I haven't talked to him."

The vet looks back at the weakened Burt and shakes his head. "Well, he's eaten something that doesn't agree with him. I can't tell you what it is."

"Could it be poison?"

"Poison?"

"Rat poison or something, bleach?"

The vet yawns. "He'd be dead by now. More than likely your brother fed him something he's not used to. Chocolate or something."

"Chocolate?"

"Dark chocolate's the worst. They can't stomach it." The vet looks at his watch. "We could keep him overnight for observation but that will cost you. I'd just make sure he drinks lots of water. Don't feed him anything for a while. See how it goes. How old is he?"

"Fourteen."

"So he's old. He's got stomach trouble. Give him a day to get over it. If he doesn't get better, bring him back in, we'll run some tests."

The visit with the all-night emergency vet costs Raymond fifty dollars.

❖

He arrives late for work, carrying Burt. The health inspector is in the dining room, helping himself to the salad bar. He glances at Raymond. "You bringing dogs in here now, Ray?"

"He's sick. I'm keeping him downstairs."

"I've always said this place is going to the dogs." The health inspector laughs at his own joke, then spears some pickles on to his plate.

Raymond stops Beth outside the dish room. "Have you got a bill for him?"

"Who?"

"Your boyfriend."

"Of course I've got a bill for him."

"You've been giving him free ice cream and coffee."

"Like maybe once."

"No. You've done it a couple of times. He comes in, sits down and you don't charge him." She's wearing lipstick today. She doesn't usually wear lipstick to work.

"We always give our best customers free refills."

"Since when is the health inspector a best customer?"

"Fuck off, Raymond." She starts to walk away.

"We don't give our best customers free ice cream," Raymond calls after her. Beth turns abruptly and points her pen at him. "You want me to ask him to check the temperatures again? You want me to tell him the bitch says the chicken is pink?"

"Just charge him like a regular customer. Don't give him special favours."

Bubba pokes his head out of the dish room. "Give who special favours?"

In the kitchen Raymond finds Jeff studying his *Star Trek Movie Memories* book. He glances up and pushes his glasses up his nose. "What's the password, Captain?"

"Gator burgers," Raymond mumbles. As he picks up his messages he notices Bruce on the take-out phone arguing loudly with his lover. "Don't get hostile," Bruce shouts into the receiver. "He's just a friend. I'm allowed to have *friends*, aren't I?"

Raymond takes Burt downstairs, puts him on the floor of his office and sets a bowl of water in front of him. But he doesn't drink. He tries Dwayne's cell again, then phones Gloria's but there is no answer. He calls a locksmith and sets up an appointment to change his apartment door lock. While debating whether or not to phone Mara, he does some ordering. He would like to tell her that he didn't send the lingerie, but he's afraid that she won't believe him, or worse, will become terrorized because his identical twin is stalking her and sending her things. He wants to call her only when it's all over, when he has succeeded in stopping Dwayne from bothering her, when he has succeeded in eliminating his biological family from his life. Then he'll explain everything. He tries to picture her reaction to the lingerie. She'd think he was absolutely out of his mind. She'd throw the stuff in the garbage and decide never to speak to him again.

Burt farts. Raymond hopes that this is a good sign.

But she did like the flowers. He wishes he'd thought of sending her flowers. He didn't think she'd like flowers. They never celebrated Valentine's Day. She said she thought it was stupid; just another "brain-wash-the-consumer-into-buying-crap day."

He calls a lawyer to set up a meeting to settle his mother's estate. Then he does nothing, wondering why he bothered to do anything before. Why he dug himself these holes.

Mrs. Bumby knocks on his door and smiles before noticing Burt. "Do you usually bring your dog to work, Raymond?"

"No. He's sick. I have to watch him." He knows that Mrs. Bumby is smelling Burt's fart. He hopes he lets loose another one.

"Raymond, I feel we got off to a bad start. I think we should have a talk, just the two of us." She looks around for somewhere to sit. There is only the one chair and Raymond is on it. Yesterday he would have found a chair for her. Not today. Today he lets her stand in her pointy shoes.

"Simon is very fond of you, I know. So fond, I think, that he turns a blind eye to certain things." Raymond just stares at her. He wonders if he should make a voodoo doll in her likeness and stick pins into her. Mara did this to her new boss. She made the doll out of stuffed nylons. She stitched wool hair on to his head and pubic area. She attached a deflated balloon for a penis. She gave him buttons for eyes but no clothes. Then she stuck pins into all of his vital organs. Her boss didn't notice, but it provided Mara with an outlet. Raymond suspects he could use an outlet.

Mrs. Bumby crosses her arms under her bosoms. "You're not listening, Raymond."

"Sure I am."

There have been people in Raymond's life who have been able to make him feel insignificant without actually telling him that he's insignificant. Mrs. Bumby is one of them. He knows that she thinks he is an irritant that must be removed — will be removed — without too much difficulty. She is presenting a friendly front in the hopes of catching him off guard. One moment, when he isn't looking, she plans to ram a spike into his back. Normally, when faced with this kind of opposition, Raymond steps back and allows his opponent to move ahead of him. But not this time. This time he's going to fight Mrs. Bumby.

She moves her handbag from one wrist to the other. “Maybe we’d be more comfortable in the dining room.”

Raymond crosses his arms. “I’m comfortable here.”

“I see, well . . . obviously my main concern is cleanliness.”

“Obviously.”

“In the kitchen, of course, but also the dining room and washrooms.”

“Feel free to clean them.”

“What?”

“Dr. Kalbfleisch wants to keep staff costs low. So we don’t have cleaners. Staff does cleaning when we have the time.”

“Well, if that’s the case, I have noticed that staff members do have time. In fact, they seem more interested in gossiping than actually performing duties.”

“So talk to them.”

“That’s not my job, Raymond. You’re the manager.”

“What *is* your job?”

“Excuse me?”

“Do you have a job here? Dr. Kalbfleisch hasn’t told me to put you on payroll.”

Jeff shouts down from the kitchen. “Boss, some guy called Arthur wants to talk to you. He says you know him.”

Raymond gets up and steps past Mrs. Bumby. “Excuse me.”

Arthur, pulling on his goatee, stands inside the front doors by the Chicken Deal-icious sign. “Good day, Raymond.”

“Do you want to sit down?”

“Perhaps that would be best.”

They sit at a table in Beth’s section. Raymond knows that she will ignore them because she’s talking with the health inspector. She hurries over to the salad bar to get him more baby corns.

“Raymond,” Arthur begins, “what are your intentions where my sister is concerned?”

“I don’t have any.”

“Then why, if you don’t mind my asking, are you sending her gifts?”

“I miss her.” Arthur is another one of those people who can make Raymond feel insignificant. Even though Raymond knows that Arthur is a failed investment dealer who put Easy-Off on his pimple, he still feels intimidated by him.

"That's all very well," Arthur says. "But you upset her, you understand. She's going through a difficult time right now. I don't think that your gifts are helping her."

"Well I'm not sending any more."

"Really?"

"Really."

"Oh, well I'm glad to hear it. I think you'll find it's for the best. I think you both need time to yourselves."

"Yes." Raymond can see that Arthur expected a fight, which explains why he came to a public place to talk. If he'd come to the apartment, Raymond might have strangled him.

"It's awkward for her, you understand, because she doesn't want to get the police involved. She's hoping that this is something we can settle amicably."

Mrs. Bumby picks up the bar phone and wipes the receiver with a Kleenex.

"It's settled," Raymond says. "I'm not sending her anything else."

"Or calling her? Or stalking her?"

"Right." He suspects that Mrs. Bumby is calling Dr. Kalbfleisch. He suspects that soon he will be out of a job.

Arthur pulls on his goatee. "Well, I'll tell Mara not to worry then."

"Good idea." Mrs. Bumby is becoming very agitated on the phone. Her head bobs and her bosoms quake. Raymond stands. "I've got work to do, Arthur."

"Of course. I must be on my way." Raymond knows that he has nowhere to go, that he will sit in a café and offer financial advice to anyone who will listen.

"Give my regards to Mara," Raymond says.

"Of course."

Mrs. Bumby lowers her voice as Raymond passes the bar on his way to the kitchen. Seymour's at the take-out counter telling Bruce and Bubba about Irish farming practices. "Weasels and dogs are not natural predators," he explains. "So the farmers put a pair of them into a burlap sack. Because they're forced on one another, with no hope of escape, they fight. Usually the dogs win and kill the weasels. Once out of the sack the dogs never forget about being trapped with the weasels. So they hate them, hunt and kill them. Animals they had no dispute with before man forced them into a confined space. Any creature will fight another creature in a confined space."

Raymond thinks about being confined in Gloria's uterus with Dwayne. Punching and kicking him, learning to hate him.

"That is inhumane," Bruce comments.

Bubba blows his nose on a napkin. "Why'd they have to kill the weasels?"

"They destroy the crops," Seymour says. "A farmer has to guard his crops."

"Wow."

Raymond's office smells of Mrs. Bumby's perfume. He can see that she's still on the bar phone because the line is illuminated. In the confined space of the restaurant, he wants to kill this woman. He leans back in his chair and looks at Burt. He hasn't drunk any of the water and still isn't moving. Raymond kneels beside him. "What's up, big guy?" He rubs his belly, expecting Burt to wake and look at him, roll over on to his back exposing more belly for rubbing. But he doesn't. He lies still. Raymond presses his ear against Burt's chest. He waits for a heartbeat, some rib expansion, anything. He cradles Burt's head in his hands and tries to lift his eyelids with his thumbs. He shakes him, gently at first but then more violently. When he gets no response Raymond starts to scream. He has never screamed before. The sensation is unfamiliar to him; a complete loss of control. He wants to shatter the walls with his screams, cave in the roof, crack open the floor. He wants it to end.

eighteen

Raymond floats on his back in the pool. He is not alone today. Two elderly women sit on deck chairs, staring at him while they discuss their daughters' weddings. "He was kissing all the bridesmaids," one of them complains. "I told him he was making a fool of himself." Raymond rolls over and dives below the surface, thinking about the woman he saw kissing the dead cat at Old Friends Pet Crematorium. She was crying. The man behind the counter suggested that she meet with his grief counsellor. The man seemed peculiar to Raymond. While he talked he folded his right ear with his fingers and tugged on it as though he were trying to pull it off. But he was pleasant and didn't argue when Raymond explained that he didn't want a chapel service or a casket or a headstone, that he just wanted Burt burned and put in a tin. The lady with the cat did want a chapel service and a casket and a headstone. She also agreed to meet the grief counsellor.

Raymond is supposed to pick up the ashes tomorrow afternoon. He plans to keep them with his mother's.

He has pinned the new key to his apartment inside his swimming trunks. He can feel its sharp edges while he swims. He's been avoiding his apartment because Burt isn't there, and because Dwayne's head keeps appearing on the TV screen.

He tries to think about other things: Seymour shitting blood. He told Raymond he will have to go to the hospital for tests. Doctors will insert instruments up his rectum. "A microscope," he explained, "so they can see what's going on."

"Wow," Bubba remarked.

But Seymour's lucky, Raymond thinks. Even if he is shitting blood. Because he doesn't love any human or animal. His home is always empty except for his VCR and movie star biographies. No one can hurt him by hurting an animal or a human he loves. Loving means you have no control, because you can't control this other being. You worry about it, you fear for it, but there's nothing you can do. Much better to be loveless. Much better to read about Vivien Leigh and eat yourself to death. He breaks the surface of the water again.

"She wants it to be traditional," one of the deck-chair women explains. "I told her that's going to cost more. What with the train and everything. I told her a modern look would be better."

"No veil?"

"Why not a nice hat? You know, a little pillbox. Those are cute. I told her, forget traditional."

Raymond's new lock was expensive. And it's difficult to open even with the key. But Raymond felt that he needed a difficult lock. A lock that would outsmart his brother.

This afternoon he saw a little boy cradling in his arms the puppy Raymond nearly ran over. The little boy held it with great care. His upper body curved around the puppy, shielding it. While crossing the street the boy watched for cars. Raymond, in his car, stopped, halting traffic. The boy, completely absorbed in protecting his puppy, seemed not to hear the horns. He had a beatific expression. Raymond suspected that he himself had worn such an expression while holding his puppy, Buster; before he'd kicked him. Before he'd kicked him, Buster had trusted, adored and loved him. And it had been easy for Raymond to reciprocate this love. He and Buster had a bond, a knowledge of each other, that Raymond has never shared with a human. Except with his twin, before he met him.

Now Raymond would be afraid to have a puppy, love a puppy. He couldn't do it any more. There would be too many dangers. While watching the boy, he'd envied the emotions he was feeling. But at the same time he knew that he could never feel them again. Every emotion he feels now is edged with fear. Even when he thinks about Mara, he feels fear. Not just because of what Dwayne might do to her but because of what she might do to him, Raymond. She could destroy him. He feels that fragile. One hostile look from her and he would crumble. He couldn't take it. He must solve the Dwayne problem first. Then he can return to her a hero, strengthened by his actions. He called Gloria. She said Dwayne usually goes to the sports bar on Friday night for the karaoke. After his swim, when he is calmer, Raymond plans to go there.

"Diets don't work," one of the deck-chair women insists. "I told her, forget dieting. Buy a dress that fits. I'm not spending six months with her cranky because she can't get into her wedding dress."

Raymond can't imagine getting married again, can't imagine believing that he could love and cherish a person until death did them part again. Beth announced today that she is engaged to the health inspector. Nobody believed her, but she insisted it was true. The health inspector just hasn't found the right ring yet, she said. Raymond intends to talk to her, like a brother. He wants to caution her.

He wishes he could forget the dream; the blood, the gore. He was wearing spiked shoes and stamping on Dwayne's face. Only it looked like his own face. He wasn't sure whose face it was. He felt the skull fracture and the brain turn to pulp. He felt blood seeping through the seams of his spiked shoes. Suddenly he noticed that the hair tangled in the spikes was grey. Dwayne's hair wasn't grey, nor was his own. The face he was stamping on belonged to someone with grey hair who looked like Dwayne and himself. When he realized that the head belonged to his biological father, he looked up and saw Dwayne laughing at him. He was swinging from a tree, like Mara's naked neighbour. Raymond ran after him, trying to pull him down from the rope, but he couldn't catch him. Meanwhile his biological father was dead. He had killed him: a man he didn't even know, didn't even hate. This realization left him feeling completely spineless. His knees buckled and he fell to the ground. One of his hands landed on the pudding of his father's brains. Still swinging from the tree, Dwayne laughed.

He doesn't look at the TV. He changes, grabs his keys and leaves. Outside, the man in the baseball cap, sitting cross-legged with his shirt unbuttoned to his navel, greets him, "Good evening to you, sir." Raymond nods. The man nods back. "So kind of you, sir. God bless you. Happy holidays to you and your family."

❖

In the sports bar Dwayne is gripping a microphone and singing, "It's so easy, it's so easy." People sitting at the tables chime in, "It's so easy, it's so easy." Raymond gets a beer from the bar and sits down in a dark corner on a chair that's shaped like a baseball glove. He observes that the people at the tables are enjoying Dwayne's performance. Many of the women smile and sing along, clapping their hands. Raymond can't understand how they can be entertained by a man who kills dogs and bunnies. He tries to see what they see in Dwayne. They seem to like it when he swivels his pelvis and jerks one knee.

"Way to go, Elvis!" a man shouts.

Raymond doesn't think that Dwayne sings very well. He reminds him of himself when he sings in the car. He would never sing in public. Dwayne winks at some of the ladies who giggle.

It bothers Raymond that these people don't know who his brother really is. He suspects that if he told them that his brother kills bunnies and dogs, they wouldn't believe him. They would call him a liar and chase him out of the sports bar. That people can be fooled so easily unsettles Raymond. He has never felt that he could fool anybody, has always felt that people could see right through him. For this reason he has never pretended to be anyone but himself. Watching his brother, he feels that he should have pretended to be someone else. Because his brother is having a good time. His brother plays many parts and nobody cares. They applaud him. He remembers Tory saying that her friend reported that Dwayne was amazing in bed. Raymond feels certain that no one has ever described himself as amazing in bed.

Dwayne falls to his knees, still clutching the microphone. He winces during a high note. Raymond goes to the bar for another beer. The bartender is watching wrestling on a TV bolted to the wall above the trophies. "Are you Julio?" Raymond asks.

"Am I who?"

"Julio."

The bartender shakes his head as he hands Raymond his beer. "Does Julio work here?" Raymond persists.

"Never heard of him," the bartender says, looking back at the TV.

Raymond returns to his baseball-glove chair. Dwayne has stopped singing and is joining a group of people at a table. The man who shouted "Way to go, Elvis!" pats him on the back. A woman caresses the back of his neck with her hand. Dwayne says something and they all laugh. Raymond hates him. He rubs his forehead with his hand, trying to figure out what to do. He doesn't want to cause a scene. But if he doesn't confront Dwayne now about Burt, he may not get another chance. He wants to settle this. He wants his brother to admit that he's a murderer. He wants his brother to repent.

A woman wearing a miniskirt and high-heeled boots that go above her knees is singing about honesty being such a lonely word. People pay less attention to her than they did to Dwayne. After finishing his beer Raymond goes over to Dwayne's table and waits to be noticed. The man who said "Way to go, Elvis!" sees him first. "What the fuck . . . ?" he mutters. The people at the table, and some of the people at other tables, stare at Raymond and Dwayne. Some of them swear, some of them gasp.

"Howdy, brother," Dwayne says.

"What did you do to my dog?"

Dwayne squints. "Your what?"

"My dog. You poisoned him."

Dwayne gestures towards Raymond. "Folks, meet my identical twin."

"Far out," the Elvis man says.

Dwayne grips Raymond's arm. "We've been reunited after being separated at birth." Raymond tries to shake Dwayne off but he can't. "We're just getting reacquainted."

"How wonderful for you," the woman who caressed Dwayne's neck remarks.

"It's just like a movie," a bug-eyed woman comments.

"What did you do to my dog?" Raymond repeats.

"Nothing. I haven't seen your dog."

"You got the key from the super and took him out."

Dwayne appears baffled, as though he has no idea what Raymond is talking about.

"You fed him human food," Raymond persists. Now it seems to him that everybody in the bar is watching them. The woman in the high boots has stopped singing even though the music is still playing.

"Calm down, Raymond," Dwayne says.

"You fed him dark chocolate and it made him sick."

Dwayne looks around at the people at his table. "Sometimes he gets a little confused."

"I am not confused. You killed my dog."

"Don't get psycho on me, Ray."

"You fucker, you killed my dog."

"Take it easy now," the Elvis man cautions. Raymond sees the bartender coming out from behind the bar. He's very large.

Dwayne releases Raymond's arm. "I didn't touch your dog."

"You did too, you took him out and you poisoned him. *My* dog." Raymond can't believe that he's having no effect, that no one here believes him. He feels immobilized, as though wrapped in duct tape.

"Okay, pal," the bartender says. "The man said he didn't touch your dog."

"He's lying. He's a liar. All he does is lie."

The bartender takes his arm. "I think maybe you should go outside and cool off. We don't like fighting in here."

Raymond tries to kick Dwayne, but he stubs his toe on a chair leg. "There is no Julio," he shouts. The bartender starts to pull him towards the door. Limping, Raymond looks around and sees that everyone is staring at him as though he is insane. He can't believe this, when it is his brother who is insane. "He's crazy," he insists.

"Yeah, well, we all get a little crazy sometimes," the bartender offers, still firmly pulling him towards the door. Raymond knows that he has no choice but to surrender. Before stepping outside he looks over his shoulder at Dwayne. He's talking to the people at his table again — as though Raymond had never been there.

The bartender gives his shoulder one last shove. "Go home now, buddy. Sleep it off."

There's nowhere to go. He could wait here, in his car in the parking lot. He could wait for Dwayne to come out. Then what? More tape seems to be binding his arms to his sides. He feels completely stuck. He thinks of flies stuck on flypaper. They never give up the struggle. Even at the end, when they are coated in glue, they twitch a leg or a wing in defiance. How pointless.

The door of the sports bar flings open and a woman storms out, followed by a man. "You motherfucker!" she shouts.

"Where do you think you're going?" the man demands.

"None of your fucking business." She hurries down the street but the man chases her. Listening to their shouts recede, Raymond wonders if the man will kill the woman and if it matters, if anyone will notice. There was a time when he would have been concerned. He would have followed the man and woman and made sure that nobody got hurt. Now he doesn't care. Maybe the woman deserves to die. Or maybe she'll kill the man. She'll pull out a hairpin and jab his throat. Maybe they'll kill each other and stop making so much noise. Raymond would like that. He would like some quiet now, some silence. The bass beat pounding from the speakers in the sports bar reverberates outside the building. Raymond can feel it resonating through his tires into his body. It's making him quake. He must get away from here.

❖

He parks down the street from Mara's. It relieves him to see that there is still no "Sold" sticker on her For Sale sign. The blue light flickering behind her curtains indicates that the TV is on. At least she's home. Safe. Since Dwayne is at the sports bar. Raymond can't stay here all night though, he realizes that. He should probably get something to eat because he hasn't eaten all day. Although it sickens him that he can even think about food when his dog has been killed. He shouldn't be hungry.

At Chicken Villa he looks for Claire. He can't see her. He sits down anyway, thinking that when he sees her he'll move to her section. He studies the menu, looking for something other than chicken. He decides to try the Sooper-Dooper Club without the chicken. A waitress with dark fuzz on her upper lip approaches him. "What can I get you?"

"Is Claire working tonight?"

"She doesn't work here any more."

"Really? Since when?"

"I don't know. Last week." The waitress pulls out her bill pad.

"Why did she leave?"

"Her boyfriend didn't want her working nights, and all the day shifts were taken."

"Why didn't he want her working nights?"

"He wants her home, I guess."

"To cook dinner?"

"Something like that. She's not complaining. He makes good money." She glances over her shoulder at a customer who is waving a coffee cup at her. She looks back at Raymond. "Are you ready to order?"

"Ahh . . . could I have the Sooper-Dooper without the chicken?"

"There's not much to it besides chicken."

"That's okay. Maybe they could give me extra cheese."

She scribbles on her bill pad. "Okay, I'll ask. Would you like something to drink with that?"

"A scotch, please. On the rocks."

"Sure."

What's happened to Claire? Raymond imagines her gagged and bound in her kitchen, naked except for an apron. He sees her fiancé coming home and ordering her to cook his dinner. He unties her and pulls out the gag. She coughs as she reaches into the fridge for pork chops. As she bends down to pull out the frying pan, her fiancé grabs her buttocks.

"Here you go," the moustached waitress says, setting his scotch on the table.

Raymond clears his throat. "Do you think if there were day shifts available, she'd take them?"

"I don't know. I mean, who wants to work in a *chicken* restaurant?"

"Not this one. Another one."

"Another one?"

"Yeah. I manage another chicken restaurant."

He notices that the waitress is looking at him differently, as though he is no longer respectable; as though he is luring unsuspecting waitresses into his chicken restaurant so that he can sexually harass them. "I wouldn't know," she says.

Raymond considers writing a note to Claire and asking the moustached waitress to give it to her. In the note he could offer her a job. While drinking his scotch, he writes a letter to her on the back of his placemat: *Dear Claire, You may not remember me although I am one of your regular customers. I understand that you would prefer to work days than nights. I am manager of a chicken restaurant and am looking for a day waitress. If this interests you at all, please call.*

He leaves his name and the Chez Simon number, knowing that if he leaves his home number she'll think that he's trying to pick her up. The problem is he senses that the moustached waitress doesn't trust him and may not deliver the letter. He'll have to leave her a big tip.

A hulk of a man sits at the table in front of Raymond with a woman wearing a hairstyle that makes her resemble a poodle. "I got two broken ribs," the man tells her. "Not fractured. *Broken.* And nerve damage."

"Who said?"

"At the hospital. It's on the X-rays."

The woman pulls out a comb and fluffs up her hair. "So, whose fault is that?"

"It's not my fucking fault."

"Oh so it's supposed to be my fault?"

The man picks up a menu. "He's *your* friend."

"I didn't pick a fight with him." She snatches her purse and heads for the ladies' room. The man watches her before his eyes settle on Raymond. Raymond stares back at him, expecting the man to look away, to realize that it's rude to stare. But the man doesn't look away. His eyes lock with Raymond's. Only he doesn't seem to be looking at Raymond. He's staring at him but not seeing him. Raymond feels invisible, inconsequential.

Outside in the parking lot, before he came in, he had a waking dream. He was trapped in a stone tower. He tried to scale the walls but they were coated with slime and he couldn't get a grip on them. Below him, he could hear water lapping and he knew that swimming in it was a huge lizard intent on killing him. In seconds the dream ended, splintering into the points of light Raymond knew signalled an oncoming migraine. Sitting in Chicken Villa he has another waking dream. He sees index cards that structure his life. They keep order, calming him. He refers to them before initiating any thought or action. The index cards determine who he is. Suddenly a gust of wind blows them into chaos. Raymond is lost without the cards. The points of light come back, fuzzier, more grainy.

The poodle woman returns to the table. "I'll sue the bastard," the hulking man announces.

"Go ahead," she responds.

"Who does he think he is, that's what I want to know."

Raymond drinks more scotch, pondering the index-card waking dream.

It bothers him that he felt he needed the cards, that he could not live without them. He shouldn't need them. He shouldn't need order. Order pens him in, traps him — in the tower with the lizard below.

The waitress brings him his sandwich. "He gave you extra bacon."

"Thanks," he says although he asked for extra cheese. He shouldn't be having waking dreams. He hasn't had them since he was a child. When he was a child he could fly in the waking dreams, and eat the clouds. They tasted musty.

The waitress nods at his glass. "Do you want another one?"

"No thanks. But do you think you could give this to Claire?" He holds the folded placemat out to the waitress who stares at it as though he's spit on it.

"Who do I say it's from?" she asks.

"Just a customer. The letter will explain itself."

She takes it and stuffs it in her back pocket. "Okay, well, I can't promise anything. I don't know if I'm going to see her."

"Well if you do, I'd really appreciate it."

"Enjoy your meal."

The hulking man has dropped his head to the table, resting it on his forearms. Only now does it occur to Raymond that the man resembles Mara's father who drank himself to death. Mara watched him die. The whites of his eyes turned yellow and his skin turned purple. Pus leaked from his mouth. When she touched his arm it broke the skin. She'd never liked her father but she tried to care about him in the end. She didn't though. She found him repulsive. Raymond wonders if Gord will kill himself with alcohol. And if he'll feel guilty for not being there to watch him die. He knows he will. He will always feel guilt. Why, when his brother does not? Why is he the one who fears repercussions? Why does he care when nobody else does? Nobody cares if he loses his index cards, so why does he cling to them? Why does he worry about the effect he has on people when he has no effect? The hulking man looked right through him. Mrs. Bumby thinks he's an irritant. His staff ignore him. His ex-wife doesn't want him around. So why does he care? He should stop caring. He should throw away his index cards.

❖

He stops at the all-night supermarket to pick up milk and Shreddies. Out of habit he walks to the pet food section. It's only when he's reaching for the cans that he remembers that Burt is dead. The old woman with dyed hair is there again. She thrusts a can of cat food at him. "Is this any good? Gourmet Viddles?"

"I don't know."

"It's fifty-nine cents more than this one." She shows him another can. "But this one is gourmet. What's gourmet about it?"

Raymond starts to move away. "I don't know."

"Do you think my kitty will know the difference?" Raymond can't get away. She's chasing him. "I don't see how kitties can know the difference. What's gourmet?"

"Compare the ingredients," Raymond suggests, stopping at the checkout counter.

"Could you do that for me? I don't have my glasses."

"No."

She doesn't seem to hear him. She pushes the cans at him, but he doesn't put down his Shreddies or his milk. "No," he repeats.

"Think my kitty will know the difference?"

"I don't know and I don't care," Raymond says loudly. People waiting to cash out stare at him. They don't smile, they don't frown. They just stare. The old woman appears stunned. Her mouth gapes as she continues to hold the cans out to him. "No," Raymond says. "No." In an instant, if he doesn't get out of here, he knows that he will relent and check the ingredients for her. He will waste his time for her. He will be of service and it will mean nothing. Because she doesn't care. He could be any stupid fuck she can snare at the supermarket. It won't mean that he's a better person. It will mean that he's a stupid fuck. He puts down the Shreddies and the milk and leaves the supermarket. He gets in the car, locks the door and sits very still. He tries to think of someone who owns a garage. A garage he could drive into, with a door that would slide shut behind him. A garage he could seal with tape to prevent the exhaust fumes from escaping. He can't think of anyone with a garage. He can't think of anyone.

nineteen

"You upset Mrs. Bumby, Raymond."

"I'm sorry."

Dr. Kalbfleisch stirs five teaspoons of sugar into his coffee. He's got sleep incrustations in the corners of his eyes. And he smells. "She thinks you don't like her."

"I don't dislike her, sir. But I've always reported to you when there's been a problem." Raymond feels groggy. He took two of Mara's sleeping pills last night because he couldn't sleep, even though he threw a blanket over the TV. He woke several times thinking he saw Dwayne sitting on the end of the bed, staring at him.

Dr. Kalbfleisch sucks on his dentures. "You told her to clean the toilets."

"I didn't tell her anything. I said she was welcome to clean them if she wished."

"That's not funny, Raymond."

"Well, honestly, sir, I didn't know what else to suggest. I cleaned the toilets myself after your last visit. We all have to put a hand in." He also dreamed about Gloria's budgies. They were pecking at his head.

"She's new to the business," Dr. Kalbfleisch points out.

"I understand."

"She wants what's best for the restaurant. Maybe she's a little too enthusiastic."

"Well I'm all for enthusiasm, but we simply don't have enough staff to keep the place exceptionally clean."

Dr. Kalbfleisch waves his hand indicating that Raymond need not explain further. He takes out his handkerchief and wipes his nose. "I wanted you two to like each other."

"I don't dislike her, sir. I don't know her very well."

"She's a good woman. She has a lot of energy." This is the second time that Dr. Kalbfleisch has described Mrs. Bumby in this manner. Raymond suspects that he is repeating this description in the hopes of convincing himself that it is true. Dr. Kalbfleisch puts his handkerchief back into his pocket. "She wants what's best for me. When you get old, Raymond, you need people looking out for you."

"Well we all want what's best for you, sir. We just can't keep the place exceptionally clean without hiring a cleaning staff."

Dr. Kalbfleisch holds his hands over his ears. "Don't start with the cleaning staff, Raymond."

Raymond worries that he is becoming addicted to Mara's sleeping pills. The bottle is almost empty.

"She keeps setting off the alarm system," Dr. Kalbfleisch says.

"What alarm system?"

"In the house. The police show up. They think she's crazy."

"Doesn't she know how to decode it?"

Dr. Kalbfleisch shrugs. "It's complicated."

How complicated can it be? Raymond wonders. How stupid can this woman be? And how can Dr. Kalbfleisch not see this?

"Any news on the tests?" Raymond asks.

"Nothing showed up. They want to do more tests." Raymond remembers this from when his mother became ill. She'd go for tests, the results would be inconclusive, so she'd go for more tests.

"Do you *feel* sick, sir?"

"I'm tired."

"Well, I think that's to be expected. After the death of a loved one."

"Mrs. Bumby is worried about my heart. After what happened to Ava, who can blame her. She says you can't be too careful."

There is no doubt in Raymond's mind that Mrs. Bumby wants Dr. Kalbfleisch to have a heart condition so that she can frighten him to death and inherit his worldly goods. He clears his throat. "Are you short of breath at all, sir?"

"Climbing stairs isn't so easy any more."

"If you don't mind my saying so, you seemed fine before your wife's death. Do you think you might be feeling weak because you miss her?"

Dr. Kalbfleisch grimaces at some barbecue sauce spilled on the floor. "She jumped from a moving train, Raymond. To save her baby. There were gunmen but it was night and they didn't see her. She crawled to a village. Her legs were frozen. She was in hospital for weeks. She lost her toes."

Raymond isn't certain if Dr. Kalbfleisch is referring to Mrs. Kalbfleisch or to Mrs. Bumby. He decides he must be talking about Mrs. Kalbfleisch because she was the one who spent time in the camps during the war. He tries to picture feet without toes. "Was the baby alright?"

"The baby died. Pneumonia."

"I'm sorry."

Dr. Kalbfleisch shakes his head. "Too much suffering for one person. You can only take so much."

Bubba signals "phone" to Raymond from the kitchen. "Excuse me, sir," Raymond says.

It's the peculiar man from Old Friends Pet Crematorium informing him that Burt's ashes are ready. "Thank you," Raymond tells him. "I'll come by today."

"No rush," the man assures him.

Raymond hangs up, trying to figure out what to do about Dr. Kalbfleisch. What to say to him. What to say about Mrs. Kalbfleisch jumping from the moving train to save her baby, then losing her toes. He finds it hard to believe, having met her. How could someone who has endured such hardship complain about residue on ketchup bottles? Bubba stares at him, shoving his hand into his pants pocket to adjust the crotch of his underwear. "Can't you find something to do?" Raymond asks.

"Beth's marrying the health inspector."

"I heard."

"He's a prick."

"I know."

"Can't you stop her?"

"No."

"Can't you try?"

❖

Raymond invites Beth to have a coffee with him in his office. He brings down an extra chair and even offers her pie, but she refuses.

"What's this all about?" she demands.

"Nothing. I'm just concerned."

"About what?"

"Don't you think you might be rushing things a little with the health inspector?"

"Don't be a toad."

"Seriously. I mean, you hardly know the guy."

"Ever heard of love at first sight?"

"You hated him at first sight."

"Love, hate. Same thing."

Raymond wonders if this is true. He stares at the *Star Trek* poster. William Shatner doesn't look as though he's wearing a toupee. His hair looks real.

"I didn't tell him you went soft on me," Beth says, "if that's what's bugging you. I didn't tell him nothing about us."

"That's not my concern," he insists, although it is one of them. "We just . . . all of us, think you might be rushing into this. I mean, you said yourself you hate all that wedding crap. You said it was all bullshit."

"That was before. Now I see it different. Like I don't want to grow old alone. That's what happens. You get old and people think there's something wrong with you because you're not married. It's okay when you're younger but later on it's like you're a reject. I mean, look at you, Raymond. Let's face it, you're a reject."

Raymond doesn't know how to respond to this, doesn't know if he should defend himself.

"Anyways," she adds, "I've been offered a job at Chicken Villa. The only problem is they want me to work nights."

"Please don't go," Raymond says, startled to hear himself begging.

"It's too weird here now, what with everybody knowing what's going on."

"Nobody knows what's going on. We're just worried about you."

"Yeah, right. The point is it's nobody's business but my own. And I don't like how, ever since that night, you've been treating me like a second-class citizen."

"I've been trying not to."

"And I don't like that bitch snooping around. It's bad enough with just Kalbfleisch. She told me yesterday that she's going to organize his life. She's going to get him a daytimer and mark down exactly what he should do and when. It's like she's going to tell him when to take a dump."

Raymond scratches behind his ear. "Well he hasn't married her yet. Maybe he'll change his mind."

"People don't change their minds about stuff like that. It's like they'd rather marry the person than admit that they've made a mistake."

"Is that why you're marrying the health inspector?"

She stands. "Like I said, that's none of your business. I suggest you worry about your own problems. And tell Bubba to quit staring at me. It makes me sick the way he stares."

"Are you really leaving then?"

"Let's just say if you people don't lay off me, I'm outta here."

"Nobody will bother you."

She points at him. "And you keep that bitch off me or I'm going to knock her block off."

"Of course," Raymond says, although he would like to see Beth knock Mrs. Bumby's block off.

After she leaves, he stays at his desk, listening to the washer thumping in the laundry room. It occurs to him that if Beth leaves, he could hire Claire. Maybe it would be good if Beth left. Claire would be wonderful to have around. Bubba would go crazy over her and forget about Beth. It would be a fresh start for all of them. He warns himself not to become too hopeful about Claire phoning him. He doesn't even know if the moustached waitress delivered his letter. He looks down at his adding machine and starts to punch in the day's figures. It bothers him that he is missing Belinda again; not the senile, incontinent woman she had become but the kind and decent woman she was before. She used to bring jelly doughnuts home. The two of them would sit at the kitchen table doing crosswords while eating the doughnuts and drinking tea. Jelly would drip on to the crosswords but they didn't care. They were together, working together. They were a team.

Bubba knocks on his door, even though it's open. "Did you talk to her?"

"Yeah." She used to make him stand straight by putting a broom handle across his back and telling him to hook his arms around it. He didn't mind.

He had her attention. Sometimes he would slouch on purpose to get her attention. Gloria told Raymond that Dwayne did things like killing bunnies to get attention. Raymond didn't believe her.

Bubba pushes a stick of gum into his mouth. "So . . . ?"

"Bubba, I can't tell her what to do. It's her life."

"Did you tell her what a prick he is?"

"She doesn't think he's a prick."

"She just wants to ride in his car and live in his house."

"Well, that's her prerogative."

Bubba turns away and rests his forehead against the doorjamb. He begins to make squeaking sounds. It takes Raymond a moment to realize that he's crying.

"Come on now, Bubba," he says. "There'll be other waitresses."

"Not like Beth," Bubba sputters.

"I'm thinking of hiring one from Chicken Villa. She's pretty and very nice. You'll like her."

Bubba looks at Raymond as though he has just blasphemed. "I *love* Beth," he emphasizes.

There's that *love* word again, Raymond thinks. That word people use for lack of another. That word people use as a weapon, or a line of defence. A word that justifies bad behaviour, or simply existence.

"Maybe you should tell her that," Raymond suggests.

"You think so?"

"I don't know." He remembers Beth ordering him to tell Bubba to stop staring at her because it makes her sick. He's afraid to tell Bubba this. He's afraid he'll fall apart, in his office, and he'll be short a line cook. "I'm not good at the personal stuff, Bubba. All I know is that she seems pretty determined to marry this guy."

Bubba thumps his head against the doorjamb, then turns to Raymond. He's waiting for something: advice, encouragement. He wants Raymond to tell him what to do. A week ago Raymond would have complied, tried to help him out, or at least to offer hope. But not any more. He's tired. He has to pick up Burt's ashes. "I gotta go," he says.

❖

Mara's mother killed herself when Mara was two. Mara and her sister went to live with their grandparents. She once told Raymond that she had a faint memory of her mother sitting on the floor with a pool of blood between her legs. That's all she remembers. When she was ten she insisted that her grandparents tell her exactly what had happened to her mother. Reluctantly, her grandmother explained that her mother had "laid her head down on a pillow and turned on the gas." Years later, before he died, Mara's grandfather gave her her mother's suicide note which was addressed to her father. It read, *I am doing this so that you will be haunted for the rest of your life for what you did to the girls.* Mara has never understood what her father did to her or her sister. She remembers no sexual abuse, and her sister refuses to talk about it. If Dwayne was sexually abused, how can he speak of it so easily? How can he not care that everyone knows? Wouldn't he be ashamed? Wouldn't he want to forget about it? Put it behind him? Mara's sister has a drinking problem and sleeps with many different men. She frightens Raymond because she is completely out of control. Dwayne is in control.

At Old Friends Pet Crematorium the peculiar man hands Raymond the tin containing Burt's ashes. While he waits for Raymond to get out his credit card, he folds his right ear in his fingers and tugs at it. "Nice day out?" he asks.

"Very." Raymond hands him the card.

"Makes a nice change."

Even if he was sexually abused, does that justify his actions? Does being wronged justify doing it?

"Would you care to look at some urns?" the man asks, still gripping his ear.

"No thanks. No urn." Raymond signs the credit card receipt. As he leaves he hears the man say, "Enjoy the day now."

❖

When he comes in the back door of the restaurant, Jeff grabs his arm and pulls him behind the broiler. "There's a girl out front who says you offered her a job. I must warn you, Captain, our Beth is not happy about it."

"How long has she been here?"

"Twenty minutes or so. And Mrs. Bumby is about."

"Where?"

"Last I saw she was inspecting those shelving units you assured the health inspector you would remove."

Raymond looks around. "I don't see her."

"She has a way of creeping up on you."

Beth spots Raymond and strides towards him. "What's with the bimbo you've offered a job?"

"Nothing's definite. You said you were leaving so I thought I'd interview some people."

"Bullshit. She showed me your letter."

"What letter?" Bubba asks.

"He wrote this little slut a letter begging her to come and work here."

"You said you were leaving," Raymond reminds her.

"Leaving?" Bubba asks.

"I didn't say nothing definite."

Bubba looks at Raymond. "She didn't say nothing definite."

"She isn't even a natural blonde," Beth says. "When you stuff her, take a look at her bush. I bet you it's black."

Mrs. Bumby appears from downstairs. "What's going on here?"

Beth turns on her. "None of your business, you stupid cunt." Mrs. Bumby's mouth opens and closes several times. Beth takes off her apron and throws it on the floor. "I've had it with this hole."

"Don't go," Bubba pleads.

"Quit staring at me," Beth snaps. "It makes me sick the way you stare at me. Like a dog that wants food." Bubba appears to shrink.

Raymond holds up his hands. "Alright, calm down, everyone. I'm sure we can work this out."

Beth starts downstairs. "There's nothing to work out. I'm out of here."

Jeff nods at the order shelf. "She's got dinners up."

"That's alright," Raymond says. "I'll take them out."

Bubba adjusts the crotch of his underwear. "Aren't you going to stop her?"

Raymond picks up the orders. "I can't."

Fortunately the lunch rush is over. The dining room is empty except for Beth's table and Seymour who is informing Bruce that Peter Sellers had an affair with Liza Minnelli. "She's a smoker, you know," he adds. "A friend of mine sat beside her in an airport. Apparently she reeked of cigarettes."

Raymond sets the plates down in front of Beth's customers who are teenaged girls. "I'm marrying a tall guy," one of them insists. "I hate short guys."

"Enjoy your meal," Raymond says.

Claire is sitting close to the entrance, near the weeping fig in the planter. Raymond offers her his hand. "Hi, I'm Raymond, the manager."

She doesn't take his hand but holds up his letter. "Is this legit?"

"Yes. We need a waitress. As soon as possible."

"Oh." She puts his letter on the table. He wishes she'd fold it up and put it away. It's too exposed on the table. He's too exposed.

"Do you think you could start right away?" he asks.

"You mean now?"

"Sure. It's slow. You'll get a chance to know the place." Her thumbnail is blue. It looks as though it got caught in a door, or stepped on.

"I have to be home by five-thirty." She keeps twisting a lock of her hair in her fingers. His mother used to do this.

"That's fine." She looks different to him now, outside of Chicken Villa. She no longer has the glow of a waitress anticipating a tip. Raymond wonders if her hair *is* dyed. "So," he says, "let's find you a uniform. Actually, you're supposed to provide the slacks. Dark slacks, preferably black. No jeans."

"Sure."

As they walk through the kitchen he feels Bubba and Jeff watching them. "Has Beth left yet?" he asks, attempting to sound unconcerned.

"Affirmative, Captain."

In the locker room he searches for a clean white shirt and apron while Claire continues to twist her hair. He has noticed that she isn't wearing a bra and worries that her nipples will show through a white blouse. "So you usually have just two waiters on?" she asks.

"Sometimes three. On show nights we have three. There's some theatres around here."

She nods, then stares at the floor. She seems very tired. He sees no signs of her former bubbly self. He's afraid that hiring her was a mistake. She will be despondent and needy, traumatized by her domestic life. He hands her a shirt and apron. "Here you go. Come upstairs when you're ready."

Mrs. Bumby is waiting for him in his office, holding the tin containing Burt's ashes. "What is this?"

"My dog's ashes."

"The dog that was here yesterday?"

"Yes. He died." He takes the tin from her and puts it on the desk.

"I'm sorry," she offers.

"That's alright."

"Am I to understand that we have seen the last of Beth?"

"Yes."

"This new girl, is she experienced?"

"Yes."

She takes her handbag off the desk. "I just wish you could find someone with manners."

"The new girl has some."

"I'm glad to hear it."

"I've got to show her the ropes," he says, stepping past her. He knows that she wants to say more but he doesn't want to listen.

Upstairs, Bubba avoids him by going into the savoury freezer. Jeff ignores him by putting his headset on while preparing wings for Wing Night. Even Sharif seems unusually preoccupied. Bruce is on the bar phone with his lover again. "They have violent and erotic sex," he explains, "and are empowered afterwards."

If he had friends, Raymond realizes, they would be the staff of this restaurant.

Her nipples do show through the shirt but he pretends not to notice. Her breasts don't excite him any more. They embarrass him. She embarrasses him. She was his fantasy, his dirty magazine under the bed. He thinks of Gloria peering at Dwayne's porno magazines. "He don't even hide them like normal people," she said.

Normal people.

He tries to introduce Claire to the kitchen staff but they express no interest. Bubba has lost his contact lens again and is crawling around on the floor. Claire has no difficulty adapting to the cash register or their system for calling in orders, although she does point out that Chicken Villa is computerized. "Everything goes a lot faster," she tells him.

Raymond can't understand how he could have desired this person.

What he saw in her. He must have seen what he wanted to see, what he needed to see. He remembers the conversation he overheard in the bar with Tory about impressionist painting. "What the painter sees is not necessarily what is actually there," the man had explained. Raymond realizes that he doesn't necessarily see what is actually there. He imagined Claire, as he imagined his twin and his biological mother. As he has begun to imagine his dead adoptive mother. He no longer trusts what he sees, or what he thinks he sees. Claire's not even a natural blonde. He clears the plates from the teenaged girls' table. "Pussy power," one of them emphasizes. "He doesn't get what he wants until *I* get what *I* want."

As he carries plates back to the kitchen, Raymond wonders how much pussy power Beth has over the health inspector. And if it will last until the wedding or if he'll break it off. What is the health inspector imagining in Beth, and what is Beth imagining in the health inspector? Why do humans have to imagine? Why can't they be more like dogs? See it like it is. He thinks of Burt getting excited about food and walks and tummy rubbing — concrete things. Burt wasn't dreaming about a love he couldn't have or a life he couldn't live. Burt was grounded in reality. Raymond can't even imagine what reality is any more.

He offers Claire a lift home but she says that taking public transit is no problem. He drives to Mara's house and parks on the street two houses over, behind a hedge. The "Sold" sticker on her For Sale sign stupefies him. He stares at it to ascertain that it's real. Maybe there's been some mistake. Maybe the sale didn't close and they forgot to take off the sticker. Maybe they put the sticker on the wrong sign. Then he realizes that he's imagining things again. She sold her house. He gets out of the car and approaches her lawn. He stands on the edge of her property hoping that, if she's inside, she'll notice him and invite him in for a drink. The singing neighbour is digging in his flower bed. He has shorts on but no shirt. He has a hairy back and his flabby gut jiggles while he digs. He turns to stare at Raymond, then starts to whistle. Raymond decides to be brave and confront Mara. He walks across the lawn and rings the bell. When there is no answer he looks through the window into the living room. Her furniture is gone and there are boxes everywhere. She has moved without telling him. She has moved without telling him because she doesn't want him to know where she has gone.

❖

Outside his apartment door he studies the stain left from Burt's vomit. If Burt weren't dead, he would spray carpet cleaner on it. Down the hall the obsessive-compulsive man is taking one step backwards for every three steps forwards.

He notices the light flickering on the answering machine and presses the playback button. "Raymond . . ." Mara begins. "I don't know what to say to you. I don't know what you want from me . . . what you expect me to do. Last night can't change anything. I'm sure you know that. It was nice. I'll never forget it. Somehow we were able to bypass all the shit we've been through. I liked and hated that about it . . . that we could forget. I don't think we should forget. I can't anyway. But you seemed different. Maybe you're going to be alright, start fresh or something. I can't start fresh, I really can't. I can't start, period. I just want peace. So please don't call me. Let's leave it as it was. Okay . . . ? Please . . . ?" He can tell that she's starting to cry. "Take care of yourself, Raymond. Live a healthy and prosperous life. Really. You deserve it. Just please leave me out of it." It sounds as though she has difficulty hanging up the phone; something bumps before the line goes dead.

Still holding Burt's ashes, Raymond sits on the chair. He was not with her last night. He has not been with her for a long time. He has been careful not to be with her. He has respected her request that he leave her alone, that he give her peace. Dwayne has not respected her need for peace. He has done nothing but disturb her. And now he has done more than that. Raymond isn't sure what, doesn't want to think what. Doesn't want to imagine. There is a rage erupting inside him that he's afraid he will be unable to control. There is a fury burning inside him that is causing his breath to scorch his throat, his mouth, his eyes, his nostrils. He will self-destruct from these feelings. He will ignite and burn as Belinda did. Only he will have no moment of ecstasy, no moment of orgasm. He will only suffer while burning alive. And his spirit will go nowhere. Trapped on earth, it will hover powerlessly around his twin. He will be forced to watch his twin continue to ruin his life. He will be forced to watch his twin continue to fuck his wife. Raymond starts to scream, louder than when Burt died. He wants to ignite, wants to burn the building, wants to destroy lives, his life. He wants to have an effect.

Someone's knocking on his door. "You alright in there? Open up." More pounding on the door. Raymond stops screaming. The abrupt quiet scares him. He doesn't want to be alone. He opens the door to the super. "You alright, Mr. Gage? Your neighbours heard screaming." The super tries to look around Raymond to see if there is anyone else in the apartment. Anyone being tortured.

"I was screaming," Raymond admits.

"Is that right?"

"Yes. I've stopped now."

"You won't start again?"

"No."

"It's just it disturbs the neighbours."

"Yes."

The super glances up and down the corridor. "Alright then. Good night."

"Good night." Raymond closes the door, locking his new lock. The lock that was intended to outsmart his brother. He sits back down on the chair in the hall because he doesn't want to go into the living room. He holds Burt's ashes. But after a moment he forces himself to go into the living room to get his mother's ashes. He brings them back into the hall and sits on the chair again with Belinda in one hand and Burt in the other. He grips them close to his body. Their edges press into his ribcage. He can feel their edges.

twenty

It was while Dr. Kalbfleisch and Raymond were discussing Mrs. Bumby's concern about staff attitude that Dr. Kalbfleisch had the seizure. He fell forward on to the table, crushing his hot-fudge cake and knocking over his coffee. Raymond assumed that he was having a heart attack and shouted at Claire to dial 911. Some of the coffee had spilled on to Raymond's trousers, burning him. The reality of his own pain kept interfering with the reality of Dr. Kalbfleisch's unconsciousness. While he was trying to figure out what to do about Dr. Kalbfleisch, he held the fabric of his trousers away from his skin to reduce the burning. Fortunately, Claire seemed to know what to do. After calling 911, she pulled Dr. Kalbfleisch off the chair and laid him on the floor. She checked his pulse and made sure that he was breathing. She dampened a clean dishrag and wiped the hot-fudge sauce off Dr. Kalbfleisch's shirt and jacket. She did this tenderly, as though he were a child. She'd been getting along well with Dr. Kalbfleisch. He'd been calling her "sweetie" and leaving her big tips.

That was days ago. Now everyone knows that Dr. Kalbfleisch has a malignant primary brain tumour that is inoperable. Everyone knows that, even with radiation therapy, he will probably be dead in two months. Nobody is saying much about any of this. The chicken hats lie forgotten in a box under the take-out counter. Mrs. Bumby is spending all her time with Dr. Kalbfleisch. Raymond suspects that she's making certain he rewrites his will and gives her power of attorney. It angers him that they wasted time testing Dr. Kalbfleisch's heart when the disease was in his head. He blames Mrs. Bumby, even though he realizes that she can't be held responsible. He's blaming Mrs. Bumby because there is no one else.

All of this has distracted him from his own troubles. He dreams about his biological family, and budgies and horses' heads. But he has done nothing to remedy the situation. He knows that at some point he must do something about Dwayne, that he can't just leave it. But he knows that if he reveals to Dwayne how he has succeeded in destroying him, Dwayne will feel victorious. Dwayne will have won. Raymond can't let this happen.

He also dreamed that there was a warrant out for his arrest. He was in bed with Mara and she was comforting him while advising him to turn himself in. He didn't know why he was being arrested but he knew that she was right; that he would have to turn himself in; that it was only a matter of time before they came for him.

He has tried calling her at work. They say she's been transferred. They won't tell him where. She must have instructed them to tell no one because when he tried calling again, disguising his voice, he got the same response.

Seymour has stopped shitting blood. He says he must have been taking too many aspirins. Currently he's reading about James Dean. Raymond finds it astonishing that Seymour can have been shitting blood but is fine, and Dr. Kalbfleisch can have seemed fine but has cancer. Nothing is what it seems.

So when Gloria comes into the restaurant, Raymond isn't sure how to react. He suspects that she wants free food, so he asks Claire to bring her a dinner. While she eats, he tries to appear occupied even though the lunch rush is over. But when Gloria explains to Claire that she is Raymond's mother, Claire insists that Raymond join his mother for dessert. "There's nothing to do," she points out, in front of Gloria. "Relax, Raymond. Spend some quality time with your mum."

As soon as he sits down she fixes her right eye on him. "There's some disease," she says. "They found the gene for it."

"What disease?"

"I don't know, some disease. They know what causes it."

"What?"

"They know what causes it, from the gene. They can tell if you're going to get it."

"What disease?" Raymond wonders if she is about to admit to some family history; some form of mental illness that might explain Dwayne's behaviour.

She eats some pie. "I like the pie here," she admits. "Not as good as at that Chicken Villa place. Theirs is more crusty. But this is good. More filling in it."

"Why are you talking about genes?" Raymond asks.

"What's that?"

"You were talking about genes."

"Was I?" She shakes her head. "Half the time I don't know what I'm talking about. It's living with Dwayne that's done it. I have to repeat myself all the time, see, because he don't listen. So then I forget what I'm saying, since I have to keep repeating it."

"How is Dwayne?"

"Haven't seen him. Guess he's doing alright. Otherwise he'd be eating me out of house and home."

"Do you think he'll be there for lunch on Sunday?"

"Maybe. Why, you want to come over?"

"I thought I might."

"The girls would love that. Tory thinks you don't like her. I told her, 'Raymond's reserved. It don't mean nothing. He was just brought up nice.'" She leans forward and fixes her right eye on him again. "She's used to pigs like her dad, see. She's not used to gentlemen like yourself."

"Don't tell Dwayne I'm coming."

"Why, you want to surprise him?"

"Yeah."

Gloria points her fork at him. "I'm glad you two are getting along so good. He don't got too many friends now. Just that crowd he hangs out with. I don't trust any of them. They're the ones got him into trouble. I'd just as soon they was all dead." She finishes her pie and slurps her coffee. "Tory says she's going to write a book about our family. You and Dwayne being separated at birth and whatnot, then finding each other. She asked me if I minded the whole world knowing about the rape. I said I couldn't care less. She don't like cleaning teeth, see, she wants to be a writer." She pokes her finger under her turban and scratches. "It should be a good book, maybe she could sell it to TV. It could be a movie-of-the-week type thing.

I told her she could write whatever she wanted, so long as Liz Taylor plays my part. Tory said she was too old. Wasn't that nice of her? She's a sweet girl."

Seymour told Raymond that James Dean's favourite quote was from *The Little Prince*: "What is essential is invisible to the eye." Raymond liked this quote, although he wasn't sure what it meant. Looking at Gloria, he ponders it again. She is visible to the eye but not essential. Seymour also informed him that James Dean liked it when people burned him with cigarettes. "The human ashtray" they called him. Raymond found it confusing that someone who could think that what was essential was invisible to the eye could want to be burned with cigarettes.

Gloria adjusts her turban. "You come over Sunday and I'll roast some pork. Wouldn't that be nice? With some carrots and potatoes? Roasted potatoes? Wouldn't you like that?"

Raymond nods vaguely, remembering the Siamese twins who are at this very moment being surgically separated at the hospital. They are joined at the head, sharing brain and spinal fluid. The operation will take twelve hours. The doctors said one of them will probably die once they are separated. How will the surviving twin feel, Raymond wonders. They are already two years old, already accustomed to being joined at the head. To them, being joined at the head is normal. The surviving twin will wake to find that a vital part of himself has been removed.

"And we'll get Tammy to make her cherry cheesecake. It's *so* delicious. She uses cream cheese, see, and makes a graham-cracker crust, then puts cherries on top. It's *so* good."

Raymond wonders if Gloria ever despairs. If there are days when she sits in a dark room and doesn't go out. He would like to ask her this but he can't think how to phrase it. He feels that he doesn't speak Gloria's language, that whatever he says will be misunderstood. "What about your parents?" he asks.

She scrapes her pie plate with her fork, then licks it. "What about them?"

"What were they like?"

"They was good people. They died when I was young, see. Car accident. That's why I'm glad Dwayne sold his car. I don't think he should be driving."

"Did you miss your parents?"

"Oh sure. That's natural."

"But I mean . . . how did you get over that? Losing them?"

Gloria slurps more coffee. "I've never been one to cry over spilt milk, Raymond. If things don't work out exactly right, you make do with what you got."

"Yeah, but I mean . . . they were your parents."

"So? Lots of people got parents and don't get along. Look at me and Dwayne. I gave that boy everything and look how he treats me. He used to be my pride and joy." She opens her purse and takes out a photograph of Dwayne sitting on a Santa's lap. He looks frightened. "Wasn't he cute? You must've been cute too, Raymond. Cute as a button."

The possibility that Dwayne has fornicated with Mara keeps eluding Raymond. He hopes that he's overreacting. Anything might have happened between them, other than fornication. They might have just had a drink together, and a conversation. She didn't say anything about sexual intercourse.

"I always say you got nobody to blame but yourself when things don't work out exactly right." Gloria has said this before to Raymond. He suspects that she has said it many times to Dwayne.

Raymond clears his throat and narrows his eyes. "What's wrong with your arm?"

"My arm?"

"Yeah. Your right arm is shorter than your left. Why?"

"I had a bad fall. That's what happens when you get old. You fall down." Suddenly she's looking for something in her handbag.

"Dwayne says one of your boyfriends twisted it." He doesn't know why he's provoking her. He can't stop himself.

"Nobody twisted nothing. That's him making up stories again." She pulls out a lipstick and her compact and reddens her lips.

"Why would he make up a story like that?"

"To get attention."

"Except that it's *your* arm that was broken. How would your arm being broken get him attention?"

"Don't expect me to go explaining your brother to you. Half the time I don't know what he's thinking." She tosses her makeup back into her handbag and snaps it shut. "You probably know him better than I do. Being twins and all that." Reading about identical twins Raymond learned that they like to sleep together. One article described a set of infant twins who would crawl on top of each other and sleep as they may have slept in the uterus. It also stated that male identical twins had a fifty per cent greater chance of being homosexual than male singletons. Raymond has tried to forget this information because he's afraid he might be a latent homosexual. He has never consciously desired men, but then he has never felt completely comfortable with women. He notices Jeff signalling him from the kitchen. "Excuse me," he tells Gloria as he gets up from the table. Jeff stands very rigid by the dish room, wearing gloves coated in chicken blood. "Bubba phoned in sick. He's never phoned in sick."

"What's wrong with him?"

"He's upset about Beth. You better talk to him. Man to man. Otherwise I think you might be looking for a new line cook."

"Shit."

"He thinks you're one."

Raymond pays for Gloria's dinner and promises to be there on Sunday. He drives to Bubba's. His apartment smells of dirty socks, sour milk and crème de menthe. Bubba smells of crème de menthe. "Can I buy you a beer?" Raymond asks.

"What for?"

"So we can talk?"

"I've got nothing to say to you." Bubba kicks a pile of clothing on the floor. Raymond notices more clothing strewn throughout the apartment. He clears his throat and narrows his eyes. "Well . . . I'd like to talk to you. Maybe we could grab a bite to eat. Is there somewhere around here you'd like to go?"

❖

The two of them sit in a booth in a restaurant that is designed to look like a fifties diner. The waitresses wear close-fitting pink uniforms and frilly aprons. The one serving them has runs in her nylons. Bubba gets up to insert quarters into the jukebox. He plays Elvis singing "Are You Lonesome Tonight?" He sits back down and grips his beer mug with both hands. "My horoscope was supposed to be really good this month."

"The month isn't over yet. Maybe it'll get better."

Bubba stares fiercely at a blister on his index finger. He touches it gingerly with his thumb. Outside the diner, policemen are putting handcuffs on a man. He doesn't resist as they push him into the cruiser and close the door. Bubba shakes his head abruptly, as though he were trying to shake water from his ears. "I've got no respect for you," he declares.

"You don't have to respect me. I just don't want you to quit. We need you."

"Horse piss."

"It's true. Jeff doesn't like working with anyone else."

"I hate that place."

The handcuffed man begins shouting behind the passenger window of the cruiser. The three policemen ignore him. Elvis sings plaintively. Raymond scratches behind his ear. "The thing about Beth . . ."

"What thing about Beth? You don't know anything about Beth."

"I know that you liked her."

"And she liked me, before you screwed everything up. Everything was going great before you had to go and try to poke her."

"That was my mistake. I'm sorry."

"Horse piss."

The policemen, standing around the cruiser, appear to be in no hurry to go anywhere. The handcuffed man begins to bang his head against the window. The policemen pay no attention to him.

Bubba sniffs. "She said I reminded her of a dog waiting for food."

"She was upset."

"She said it made her sick the way I looked at her."

The man continues to bang his head against the window. Raymond expects it to break. "Sometimes," he offers, "when people are upset, they say things they don't mean."

"Horse piss."

"This is just an idea, but . . . do you think it's possible that maybe you didn't really love her? That maybe you imagined that you loved her? I know I do that. Imagine things."

"Like what?"

"That I love somebody. I really want to love somebody, so I imagine things about them. So that I can love them."

"Like what?"

"Like they love me. I *imagine* that they love me. It's all in my head. The whole relationship. It has nothing to do with reality."

Bubba appears to be considering this information. He pokes his index finger into his ear. "Reality as we know it."

"Right."

"I just don't get how she can go off with that pissy-assed prick."

"Maybe she's imagining him."

"He's got a house and a car. She doesn't have to imagine that."

"It's a government vehicle. He doesn't own the car." Raymond thinks that he can see blood on the handcuffed man's head. He doesn't understand why the policemen continue to stand around while the man is bleeding. Why don't they take him to the station?

Bubba ponders his blister again. "You didn't have to go and fire her though."

"She wanted to quit," Raymond explains. "She told me she got offered a job at Chicken Villa."

"She did?"

Raymond nods.

"Wow. That's a nice place."

Raymond experiences a brief moment in which he thinks he should make time to visit Belinda. He's been experiencing these quite often since he's always had to make time to visit her. Just as he's always had to make time to walk Burt, or visit Mara. Now he no longer has to make time for anybody. Nobody cares.

"That new waitress is phoney," Bubba says.

"Kalbfleisch likes her."

"She thinks she's some kind of princess."

"She's a good waitress."

"Not as good as Beth."

"She smiles more."

"Beth was the best."

Raymond had hoped to dispel Bubba's illusions about Beth. He'd hoped to eliminate the distorted shit from Bubba's mind. But now he senses that this isn't necessary; that without the illusions, Bubba would fall apart. It's almost better that Beth has left Chez Simon. This way Bubba will be protected from her harsh words. This way he will be allowed to dream.

"You coming back to work?" Raymond asks.

"I guess."

❖

Seymour's at the take-out counter telling Jeff about South Africans torturing other South Africans by leaving them neck-deep in tanks of ice water for days. Jeff and Bubba greet each other with high-five handshakes. Then Jeff studies Raymond. "Code name?"

"Gator burgers."

Jeff nods. "Mrs. Bumby's waiting for you below deck."

"Alright." He's too tired to face her. First he goes to the bar and pours himself a drink — vodka, so she won't smell it on his breath. He has never drunk on the job before. He pours another shot. Two women sit at the table beside the bar. One of them fondles her dangling earrings while she talks. "He went on and on," she says. "It was very convoluted. I didn't know what he was talking about."

"He's totally self-absorbed," the other woman remarks.

"He kept looking at my feet. He said they were the most beautiful feet he'd ever seen."

"He told me the same thing."

A regular customer, who wears a headband and talks incessantly about Marshall McLuhan, leans over the bar and stares at Raymond. "The medium is the message," he tells him. Raymond returns to the kitchen, nearly bumping into Claire. He notices a bruise on her temple. "You okay?" he asks.

"Why wouldn't I be?"

Sharif comes out of the dish room and hands her some finger bowls. In another dream last night, Raymond gave Belinda a ceramic bowl he had made — although, in reality, he has never made a ceramic bowl. It pleased her in a way he had never succeeded in pleasing her in reality. She suggested putting a small candle into the bowl and lighting it when she missed him. He woke from this dream happy because he had pleased her. Then he remembered that she was dead.

Mrs. Bumby's perfume leaks into the hall. He can hear her sobbing as he approaches. She's sitting at his desk with her face in her hands. She doesn't look real to him. With her yellow hair piled high on her head she looks like an aging starlet. Her eyelids droop as she looks up at him. "It's all so terrible, Raymond."

"What?"

"Simon. They don't think he has much time."

Raymond nods and flicks absently through his rolodex. He doesn't believe her. She's trying to manipulate him, make him feel sorry for her. Make him forget that she's aiming a spike at his back. He notices that her eyes are red. Still he doesn't believe her. Aging starlets can manufacture tears.

"It's horrible the way he's wasting away," she continues. "He's given up." She pulls a Kleenex from her purse and wipes her eyes, carefully avoiding her makeup. Raymond feels the vodka heating his face and worries that she will see that he's drunk. He remains focused on her, knowing that she expects him to say something, offer condolences. But all he can think about are the lies. If he has any sympathy for her at all, it is because she's an aging starlet desperate for a leading role. Her last leading role. "He's asked me to keep you on," she says.

"Keep me on?"

"It's his wish that you remain here."

"He's not dead yet."

"No. But that is his wish."

Raymond nods and stares at the *Star Trek* poster. His teeth are clenched so tightly it feels as though they might shatter. Already he can feel the broken pieces in his mouth, sliding down his throat, choking him. He turns and walks down the corridor, hearing his footsteps echo off the walls. Her voice trails him. "Raymond . . . ? Raymond . . . ? Where are you going?"

He deliberately doesn't put on his seatbelt. He drives fast out of the parking lot, away from Chez Simon. He nearly runs over a woman pushing a stroller. She screams "Asshole!" at him. He stops at the general's memorial, gets out of the car and looks up at him. He climbs on to the base of the statue, wraps his hands around the general's boots, then his thighs, his waist. He grips the general's rifle, then his shoulder, and pulls himself up, wrapping his arms around the general's neck. He looks into his blank eyes. He must know something. He must. Abruptly air escapes Raymond. It's as though one of his lungs has been punctured. He feels faint and rests his forehead against the general's cold shoulder. He hears footsteps below. "What are you, some kind of pervert?" a man inquires. Raymond won't look down. He doesn't want to come down.

twenty-one

One of the baby Siamese twins died. His brain began to swell and he had a stroke. They kept him on a respirator but his heart stopped. The surviving twin is in stable condition, with a head wound where his brother used to be. Who decided, Raymond wants to know, which twin should die? The horses' heads that Tammy painted bear down on him, their bulging eyes immovable. The air in Gloria's house is stifling. He sinks into the couch, feeling it engulfing him, restraining him. Gloria and Tory have been arguing since he arrived. He doesn't want to listen to them but he doesn't feel ready to confront Dwayne. He feels that he is unravelling. His mother used to make him help her unravel sweaters she'd knitted. She would be unhappy with a stitch or a pattern and would want to redo it. He'd hold the sweater while she pulled at the yarn. The sweater would fall apart in his hands.

"What do *you* think, Raymond?" Gloria demands.

"About what?"

"Tory going off and using any Tom, Dick or Harry's sperm to get pregnant."

"It's not any Tom, Dick or Harry's," Tory points out. "They screen it for diseases. They're going to show me computer diagrams of the shape of his head and nose and everything. I get to choose his hair and eye colour."

"Who's to say they're telling you the truth? They could be showing you anybody's head. There's no law saying they have to show you the real head."

"I'm sorry I mentioned it," Tory says. "I shouldn't have told you."

Dwayne is in the backyard, floating on his dolphin in the pool. Gloria told Raymond that he has one of his sinus headaches.

"Why can't you find a nice man to marry?"

"It's not like I haven't tried," Tory reminds her.

"You were going to marry, weren't you?" Raymond asks, hoping to defuse the argument. "Your fiancé died, didn't he?"

"That's correct. My mother keeps forgetting that rather important detail."

Gloria adjusts her turban. "You can't go crying over spilt milk."

They hear Tammy screaming at her children in the kitchen. She's supposed to be making scalloped potatoes. Raymond expects Gloria or Tory to show some concern about the screaming, but they seem not to hear it. The budgies do, though, and begin to squawk and flap their wings. "Calm down, Chow-Chow," Gloria urges, taking a handful of potato chips from a bowl on the coffee table. She points a chip at Tory. "What're you going to do with a kiddie and no dad?"

"Lots of children grow up without fathers," Tory argues.

"Dwayne, for instance," Raymond offers.

"Dwayne always had men around to help out," Gloria corrects him. "They was always fixing his airplanes and whatnot." She crumbles some potato chips into each of the budgie cages. "What about you, Raymond? How would you have felt if you didn't have a dad?"

"I don't know."

"Seems to me you're a gentleman *because* you had a dad."

"I don't think so. I think I have my mother to thank for that. She always believed in the importance of common courtesy."

Gloria squints. "The what?"

"Being polite and considerate of others."

"Oh." She scratches under her turban. "But your dad must have been nice."

"Not really."

"See?" Tory says. "He probably would have been better off without him. Personally, I think fathers are overrated."

Tammy screams louder at her children, and they scream back. Gloria picks up her converter and switches on the TV. She surfs until she finds the weather channel. "I'm worried about that jet stream," she tells them. "Don't want that cold air hurting my lilacs." She turns up the volume to block out the fighting in the kitchen. Raymond feels himself becoming more tense. He can't understand why Tammy is screaming at her children. Belinda screamed at him only once, when he was small and wanted a fudgsicle. She refused to give him money for it, so while she was putting curlers in her hair, he took two dollars from her purse and went to the corner store. When he returned with the fudgsicle he handed her the change. She became very upset, called him "horrible boy" and "wicked" and insisted that he would have to be "sent away." She grabbed a suitcase and began packing his clothes. Her behaviour shocked Raymond because he had never seen her so angry before. Gord had left the night before and usually this would mean a period of calm. He and his mother would play cards or watch TV. She'd drink some sherry. After she had the suitcase packed she grabbed his arm and dragged him down the hall to the elevator and out of the building. He was so stunned he kept forgetting to lick his fudgsicle and it was melting all over his hands. At the bus stop he began to wail and plead with Belinda to let him stay. He knelt on the sidewalk with his face in his hands, heaving sobs that shook his entire body. When the bus pulled up, he waited for her to force him to get on it. But she didn't. She said he could stay if he promised never to steal again.

Afterwards, depleted of energy, he curled up on his bed with his arms wrapped around his knees. He couldn't stop shaking. He felt Belinda lie down beside him and place her arms around him. He didn't want this, didn't trust this, when moments ago she had been sending him away.

"Dwayne's got one of those pimples behind his ear, right on the bone," Gloria informs him. "Do you ever get those?"

"No."

"Right on the bone. He says it hurts like hell. He's always trying to squeeze it. I tell him, 'Leave it alone or it'll get infected.' But he don't listen to me."

"Did you tell him I was coming?" Raymond asks.

Gloria shakes her head. "You told me you wanted to surprise him."

"That's right."

"He said he don't want lunch. No wonder, since he ate a whole packet of Cinnamon Swirls. Didn't leave none for the kiddies." She nods at the weatherman on TV. "He's talking about a cold front now. Yesterday he was talking about a warm front. Why can't they make up their minds?"

"They forecast the weather, Mother," Tory explains. "They can't say definitely what's going to happen."

"What's the point of me watching it if they can't say definitely what's going to happen? I might just as well look out my window."

Tory sighs. Gloria waves her converter at the TV. "They act like they know what they're talking about. That's what I don't like. Why don't they just own up and admit they don't know nothing?" Raymond wonders how she can be so offended by the fallibility of the weatherman when she herself constantly lies.

"They don't 'own up,'" Tory tells her, "because they know people like you will keep tuning in regardless of whether or not they're accurate."

They hear a crash from the kitchen and Gloria jumps up. "There she goes breaking my china again." She hurries into the kitchen. Tory sips her mineral water, then smiles at Raymond. Again he is impressed by the whiteness of her teeth. "I hear you and Dwayne are getting along great."

"Where'd you hear that?"

"Dwayne."

"Really?"

"It's not true?"

Now that Gloria and Tammy are fighting, the budgies become even more agitated and start to peck at the bars of their cages. Raymond gets up. "I've got to go talk to him." He doesn't know what he's going to say or what he's going to do.

He has to step over obstacles to get to the pool: toys, hoses, gnomes. He climbs the ladder and watches his brother floating peacefully. Raymond envies his calm. The breeze nudges the dolphin but Dwayne remains undisturbed. For a moment Raymond sees himself in his brother and wants to forgive him, as he wants to forgive himself. He wants to hold his brother, absorb him, to stop him from hurting either of them. He clears his throat. "Dwayne?"

"Raymond?" He doesn't open his eyes.

"We need to talk."

"I'm listening." His hands remain folded over his chest.

"Mara phoned me. She said you were at her house."

"She did?"

Squirrels scramble up the tree beside the pool. "I asked you to leave her alone."

"She invited me in."

"She thought you were me."

Dwayne smiles. "You hope."

"What's that supposed to mean?"

"It means that if she didn't think I was you, she's inviting strange men into her house."

"She wouldn't do that."

"No?"

The squirrels fight on a branch, making high-pitched guttural sounds. Raymond scratches behind his ear. "What did you say to her?"

"About what?"

"Anything."

"She did most of the talking. She's a very unhappy lady."

"Why didn't you tell her who you were?"

"She seemed pretty upset. I didn't think it would be appropriate."

"So what was appropriate?"

Still with his eyes closed, Dwayne swats at a fly on his face. "I fucked her, Raymond. That's what you want to know, isn't it? And you know something? She really needed it. She was hungry for it. She was like a cat."

Raymond is in the water before he thinks to get in the water. He surges to the dolphin, flips it over and grabs his brother's head. He forces it between his knees and holds it there. Underwater his brother swipes at him, but Raymond is able to twist first one arm, then the other, behind his back. They both sink in this awkward embrace. Raymond feels completely lucid with his brother's head clamped between his knees. He expects to need air but he doesn't. He watches the bubbles erupt around his brother's head and contemplates how weak he is: how he can't even hold his breath, can't even put up a fight. All that talk, all that tormenting, and this is what remains. Raymond starts to laugh. Water gushes into his mouth and nose, choking him. He releases his hold on his brother and swims to the surface. He sputters and coughs, hooking one arm over the side of the pool. Sun ignites the water, blinding him. He rubs his eyes, waiting for Dwayne to surface. When he surfaces he will understand that Raymond has won. When he surfaces, he will repent.

❖

Raymond's clothes have dried but they feel stiff. He watches Gloria pace the waiting area. People sitting on chairs stare at her. Raymond had forgotten how strange she looks. He'd grown accustomed to her turban and heavily made-up face. Now he sees her as though for the first time and is ashamed that she is his mother. Every twenty minutes she goes downstairs to smoke outside the main lobby. She doesn't understand what has happened and Raymond hasn't explained it to her. He doesn't understand it himself. He was fooling around. They were fooling around. That's what he has told everyone. The doctors don't care what happened, they're just trying to save Dwayne. They're concerned that there might be a ruptured aneurysm. They're doing a CAT scan.

Comatose, Dwayne looked very different to Raymond. The cruel lines were gone from his face.

He can't stop thinking about the baby twin waking up without his brother attached to his head. It will feel cold where his brother had been. The baby twin will constantly feel the chill. He will spend his life trying to get warm. Why was he the one allowed to live, he will wonder. He will feel guilt for having survived. As Raymond has felt guilt for being the stronger twin and strangling his brother in the womb. Only he didn't strangle him. He was wrong to feel guilt. He had nothing to do with the plight of his brother. Until now.

Gloria sits beside him. "What's going to happen if he's a vegetable, that's what I want to know. Who's supposed to look after him?"

"I will."

She fixes her right eye on him. "You serious?"

"Yes."

"You'd need all kinds of special equipment and whatnot."

"We don't know how affected he is. It might not be that bad."

"I always told him not to go diving in that pool. But he don't listen to me."

She has mentioned "diving" twice — when they were in the ambulance and again while they were waiting in emergency. Raymond doesn't know where she got the idea that Dwayne dove into the pool and bumped his head. But she seems to have convinced herself that this is what occurred.

She seems to be unwilling to believe otherwise.

"It's too damn shallow," she adds, "for a grown man to be playing around in. I told him, 'Go to the YMCA.' But he don't like swimming in water other people have swimmed in. He says he can see their bodily fluids in it, excretions and whatnot. That's what he says." She has not stopped talking about Dwayne since they were told that he was in a coma. Raymond suspects that she believes that if she continues to talk about him, Dwayne will not become a vegetable. At times it seems to Raymond that she mistakes him for Dwayne. She'll say something very familiar to him, not expecting a response. Or she'll refer to someone Raymond doesn't know as though he does.

She shakes her head. "He never used to mind public pools. He was always in them. Doing handstands and whatnot. He'd just come home for a fudgsicle. The only way I could get him home was with fudgsicles. So I always had them."

Just as he was surprised by Dwayne's carefully made bed, carefully stacked shoes and obsessive cleaning, so is he surprised by his brother's fondness for fudgsicles.

"And those little green worms," Gloria adds. "You know those jelly worms? They're like jujubes, only they're shaped like worms. He only wanted the green ones. Well they don't sell packets of just *green* ones, know what I mean? So I had to go buy a whole packet." She shakes her head. "What I did for that boy. And all I got was trouble."

Raymond also preferred the green ones, because they were tart and sweet at the same time. When he was candy boy, they weren't stored in packets but in a bin. He'd only take the green ones. He feels sweat beading on his upper lip.

"What's the matter with you, Raymond? You look pale. You should eat something. Maybe your blood sugar's dropped. You want me to get you a candy bar or something?"

"I feel sick."

"That's what I mean. Your blood sugar's low. You got to eat something. I'll be right back." As he watches her trudge away, the reality that they were formed inside her disgusts him. He leans forward and puts his head between his legs because the room is revolving and he's afraid that he's going to faint. He doesn't know what he's done. He is not a violent man. He cannot have hurt his brother. Suddenly he feels a cold spot on his head where his brother used to be. He puts his hands over it and sways from side to side on his chair. He can't stop unravelling.

❖

The CAT scan revealed bleeding in Dwayne's brain. Then an arteriogram was done to locate the subarachnoid hemorrhage. Tory explained that this meant they had to inject radioactive dye into an artery in Dwayne's groin, then pump it up to his head. This revealed that the aneurysm was in the anterior communicating artery. Now they're drilling holes in Dwayne's skull, and sawing off a "bone flap." Raymond feels the pain, a burning, and the vibration from the drill. He bangs his head against the wall like the handcuffed man banged his head against the police-car window. Someone puts a hand on his shoulder. "Calm down, Raymond," Tory says. "We have to help each other through this." She isn't smiling. Her lips hang loosely like the lips of a fish. Raymond closes his eyes again. The doctors wanted to know if there was a history of aneurysms in the family because vascular malformation can be hereditary. Gloria insisted that nobody in her family ever had any trouble with their brains. The doctors informed them of the the risks of surgery: death, stroke, a neurological deficit causing loss of power, speech, mental capacity, vision. They also explained that without the surgery there would be repeated hemorrhages. They suggested that Dwayne was fortunate that the rupture occurred while his brother was present because without immediate help, he would have been in worse shape, possibly dead. Raymond's trying to understand if this means he saved his brother; if his brother would have died one day — suddenly — if Raymond hadn't held his head underwater. Died as he wanted to die. Like jumping from the bridge, it would have been over in seconds. Now it will take days, weeks, maybe years for him to die. Raymond has saved his brother's life.

"Maybe you should go home, Raymond," Tory says. "They said it's going to take hours."

"Why?"

"It's in a delicate area, between the two hemispheres. They have to move the brain around to get at the artery so they can attach the metal clip. It's not like they can just go in there and fix it. They have to use a microscope."

She shakes her head. "They say it might cause spasms through other arteries, can you believe that?"

Raymond doesn't want to think about it, can't think about it. When he carried him out of the pool he felt as though he were carrying himself. They were his arms and legs that he was holding. His head that was lolling around. His belly button with the soft hair growing out of it. His belly button.

"Raymond . . . ? I think you better go home."

❖

He stares up at the general. If he could give his life to his brother, he would. If he could give his brain to his brother, he would. He sees him on the operating table, obscured by surgical drapes, just the opening in his skull revealed, drained of blood. Doctors poking around in there with sharp instruments, a metal clamp, a microscope. Doctors who care only about his brain, not who he was, what he did. Deliberate cruelty. Why? What had Raymond ever done to him? And what is he supposed to do now? How is he supposed to face himself? Before, he was afraid of his brother. Now, he is afraid of himself. He kneels on the concrete at the general's feet. Litter surrounds him. He grips his hands over the cold spot on his head. He feels his brain bleeding into his skull.

twenty-two

Raymond stayed over last night. He couldn't go home, couldn't face his apartment devoid of Burt. He and Gloria ate popcorn and watched a Mickey Rooney movie. Mickey was very young and excited about putting on a show. Raymond barely noticed him. He stared at the TV and ate the popcorn, but nothing registered. He couldn't stop thinking about his brother, still unconscious, with nurses fluttering around him. They'd shaved the front half of his head. Nearly bald, with his head bandaged, he looked like Gloria in her turban. Raymond stood beside him waiting, hoping that he would open his eyes. He prayed that he would open his eyes.

Chow-Chow the budgie died in Gloria's lap. "Too much excitement," Gloria said. After Raymond buried the bird in one of the flower beds, he paced around the pool. He wanted to slash it with a knife but was afraid this might cause a disturbance. The dolphin was still floating in it.

The doctors aren't revealing much about the surgery. "It's too early to say," they told them. "His vital signs are stable. We'll just have to wait and see." Tory explained that, in any case, there would probably be weeks or months of rehab. "You don't bounce back from brain surgery," she warned.

Raymond was supposed to sleep in Dwayne's room, on the bed made up exactly like his own. But he couldn't, he didn't belong there, wasn't welcome there. Gloria's snores penetrated the wall and Raymond wondered if this used to disturb Dwayne.

Pacing her airless house he tried to blame her so that he could stop blaming himself. He looked in drawers and closets for clues. Clues to what, he wasn't sure. He found none. He turned the TV back on and watched infomercials. He turned it off and tried to read a *National Enquirer.* A baby was born with two heads. Raymond stared hard at the photo to ascertain if it was real. It made him think of the surviving baby twin again, who will have to learn to stand and walk on his own without the support of his brother.

He opened the fridge several times and stared at the packets of meat. They looked like body parts to him. He ate some olives. Back in the living room he stared at Tee-Kee, the remaining budgie, and Tee-Kee stared back at him. What was he thinking, Raymond wondered, now that Chow-Chow was dead? Did he feel in any way responsible, since he'd tried to have "his way" with Chow-Chow? Did he miss Chow-Chow? Was he in mourning? Tee-Kee offered Raymond no clues. He did not ruffle one feather or make one sound.

Tonight is no different, he can't sleep. He went to Chez Simon today and did his job as best he could. Everyone was very considerate of him, even Mrs. Bumby. She asked him about ordering. He knows she's trying to learn how to do his job so that she can fire him. But he doesn't care.

He tried going to his apartment although he knew it would be filled with his past life. His mother's belongings sat in boxes in the living room. He still hasn't figured out what to do with them: if he should sort through them or just give it all to charity. He tried looking in one box but it contained clothes that he recognized, clothes he'd seen her wear that were now empty and that she would never again fill. He closed the box and returned to Gloria's. They ate Kraft Dinner together.

Submerged in all of his remorse there is still anger. He would have thought that after nearly killing his brother he would no longer feel anger towards him. But he just has to remember Mara — what Dwayne did to Mara — and he wants him to die; the previous Dwayne, not the one he saw today in the turban without the cruel lines in his face.

The doctors advised them to expect possible changes in his personality, given the location of the aneurysm. They couldn't say what those changes would be. "It's highly variable," they told them. Tory explained that it had to do with the part of his brain that was affected. The ruptured artery was in the front of his brain. The frontal lobes control personality, she said.

So they must wait. Raymond's eyelids are burning from lack of sleep. He stares at Gloria's bookshelves although there aren't many books on them. He discovers an old high school yearbook and searches for Dwayne. He finds him, wearing a ponytail but no smile. Under his photo, Raymond reads, "The evil that men do lives after them. The good is oft interred with their bones."

"What are you up to?" Gloria asks, wearing her fluffy pink bathrobe and matching turban.

"I didn't realize he graduated from high school," Raymond says.

"Just barely. All he got was passes."

"At least he graduated."

"He had a head, he just didn't use it, know what I mean?"

Raymond nods, considering his own head and how he doesn't use it.

"You want some cocoa?" Gloria asks.

"No, thanks."

She walks over to Tee-Kee's cage. "What are *you* thinking about? Think maybe you were a little too hard on her? What'd you expect, you was bigger than she was."

As Raymond was bigger than Dwayne.

Tee-Kee ruffles his feathers and squawks. Raymond clears his throat. "Are you worried?"

"Of course. But it's a good hospital. I'm sure they'll do what's right."

"They've already done it."

"That's what I mean. They did their best."

He watched Gloria sign the papers that permitted them to drill into Dwayne's head. He saw her hesitate, saw her confusion. So did Tory who put her arm around her. "It's okay, Mum," she kept saying, "it'll be okay."

"Gloria . . ." Raymond begins. "He didn't dive into the pool."

"I don't want to hear about it, Raymond. What's done is done. What you boys get up to is your own business. I don't want to hear about it."

The evil that men do lives after them. "I just don't want you to misunderstand."

"I'm not misunderstanding nothing. You boys was fooling around. Simple as that."

Maybe this is brave of her, Raymond thinks. She is finding a way to cope, to adapt, as she has always adapted. The truth doesn't matter. Raymond has been so concerned with the truth. What is the truth? Maybe she's right. Maybe they were just fooling around. Anyway, it's her truth. It works for her. Raymond should find his own truth and stop worrying about everyone else's.

Gloria adjusts her turban. "Tammy's all upset because Hubert stole her cat."

"Who's Hubert?"

"You know Hubert. He came to one of the pool parties."

"What pool parties?" He realizes that she's confusing him with Dwayne again.

"Dickie's friend, Hubert. He was the guy putting underpants on his head."

"I wasn't there."

"What?" Gloria stares at him.

"I was never at a pool party. I'm Raymond."

"For goodness' sake, there was me thinking you was Dwayne."

"So why did Hubert steal her cat?"

"I told her maybe he was joking around. He's always joking around. She said he put the kitty in his gym bag. He's always liked that cat, see, because it's orange and so fat."

"Why doesn't she tell him to give it back?"

"He says he don't got it. She's worried because he's got a gall bladder problem, see. He needs his medicine."

"Who's got a gall bladder problem?"

"The kitty." She covers Tee-Kee's cage with a sheet. "You go to sleep now." She turns and fixes her right eye on Raymond. "You too, Raymond. It's no good not sleeping. What's done is done. You want anything from the fridge, you help yourself."

"Thanks." He listens to her climb the stairs and wonders how different a person he would have been if she had raised him. If he would have become cruel like Dwayne.

He notices some jujubes in a dish by the lamp. He takes some green ones and chews them one at a time, feeling them cling to his dental work.

The parents aren't going to tell the surviving baby twin about his brother. They believe it will be easier for him to grow up believing that he was born alone. Raymond can't understand how they can possibly imagine that the baby twin won't know on some level that he was one of two; that he will constantly mourn the loss of his twin, only he won't understand what he is mourning. He will only feel the cold space beside him.

❖

The hospital phones early to tell them that Dwayne has woken from the coma. As soon as he became conscious he asked for a Coke. He has already drunk three cans but will not touch food. Raymond and Gloria eat a piece of toast, then hurry to the hospital. Surrounded by doctors, Dwayne sees Gloria first and emits a primordial scream. "Mummy," he shouts, reaching towards her. Gloria offers him her hand which he grips to his chest. Raymond has never heard Dwayne refer to Gloria as "Mummy." He can see that Gloria is as surprised by Dwayne's behaviour as he is. They've taken the tube out of his mouth but he still has an IV in his arm. A doctor begins to pinch his legs. "Feel that, Dwayne?"

"A little."

The doctor puts a pencil between Dwayne's big and second toe, then squeezes them together. "Feel that?"

"A little."

The doctor squeezes harder. Raymond worries that he is hurting Dwayne, but Dwayne doesn't seem to mind. The doctor exchanges a look with another doctor, then puts the pencil between the toes of Dwayne's other foot and, watching Dwayne's face, repeats the squeezing procedure. "Ouch," Dwayne says finally.

"Good," the doctor remarks and jots something on a chart. The other doctors nod, then begin to file out of the room. The toe-squeezing doctor ushers Raymond and Gloria into the corridor. "We're just a little bit worried about his legs," he admits. "There seems to be some residual deficit, a slight spasticity."

Gloria fixes her right eye on him. "You mean, he can't walk?"

"Not immediately. He'll be using a wheelchair for a while. Rehab should have him up and using a cane in a few weeks. In a few months he may not even require that."

"Otherwise he's alright?" Raymond asks.

"As far as we can tell."

Gloria scratches under her turban. "So what you're saying is he could be normal, after a while."

"He could."

Gloria smiles a smile Raymond has never seen before. Then it occurs to him he has never seen her smile. She looks youthful, almost girlish. "I'm gonna go tell him." She hurries back inside and Raymond follows, after thanking the doctor.

Gloria leans close to Dwayne. "How you doing?"

"Okay."

"They say there's nothing wrong with you. You're not paralysed or nothing."

"There's nothing wrong with me?" He speaks more slowly than before, without the sneer. He looks very different to Raymond, confused and frightened, like the little boy in the photograph standing in front of the sandcastle.

"That's right," Gloria says. "That's what they said. It'll be a while before you can walk, though. You got to take it easy for a bit."

"Okay."

Raymond steps closer to the bed, waiting for Dwayne to notice him, reproach him. He doesn't.

"They say you're not eating nothing," Gloria adds. "You got to eat. It's not like you not to eat. What about some pudding? Wouldn't you like some pudding?" A nurse hurries in to check on the patient in the neighbouring bed. "Have you got pudding?" Gloria asks her. "If you want him to eat, you got to get him some pudding."

The nurse reaches under the man in the next bed and pulls out a bedpan. "I'll see what I can do."

"I want more Coke," Dwayne says.

"We'll get you some," Gloria assures him.

"I'll go get some now," Raymond offers.

He leaves the hospital to find a convenience store. Morning rush-hour traffic congests the street. Clouds of exhaust billow around him. He walks several blocks before finding a store. Inside, an old man is buying lottery tickets. Raymond has to wait for him to select his numbers. The man has two huge boils on the back of his neck. He breathes heavily, deep in concentration, as he studies the tickets. What is he dreaming of? Raymond wonders. How does he imagine his life will change if he wins? He will be the same man, except that he'll be able to buy more things, a huge house that he will be unable to fill. He'll pace its rooms, feeling the boils on his neck, breathing heavily, wondering why winning the lottery didn't make him happy. Maybe winning would be the worst thing that could happen to him. Once he's won he has nothing to hope for, to imagine. Raymond has won. He has reduced his brother to a childlike state at no cost to himself. He thinks it may be the worst thing that could have happened to him.

❖

He watches Dwayne drink from a can of Coke. He's not sure if he's ignoring him or not recognizing him. He seems only interested in Gloria. When she moves away from the bed, his eyes follow her. He seems afraid that she will leave.

"We should maybe lace the Coke with vitamins," she whispers to Raymond, "since he's not eating nothing." She picks up a bowl of pudding. "This is nice, Dwayne. Vanilla pudding. You like pudding."

"I'm not hungry."

"You got to eat."

"Are you leaving?"

"Raymond's got to go to work."

"*You* don't have to go."

She scratches under her turban. "I tell you what. You eat something and I'll stay."

To Raymond's amazement, Dwayne starts to cry.

"Now, now, don't go getting upset," Gloria tells him. "That won't do no good. I'm just worried about you, that's all."

"I'm not hungry."

"Forget about it. Maybe we'll try some soup a little later on. You want to watch TV?" She turns on the TV and adjusts it so that Dwayne can see it. She stands beside him, leaning on the bed rail. "'Geraldo' is on. You want to see who's on 'Geraldo'? Yesterday there was skinny men on said they liked fat women. They was so fat they had to sit on two chairs."

In their turbans, watching the TV, they form a couple. Raymond feels that he is intruding. When he leaves, they don't even notice.

❖

Mrs. Bumby and Claire seem to be getting along. Mrs. Bumby calls her "dear" and Claire calls her Barb. They're changing the restaurant, moving plants around, hanging more plants. Stained-glass windows have been suspended from the ceiling on either side of the front entrance. "Hello, Raymond," Mrs. Bumby says, smiling. "Everything alright?"

"Fine." He goes straight downstairs and is surprised to find Dr. Kalbfleisch sitting in his office. "Hello, sir."

"Is she still here?"

"Yes."

Dr. Kalbfleisch nods. He doesn't look any different. Raymond finds it hard to believe that there is a malignant primary brain tumour growing inside his head.

"I'm glad to see you back, sir."

"Not for long, Raymond. They won't let me out for long."

"Just the same, it's good to see you."

"I wanted to talk to you about a few things."

"Yes?"

"I'm marrying Mrs. Bumby. It's for the best, Raymond. She'll look after things."

What does it matter, Raymond wants to ask, since you'll be dead? "Congratulations, sir." Standing there he has one of his waking dreams. There's a pile of bricks. He lifts one and a rattlesnake slithers out from the pile, rattling.

"She's a good woman," Dr. Kalbfleisch emphasizes.

"I have to tell you, sir, that I will be leaving Chez Simon."

"Don't say that."

"I'm sure Mrs. Bumby can look after things." He hears her down the hall instructing Sharif on how to clean the toilets.

Dr. Kalbfleisch holds one hand over his eyes. Raymond notices it trembling slightly. He wonders if Dr. Kalbfleisch is experiencing tremors because of the tumour. "Are you alright, sir?"

"I want the restaurant to go on."

Why, Raymond wants to ask, since you'll be dead? "I'm sure it will, sir."

"Not without you, Raymond. You know the chicken business. Mrs.

Bumby has big ideas. She needs you to explain the business to her. Please, Raymond."

Is this a dying man's plea for immortality? With his name in lights, does Dr. Kalbfleisch imagine that he will live for ever?

"Oh there you are," Mrs. Bumby interrupts. "Simon, we have to get you to the hospital. Raymond, there are too many apple pies in the freezer. Why did you order so many?"

"We used to run out of them."

"Really? How curious. Well, please don't order any more."

Raymond watches Dr. Kalbfleisch to see if he remembers Mrs. Kalbfleisch's passion for apple pie. He seems unaffected, only pulls out his handkerchief, wraps it around his index finger and pokes it into one nostril.

"Claire's going to organize some cleaning," Mrs. Bumby adds. "Bruce is going to help her."

"Does *he* know that?"

"Not yet."

Raymond suspects that with Mrs. Bumby in charge, Bruce too will be leaving. And probably Jeff, then Bubba. They will all go to work at Chicken Villa. Slowly the lights will fade at Chez Simon.

"Good luck to you, sir."

"You'll do that for me, Raymond, what I said?"

"I will." He can lie to him now, since he's dying.

❖

Gloria is asleep in the chair beside Dwayne's bed. She's snoring, so is Dwayne. They've removed the bandages, revealing the incision on the right side of his head. Raymond stares in disbelief at the staples holding his brother's skin together. They form a curve, almost like a horseshoe. The hair at the back of his head stands out in tufts. He looks like a monster waiting calmly to be wakened, to wreak havoc on earth. Raymond studies the face that could be his own. Mr. Hewitt in the neighbouring bed groans.

"Psst," Gloria says. "Raymond, come over here." She walks towards the washroom, Raymond follows. "That fellah's been spanking his monkey in here." She nods towards the toilet. Raymond can see the residue of what could be dried semen against the wall.

"What do you want me to do about it?"

"He's got a heart condition, see. I don't think he should be doing that. Besides it's not very hygienic. Dwayne wouldn't like it."

"He's not using the washroom, anyway."

"Soon he will. They say soon we can try to get him in a wheelchair. I don't want him going to the bathroom and seeing that."

"Well then tell the nurses."

"I don't want to embarrass the fellah, know what I mean? I don't want us being enemies, what with us sharing the room and whatnot."

"So what do you want me to do?"

"I thought maybe you could get us some Fantastik or something and clean it up. Nobody has to know."

Raymond is beginning to understand that the rest of his life could be spent running errands for his brother, performing duties for his brother who no longer sees him, who no longer cares. The rest of his life could be spent trying to make amends.

"Alright," he says. He goes back to the convenience store to buy Fantastik.

twenty-three

For weeks Raymond has watched his brother, waiting for recognition, recrimination, anything. The doctors maintain that Dwayne has made a remarkable recovery. They claim that the loss of short-term memory is probably only temporary. At the rehabilitation centre the staff are pleased that Dwayne's leg function is improving. He's walking with a cane now but they expect that soon he won't even require that. As the scars on his brother's scalp fade, so does Raymond's memory of what actually happened. Gloria has been telling everyone that Raymond saved Dwayne's life. "You should've seen him," she says. "He jumped in with his clothes on and pulled him out of the water. Dwayne would be dead if it weren't for Raymond." She doesn't seem to mind or notice the changes in Dwayne. She seems to like it that he no longer leaves the house, that he follows her around. She has begun to call him "Pussy Cat" and "Sparky." The only thing she is not happy about is the showers. Dwayne takes three a day and they're getting longer. He occupies the bathroom for an hour, using up all the hot water. When she scolds him, he says that he's sorry, that he didn't realize he was in the shower for so long. They've mentioned this to the doctors but they only shrug. "These are minor problems," they say. Because they didn't know Dwayne before the accident, they don't see the changes in him.

He won't eat with Gloria and Raymond. He eats at night, when no one's looking. He forages in the fridge and eats items one at a time. He'll start with potato salad, eat the entire bowl, then move on to the meat loaf. He'll finish that before starting on the pudding. Raymond, who has been sleeping on the hide-a-bed, has discovered Dwayne in the kitchen in the dark several times. Dwayne's fright at being discovered reminds Raymond of an animal. He freezes, clutching the food. And even though Raymond insists that it's good that he's eating, Dwayne stops and glances furtively over his shoulder, as if checking for other predators. If Raymond turns the light on, Dwayne shoves the food back in the fridge and scurries to his room. In the morning there are no traces of the night's foraging. Gloria has accepted this pattern of behaviour with no qualms. Nightly she makes certain that there is plenty of food Dwayne likes in the fridge. "He's eating," she points out. "That's the important thing." He particularly enjoys pudding and she's been making all kinds, lacing them with liquid vitamins.

He has expressed no interest in the swimming pool, or even in going out to the backyard. He prefers to stay inside and watch TV, or play with his electric trains in the basement. According to Gloria, when he played with his trains before the accident he would harangue her about the clutter in the basement. Sometimes, in his frustration, he would crash the trains into one another. Now he simply constructs his tracks over and around her clutter. He uses matchbooks to make the tracks level on uneven terrain. This is different from before, Gloria admits. Before, if he couldn't find level ground, he would scream at her to clear out her "junk." Raymond has sat on the basement steps watching Dwayne construct little villages around the tracks. Anything new he builds does not have the symmetrical lines of the structures he completed before the brain damage. But he doesn't seem to notice. He lines up perfect little houses beside slightly crooked ones. Sometimes he just sits, holding his diesel locomotive in his lap. Gloria told Raymond that he has always favoured his diesel locomotive

These are considered small changes in an otherwise phenomenal recovery. He can speak when spoken to, can look after himself, and even help Gloria with the housecleaning. She's been trying to get him to cut the grass but he remains reluctant to go outside. He no longer shouts at Tammy, Tory or the kids when they come by. He won't sit down to eat with them only because he claims that he is not hungry. Usually he watches TV or goes down to the basement. Gloria has begun to touch him. She strokes his head, pats his shoulder or hugs him. He doesn't seem to mind.

The nightly kitchen encounters are the only interaction Raymond has with his brother. During the day, when Dwayne is cleaning his room, taking showers, following Gloria or in the basement with his trains, he seems not to notice Raymond. It's not that he's ignoring him; Raymond just doesn't seem to exist for him. If Raymond tries to start a conversation with him, he responds with little interest. He responds as he would to a complete stranger.

Dwayne has been baking brownies on a regular basis and this pleases Gloria. The three of them eat the brownies while watching TV. In Dwayne's company, Gloria seems to forget about Raymond. He is reminded of how he felt when his father and mother were together; how he ceased to exist.

But he continues to stay over on the hide-a-bed because he doesn't know what else to do. He has great difficulty sleeping, and tosses and turns most of the night, listening to Gloria's house creaking and her clock ticking. The horses' heads seem to glow in the dark and he feels them staring down at him. Sometimes Tee-Kee starts squawking for no apparent reason. Sometimes Raymond hears scratching in the walls which he assumes to be mice.

He has stopped going to work. Nobody from Chez Simon knows where he is. He feels in limbo. He's waiting for something; he doesn't know what.

"You ready?" Gloria asks him. Raymond nods. Gloria shouts down to the basement. "Sparky . . . ? Raymond and me are going to go do some shopping. You going to be alright?"

"Yeah," Dwayne shouts back.

"Maybe later you could mix up some brownies."

"Okay."

❖

During the past weeks Raymond and Gloria have worked out a system at the supermarket. It's as though they've been doing it for years. Almost without looking, she tosses packages into the cart. She trudges down the aisles with her chin jutting forward, periodically tugging her blouse down over her hips. He follows close behind, pushing the cart, listening to her slip-on sandals flap against her heels. She'll ask him if he wants certain items but won't wait for his response. Often she insists that he likes certain things which he doesn't, particularly meat products, and he knows that she's confusing him with Dwayne. But he has stopped advising her of this. He no longer has the energy to distinguish himself from his brother.

Leaning over the meats, she again discusses people Raymond doesn't know. "They was all excited about moving to the country, see. To get away from all the crime and whatnot. Now they're scared to leave their trailer home. Patty says it's right in the middle of nowhere, and one night, when Geordie was out, she swears she saw the door handle turn real slow. She was scared out of her wits, she said." She holds up a packet of pork tenderloin and scrutinizes it with her right eye. "I said right at the beginning, remember what I told them? I said the only difference between the city and the country is that the criminals need cars to get around." She puts the pork into the cart, then begins to study packets of chicken. "It's too bad because they was always dreaming about the country. It just goes to show how you're better off just dreaming. There's sewage problems too, see, in a trailer home. Specially in winter. I worry about those kiddies." She puts a packet of chicken legs into the cart and resumes surveying the meats. "What about liver and onions? You like that. Lots of iron."

"I'm not Dwayne," Raymond interjects.

"What's that?"

"I'm Raymond."

"For goodness' sake, there was me thinking you was Dwayne."

Is it because he has no personality that he can fade so easily into his brother?

"It's because you look like him, see."

"He looks like *me*."

"Whatever." She drops the liver into the cart and proceeds towards the freezers. "What about ice cream, you like ice cream. It's good for you. Lots of calcium."

"I don't like ice cream. I hate ice cream."

"Now don't go getting excited." She reaches into a freezer and pulls out a carton of ice cream.

"I'm not. Just don't think you know what I want just because you know what Dwayne wants."

"I don't think nothing, Raymond. Just sometimes I get a little confused, that's all, what with you being just like him. Don't take it personal."

"I'm not just like him."

"Okay then. So we'll get ice cream for him and something else for you." She fixes her right eye on him. "What do *you* want?"

He can't think of anything. He doesn't hate ice cream. Gloria has selected butter pecan, his favourite.

"Is that his favourite?" he asks.

"What's that?"

"Butter pecan. Is that his favourite flavour?"

"Yeah, why? You want us to get something else?"

"No, that's fine."

On the drive home she talks more about people he doesn't know. When she pauses to check her lipstick, he clears his throat and narrows his eyes. "You've never told me if you have any brothers or sisters."

"I had a brother but he died. Cancer."

"What kind of cancer?" Raymond asks, wondering if this will reveal something regarding his genetic makeup.

"Bowel. He was a travelling salesman, see. Didn't get to go whenever he wanted because he was always on the road. So he'd hold it in, know what I mean?"

"That isn't necessarily why he got cancer. It could be in the family."

Gloria shakes her head. "All that stuff clogging your bowel can kill you, all those toxins and whatnot." She puts her compact back into her purse. "That was Tammy called before we left. Hubert's holding Rusty ransom. He wants a hundred dollars for that kitty. Tammy's fit to be tied."

"I thought you said the cat would die without its medicine."

"Just because it isn't dead yet don't mean nothing. Could be it's dead already and Hubert isn't telling us about it." She shakes her head. "What kind of person would go kidnapping a kitty?"

"Dwayne kidnapped my dog."

"He did not."

"He did. He got the keys from my super, then went into my apartment and stole my dog. He poisoned him."

"Now, Raymond, you don't know for sure Dwayne did it."

"My super said the guy looked like me. Not too many men look like me."

"Could be he just took the dog for a walk and the dog ate something. Dogs are always eating out of trash cans and whatnot. Maybe he ate a chicken bone. Could be he choked on a bone."

Just like his parents, Raymond realizes, Gloria and Dwayne will always stand united against him.

❖

He leaves them at the kitchen table eating the ice cream and playing cards. They don't say goodbye. They don't observe that he is leaving nothing behind. He gets in the car and drives to the restaurant he and Mara used to frequent for nachos. He sits at the bar and orders a scotch. The mariachi music unsettles him. The cheerful horns make him feel as though he should be celebrating something. The bartender moves to the music as though he's shaking maracas.

The man beside Raymond seems quite drunk. He keeps sliding off his stool as if he's about to leave. But finding himself unsteady on his feet, he sits back down. He notices Raymond watching him and stares back. "I have to go to a detox centre," he explains. "Is that a drag or what?"

"That's a drag," Raymond agrees. The dancing bartender winks at him. Raymond isn't sure why. The drunk man continues to stare at him. "You look like an executive type," he observes.

"I'm not," Raymond replies.

"Sure you are. You're an executive." He slides off the stool again, wavers, then gets back on it. "*I* used to be an executive." The bartender winks at Raymond again. "I used to work for a big corporation," the man adds, "I used to be a *company* man. And you know something? They had my balls in a vice." He clenches his fist and holds it out to Raymond, demonstrating the vice grip. "They doing that to you yet?"

"Who?"

"The fucking VPs."

"No. I'm not an executive."

"You know what you can tell them?" He slides off the stool again. "You can tell them to go fuck themselves."

"What time's your meeting, Lloyd?" the bartender inquires.

"What meeting?"

"At the detox centre."

"Ah *fuck* them." He sits back down. At one of the tables a napkin catches fire. Customers gasp and stare at the flames. The owner of the napkin looks sheepish as he drops it on to a plate and waits for it to burn itself out. "It's those fucking candles," Lloyd comments before turning back to the bartender. "Why do you have those fucking candles on the table?"

"Romance, Lloyd. Ever heard of it?"

"It's a *fucking* fire hazard."

Raymond pays for his scotch and leaves. He contemplates Lloyd's bitterness: how it isn't helping him to detoxify. He contemplates his own bitterness and how it isn't helping him to live. Belinda used to talk about "chapters" in her life. "Thank God that chapter's over," she'd remark, or "That's the end of that chapter." Raymond wonders if she really was able to end her chapters. Or if they continued to bleed into one another, internally, imperceptibly.

❖

Sharif seemed surprised that Raymond, his former boss, wanted to come to the hospital to visit his son. Raymond picked him up outside the unemployment centre. Even Sharif hates Mrs. Bumby and is looking for a new job.

His baby weighs two and a half pounds and is the length of Raymond's hand. Very thin, with almost translucent skin, he lies asleep in the incubator. Soft, downy hairs which full-term babies shed before birth still cover his shoulders, arms and legs. A nasal tracheal tube feeds him oxygen through a nostril. An IV unit has been attached to a catheter inserted into an umbilical artery. Three tiny electrodes, taped to his chest, connect him to a heart monitor.

Sharif fits his arm through the porthole in the incubator and slides his fingers into the attached sleeve and glove. Gently, he lays his hand on Taha. The baby seems to respond, stirring slightly. Raymond watches, holding the stuffed owl he bought. He wanted to offer a gift but couldn't think of what would be appropriate. He stood perplexed in the toy store, staring at the abundance of stuffed animals. The owl gazed down at him, calming him.

Sharif strokes his son's tiny head while speaking softly to him in Urdu. Watching the subtle interaction between father and son, Raymond longs to have such a relationship. Surrounded by white noise, in the sterile surroundings, he can't help but remember his dead babies. The ulcer that is his grief ruptures and the pain that Raymond has suppressed recurs with force. He feels as if he might choke, as if he might cough up blood.

Sharif, watching him, carefully withdraws his arm from the incubator. "You alright, sir?"

Raymond nods. "He's beautiful."

"Would you like to touch him?"

"Oh, I don't think I should."

Sharif nods. "Please."

Raymond's afraid to touch the baby, afraid he might curse it, kill it. The nursery is warm, making him sweat. The owl's fluff becomes damp in his grip.

"Please," Sharif repeats, taking the owl. Raymond realizes that if he doesn't touch Taha, Sharif may be insulted. So he carefully slides his arm through the porthole and fits his fingers into the glove. Taha has curled his hands under his chin and pulled his legs into his chest. Raymond gently strokes his shoulder with his index and middle finger. He's alarmed by the infant's fragility. His tiny ribs could belong to a bird. He places his fingers where he thinks the baby's heart should be and is relieved to feel it fluttering. Abruptly Taha grabs Raymond's index finger, opens his eyes and stares at him. It is not the defenceless look Raymond would have expected from a newborn. It is a serene gaze, full of wisdom. It is as though Taha can see inside him. As though he, who has had to fight for life, understands Raymond's sorrow and shame. Without guile or motive the infant's stare seems to be saying, "You will go on."

❖

Raymond parks near the general and sits on the bench, looking up at him. He wonders how different the general's life would have been if he'd had an identical twin. Would he have fought so bravely? Would he have been such an outstanding individual if he had been one of two? Would he have been worthy of a memorial?

A squirrel hops towards Raymond and sits on its haunches watching him, waiting to see if he has any food to offer. Its tail has been cut off, leaving a small stump, but the squirrel doesn't seem to mind. He looks fat and healthy. He's not bitter because somebody cut off a piece of him. He has adapted, as an amputee adapts to the loss of a limb. As the baby twin will adapt to the loss of his brother. Raymond realizes that he keeps waiting for other people to make him feel complete. It's as though he can only see himself reflected in other people. Without them, he feels invisible. His father used to call him "the invisible man" because he wouldn't notice that he was there. Gord would be saying something to Belinda that Raymond suspected he wasn't supposed to hear. But it was too late to make himself scarce. So he would keep still, hoping that his father wouldn't notice him. He would eventually, and would tell him to go to his room where Raymond would sit alone doing crosswords, missing Belinda.

The day after Gord sent him to his room for stealing his cigarettes, Raymond felt so invisible he went to the community pool and dove off the high-board. He'd never done this before because he was only ten. But he felt so worthless, so insignificant, that he decided he might as well dive off the high-board and see if it would kill him. Although he was frightened, he couldn't dawdle on the ladder because the older boys were climbing up behind him, eager for their turns to jump. So at the end of the board, feeling its spring, Raymond had no choice but to plummet towards the water. He could have tried a jackknife, or a cannonball or even a regular jump, but he was determined to dive head first into the depths below. In the air he could feel his body twisting and he knew that he would bellyflop. It seemed to take forever to hit the water. He could hear the sounds of the pool: splashing, laughter, transistor radios. Then he felt the smack, and silence surrounded him. Stinging from the bellyflop, he felt himself propelled deep down to the bottom of the pool. He couldn't stop, he was afraid that he would crack his skull on the cement floor. He imagined himself dead, floating to the surface with a bleeding skull. Suddenly he didn't want to die. But he couldn't get his bearings in the water. Gasping and swallowing, he flailed his arms and legs, trying to find the bottom or the edges of the pool. Finally his toe grazed the bottom and he knew that if he pushed off with all of his power, he might make it to the surface. He looked up and saw the bright blue light. He swam as hard as he could towards the light.

Afterwards he lay shivering on his towel until the sun warmed him. His throat was sore from swallowing chlorinated water, so he sat up and drank the Orange Crush he'd brought from home. He didn't mind that the activity around him had nothing to do with him; that no one had noticed that he had almost died. He felt proud of himself for having dived off the board and he forgot his father's treachery. He thought about the future: how many more times he would dive off the high-board, how many more bottles of Orange Crush he would drink. And he felt comfortable inside himself.

In the company of the general and the squirrel who have both endured abuse and many storms, and with Taha's gaze in his mind, Raymond believes he will feel comfortable inside himself again. He doesn't know when or how. He suspects that the feeling will come upon him when he least expects it. He can't anticipate or manufacture the feeling. He can only believe that at some point it will happen. Even though it seems impossible — as impossible as Taha surviving a premature birth on a bathroom floor. If Raymond lets go of his index cards, if he stops digging himself these holes, it will happen again. Taha told him so.